Roy McLarty left school at fifteen and was glad to go; he worked on farms and shops, sang in a group, married and had two children. Returned to education in his thirties, he became a Lecturer and made frequent appearances on TV and radio.

In 1980 he removed to Norfolk where he taught and directed thousands of students, found time to write papers and sit on several Boards where he saw a lot of the City. He is the author of the acclaimed *Snake in the City*. Roy likes walking, meeting people, and finds something new every day in life.

Dr McLarty is Emeritus Professor at Boston University. He is also a visiting Professor at various international universities.

THE RELUCTANT PLOTTER

To my wife Mary, my family and friends

Roy McLarty

THE RELUCTANT PLOTTER

AUSTIN MACAULEY
PUBLISHERS LTD.

A CIP catalogue record for this title is available from the British Library.

ISBN 978 184963 400 7

www.austinmacauley.com

First Published (2013)
Austin Macauley Publishers Ltd.
25 Canada Square
Canary Wharf
London
E14 5LB

Printed and Bound in Great Britain

Acknowledgments

Written in collaboration with my brother John. Also, many thanks to various friends for encouragement and kind suggestions.

1

'What it comes down to,' he said, giving me a quick glance, 'is that we may want Harry Hetland taken care of. It's something we have to consider – a last resort. So far every legitimate effort has failed and I want you to look at it – give us a report to military standards, covering all the aspects.'

I stared at the floor for a long moment.

'A tall order, Sir Lance.'

'No reason why we shouldn't *look* at it. All options must be considered, a professional view of the prospects, an overview of the whole scenario.'

I allowed him a moment's silence. We don't liquidate politicians in this fair land of ours. These things are always wrong, their outcome is unpredictable, the perpetrators are likely to be caught and surely a decent old man like Sir Lance knew that better than I did. And as an old hand, I certainly knew better than to get involved in something so rash, but I quenched the refusal that welled in my gut. He wanted a report, something I'd done at various times in my career, and what's the harm in that? In the military world there are reports on nearly everything and contingencies for almost every conceivable emergency. This would just have to be another one.

'Well I can certainly look at it,' I said. 'But it's not going to be easy.'

This he acknowledged with a shrug. In the military world (and it seemed we were playing at soldiers today) the concept of easy doesn't come into the calculations.

'I want you to look at it,' he muttered with the hint of an apology. 'Things are out of hand and getting worse. He's a terrible man, utterly ruthless, a known killer.'

'That's true.'

We were silent for a full minute. It seemed Sir Lance was in no hurry to elucidate. The room was comfortable and there was plenty of time, though I wasn't exactly relaxed. Outside, the crescent moon could be glimpsed through heavy cloud which was more than could be said for the great man, who was wreathed in shadow beside the window's curtains. A table lamp at the far corner provided the sole lighting while the main lounge, two doors away, was illuminated one notch below the maximum for a country mansion. No one would know we were in his study: he was a man of some subtlety.

'We want you involved. And you gotta see him first. Press images never give the right impression. What d'you say?'

I shifted in my chair.

'Best not... I wouldn't mind *observing* him from a distance.'

'That's exactly what I mean. You'd stay in the background.'

'Yes, but where would this meeting –?'

'Oh, the House. It's the only predictable place in his itinerary. I won't be introducing you. Shouldn't be too unpleasant. And you gotta see him. What d'you say?'

Ideally I'd have wanted to mull it over first, there were many angles to be considered and it was a humdinger of a proposition. By accepting his offer I'd begin to be involved, steamrollered into a pattern of events that promised to be challenging. But I needed the money.

'Well –'

'Meet me at the House,' he said, becoming decisive. 'How about tomorrow?'

2

My particular discipline discourages the frank exchange of information and I didn't tell him that Harry and I had already met in somewhat unpleasant circumstances that still rankled.

It was two in the morning and I was home on leave when the phone burst into life. Had it been in any other room I'd have left it unanswered. Without a doubt I should have done just that, but by this time I was awake and its strident tones couldn't be ignored. I put it to my ear without uttering a word.

'Is that you, Mat?' said a voice, which I recognised as Big Andy's. He seemed anxious. I said nothing. 'Mat, can you hear me? Mat?'

'What is it?'

'Come and get me, I'm in bad trouble.'

'You usually are.'

'This is desperate – I'm stuck in a warehouse.'

When you've just awakened you can be pardoned for wanting to avoid some of Andy's excesses, but sometimes they're unavoidable. He's a big man with bad judgement who throws his weight around and makes demands on his friends without being helpful in return. A lot of people won't talk to him, but that option wasn't open to me. He was a colleague and there's an understanding that we must assist each other.

'What are you doing?'

'I got in a window and can't get out, you gotta help me –'

As my eyes adjusted to the darkness of the room, I winced at the 'you gotta help me' as though I'd sent him there in the first place. Andy is a peculiarly awkward man who walks with a clumsy stride and is forever falling over things. At that point I was on leave from the unit, taking a holiday at my flat and trying to cope with the rotten weather. Surely I was entitled to some sleep.

'How?'

'You'll have to come and get me out,' he said, his voice

rising.

'Whose phone are you using?'

'Theirs – they can't trace it. Here's the address...' And he recited a place an hour's drive away.

I may appear to lead a colourful life but that's an illusion. Almost every part of my existence is dull, so much so that I never stray from law and order. I am not a criminal, I am not criminally inclined, nor would I want to be. At that point in my career a conviction in Court would have resulted in a dismissal that would have ruined the rest of my life. Yet here was a man – a colleague of several years – requesting help for what sounded like a madcap burglary.

'There's no time to spare, leave right away.'

For a man who was not in a position to dictate, this was a bit rich. I allowed a ten second gap before saying: 'Okay.'

'Park on the main road. Walk round the back, it's got a red roof.'

Slamming the phone down, I got dressed and, it being a damp night, had some trouble starting the car. By that time the roads were quiet, though they became progressively busier as I neared London. I'd said an hour, but it took thirty five minutes to reach the industrial estate, one of the biggest I'd ever seen, with most of its factories closed for the night, something that made a solitary car obvious. Cops were one thing, night watchmen and CCTV cameras were another. I'd a chance of getting my number logged if something went wrong and with Andy that was all too likely.

Rather than park on the street, I chose a convenient bay at a factory on the night shift with a busy car park and strolled towards Big Andy's problem. Surprisingly it was a publishing company that was receiving his crazed attention. What was worth stealing in a publisher's warehouse? Only books, and you need a truck for that. It seemed depressingly prosperous, a huge building with the look of some serious security.

Walking at the edge of the pavement, I tried to be inconspicuous, though a light fall of rain began to make me look like a downright fool. Who goes walking in the rain at that time in the morning? And this was not the place to attract walkers even in the best of weather. I was the sole pedestrian, strolling slowly with my hands in my pockets hoping to be mistaken for a nightshift worker out for a quick smoke.

The warehouse had an empty car park to the front and a short road flanking its north side that probably fed loading bays at the back. Such was the size of the frontage that it took an age to cover the distance, during which I must have been visible for a mile under the street lighting. It would be difficult to explain to a passing cop why I'd left my bed to walk in that odd place and of course there was the chance I was being recorded by any one of a dozen cameras. Here I made a move to the north side that gave a view of the main road outside with convoys of trucks thundering along its length. That meant I was visible from outside the estate too, a solitary man sneaking up on a closed factory. On the opposite side of this street, there were a couple of workshops in darkness, with no cars in front of them. I cursed when I looked to the left to see a small car at the back of the big warehouse, almost certainly belonging to a night watchman's. That was all I needed.

Now the building with the red roof came into view, an annexe that looked like an afterthought on the planner's part. It wasn't small, although the warehouse dwarfed it. At least it was sufficiently set back from the road to be nearly out of sight. It presented several windows to the world, all of which were intact and had clearly not been forced. I rapped on the central one and waited, cursing myself for getting involved. What would happen if a patrol car arrived?

'Mat,' said someone and I looked up to see Andy looking down at me from the first floor window. 'I'm in here.'

He had a hook nose and the face of a madman. His hair was unkempt and his eyes were bloodshot, which probably meant he'd been drinking. He was dressed in baggy clothes that were sure to get caught on sharp corners. If there was a wrong way to do a thing, Andy would do it every time. Presumably he'd been trapped for some time before phoning me; perhaps saner people had refused to help. We began a conversation in whispers.

'What do I do?'

'The key's on the other side of my door.'

Rain was running down my face as I looked up at the big fool, trying to decipher this remark. Then I understood. He wanted me to break in and unlock his door.

'I can't break in!'

'Nothing else for it.'

Assisting a friend was one thing (though in legal terms it made me a party to his crime). Breaking in was something else. And there were sure to be sophisticated alarms in the place; it was a wonder he hadn't set them off. Anyway, I couldn't break in. I'd no tools aside from my Swiss army knife and I knew nothing about the building's geography.

'How did you get in?'

'The side street; it's no good, you can't get out.'

Walking to the side street I found the first floor window immediately. It was wide open – an act of monumental stupidity. Any passing cop or watchman would recognise it as a break-in from several hundred metres: in fact it was visible from the main road beyond the estate. Underneath the window was a broad pipe, big enough to walk on, which he'd used to get in. Not particularly difficult, even for big Andy and no doubt it hadn't been raining at the time, but he was too clumsy to get out by the same route and that wouldn't have occurred to him until it was too late.

This is where it got dangerous. I looked around to make sure the area was free of both cars and people. Beyond the building, the street came to a stop at a hedge where there was a gap for a footpath. If something went wrong I could run there and find somewhere to hide. Of course I'd have to wait until the fuss had died down before retrieving my car. Not much of a plan, but at least it offered an option.

The rain was still falling. The pipe promised to be slippery. I'd have to hope my old skills were still on tap. Putting on gloves, I climbed up the pipe, my shoes gripping well, and was in the room in a matter of seconds. Unlike Andy, I had the option of getting out by the same method.

He was towering over me, all anxious.

'How are you going to get out now?' he asked as I closed the window. I didn't know how he'd got it open. Andy isn't good with his hands and there had been no damage to the lock, so someone must have left it open. That was probably what had happened. Andy wouldn't think of it himself. No doubt an insider at the pub had come up with the brilliant scheme and he'd leapt at it without further thought.

'What are you going to do now?' he asked.

The room was a fair size. It looked as though it was in constant use as a store for packing materials, with several windows which let in a fair amount of light from the street. Along the walls there were thousands of corrugated cartons, all flat packed, as well as several tables, most of them covered by dust sheets. There were laser printers and duplicators that looked as if they'd had a lot of use as well as two trolleys for moving loads and a goods hoist for the far corner – not a bad thing, it might give me the chance of an exit if all else failed, through such things are usually slow and noisy.

I wiped my wet shoes on a dustsheet. One thing you must avoid is wet footprints on the floor.

With nothing to talk about, I walked to the door to find a mortice lock with a key in the other side. There were several ways to get round the problem, but I hesitated. Why, in a big smart company, would someone lock the door on the outside and leave the key in it? Usually keys are held by the duty officer and while there's no accounting for human sensibilities, they are seldom left in the door overnight.

'Alright, what's the story?' I asked.

'I came in the window and that door was locked.'

'Did someone lock it *after* you came in?'

'No, it was like that when I got here.'

'What were you after?'

'They're pirating *Windows* labels. I can get a fortune for them.'

For a moment the ground shifted under my feet. This was not the time to chat about the disadvantages of his brilliant wheeze. I'd no great sympathy with Mr Bill Gates and the odd million would make no discernible difference to his chances, but if the firm was engaged in piracy, that meant it was almost certainly run by gangsters, who would take a dim view of Andy's enterprise.

'Can we get out by the main door if I open this? You're sure it's not alarmed?'

'This place isn't alarmed. I know a worker.'

'You're sure?'

He nodded.

Turning to the door, I got out my Swiss army knife and was about to start work on the lock when I heard a door slam.

There were some footsteps.

'Security,' whispered Andy. 'He's been in twice. Doesn't come upstairs.'

More footsteps. Another pause, and then I heard them begin to ascend a metal stairway which obviously led to our room. I swung round and gestured Andy against the wall. The key was in the door and this room was the guard's probable destination. Andy is so big that the guard might notice his bulk before the door was properly open. If the alarm were pressed we were done for. In desperation, I looked for a weapon and saw nothing. It would have to be fisticuffs, and still that might not stop him pressing the button.

The footsteps arrived at our level and the floor creaked as the security guard walked past our door, continuing to the end of the corridor before coming back and descending the stairs, slightly out of breath. There was a ten second pause before the outer door slammed. Plainly he'd pressed a security code before opening it.

'You great nitwit,' I said. 'This place *is* alarmed.'

'I didn't know.'

I went to the window to look out. There was no problem about my getting away. Wet or not, I'd use the pipe, or there was the soft earth in the flower bed below me if I wanted to jump. I turned to the big idiot. He was the problem.

'I'll drop you out,' I said. 'After that you'll walk slowly to your car and drive off. We don't leave together, okay?'

'Right, do it.'

I grabbed a dust sheet, rolled it into a rope, and lowered it out of the window after looping it to a radiator. Then I got the window open. Outside the rain had stopped.

'Oh, I see. Good.'

Andy's had the same training as me and should have done this hours ago. The reality was that he'd had several options at his fingertips and had failed to use any of them. Unsteadily, he climbed on to the sill and slowly lowered himself on to the pipe with lots of huffing and puffing. Then he grasped the sheet and slid down until he hit the soft earth, rolled over and stood up in one movement. At least he hadn't broken his ankle, though he'd messed up the flower bed and got soil on his clothes. He walked off with a wave and shortly afterwards I saw an old banger drive off.

Glad to see him gone, I pulled the sheet back and returned it to its original position. Then I rubbed Andy's fingerprints off the sill, had a quick look to make sure nothing incriminating had been left and got ready to leave when there was the unmistakeable sound of a vehicle decelerating.

Jumping back, I slammed the window shut as a security van, driving in no great hurry, pulled up and parked outside.. Two minutes earlier and they'd have had Big Andy. I stepped back, well aware that a white face in a dark room is easy to spot. Outside, doors slammed as three people got out and walked off at a smartish pace.

What was happening? I remembered the key in the door, and the empty tables in the room. Perhaps they processed the labels in this very room. These, of course would be more than labels. They would bear security codes and serial numbers duplicating Microsoft's own and be marketed with identical packaging. Obviously this would require sophisticated equipment and somewhere there must be a replication plant to turn out the discs themselves. It was quite likely that the guards had come to sort the labels before the next stage. This was the kind of room they'd use, with its tables and packaging facilities. And of course they'd do it at night when the place was quiet. The night watchman had thoughtfully left the key in the door.

I crawled into the far corner behind the biggest pile of cartons. With a bit of luck I'd never be noticed. It seemed likely they would work quickly and be gone in minutes.

Half an hour later, I was getting cramp and still the outer door hadn't slammed; there'd been no footsteps, no talking and no activity of any kind. So they were not in this part of the complex and there was nothing to be gained by hiding. I got out and looked. The roof of the van was still visible, but there was no sign of activity. But the windscreen was slightly shaded and it would be unsafe to assume there was no one in the cabin. I waited in silence, furious with the big idiot for getting me into this mess, and trying to see an escape route. My watch said it was now three thirty in the morning. Time passed very slowly.

In desperation, I searched the room to find nothing that was any good to me. This was the despatch department and it contained only packing materials. There was no sign of the *Windows* labels, nor was there any indication of other work. Most such places are on the ground floor, but here the management had apparently elected to have it upstairs away from prying eyes.

Four o'clock and the van was still there. Soon early morning staff would arrive and I'd be trapped in a gangsters' storeroom.

At last there was the sound of a van moving. But it was a second one coming in from the main road to park behind the first. Doors slammed as three guards disappeared into an unseen point in the warehouse, walking fast. This made me look at the first van again. Perhaps there wasn't a watcher in its cabin after all, or the new arrivals would have identified themselves.. So I'd have to take the risk and leave before things got worse. I opened the window and was about to climb when I heard slow footsteps on the street at a point beyond my vision. It sounded like a guard on duty. He was either guarding the vans or acting as a look out. Of course the main road was in sight and he'd see the approach of any police vehicles. They'd get a minute's warning in the warehouse. They were organised, and that was possibly why there was a key in the door. In the event of bad weather the guard could watch from the window. And it had been raining earlier. He might have arrived in this very room!

Again I retreated, comforting myself with the thought that since they were involved in something shady they'd be gone before the day workers arrived. No need to panic. Organised gangsters don't take unnecessary risks. Soon they'd be off and I could get out there.

Then I heard the sound of another engine.

It was a third van, which parked behind the first two. Doors slammed as another three people got out: two men and a woman. One of them spoke to the unseen person before disappearing through the side door of the warehouse as though they'd a lot of work to do. Now three identical vans were sitting outside the window. At least nine people were involved , not including the guard on duty outside. Not good.

Another half hour passed. Already the sky was lightening in the east, several cars and vans had driven along the main road into the estate, presumably to get preliminary work done in other factories. The dawn was breaking, workers were driving to other parts of the Industrial Estate and the risk of being spotted when exiting the window was reaching new heights.

You certainly don't walk out and surrender to gangsters. One viable alternative – albeit a drastic one – would be to hide in the loft of the building until the following night. No picnic, but it would be better than being dead. My instructors had often mentioned that almost every building has a suitable place for water cisterns and paraphernalia seldom approached by the management. But first I'd have to get out of this room. By now the security guard was overdue for an inspection and I'd have to hope I'd hear his footsteps in time to take evasive action. I took my Swiss army knife and worked on the lock. Within five minutes the door was open to reveal a twenty metre corridor.

But my plan to hide in the loft failed too. The entire length of the ceiling was uninterrupted, meaning the loft in this part of the building was impossible to enter. There were several doors, all with keys in their locks. None gave access to the upper floor and none of them contained anything helpful to me.

Back in the first room, I returned the lock to its original condition before staring in fury at the three vans. Big stupid Andy had landed me in a potentially fatal mess.

Five o'clock (and still no security check; it didn't look like there'd be one now) and there were sounds of an engine, but it wasn't the vans, a truck had arrived and was reversing into a loading bay that was out of sight.

Alright, I had to face it. I was done for. I wasn't going to get away. There were too many people about, factory workers would be arriving shortly and the place was crawling with guards. If I was going to live I'd have to bluff my way out.

I went downstairs to find a neat reception area that led to an office marked Mr Gundy, General Manager. It was a smart place with fine furniture and all the accoutrements of modern business. Usually the boss likes to be in the centre of things, but here Mr Gundy was isolated from his workforce. No surprise. When you're dealing in contraband, you don't want your secretary to see too much. There were facilities at the back where I washed my face and made myself as presentable as possible. I brushed the dust from my clothes and got my fingernails clean. One instructor used to tell us that with the right attitude you could convince anyone about anything. Why he'd never become a General remained unclear.

There was a bug in my pocket the size of a clothes button with two short trailing wires, its battery long dead. It was the souvenir of a past incident which I'd always known would be useful. I put it through my top with just the tail-end of a wire visible. Then I looked at my anxious, too white, face and wondered if I'd be alive by ten in the morning.

Taking a seat at the desk in a comfortable chair, I began looking about. Nothing was locked. The filing cabinet was full of papers and I did a lot of reading, though I have to admit there was nothing that looked remotely illegal. Of course they wouldn't put sensitive stuff in writing. I even brewed myself a cup of tea and ate a biscuit from Gundy's personal canteen.

Time passed. Around seven a guard came in to the vestibule and switched the alarms. He didn't patrol the building or look into the office. I went on with my reading. At least, I tried to, but it was hard to know what the words meant and my nerves were getting so bad that sometimes I was holding the paper upside down. Difficult to know what was going on outside and none of the vans had moved.

It was not until eight thirty that Gundy himself arrived. He was a man of about forty-five dressed in a mohair suit. He was thickset and looked none too bright, though I suspected he'd be good with his fists. There was a carton in his hands. He pushed the door open to find me sitting with my feet on his desk.

'Who the hell are YOU?' he bawled.

Behind him I could see part of a loading bay at the end wall of the big building. A workman who had been going across the tarmac looked round briefly, looked away even quicker, and continued walking. There was probably a lot of shouting in the firm and no doubt it was good policy to ignore it.

'Microsoft,' I said.

Gundy was about average height with the beginnings of a beer belly and from his stance it was easy to see that he was not quick witted. At this point the door was still open and I wondered if he was considering running for the guards. Then at last his brain creaked into life and he reacted.

'Who?'

'Microsoft. Put that carton on the desk, please.'

Perhaps it was sensitive. When I'd first spoken, he'd wrapped his arms around it like a child with a precious toy. It seemed he'd been doing some work in the main building before coming to his office. Very likely. You can hardly print *Windows* labels in the light of day without attracting the wrong kind of attention. The job would be done at night by a trusted few – no doubt he'd wanted to tidy up in case an embarrassing example of their piracy had been left in plain view.

'Get out of my office,' he said, trying to make it sound like a snarl.

That was very much my intention, but I doubted if I'd get ten paces, or even five, before he changed his mind.

'In due course,' I said, trying to keep a wobble out of my voice. 'After we've done some business. Put that down, please.'

He let the door close behind him and looked at me.

'Who are you?' and now there was a whine in his voice. He sounded more nervous than I did.

'Please, you heard me. Put that carton down and take a seat.'

But he remained standing.

'How long have you been here?'

By this time we'd reached a pivotal point in the preliminaries. Now he was beginning to ask the questions and I'd have to watch.

'Long enough to know everything. Let me see that, please.'

With a great sigh he reached over and placed the carton on the desk respectfully. It was packed with a variety of printed cards, none of which made any sense to me and none of which had anything to do with Microsoft. No doubt they ran a lot of profitable lines.

But he was getting his confidence back.

'You're not Microsoft. Why would you be alone?'

I smiled and pointed to the bug in my top.

'Modern technology,' I said. 'I'm not alone. There are security people recording every word. Isn't science great? This is the twenty first century, you know. They can be here in seconds.'

He produced a handkerchief and wiped some perspiration from his face, which was turning red. Then he sat down and put his face in his hands. I noticed a bald patch, and a gold ring on his finger.

'What's this in aid of?'

'We know about the copies, we know how you're doing it, how you're marketing them and who your customers are. It's all on the computer – I want to negotiate.'

'Negotiate?' he said, looking up in surprise. 'What d'you mean?'

'It's your lucky day. Destroy the labels and we'll forget it.'

His dark jacket was badly creased, but looked expensive. The lapel bore a badge marked Chief Executive. He was showing the right amount of cuff, but it was slightly soiled. He looked up to see if I was serious.

'Forget about it?' he sneered, though there was a wobble in his voice. 'As easy as that?'

'Oh, we don't want publicity. Every time this goes to Court there's a wave of imitators and that makes it worse. We are prepared to offer an amnesty provided you destroy all pirated material and undertake not to do it again.'

His mouth opened and closed in suspicion.

'How come you sued some people up North?'

'They refused to cooperate. The idiots thought a bent Inspector could save them. I deal on a higher level.'

'Uh, well I can't promise –'

'You'll have to. This is serious. You can get years for this.'

He cleared his throat and said with some sincerity:

'I'm the General Manager, but I'm not the real boss. He's coming in this morning. You'll need to speak to him.'

I stared at his fat face in consternation. So far my tactics had been effective and he was reasonably pliant. But that was anything but absolute and a new nervousness made my hands shake so badly I had to put them in my pockets. Microsoft was no part of my agenda; all I wanted was a convincing cover for my getaway. One thing I didn't need was a boss who was certain to be a stage or two above Mr Gundy's powers of perception.

'When is your boss due, Mr Gundy?'

He looked at his watch and said:

'Any time. I've seen him here at seven, but sometimes it's eleven. If you wish I could phone –'

'Best not.'

A warning would do me no good. Perhaps it would be possible to make a retreat and say I'd be back later, but how would that go down? Surely a senior investigator would wait until the job was done? No – I'd have to wait and bluff it out. My performance so far had been nothing more than bluster in front of a dolt. Clearly Mr Gundy was a mere buffer between the factory and the head honcho. What kind of things would I have to say to convince his boss, and how could I conclude it before driving off in my old banger? I was done for.

'He's a busy man,' I said. Now I was almost keeping in with him.

'Big bosses usually are. Do you know Bill Gates?'

'I've met him,' I improvised. 'But he's not as nice as he looks –'

Then the phone burst into life like an exploding bomb and for a few seconds we stared at it, knowing that it could herald big changes to the situation. He reached out and looked at me respectfully. I nodded, he lifted it and said: 'Hello.'

A female voice said something.

'Ask him to come here. It's urgent.' He put the phone down and said: 'We're in luck, he's just arrived.'

But it didn't sound like luck to me. If the place hadn't been surrounded by guards it might have been possible to do a runner, but I'm not getting any younger and there would certainly be an athlete among them. I'd have to face the music.

'He's very smart to deal with,' said Gundy. 'You'll be

impressed.'

A trickle of perspiration ran down my face.

Outside there were footsteps and I looked up to see Harry Hetland (though at that point I didn't know who he was) come into the room with a big guard behind him. Later, I would find out it was Gundy's use of the word 'urgent' that had done it. Harry had a sensitive ear and didn't miss a trick. His eyes were intelligent and they were focussed on me, sitting on his General Manager's chair.

'He's Microsoft,' said Gundy, looking up at his boss.

'How nice,' said Harry. 'Perhaps he's bought the company?'

Mr Hetland had a well shaped head and black hair. His face promised a lot of mental energy. His shoulders were wide, his eyes were dark and there was something about his face that was downright malevolent. The mention of Microsoft had left him undaunted, though there had been a brief moment of uncertainty as he tried to puzzle my role. He was too important for this emergency and he had nothing but contempt for me.

'No chance of that,' I said, irritated by his disdain. Had he been polite I might have been finished but suddenly the ball was at my feet again. 'We know what's going on. And we don't need a security guard.'

'And you're in a position to dictate?'

I stared at him.

After twenty seconds he turned to the big man and said:

'Alright, Bert, wait outside the door.'

The big fellow went out and we were alone. He seemed glad to go and I envied him his freedom.

I said: 'First, I should warn you that this conversation is being recorded.' Harry, I noticed, had already located the bug by the time he'd ordered the guard out. No doubt he'd also noted a few other things to my disadvantage. At that moment something happened to me. I'd nothing left to say. My mind had gone blank.

'Well?'

Shrewd eyes were turned on me and they were utterly calm. Harry was no panic merchant. Without doubt I'd seen this man on TV and in the papers, though I couldn't identify him. His tasteful navy blue jacket, tie and silk handkerchief were immaculate, without a crease, but as an army man, I recognised a bulky shape about his jacket that meant he was clad in a bullet proof vest. 'We know about your piracy,' I began, carefully avoiding his eye. 'It's got to stop. I'm here in an informal capacity to negotiate a deal. Destroy all your *Windows* labels and we'll forget it. That means the masters, the artwork and the data files. All pirate material must be shredded and you must sign a legal undertaking not to do it again.'

He stared at me for ten seconds during which my life passed before me.

'*Windows*?' said Harry, seemingly baffled, with honest surprise in his face. 'Oh, *Windows*! So that's what this is about. We're in perfect agreement. There's no need for the melodrama. I believe I have a license for every computer in the building. If there's any discrepancy I'll write a cheque this very morning.'

'You're running thousands of counterfeit discs' I said, all too aware that the source for this was Big Andy, a man who hadn't even realised the door was alarmed.

'Discs. Thousands?' said Harry with a puzzled frown. He was playing with me. 'What's going on? Do you know anything about this, Mr Gundy?'

'No.'

'We have no facilities for duplicating discs, have we?' The question had an air of honest puzzlement that would have made an actor proud.

'No, none at all, Mr Hetland.'

I heard this with a jolt, recognising him at last. The name of Harry Hetland would strike fear in the stoutest hearts. Everybody knew he was a gangster, though his ratings were beginning to rise now that he'd become an MP. When he looked at me I had to stop myself wincing.

'Do you have evidence of this? Perhaps some copies I can examine? We've never printed a *Windows* label in our lives, have we, Gundy?'

'No, Mr Hetland.'

So the General Manager who had more or less admitted the offence a few moments ago was now singing his master's song. But I could hardly blame him for siding with the ball of fire beside him. I'd have done the same.

Then Harry's eyes went to the bug and he gave me half a smile and adopted a friendly tone. Intimidate them first and then turn on the charm. There were no flies on this man. Now he was a smart young lawyer who'd just concluded a deal:

'What is your name, sir? Who am I dealing with?'

'Murgatroyd. Sid Murgatroyd,' I blurted. In the tension of the moment I'd almost said Mat Hill.

'Well, Mr Murgatroyd, let me put my cards on the table. I am a totally honourable businessman with a blameless record. I pay my taxes and all my debts. You have come to my office to claim that I'm pirating your product. I am not, but I also accept that you reasonably believe I am, otherwise you wouldn't be here. Presumably you have evidence to encourage this view and in all fairness I'm entitled to see it before the matter goes any further. I can understand that you wouldn't bring important evidence in an informal capacity. But I have to see it.'

I remember my Commanding Officer arguing with another officer. He was quite wrong but he won the exchange by saying as little as possible. I'd learnt a lot from watching officers. I'd have to take a leaf from his book.

'We don't want fuss,' I said, trying to get the initiative again. 'This is informal.'

'Oh, I welcome that, Mr Murgatroyd. That is the only way to handle the difficulty,' said Harry, all sweet reason. 'I don't welcome a fuss either, absolutely not. But recently we found our name used by an unscrupulous individual and I had to use my influence to correct a damaging situation. This may be the explanation of your – um – misunderstanding.'

'The evidence is strong.'

'I suppose it is, otherwise you wouldn't be here. But I will fight it with all my resources; so let's bypass the formalities. You must bring me samples of these – er – pirated discs. If we're in any way at fault I'll do something about it immediately. Perhaps an employee has been using my facilities. I've heard of that happening elsewhere, but never here. If so, I'll deal with it right away. You have made a verbal complaint, but with respect, that's not enough. Not on the scale we're dealing on. I employ hundreds of people and their welfare has got to be considered. For the moment I must ask for proof.'

During this, Harry had moved and I saw what might have been the outline of a gun in a shoulder rig, something I'm trained to watch for. Gundy looked a poor figure beside his boss. His face was red, his hands were clenched and he was sweating. It seemed likely that he wasn't starting a shift, but concluding one. He'd been up all night.

'Proof?' I said. 'But that can't leave our office.'

'Oh yes it can, Mr Murgatroyd. You said labels – you spoke in the plural. Bring me one, that's all I ask. I don't need more. It's not a lot to ask. Of course I'll expect a written statement of where you obtained it and when, also a forensic breakdown, but your legal department will understand that.'

'I'd hoped to resolve this –'

'And we surely will when you bring it.'

'Very well,' I said, but possibly it was a mistake to concede so soon. Surely no investigator would be so ineffectual? 'Perhaps tomorrow?'

The cool eyes looked at me as his head shook.

'I won't be here tomorrow. How about Friday?'

He was certainly used to unnerving his opponents, and it was obvious he considered me a pure weakling. Was I too pliant to be true?

'Yes. Friday at nine?'

'Well, that's a deal, then,' he said, standing up. 'Now, I'm busy. The auditors are waiting in the main building.'

I stood up too, suddenly aware that my tensed muscles had almost seized. Harry had an expression of triumph on his face that made me suspect he'd seen through me and was about to seal my fate. The guard was still at the door. Gundy's gaze was switching between me and his master.

'We've compromised,' I said, in a last desperate bid to get the upper hand. 'Bend a little in my direction, Mr Hetland. Let me see through your factory before I go.'

That is what saved me. For the briefest second a twinge crossed his face. Gundy was looking at me with a startled expression, his mouth open, while his boss held out his hands to stop me.

'Any other time than this, Mr Murgatroyd,' said Harry, all business-like. 'We'll show you round on Friday, not before. With respect, you haven't established your credentials, you don't have a warrant and I have a partner from Price Waterhouse waiting for me. In any event, as an investigator you must be aware that even if we were pirating your material, which I assure you we are not, we'd hardly have it lying about on display.' During this, he had avoided my eye, now his forehead furrowed for a minute as he looked at me. 'But we'll cooperate on Friday. I'll show you around with great pleasure. Don't go and get a warrant, now. That won't be necessary. You'll have my full support. You'll see the entire building, every nook and cranny.'

3

'This is not a coup,' continued Sir Lance, 'not in any sense of the word. We've no intention of putting anybody in his place, none at all.'

I gave him a nod, none too surprised. In my book a coup was neither here nor there. He was merely assuring me that the plotters had no intentions of seizing power and I knew that already. Whatever his qualities, Sir Lance was not an aspirant for Number Ten. The whole thing was to bring down Harry and that was enough to be going on with. And of course we don't do coups in the UK.

'And what did you want me to, um, do?'

'Oh, you're not involved in the... action, if there is any. We want the possibilities aired, that's all. Give us a detailed, comprehensive report to military standards. We've got to look at the options without personal bias. You know how to do it. You've done it in Special Forces.'

Like many desk men, Sir Lance was impressed by vague references to Special Forces. But I'd no great experience of this kind of thing. It sounded a bit over the top and the UK was probably the worst place on earth to try it. That said, I'd always regarded him as a sane man who had never once disgraced himself. And the money was good.

'Well, I can do that; a preliminary report first, then zero in on the detail?'

'Yes, that kind of thing. A look at the options. And we want it soon. I'll give you a disc with a lot of his personal details, all of them less than six months old, to give you a look at his lifestyle.'

'He's going to be a tough nut.'

'Yes, but he's got to go,' said Sir Lance, like a vet getting ready to put the dog down. 'Ideally he should be exposed on the political front, but he's got the press tied up. We've got to consider other options. Hopefully it won't be necessary, but we need a contingency plan. I mean, he could be the next prime minister and then there'd be some fun. He'd flout the Electoral System like he's flouted everything else. Once in power he'd be difficult to unseat, maybe impossible. Damn it, man, he could be the next Hitler.' Then he added: 'That's why we want you involved – a decent man. I've known your family for thirty years.'

Here I reminded myself that I was in the company of a serious player. Sir Lance was a trained lawyer, possibly a brilliant one (if there is such a thing) though he was surely past his best at seventy. A one-time Cabinet Minister, he was now a backbencher who knew a lot about politics. But that didn't mean he wasn't out of his depth

'Well, I'll study the disc and have a look at his background. To be honest I'm not into, um, liquidations.'

In the shadows, Sir Lance nodded his head with some vehemence. It seemed we both had a distaste for the dirty work.

'Nor am I. None of us have any experience of this, or the inclination. But something's got to be done, and soon. We'll go into that later. He's got a deadline coming up, the launch of a campaign that'll focus the public's mind on his ambitions, make it clear he's heading for Downing Street. Big PR firms are working on it, planting stories about what a nice fellow he is – it's costing a fortune. And he was in that TV programme, that soap, as the loveable man next door. Damn near made me sick. How did he get into *that*? And in a strong role too. Better men than him aren't even considered. Of course we know the reason. Money – and I hear he took care of someone who'd been annoying the producer. The worst thing is that the viewing figures were up for the night. Up! He's now the most popular politician in the country. He's had speech lessons and taken courses in acting and deportment. He can't grin so they're teaching him to smile. He's reinvented himself from street fighter to media personality. The average member of the public doesn't believe he was ever a gangster or even connected with the underworld. They're giving him a clean sheet.'

'And he's a big businessman.'

'He certainly is,' said Sir Lance, shaking his head at the scale of it all. 'Newspapers and a lot of media companies. He's even got an airline now.'

Possibly Sir Lance had misunderstood my military past. After a dull career in the service, of which ninety per cent had been boring beyond belief, some colourful operations had arisen and somehow by sheer luck I'd never once messed up. On the front, you can keep your head down but there's no guarantee you won't stop a bullet. I had never messed up, but twice I'd given myself up for dead, only to find that I was in the winning team after all. But nine lives don't last forever.

'He's some man.'

'I detest this whole business. Never dreamed there'd come a time when I'd consider an assassination. Hate the very idea. But he's got to be stopped. We're calling this Operation Garden – Garden for short. In an emergency you can phone me at the Commons, or wherever, and a casual mention of the word is all you'll need. But we're going softly here, the stakes are high. Nothing sensitive is to be mentioned, of course. You merely say the word and I'll get back to you. The lines could be tapped. They probably are.'

'Oh, I'm an old hand.'

I risked a glance at his wiry frame. His family have owned our local manor, the forty-room Dalespun Towers, for centuries. That didn't mean I had to trust his judgement, though there was little doubt that Harry Hetland was a rogue and the world would be safer without him. Sir Lance's face was in shadow and he was frowning severely. These were weighty matters and he had always been little uncertain of me. I suppose he thought there was the chance I had contacts in MI5, though no doubt he'd made some discreet enquiries first. That's the trouble with plots; you can never be entirely sure of your fellows.

I got business-like.

'So, I'll have a look at the prospects, mull over a few possibilities and come back to you?'

There was a lawyerly pause after his candour. For a man who seldom utters unguarded comments, he had made some big disclosures. Now he was all sweet reason. He cleared his throat.

'Yes, all the possibilities have to be aired. Maybe we'll do nothing, but we want to know the angles. If there's a good opportunity we'll certainly look at it. We need you on board.' I said nothing. The invitation was best ignored, for the present. I would confine myself to a report without getting further involved.

'Shortly he'll make an assault on his party leadership. Once past that hurdle he's in line to be the next prime minister. A gangster who's been jailed for manslaughter.'

'Terrible.'

Sir Lance's voice dropped an octave and he leaned forward in the darkness. 'How would you do it? I mean, just off the top of your head. We've tried everything. Big exposures in the press which never get printed, TV documentaries which have been stopped. To be honest, we've been at it for years. Locks like it's got to be the heavy treatment. What would you suggest?' Then he sat back and looked at me.

I've had that kind of question before, though nearly always from professionals whose discretion can be relied on. You don't do it in private homes with ordinary members of the public, even if this was a rich home and Sir Lance was an important man.

I said: 'He's a high profile figure, protected everywhere he goes by bodyguards and security men. I'd have thought MI5 could give you all the information you needed.'

Wrong reply, even if it was technically correct. But I learnt something from his reaction.

'Not a bit of it! He's got fingers in a lot of pies. If I approached MI5 it would be leaked to Hetland within an first hour.'

'And that would be bad for the health.'

'It certainly would. Look what happened to Harpur.'

'Harpur? But that was a burglary that went wrong.'

'Don't you believe it. The whole thing was handled so well we were all duped. Harpur was Hetland's fiercest critic, the only one who would openly oppose him. And what about that Murray business last year, eh? Another critic comes a cropper.'

There was a pause. I could hear an owl hooting outside. I looked at the carpet and wondered why it was so ugly. I concluded that it was probably Persian and hundreds of years old.

'We'd better be careful.'

But it's a dicey job being a political assassin (that goes for the planning, too) and I didn't fancy my chances one little bit. Never mind that the nation would benefit from the death, the assassin's prospects are always poor. Inevitably he'll be caught, and if he's still alive seven days later, he's doing well. Politicians become popular the moment they're hit; that's their greatest career move. Their faults are forgotten while the public sheds its tears. And I've never ceased to be amazed at how efficient a state can become in the aftermath of an assassination. The services interlock, efficiency reaches unheard of heights, Security just happens to remember things they'd previously ignored, and hey presto, the villain's in hand cuffs before the kettle's boiled. If he's still alive.

'I'll have to study his lifestyle.'

'Of course you will. And I'll tell you that's not going to be easy. He's elusive, almost impossible to track.'

'Yes, but I've got to get it, Sir Lance.'

'We'll give you all the help we can. All legitimate expenses will be paid. I'll give you a thousand in advance today. It's in fifties for convenience, but you'll be able to change them okay. To put it bluntly, we want him out of it, but not necessarily by force. As I said, I'm not asking you to be the executioner. I'm asking you how to do it.'

The money was tremendously welcome, but even so, it should have been in inconspicuous denominations. A wad of fifties gets noticed anywhere. A lot of shops won't accept them, and even if they do, there's the risk of drawing attention to yourself. Used tenners would have been far more sensible, but there was no chance of my refusing.

'I'll work from home first. Later, I'll need to go to town.'

So he wasn't proposing a suicidal assault on Mr Hetland's bull neck, at least not yet. Nor was he asking me to wield the dagger. The prospect of a report wasn't so bad and I would certainly err on the side of caution. The case for abandoning the notion was obvious and I'd be quick to suggest it.

But this was really something: a one-time Cabinet Minister plotting to execute a prominent politician. And there was the question of whether I'd be allowed to walk away if I refused to be involved. Sir Lance was a decent man, but perhaps he was merely the mouthpiece of an unknown group, probably fiercer than he was. No plotter can afford to have a refusenik in the background. There was the question of whether those behind him would let me go if I declined to be involved. But I'm a survivor. I'd take the safest route by going along with them for the moment.

'You know how to do it.'

I was tempted to ask how he knew anything of my work, much of which was supposedly under lock and key, but there's no point in asking useless questions.

'First,' I said, 'I'll outline methods of approach, and the risks. Sometimes it needs a team to get the fine detail. But I know how it is, there's a limit to the personnel available, so I'll work under these constraints. But that heightens the risk of error. There are a lot of difficulties there.'

'Yes, yes, I understand. Do you see any possibilities, just off the cuff?'

'We'll have to be careful,' I said, wincing at the 'we' – did that make me a plotter too? 'It depends on the facilities. Poison gas, or deadly drugs –'

Sir Lance winced and held up his hand.

'We've listed some things on the disc. Sensitive military stuff, but let's avoid the exotic for the moment. How would you do it using the standard tools of the, er, trade?'

So he didn't want to know about the gory details, and when push came to shove, neither did I, but sometimes there's no alternative.

'Well, drugs are probably best. A heart attack induced by an undetectable pill. But there's the problem of administering it. It's easiest if he takes recreational drugs, but I don't know if he's into that. Shooting's far too risky, at least in this country. A little accident when he's with his supporters, perhaps. Or his car might catch fire. If he goes sailing, his boat might sink. Of course it's always best if that happens when he's abroad, but he's not much of a traveller, is he?'

Sir Lance winced again and looked at me for a long time, before nodding.

'How many people know about this?' I said.

He shook his head.

'Can't tell you that, my boy. It's a small number and we've a lot to lose.'

'How would you reply if they asked why you phoned me tonight?'

But questions like that shouldn't be addressed to a consummate politician.

'Oh you're an old family friend. Your father was our gardener for thirty years. I told you I was considering having a dinner for old friends of the estate.'

'Alright, that might work. But how many other phone calls have you made?'

He held his hand up to stop my questions.

'None. We know what we're doing. You're the only person we've approached.'

I don't know why, but when someone says that kind of thing I always get tense. It implies a hedging of bets, though I didn't doubt Sir Lance was being straight with me.

'First I want you to see Harry Hetland,' he said. 'Meet me in London at the House tomorrow. Use a false name. How about Bob Browne?'

I wasn't in a position to refuse. I said yes and we decided to meet at three.

4

At that time, my girlfriend Adele, she worked for the police and she preferred the tall young coppers. Lately, I'd noticed contempt in her voice when she spoke to me and I can't altogether blame her. In her shoes, I might have done the same.

'Where have *you* been?' she asked when I finally got back to our flat.

I could hardly tell her about Sir Lance, and anyway I'm not in the habit of reciting my life in blow-by-blow detail. Besides, Adele wasn't all that frank about her own activities.

'Walking up the river,' I said, looking at my muddy shoes and telling the absolute truth. Dalespun Towers has a fine avenue of trees with a gardener's lodge at the bottom, whose occupants include a Doberman dog with a notorious temper and a bark that can be heard for miles. Rather than subject myself to a confrontation, I'd opted for the footpath beside the river, much loved by fishermen. I had known it since I was a kid, and it neatly avoided the attentions of both the gardener and his canine companion. I'd even mentioned it to Sir Lance when he saw me off, but he was preoccupied with his plot and nodded uncertainly when I left.

'I like walking up the river.'

'In the dark? Since when?'

'I just felt like it. What's for supper?'

One thing she has never accused me of is having another woman. She has long since concluded that my powers of attraction were close to zero, though she might be aware that I'd dressed up out of respect for the great man. I began to unlace my shoes.

'Get your own. I'm going out.'

Sure enough, she was dressed up for an evening on the town, though she wouldn't be the night's beauty queen, having applied her make-up with zeal rather than judgement. She'd also erred with tight trousers that rendered her hindquarters in an unflattering light. But what do I know? I've often been told I haven't a clue.

'Where are you going?'

'Out.'

'Will you be late, dear?'

'Yes, and don't dear me!'

I deduced from her aggressive tone that she was going out with her friend Hazel. Adele has a hard time with people. She tends not to like anyone, and that sometimes includes Hazel too. They have frequent rows which end in months of not speaking-, before making up. Hazel works in a dress shop and is oddly bad at choosing clothes. She's buxom and proud of it and wears garish outfits, sometimes in strong checks, which emphasise her size. They've had arguments about her clothes, they've had disputes about men, and they've had rows about everything else. Sometime life's like that.

The door banged.

I laced my shoes again and went out for carry-out, which I ate while studying the disc. It was labelled *'Early Medieval Madrigals Vol: 8'* and contained some boring lute music. The file on Harry Hetland was difficult to extract, and never referred to him by name. It was remarkably circumspect in its tone. It had been well produced by professionals and had clearly cost money. Then I looked at the internet to find that Harry had a massive number of entries, easily exceeding the Prime Minister. They fell into two categories. There were scarcely any neutral comments. The correspondents were either for him, blaming conspirators for the bad press, or very much against him. The latter had the hallmarks of the truth.

Harry's early life had been vicious. At the age of twenty, he'd come to public notice when he'd been sentenced to ten years for the manslaughter of a nineteen year old youth. Later he'd been released on a technicality. During the next five years he'd begun to acquire his fortune, and according to one website was questioned by police on seventeen occasions without once being charged. He was reputed to have killed several gangsters in a turf war. According to rumour, he'd burnt down a warehouse and prevented fire crews from reaching it, and was also said to have wrecked a chain of massage parlours that were competing with his own. He'd sued a national newspaper for writing a critical article about him and won a fortune. At the age of twenty five, he was king of London's underworld, feared in all quarters. Harry was ruthless, but he was loyal to his gangsters. Like the ancient Romans, he'd discovered they fought better when there was back-up and he'd used top lawyers to free his henchmen when they were convicted.

There were several sanitized versions of this. As a disadvantaged young man he'd been enticed into a London gang and had taken the rap for the death of a youth he'd never met. He was an easy target. The police action had been completely over the top and it was only when the Appeals Court examined the evidence that his complete innocence was established. Subsequent difficulties with the law were no fault of his; everybody knew the cops couldn't bear to see anyone getting out of their clutches. They had been guilty of harassment and had blatantly refused to apologise for his wrongful arrest. Yes, there had been gangland deaths. There are always gangland deaths, but not one had been linked to him and never once had he been involved in them. Harry himself had admitted to being naïve in maintaining friendships with his gangland acquaintances. But they were his pals, the only ones he knew, and to be on nodding terms with these disadvantaged young people was no crime. Social science was now more sensitive of these issues and after taking advice Harry had built a community hall, at his own expense, which aimed to take young people off the streets. The opening had been attended by the Chief Constable himself and there was a photograph of them shaking hands. Harry Hetland is a generous man who never bears grudges.

Apparently he was an unexcitable person (I could verify that bit) with a cool head, who could see the world as it really was. He lived well but not extravagantly. His home in London was comparatively modest and he avoided flashy cars and flashy people. There were no reports of wild parties. In fact, there were no records of Harry even attending a party, let alone organising one. But where was he going and what was his ultimate goal? At the age of twenty five he was a multi-millionaire with an expanding empire at his finger tips. His managers were very efficient and even the most reckless wouldn't dream of embezzling a penny. His future was assured. He'd be a billionaire one day, but was that what he really wanted? In fact he had a terrible disdain for money – not that he ever refused a penny – and low-brow greed was something he scorned, as he did the myriad of rich people he had to deal with every day. Surely there were higher goals than mere money?

At this point his career made a dramatic change. He was a rich man who wanted to become respectable. Now he owned legitimate, tax-paying companies, so he employed PR men to reinvent his image. After five years of listing his misdemeanours, the tabloids reconsidered their attitudes. They'd had no alternative. Harry's companies had advertising budgets and he had muscle as well as influence.

I remembered that he'd been released from jail on a technicality. That meant he had a clean slate and his criminal record had been quashed, making him eligible to become an MP. Despite Harry's lack of political know-how he was selected for a safe seat in the Commons and had never looked back. Whatever his faults, he was good with his constituents and had been re-elected at every subsequent election, despite being a poor speaker and often at odds with his own party. In fact, he was probably the worst orator in Parliament, but the public had become disenchanted with verbosity and on the odd occasion when he made a comment, his East London accent went down well. Also he never used two words when one would do – a trick that most politicians have never mastered.

Reading between the lines, his appointment to Parliament had been little more than an attempt to gain respectability and it was only after his second election that his political ambitious grew. Until that point he'd been a gangster, and even while sitting as an MP he'd been questioned by the police about several major hauls. These things stopped at his second election. From that point on there were no complaints of his behaviour and no reported police enquiries.

A study of Hetland the politician revealed a different man, whose voting record and policies were sensible and down to earth. Now it seemed there was nothing in his life that smacked of the gangster-made-good. It was difficult to believe that the two were the same person, and suddenly I began to see what was worrying Sir Lance. On paper, Harry Hetland had a good chance of becoming the next Prime Minister. He was seldom attacked from the opposite benches and never from his own. On the occasion of his third election, the newspapers were mostly in his favour and not one even mentioned his colourful past. The boy from the East End had made good.

I continued through the contents of the disc to find that the plotters had a lot of facilities available, ranging from nerve gas to fierce poisons – where they'd got them things was a mystery.

But there was a poverty of information about Hetland himself. Various operatives had tried to shadow him without success. He didn't use flashy cars and when he went to a meeting he'd often leave in a second car even though the first one was still waiting with its engine running. It was always difficult to pinpoint the exact time of his arrival, and I could verify that myself. Sometimes it was impossible to know which car he was inside. One operative had complained that they would need a convoy of vehicles to shadow him and that was clearly impractical, as he was frequently escorted by his detectives on Parliamentary business. It seemed that no single day in Harry's life had ever been logged. No one knew what he did with his time. Even his personal detectives (yes, they'd been approached too) were puzzled. Then there was the problem of his friends. He had none. Harry didn't take a six-pack round to Fred's and criticise the local team, and there was nobody who made regular phone calls to him. The information regarding his love life was just as sparse. He seemed to have no lovers. Harry owned a chain of massage parlours – or rather, they were owned by a Mr Goodal, but astute observers were confident that Harry was the real owner. They were no doubt full of beautiful women, but apparently Harry had never visited one. Perhaps he was homosexual? But no gay club had been graced by his presence, and there was nothing in his manner to suggest that he was gay. It seemed that Harry was totally asexual.

All of this was maddening. How could I write a report about

a man of whom they knew so little? At this point I should have contacted Sir Lance and asked for more information, or refunded his money, but I did neither.

I am not a political man. I don't vote. I don't trust politicians. I don't think they are all rogues, and nor do I object to their ability to water down their promises. As one wag said, the world would be radioactive dust if they kept their promises. But I could see that Harry Hetland was a cold murderer as well as a competent politician who could well finish up in Downing Street

Then the phone rang.

5

Until recently, Sir Lance had a chauffeur, a big fellow named Lowry. A former Sergeant Major, Lowry was entrusted with his master's secrets – a shrewd move, since he was probably the most taciturn man in the country. He was single and lived in a flat at the back of the Towers. He only had one friend, and that was the bottle. Drink is a bad career move for a chauffeur, yet he held his job. Like many of the British aristocracy Sir Lance paid his servants badly but had a strange loyalty to them.

Some months ago, Lowry came to see me. I'd been painting the ceiling at the time and had ignored the first rap on the door. I'd eventually answered it with bad grace after a series of loud blows that threatened to bring it down.

'We're needin' something done.'

I didn't ask any questions, and truth be told I was glad to be needed; it might even mean some money.

Since the main room was uninhabitable with paint dripping on to dust sheets, we went to the kitchen. In an attempt to be matey, I asked him how things were going and as usual received no reply. It occurred to be that he might have been drunk, although I doubt a teetotal Lowry would have been the life and soul of the party either,

'Look at this,' he said, producing some papers from his leather jacket. He showed me the print of a cottage that I recognised as a prime dwelling on the Dalespun Estate. About two miles from the town, it was on the river bank and had recently been renovated. Now in demand as a holiday cottage for the summer months, it was an ideal place for a dirty weekend – utterly beautiful, with every comfort and absolutely no nosy neighbours. There was a lot of speculation in the town about the goings on there. An internationally known actress had twice been seen driving to the cottage in a Mercedes Coupe and several people claimed to have seen Mick Jagger in the locality. It was said to be booked for months in advance. Sir Lance must have made a killing out of it.

'You know the place?'

I said I did.

'Mr Oxford Yates has been there for the last three weeks.'

'The Government Minister?'

A nod.

'I doubt if he was alone..'

Another nod

'He's there this weekend.'

'What do you want?' I said.

Lowry produced a photocopy of an A4 envelope addressed in elegant female script to *Mr Oxford Yates, c/o Riverburn Cottage, Dalespun Estate.*

'That's been delivered. Yates is there tomorrow – we don't want him to get it. You'll get a hundred for this.'

This was music to my ears, but there would be a challenge or two to be overcome.

'Fine. Get the envelope and go. You've got the key?'

'No. It's high-security. There's only one key and he's got it.'

I stared at it.

'Should be no trouble,' I said. 'One of the back windows then – in and out in five minutes.'

'No, the alarm goes to the cops.'

'Then I need a key.'

'There's none. I've got a bunch of keys you could try.'

I was silent. In Special Services we've gone into those things in some detail. This was a situation to avoid. It was a near certainty that none of the keys would fit, otherwise Lowry wouldn't be here.

'Alright,' I said, 'a motor bike, then, and a heavy hammer. In and out in ten seconds flat. Force the door and skedaddle before the cops get there?'

'That'll do.'

'I don't have a bike.'

'We've got one.'

'Can the door be forced alright, or is it metalled?'

'You can force it.'

But something in his tone made me distrust his answer. Many

doors can be forced by a blow. Nearly all domestic ones are easy casualties, but not security ones; they often have metal ribs and spoilers hidden in their frame. That said, I'm good with a hammer.

'You're sure the envelope's there? The post's not all that reliable.'

'Delivered by hand. The mail's on the floor. It's lying in the hallway.'

'Hand delivered? What's in it?'

'Ask no questions.'

'Wait a minute, mate. I could get years for this. I'm entitled to know.'

'Blackmail.'

'Who's doing the blackmailing?'

'Forget it – there are things you don't know.'

Yes, there certainly were. I looked at his big face and wondered. For a fraction of a second, I thought he looked unwell. His lips were moving, he was swaying slightly and his eyes were unfocussed. He belonged to a world where you asked no questions, and that was a problem. I was being asked to commit an illegal act without the benefit of the facts. I had no loyalty to Yates. Sir Lance was another matter. I'd some respect for the man. My father had worked for him for years and he was a useful friend who gave the impression (or perhaps it was the illusion) of being willing to help if I was in trouble.

Was someone trying to blackmail Yates and wanted an envelope removed from his weekend house? Surely Sir Lance wasn't the blackmailer? No, that was unthinkable. He was far too rich and far too old to get involved in such a dicey business. But he had to be involved, or Lowry wouldn't be standing in my house with instructions. And they had a photocopy of the envelope. Who photocopies envelopes before they deliver them by hand?

'Is Sir Lance at home?'

'No.'

The handwriting on the envelope was glamorous. It didn't look like a Government missive. A smart lady had written it. The script seemed slightly familiar. There had to be something momentous inside it to warrant such interest.

'You know for certain the envelope's there?'

A nod.

But there was an uncertainty in the nod. I got a feeling he hadn't bothered, and I couldn't see Sir Lance, an ex-Cabinet Minister, phoning Lowry with instructions to break into a house. But perhaps I was getting too pernickety. A hundred pounds is no fortune, but it would be useful.

'Okay, I'll be ready in an hour–'

'No, now.'

'But I'm painting.'

'Leave it. Come on.'

Lowry's eyes were wide and his head was raised in impatience. He was a Sergeant Major again and I buckled down.

'Alright, but I'll wash first.'

I might take the occasional risk, but leaving dabs of paint at a crime scene is best avoided. Have a good wash before the action and an even better one afterwards. The cops are dangerous when they get clues, so the trick is to leave none. One hammer mark on the door would do nicely. They'd never know there had been an envelope and they probably wouldn't care. Oxford Yates certainly wouldn't make a fuss, not on a dirty weekend. This would go into the Mindless Vandalism file and be forgotten forever.

'The bike works alright?' I asked.. 'And I'll need a good hammer and a helmet.'

This was answered with a nod and a grunt. We went to the car, an old land rover, and drove to Dalespun Towers without a further word.

At the beginning, he had been worried I'd refuse and now that I'd accepted he wasn't any happier. I wondered at the poverty of his life, an existence in a flat at the back of the mansion with the inevitable bottle of whisky and utterly no human contact, but each to his own. I've met people who'd say that was a heavenly prospect.

We pulled up at the back of the Towers and got out.

'Try it,' he grunted, indicating a bike he'd wheeled out of the stables. Where it had come from and how it had become the property of Sir Lance was an unanswered question. There was no likelihood of the great man being seen on it. But that is one of the strange things about the Towers and probably another thousand such mansions. They contained hundreds of objects that their owners had acquired over the years and which are seldom used. The bike started at the first turn and I drove to the lodge gate and back, annoying the Doberman. It was in good order, with the tyres at the right pressure and the engine purring nicely. I was impressed. Obviously Lowry had given it a once over.

There were three hammers to choose from. I selected one with a metre-long handle that would give me a good swing at the door. We strapped it to the rear of the bike. Then I donned a helmet and left with a gentle rev.

There's a network of roads around Dalespun Towers which often confuses visitors. These have been in existence for hundreds of years and none of them are signposted. Fortunately I know them all. I swung to the left and then to the right on to the south road, which was two miles long and fed various cottages and farms along the way.

In all, Sir Lance had about forty dwellings, which must have provided a good income. He no longer had a Factor; all the Estate's affairs had been managed until recently by a Mrs Hunt who had begun to adopt a superior attitude, as though she owned it all. Had this been daytime, she'd have rebuked me for lowering the tone of the place with a motorbike. Fortunately she was no longer in his employment.

Within five minutes I reached the cottage.

As expected, it was in darkness. Keeping the revs down in case there was a fisherman about, I swung round, taking care to make no tracks in the mud.

A neat little sign said 'Riverburn Cottage'. It was white, with a red tile roof and a reasonably tidy garden. It appeared deserted. I unfastened the hammer and went up the path of paving slabs to discover the door was nothing more than a domestic one. Nor were there any signs of burglar alarms. The nearest window revealed an unlit room with some unremarkable furniture. A glance through the letter box showed nothing. But it was dark and that's only to be expected.

In the best regulation manner, I stood back, gripped the handle with both hands and then swung at the lock with an almighty blow that would have earned the praise of my old training sergeant. There was a tremendous thump and the door flew open with ease.

But what was this? There was no mail on the floor. Lights came on. A middle aged woman put her head around the corner and gave a scream that almost damaged my hearing. I was looking at someone's house, with coats hanging on the wall, flowers in a vase and today's papers neatly folded on a table. It was the wrong house.

Then my training kicked in. Soldiers are forever being sent to false destinations and become experts at retrieving situations. Strategic withdrawal is all part of the act. First, you utter no sound that would identify you, second you leave nothing behind and third, you get the hell out of it. I went for the bike, which was still running, threw a leg over it, and roared away with the hammer across the bar. But that was a mistake. Unsecured, the hammer slid off after less than a hundred metres. Since it was evidence and couldn't be left behind, I swung round and reached for it, managing to upset the bike and land it on top of me. Struggling out, I righted the bike, strapped on the hammer and mounted the machine again. Then I began to think. Haring off in the direction of Dalespun Towers was not the ideal solution. The cops would follow that road, Lowry would be unable to stop them looking around and the bike (which would still be warm) would be easy to spot in the stable. No – it was better to head in the opposite direction. Granted, there was a chance of meeting a patrol car on the way in but that was a more acceptable risk. Headlights would warn me and I could take evasive action.

Seven minutes later I'd returned to Dalespun Towers via the north road, which I'd joined after two miles on the public road. I'd seen nobody on the whole journey.

'You blithering idiot!' I yelled at Lowry when I'd got into his flat. 'That was the wrong house. You'll get me done.'

Lowry had an expression of great pain on his face. He was swaying slightly and allowing no word to escape his lips. I'd left the bike in a garden shed behind the Towers and sprinted to his flat, in the earnest hope that the cops hadn't arrived yet. I went to the window and swept the curtain aside to see if there were any approaching lights. By this time I'd worked out that the envelope might be in the hands of Riverburn Cottage's rightful tenants, but I said nothing. A hundred is a lot to lose.

'It musta been Riverbar Cottage. The envelope's wrong.'

When riding back on the bike, this brilliant observation had occurred to me too. It would have been useful to have had it in advance. It also gave the lie to his claim that he'd seen the package in the cottage. Sir Lance's great-grandfather had built two cottages with identical designs on the northern and southern sides of his Estate, both beside riverbanks. One was called Riverburn Cottage and the other Riverbar Cottage.

'Now you tell me.'

'You gotta get it,' said Lowry, unbothered by my anger.

'The cops will be there!'

There was no guarantee of that, of course. They were a law unto themselves, and anyway, they'd be at the first house, which was miles away.

'You gotta get it.'

It was an order and I needed the money.

With bad grace, I stepped out and ran for the bike. Life being what it is, I couldn't be certain that the cops would have arrived at the first crime scene yet. Shortly there was going to be a second one, and the Estate might be swarming.

I wheeled the bike out, checked the hammer was safely strapped in, and made off, turning right at the crossroads. As a road, this was less satisfactory. It passed three cottages and two farmsteads and it would be too easy to get noticed. Of course I'd driven the same route five minutes earlier and seen no-one (both farm buildings had been unlit) but there were probably people about.

There was blissful silence on all the approach roads. My destination lay off road; I was not so familiar with the area and had to retrace part of the journey to find Riverbar Cottage. It lay at the bottom of a drive, facing away from the road, and was almost out of direct sight until you were right on top of it. I could see why it was so popular. It was neatly camouflaged.

I could see that all the lights were out as I approached at low revs, noting that there were no cars and no signs of habitation. A well painted sign said Riverbar Cottage. It was otherwise identical to the first, although in better condition. Here there were security devices on the walls. The garden was composed of shrubs and there was a smaller river gurgling behind me. The windows were double glazed and the door looked solid.

Leaving the bike running and facing outwards for a quick getaway, I unstrapped the hammer and looked at the door. It was a superior hard wood with an expensive lock, mounted on a rigid frame. I looked into the letter box and saw nothing. Lowry had thought that it could be opened with one blow, but that was doubtful. I went to the windows and saw fine rooms with expensive furniture. The cottage was unoccupied. I looked through the letterbox again and opted to go ahead.

Gripping the hammer tightly, I delivered a blow that must have been audible at the Towers but which left the door unaffected. It didn't so much as move. Plainly there were expensive metal fittings holding it in place. It might take all of thirty minutes to get inside. For all I knew, alarms were already ringing at the police station.

Forget the door. Almost all windows can be forced in seconds. Security people forget about those. I went to the one on my right and whacked it. The whole frame shifted and alarms blazed out. I hit it again and it moved still further. Then I walloped the opposite corner and the whole thing, frame and all, fell into the room. The alarm was deafening and must have been audible for miles. I climbed in, taking some care. All you need to do is cut yourself on a splinter and they'll have you.

In the hall, I spluttered in amazement. There were no letters, cards or junk mail of any description. The alarm kept blaring as I flicked the mat at my feet and shone the torch all over in case the envelope had skidded into a hidden place. But there was nothing. I'd have to go.

I climbed back out of the window, grabbed the hammer and fastened it to the bike, glad to be away from the worst of the din. At that point I noticed that the river, had been landscaped into a pool with a ford that formed a junction with a lane on the other side. Rather than risk meeting the cops on the north road I opted for this alternative and was on the lane in seconds. My headlights were on but at the first sign of approaching vehicles they'd be extinguished. Plainly the lane was used only by tractors and farm implements. It went in the right direction, though it was in a poor condition and I had to move slowly. Shortly it terminated at a gate on to the public road. It was quiet, with no traffic.

But the situation demanded caution. Patrol cars, answering the alarm, might be coming in that direction. It would be bad to be seen on a motorbike with a heavy hammer strapped to the back. In the distance behind me, lights began to emerge along the north road, leaving me no choice. It would have to be the public road and I'd take the long way home. Two miles on, I unstrapped the hammer and hid it under a hedge.

Lowry was standing on the west side of Dalespun Towers, his back to me, looking at the north road when I came up behind him. He jumped when I said:

'The envelope wasn't there.'

He turned and looked at me.

'It wasn't there,' I repeated.

'Did you look properly?' he didn't believe me.

'I didn't half. Under the mat, over the hall. Nothing, no junk mail, nothing, what's going on? You said you saw it.'

'Where's the bike?'

'I've hidden it.'

'The cops have been here.'

'Did they find anything?'

'No.'

'What's this about?' I said. 'Why send me on a wild goose chase?'

'You're sure it wasn't there?'

'It definitely wasn't. What's this all about?'

When walking back by the river, I formed a theory that made sense. It concerned Mrs Hunt, the secretary, and her attitude. Almost certainly the writing on the envelope had been hers. The lady had just resigned her job. What if she'd been caught on the fiddle? —She was a classic case for it, with an absentee boss and loads of lovely money about. – Perhaps she'd sent some embarrassing papers to Mr Oxford-Yates by way of retaliation? Only she hadn't sent them. It had all been a bluff.

A week later a nice new secretary arrived and everything returned to normal.

From the local newspaper:

Mad Hammer Man

Residents on the Dalespun Estate have been alarmed by reports of a vandal with a hammer. One tenant, who didn't want to be named, said: 'It was terrible. There was an awful bang and when I looked into the hall an evil man was standing at the door with a big hammer. He was glaring at me.' There have been unconfirmed reports that another cottage has also been the victim of an attack. Yesterday, there was no one at Dalespun Towers to comment. The police said their enquiries were continuing.

On the evening of the next day, Lowry pushed an envelope through my door with sixty pounds in it. I suspect there had been a hundred pounds, but he'd taken forty.

Looking back on the event, I wondered if the 'blackmail' had involved the great man and his little plot. Harry Hetland had been a rising star for years and Sir Lance himself had admitted he'd been in his sights for a while. Of course he wouldn't share his secrets with Mrs Hunt. But private secretaries have a long tradition of uncovering dirty dealings and perhaps she had augmented her income by sharing the odd secret with Harry, who was reputed to be generous with such persons. Certainly many things were to happen in the course of the next few days that would suggest it. Incidentally, Riverbar Cottage was sold several months ago, possibly to bank roll Operation Garden. It was the first property on the Estate that Sir Lance had ever sold.

6

I lifted the phone.

'Mat,' came Hazel's voice. She always sounded as if she had too much energy, and tonight she was reaching new extremes. 'I think you should go to the Square and see your car.'

She sounded very concerned.

'Why, what's wrong with it?'

'Nothing, but I think you should see it.'

My car is no more than an old banger with a good engine, but it has never once let me down. I don't know if I like it and I certainly don't love it. The prospect of seeing my car didn't excite me in the least. But perhaps this was an innuendo on Hazel's part; possibly there was something else to see.

'Is Adele alright?'

'Yes, but you'll have to see it.'

'You'll have to tell me why, Hazel.'

'Oh, I can't, but you'll need to go down and see it.'

'C'mon, what is it?'

At that point the phone went dead.

For the second time in two hours, I laced my shoes and stepped out into the evening air. There was some traffic about, but the streets were relatively quiet and I covered the distance in less than ten minutes to find my car parked at an odd angle. Despite being a policewoman, Adele seldom parks exactly in the squares. It was locked, but I always carry my own key.

I'd already seen the envelope on the driver's seat and had guessed its nature before I'd got the door open.

Dear Mat,

I'm going off with Bob I hope you have a nice life. I know I will.

I put it back in its envelope and slipped it into my pocket. The writer had forgotten to sign the missive but it was a fair bet that it was Adele. Then I slid into the driver's seat and put the key into the ignition, but I wasn't going to get away that easily. A bright red shape appeared at my window and I wound it down to find myself staring at Hazel, clad in a scarlet outfit likely to fuse CCTV cameras.

'Oh, Mat, I'm terribly sorry.'

'Thanks, Hazel, but I'd rather expected it. These things do happen.'

'You must be awfully upset.'

'Well, Adele will probably be a lot happier.'

'I don't think so. I told her not to go off with Andy. He's too young.'

'Well, um, thanks. Who is Bob, by the way?'

'He's one of the new policemen and his wife's a right bitch.'

'Oh dear, that's a –'

'Adele won't be back, you know. She's away for good. She moved all her stuff out this afternoon.'

'Well she's entitled –'

'Mat, I think I should come home and look after you.'

'Hazel, you're far too kind, but –'

'I mean, you need a woman in your life and I think I'm the one. I've always thought you were great. Adele will never be happy with anybody –'

'Now, now, Hazel,' I said to quieten her down. Two couples on the opposite side of the square were listening with glee and she was getting louder by the second. 'We mustn't do anything hasty. You need a younger man. I'm too old for a nice girl like you.'

'But I'm older than Adele,' she wailed. 'I just look younger!'

'And you look well, too, but I need a quiet night to think things over.'

'I'll come up and see you tomorrow.'

'Hazel, no. I've got work. I might be away for a day or two. Thanks anyway.'

7

On the rare occasions I've met them, MPs have seemed absent-minded to me. Possibly that's because matters of state drive all common sense out of their heads, or perhaps they just have no sense in the first place.

In fact there's a prosaic reason for this. Once they've survived the Selection Committee and the hustings, they arrive in Parliament to discover it's something less than nirvana. There are hundreds just like them, and they can't make an impact. They become aware that they're only good at politics when they're with the amateurs, and they've no role to play in Parliament aside from casting their vote. Back home, they might have been the uncrowned king of the debating society, but being number six hundred and three takes the jauntiness out of their step. The old slogans that were once so effective are now close to redundant, and they have to reinvent themselves, or try to, and when they fail it's no wonder they walk with their heads down and become introspective.

From my position in the queue, I watched them doddering in and out of the great building. Some of them well known, but they were not impressive to look at and they were nearly always older than I'd expected. There's a limit to what you can get from a bunch of ageing aspirants. They may look younger on the box but that's thanks to make-up and of course their publicity shots omit the odd wrinkle or three.

After nearly an hour's watching, I was thoroughly disenchanted. There were about a hundred of us queuing, prevented from entering the hallowed halls by the massive security operation. To get in, you must first be known. I saw familiar faces approach the door to find it open before they'd got there. But there was no such treatment for me and I was becoming irritated. Didn't I have an appointment with a one-time Cabinet Minister?

Eventually a figure approached with the air of a man with more worries than he can cope with, and I recognised Sir Lance. He had a briefcase in his left hand and his shoulders were hunched. I recalled that he seldom did anything without forethought. He spoke to Security, they called my name, and I went forward.

'You're late, Mr Browne,' he muttered, while the security man looked on, blank faced. 'Come on.'

'Sir Lance, I've been here for ages.'

'Well you should have made a fuss. They didn't tell me.'

We went to the security desk where he signed my entry form. There was a discreet camera overhead and another one on my left. Two police sergeants with their hands behind their backs were discussing last night's TV. I was frisked for the second time and they put a badge on my lapel. Then the gate swung open and we went in.

'Through you come, Mr Browne.'

Yes it was all for the benefit of the gallery. I was relieved to note that he wasn't behaving suspiciously. Nobody would have thought him capable of conspiracy. I might survive after all.

But I'd been impressed by the security of the place and how carefully they watched their MPs. Without a doubt, it was efficient. It was likely that this was only a small part of a greater system, a surveillance regime that was easily the best in the country. Plainly it would be no easy matter to hit Harry Hetland, though Sir Lance was not proposing, I hoped, to do that inside Parliament itself. In fact he wasn't proposing to hit him at all – what he wanted was a report about the possibility of a hit and that's a different matter. But the protection was so thorough that it would make any hit man pause for thought. Undoubtedly MPs were monitored outside Parliament too – perhaps not so thoroughly – by the plain-clothes police I'd glimpsed in the background.

We walked along an ordinary and not particularly ancient corridor. It was relatively busy. People bustled about with their papers. Only a few of them were MPs and almost all of them nodded to Sir Lance. Some of them bore visitor's badges like me while others, possibly the majority, were among the several thousand civil servants associated with the House. Again, most didn't look impressive, though I reminded myself that I shouldn't take people at face value and they were probably abler than me. Nevertheless, I could see why Harry had some serious ambitions. He could have had the lot for dinner.

We went into a side room that turned out to be a pub.

'He usually comes here,' said Sir Lance, *sotto voce*, after we'd taken a seat in one of the poshest bars I'd ever been in. 'He's due shortly. Now, what can I get you?'

I opted for a cheese salad and sat back to look at the people around me. Again, they weren't all MPs and they didn't look remotely absent-minded. Possibly they were only switched on inside the House. Three men were discussing a project in Singapore, a solitary man at a far table was bent over his phone, and two women in designer clothes were fiercely criticising someone over their pints of beer. At another table, a well known TV man who I had always regarded as mediocre was talking to a woman in a striped suit.

'He's the devil of an odd character,' said Sir Lance, speaking so quietly that I had to incline my head towards him. He was wearing a grey suit that looked ten years old and his face was on the grey side too. He seemed subdued. I suspected he was partly proud of Parliament and utterly bored with it too. He was an old man with no joy in his attitude, though there was no pain either. Everybody nodded to him. 'He can be surprisingly matey, but other times you'd think he was ready to kill you. You've got to watch him. Don't draw attention to yourself and don't stare. Whatever else he is, he's no fool.'

'Oh, he's no fool.'

'You'd expect him to be friendly with his leaders, but he isn't really. He seldom speaks to the top brass and as often as not he's discourteous – he doesn't bother being Mister Charm if he doesn't feel like it. He's wary of being pulled into committees. Doesn't want to be tainted by association with their chairs, though that's what politics is all about. He wants to be an absolute leader. He's not interested in discussing anything with anybody. That kind of megalomania is fatal. It never works. Uncle Joe proved that. You can't run a government in the way you'd run a gang. In a democracy you've got to consult people, and that means MPs as well as constituents. If he's friendly, it's usually with the junior ranks or the minor civil servants who can do him no harm.'

'He won't like disagreement.'

'No – although the man's able. I can't dispute that. But he's a pure megalomaniac and that puts the fear of death in a lot of people, including those on his own side.'

Sir Lance produced a small tin from his waistcoat pocket and took a pinch of snuff. 'One of my bad habits,' he said.

'Your only bad habit, I'm sure,' I said, kicking myself for being so obsequious. Why was I saying that? Old soldiers don't go in for small talk. The political atmosphere must have been affecting me. In reality, Sir Lance had a number of bad habits, though they might well have improved with age.

It was hard to believe that this old man had once been a celebrated debonair. He'd married a beauty, Lady Leticia, and kept the gossip columnists going for years. No society wedding or party was complete without his name on the guest list. His name was associated with a number of actresses and models, he'd attended parties with royalty, and had been considered one of the handsomest men in the land. I suppose his marriage changed a lot of that, although it was before my time, of course. He had a son with Leticia – Julian, now a junky. –Sir Lance became an MP and Leticia had often been seen in the company of young men, until at last she ran off with a rich builder who went bankrupt the following year. She still sometimes appeared at Dalespun Towers, a forbidding old bird with a waspish tongue. She didn't like me.

'Is Harry here every day?'

'Not necessarily. He's got a contempt for the place. Mind you, he's usually in his office at some time or other – I'll bet some fancy things go on there. He doesn't mix with us and of course he doesn't court the big wigs. They keep in with him, though. He's the only ambitious man I've ever seen who can do that.'

'Are you afraid of him?'

His head went back and he stared at me for a moment.

'It's what he's going to do to the country that worries me. Anyone other than him and I'd ignore the whole thing. But he's won every battle so far. He's unstoppable. And he makes no secret of his ambitions. He could be a dictator within five years.'

I stared at the floor, wondering if this was sheer overstatement. We don't do dictators in the UK. Harry might be a bad egg, but I saw him in less colourful terms – though Sir Lance knew a lot more about politics than me and was not noted for hyperbole.

'Surely he can do nothing,' I objected, 'without the army on his side?'

'To an extent, but the scenario's more complicated than that. With anybody else I'd be relaxed about his chances, but so far he's carried everything before him. I'd look on the gloomy side. Yes, he'd carry the army. That's him!'

Several young men, carrying papers, had come in with a short man of about forty who I recognised as Harry Hetland, with his black hair, good suit, and tidy presentation. Of course he'd aged since I'd last met him, but he was still switched on, and gave the impression of being busy with no time to waste. Presumably his companions were aides or political researchers. They were not muscular and had none of the look-about attitude of security people; it seemed, therefore, that they didn't double as body guards. They were certainly attentive to their boss. In the space of a few seconds the tallest man, a thin fellow with a shaved head, had fetched a drink and pressed it into his master's hand, a service that drew no thanks. Then all their heads were together as they considered an arcane point with much nodding and shaking of heads. They fell silent every time Harry spoke. At one point notebooks were produced and there was some hasty scribbling. I noted that Harry didn't make a target of himself. A hit man would have found him difficult to surprise. Even in this select bar he was surrounded by his aides. Had someone produced a gun and opened up, Harry would have escaped unscathed, though his attendants would have been less fortunate.

Everybody was watching him. The three men had stopped talking about Singapore, the TV personality was taking an interest, the telephoner had put his phone away and the two fancy ladies had fallen silent. Even Sir Lance, after warning me not to stare, was doing just that. They were looking at power. They knew he could be the next Prime Minister and they were envious of it. In fact, I was the only person who wasn't staring at the monster, and I'd been brought in specially to see him.

From the corner of my eyes I'd noted the movements of his head, his way of making decisions, his quick wits, and above all, his economy of movement – always the sign of a well-disciplined individual. All of which confirmed my impressions. This man had an agenda that he'd adhere to, and he wouldn't allow petty things to get in the way. Most gangsters shoot first and ask questions later, which can be hazardous and might explain why his main rivals were now resting in peace. Harry was said to have sent a generous wreath to each of their funerals. But it wasn't only his head that I'd noticed. From the shape of his shoulders it was obvious he was in prime condition and could make a good case for himself in a fight. I certainly wouldn't challenge him to a round of fisticuffs.

'Impressive, eh?' asked Sir Lance, speaking very quietly.

I said nothing. My final observation was of his ego. Harry was the ablest guy in town with an opinion of himself to match. He occupied a class of his own. He was a Julius Caesar in poor company (though he was prepared to tolerate that poor company on his way up). Yes, I remembered reading something from a journalist who'd been surprised by his mental agility. There were plenty of egotists around, but there were few with Harry's practical ability. Some people have a lot of talent, and there's a potential genius in every street, but without a driving ego that light may never shine.

'He's horrible to deal with.'

Yes, Sir Lance's olde worlde skills would be redundant against this steamroller, which might explain his dislike, though I could see why Harry should be kept from leadership for the general well-being of the country.

A waiter deposited our dishes with a silent flourish and I looked up in surprise to see Harry walking towards us confidently as his aides looked on. He was wearing a double-breasted suit with a hint of blue, neatly pressed trousers and a smart shirt and tie which weren't bold but somehow spoke of power. What impressed me most was the determination in his face. He stopped beside Sir Lance and made a quiet remark in his ear.

'Oh, I've no problem with that,' said Sir Lance, utterly calm.

More whispered comments.

'Yes, I'll back you there.'

Then Harry Hetland straightened up and looked at me.

'Are you enjoying your visit to the House?' he asked, looking at me with the hint of a smile. I wondered if he remembered me. There was nothing of East London in his accent now. Of course, he'd been taking lessons from a good coach. His voice could have belonged to a competent actor or even an old Etonian. I noticed that his fingers were well manicured and he was showing the right amount of cuff. But his face was a mask without a hint of feeling and I didn't like the way he was looking at me. There was no smile in his eyes.

'Yes, I am, Mr Hetland,' I said, trying to keep a whine out of my voice. I almost called him 'sir'.

'Your first visit, Mr – ah – Browne?' he said, leaning forward to read my badge. I cursed Sir Lance for choosing such an easy name. Only the amateur opts for something easy to remember. I should have gone for something more complicated, though 'Murgatroyd' would have been best avoided.

'Yes,' I said, but I had to improvise. It would be dangerous to be recognised as the hit man I might find myself becoming.. 'I admire your policies, Mr Hetland.'

Harry stepped back, unimpressed. He didn't need my support and he didn't welcome it, but he had to be polite.

'Well, Mr Browne, I represent the future. Your friend Sir Lance is a fine man with an honourable history, but he speaks for the past. It's the future that matters.'

'I don't think you'd care for Harry's European views,' said Sir Lance, dryly.

In fact I preferred his views on Europe to Sir Lance's, but that was irrelevant. My mind was racing wildly. This was a disaster. The only reason Harry Hetland had approached us was because he'd recognised me as a threat. I wore no tie or jacket and among that batch of well-fed politicos I was lean and mean, a man of action who was out of place in this comfortable bar. He'd seen the anomaly at first glance.

'Your face is vaguely familiar,' said Harry with a puzzled frown. 'I can't place it, but we've met before?'

So he'd partly forgotten me, or was that only an excuse?

'No, no, this is the first time we've –'

'Well, it's so nice to meet you,' said Harry giving a slight nod and turning back to his advisers, who all began to talk at once.

'Well, what did you make of that?' said Sir Lance with a chuckle.

I didn't answer; I was committing the experience to memory. The monster had sniffed at me and smelt blood.

There was movement to my right and I looked up to see Harry leaving with the tall man. The other two had put their notebooks away and moved to a table where they began to talk in worried whispers. Harry led the way out, walking fast, followed by baldy. Harry gave a brief nod to a fat man who was coming in, and baldy seized his phone to take a call as they exited.

'Who are they all?' I said.

'Oh, the two at the table are political assistants. They practically run his office. They're not bad, but I think they're under a lot of pressure, I don't know why they put up with it; he's a terrible boss.'

'Because they want to be MPs some day.'

'Well that's true of all researchers. The other fellow's one of his personal assistants. He interlinks with all his above-board activities, like politics and the media: a tame rep if you like. He's bright with one or two languages and he knows nothing about the other side. Hetland keeps him clean. He doesn't get the aggro the others get, he's at least one rung up the ladder. Incidentally, if the researchers have a problem they phone him, rather than Harry. Harry doesn't like distractions. He wants things running smoothly without his intervention.'

'Does he change his team very often?'

'Those two came at the last election. The bald fellow goes back a long way.'

All of which made sense. Harry wouldn't like new people around him. Too easy for a spy to infiltrate his network, and that must be avoided at all costs.

'Does he have a chauffeur, or does baldy drive?'

'I daresay baldy drives, but there's a chauffeur.'

'These researchers,' I said. 'Any chance we could get one to turn? It would need money, of course.'

Sir Lance's grey head gave a solemn shake: he'd already thought of that. It looked as though they'd tried a lot of avenues before approaching me. If they'd been unable to turn the researchers, it was likely that Harry knew about it.

'Not a hope.'

I pecked at my salad and wondered why I was trying to write a report for seventy-year-old Sir Lance when the proposed victim was so devastatingly able. I had met a lot of smart men in the army but Harry was head and shoulders above every one. Something in my gut warned me to get out before the axe fell. Harry was formidable and Sir Lance was out of his depth.

Half an hour later, they signed me out and I went home.

Back at my flat, I knew someone had been there even before the door was fully open. An ornate blind which had covered my front window was missing. Now Mrs Birhandi, my neighbour, would be able to see straight into my room. Other things of a petty nature that had been there long before Adele arrived were missing too and I was displeased. I'd bought then with my own money and now they'd been removed by a lady who had contributed nothing to their upkeep although she earned more than I did. Of course I knew what had happened. Adele and Andy had discovered their love nest needed some garnishing and she still had the key to my flat.

I turned straight around and went to the big DIY store outside town, where I bought a lock and a blind – plainer than the last, but I had no wish to live in the gold fish bowl my flat would become if I didn't have one.

I'm not bad at handiwork and they were installed in thirty minutes. Then I sat back and thought about the day's activities. There was a lot to think about.

8

It was eight o clock the following morning and I'd just finished my breakfast when the phone rang and a big voice rang out.

'Look out the window, Mat boy.'

I did, having recognised the voice immediately and noted with some misgivings that he was in a boisterous mood. That was seldom a good sign. At least he didn't sound as if he was stuck in a warehouse this time.

'Andy, there's a big guy out there impersonating you. He's got a phone too.'

Since the *Windows* incident there had been a coolness between us which he was incapable of recognising. We'd remained on speaking terms and had seen each other about once a year. In fact we'd done some work recently for which I hadn't been paid, thus confirming my view that he was a disaster to be avoided.

'You're so right. Can I come in? We need to talk, Mat boy?'

Wincing at the 'we need to talk' I agreed. Without doubt it was Andy who needed to talk and it would certainly not be for my benefit. This was big man stuff, the kind that overrides all other considerations. In a minute he was in my flat, the big chancer, shoving me aside to make himself a coffee while declaring that he was far from happy.

'Why did we leave the service, eh?'

'We'd no choice, if you remember. We'd reached a certain age. What are you up to?'

But he seldom answers a question immediately.

'What are you doing these days – where's Adele?'

'I'm doing nothing.' It would have been insane to give him a hint about Sir Lance. 'And Adele has gone off with a young cop. We can only–'

'Sympathise – yes, well, I'm not surprised. Listen, I can give you some work for a day. Interested?'

'As long as it's paid, Andy.'

'Okay, the last one was bad. Not my fault, of course. But you'll get paid for this, provided it comes off.'

'I knew there'd be a catch.'

He sat on my chair and balanced his coffee on its arm, leaving a stain that was visible across the room, but I didn't mind. I'm not a fussy man and now there was no woman to object. He was dressed like a tramp, in a shapeless jacket that must have been all of forty years old and had undoubtedly come from a charity shop. Of course he's a big man, unable to wear standard-sized clothes.

'There's no catch.'

He was staring with unseeing eyes, unconcerned about the last balls up and obviously planning another coup. His hook nose, unruly hair and unwashed face made him look like a shipwrecked sailor who'd been plucked from a rocky isle.

'This is a funny one. I got a job last week. About that bullion robbery, you know the one?'

'I read about it.'

'Gold bars stolen from a delivery van, two men injured. Cops are getting nowhere and time's going past. Anyway, they've got me on it.'

Good for them. Appointing the captain of the Titanic was guaranteed to produce some action.

'Who got you in on it?'

'The insurance, who else?' he said, unaware of my sarcasm. 'Things are at a stalemate. They know where the gold bars are, but the evidence is weak. They've identified the robbers; the gold bars were taken to an industrial estate in Romford. They're in a storage depot that's run by a crowd of hoods, but what's new? The Court has refused to issue a search warrant. What d'you reckon?'

So that was why there was a scheming look in his eye. He was planning a convincing preamble for me. Except that it wasn't convincing. No insurance company in its senses would approach Andy of all people, though possibly – and it was a far-out chance – their agent just might. This was Andy all over.

'Oh come on, man,' I said.

You have to be reasonably smart to steal gold bars, and

letting Andy know where they were stored didn't sound clever. Among his many omissions was how this information had come to light. If things were that simple, the insurance company would have had a search warrant in the blink of an eye and the miscreants would be behind bars. Anyway, the robbers wouldn't store their booty in a depot. Such places have lots of workers and gold bars were certain to get noticed. I looked at his big brutish face and wondered who had sold him the story. Like the *Windows* escapade, this was surely another yarn from the pub.

'An eighty year old nun wouldn't believe that.'

But he's impervious to irony.

'Oh, the gold bars are there alright. They asked me to scout it out. It's a big place, huge. I've seen them.'

I jolted back in my chair.

'Eh? You've seen them? You actually saw them? How did you manage that?'

'The insurance did it. The depot has a problem with its roof – water damage. They made me the loss adjuster with covering papers. The roof's bad alright –'

'Excuse me, you went there? Into a hood's den?'

''Course I did. I don't flinch in the face of the foe, you know me. I got the camera out and took a few shots of the place, accidental like. There are cartons at the back that look like the real thing. Have a gander at that.'

This seemed odd. Insurance companies seldom engage in subterfuge, especially with people like Andy. They stick to the rules on the grounds that if something goes wrong, as inevitably it will, there could be some nasty claims.

'This isn't believable.'

No, it wasn't true, it couldn't be. It was a work of fiction to rope me into something unpleasant. But he was reaching into his pocket for evidence. Evidence?

'Here.'

It was a colour print of the interior of a storage depot, an enlargement of detail that left everything in soft focus. A red circle had been drawn around a group of cartons some distance away. The cartons were small, looked sturdy and were resting on a wooden plinth and they might well have been the real thing.

I was amazed. For once in his life Andy was on to something. Gold is heavy, and the cartons have to be small and robust to prevent bruising. Of course they were mere cartons. There was no proof they contained gold and possibly there were other explanations for their size and shape.

'That's the best you can do?'

'Hell, man, I had three gangsters standing at my elbow. The insurance guys reckon that's the goods.'

'But you said you'd *seen* the gold.'

'Alright, that's packaging, but they say it's genuine, that's how it was packed. They've identified them.'

'Andy, why would the thieves have it on display?'

'I dunno, but funny things happen. The insurance boys reckon it's okay.'

'What insurance company is this?'

He leaned back and shrugged.

'Can't remember, I'm dealing with an agent.'

Yes, this was Andy all over. Big on the story, weak on the detail.

'They must've given you papers. You were a loss adjuster, remember?'

'The name escapes me.'

So it wasn't the insurance after all. Perhaps he'd been in touch with an insider. Or possibly he hadn't taken the pictures. They might be someone else's.

'So the Court is not convinced?'

I couldn't blame the Court for wanting something more substantial than Andy and a blurry picture. Obviously there was no proof the cartons contained gold bars. But why was I taking this so seriously – this had to be another piece of fiction. It was likely that the Court had never been approached and there was no case to answer.

'You said the robbers had been identified. Who are they?'

'Oh, I don't know that.'

'Who identified them?'

'I dunno, it was the insurance bloke that said it – but hell, man, you've gotta admit he's right. That's where the bars are stored. That's the proof.'

'Proof's too strong a word.'

'I just want to have a good look at the place.'

'And you want me to go to Romford with you?'

'You've said it.'

'How much is in it for me?'

'A grand, provided the last bit goes well.'

'I don't like that proviso.'

'I get nothing if we don't come up with the goods. We're only going for a look-see in my van. Are you in on it or not?'

I'd never received a penny or a word of sympathy for the Microsoft incident and last year I'd been stupid enough to get involved with him and received nothing for my pains. Despite his claims about not being paid, I was sure he'd received a down payment as well as expenses which he'd declined to share with me.

The trip to Romford was a lost cause for sure. At best, we would be going through the motions and would never even get inside the door. On the other hand it was better than doing nothing and I wanted out of the flat. Sooner or later Adele would be on the phone, and that was something I could do without.

'Yes, I don't mind a trip to Romford. Let's go.'

9

When we arrived, the industrial estate was a hive of activity. We had to follow a stream of slow traffic before reaching the depot, which turned out to be a smart place enclosed by a security fence. Andy, who seemed to know the area well, found a parking place among a host of cars at the roadside, where we got an overview of the site without being obvious to an onlooker. The building was huge, easily the biggest in the estate. It had an attractive, well-maintained facade. In the yard, there were several security vehicles and some uniformed men and women, all hard at work, there were CCTV cameras at strategic positions and the first floor office had a big window that gave a view of the entire area. The only way into the yard was by a manned barrier which looked powerful. If I'd been a robber I'd think twice before I did a ram raid.

'How do we get in there?' asked Andy.

'Well, for a start, you don't,' I said, fed up with his schoolboy posturing. 'They'll recognise you as the loss adjuster and your goose will be cooked.' Or did his question mean that he hadn't been inside the building at all?

'Could we break in at night?'

'Surely it's a twenty four hour place,' I said in reply to that crazy idea. He might as well have postulated raiding the Bank of England with a tin opener.

'Likely.'

This was exactly what I had expected. He hadn't a clue what to do and was trying to involve me in the hope I'd think of something. But here the prospects were zero. Perhaps if I'd worked in the place for a fortnight it might be possible to find a weak spot in their armour, but that wasn't on. Smart people had designed the depot with serious security on their minds.

'Why would you want to break in?'

'To get the gold bars.'

I looked at his big face with its hook nose jutting aggressively and wondered if I'd heard right.

'Have you any idea what they'd weigh?'

'Oh they'd be heavy. We'd need a truck.'

'You certainly would. And you'd need a forklift to load them, which might annoy the gangsters. Some people can be so touchy.'

'Well, if we could just prove the gold was there I'd get the reward.'

'And you'll tell the Court you broke into the place and saw the gold? You'd be charged with breaking and entering and your evidence would be null and void.'

At that moment, a car pulled up at the gate and we watched its driver present papers which the guard studied for a long moment. He made some comments to the driver, then lifted his telephone and after a brief conversation, the car was allowed to proceed into the yard, where it was met by an official who directed it to a visitors' car park. 'Is that how you got in?'

'They made me wait for ages before the manager came out. He wasn't going to let me in. I had to argue.'

Did that mean he really had gone inside the depot? I couldn't believe it. But he'd said 'argue' and that didn't sound convincing.

'Must have been nerve-wracking,' I said with a little irony.

'Oh, I can cope. He was a bit uptight – well, protective.'

'Is that him out there?'

'Nope.'

'Right, tell me the procedure. How many doors? How many people?'

'They parked me where that car is. The manager took my card and left me in the entrance hall with a guard. He probably phoned the insurance company.'

'And that was okay?'

'Musta been. After five minutes he came back and we went to the next section. It was locked. Big heavy doors. Then I was inside. It's like a hangar for jumbos. Half of it's in shelving, you saw the photo. There was ten people inside.'

'What were they doing?'

'I dunno.'

I had some training in interrogation and was supposed to be able to recognise a downright lie. There are ways of listening to the inflection in the speaker's voice that can reveal an untruth. You can then fire a question to see whether the subject departs from their earlier answer. But that only works sometimes. If the subject is delusional, you can get the wrong answers every time. I wondered if that applied to Andy.

'Who owns it? Officially.'

'I dunno. A big corporation I've never heard of.'

'And who owns them?'

He shot me an irritated look.

'Oh, come on. I don't bother with these things.'

'It pays to know. Your life might depend on it. I think it's Harry Hetland. How much are the gold bars worth?'

'Five million.'

'That's worth a lot of security. They'll kill to protect it.'

'I suppose so,' said a dispirited Andy. 'Should I forget it?'

The hopelessness was inescapable.

'I think so.'

'It don't look good,' said Andy, with a hint of anger. 'Let's go.'

10

Andy's van was in poor condition. It had clearly once been a beast of burden to a small-time builder. It stank of sweat, glass on the facia had been smashed, there were several chips on the windscreen and my seat was unsteady. The springs on the driver's side were broken which meant that Andy was barely able to see out the windscreen, and he was a big man. The ashtray was overflowing and there seemed to be something wrong with the way the gears meshed. It stalled twice before we got away.

'Is this thing legal?' I said.

'For a hundred quid it'll do me,' he said, 'Listen, I'll take the long road back. Maybe look into a pub for lunch. What say?'

'Fine by me.'

The van crept off only to halt twenty seconds later when we hit a jam caused by a huge truck trying to reverse into a very narrow gateway. Then we drove through some busy roads before heading in the direction of the M25. We didn't join it but went underneath to the east, to a smaller road where the traffic was still heavy. Then Andy branched on to a minor lane that was less congested.

'You said Harry Hetland owned it?' he said.

'Well, I was guessing.'

'But that means he did the theft.'

'He might have.'

'But, I mean, he's all respectable now. Is he still running gangs?'

'I know nothing about him,' I said, noting that even Andy had been won over by the PR. He seemed to think it was fanciful that a big politician could be into crime. In fact I'd no idea if Harry Hetland owned the depot. The strict security had made me wonder, and there was something about it which reminded me of the *Windows* incident. There was a limit to the number of gangs who could mount a five meg robbery on his patch. It was doubtful he'd store hot goods for other parties.

'I was glad to get out,' he said. 'You could get your throat cut in there.'

'I'll bet,' I said, though I still didn't know whether he'd really been inside or not.

'Maybe I should forget the whole thing?'

'You've no alternative – I'd say it was impossible.'

By this time, we were in the country and there were green fields and prosperous farms on either side of the road. On my left a Hereford bull had his big face stuck through a hedge to eye some heifers in the opposite field and there were ponies grazing in the next meadow. We approached a crossroads and Andy slowed down.

'I know a pub that does a good lunch,' he said. 'I haven't eaten today yet.'

'You should take some breakfast, man.'

'I know. This Romford thing's been on my mind.'

We turned on to a narrow lane which was full of potholes and crossed some flat country that was deserted, despite its closeness to London. Eventually we arrived, at a pub in the middle of nowhere. Apparently it had been five years since Andy's last visit. There was a new landlord and everything had changed for the worse. The floor hadn't even been swept and the tables were cluttered with last night's glasses. We took a place at an empty table where I ordered a club sandwich and Andy opted for a pie. It took an age before the goods were produced but it was nice to relax. The room was comfortable and we talked a lot about our past experiences in the Service. Now life had become dull for both of us and we were making heavy weather of the civilian world. Andy was long divorced and was now estranged from his two sons who had accused him of taking their money. By the time we'd finished our lunch, two men and a party of women had arrived to swell the numbers.

'You fancy a walk?' asked Andy when we left, after he'd somehow manoeuvred me into paying the bill. 'There's a path five minutes down the road. It's a round trip of about six miles through some nice woodland.'

I said that sounded good.

'Let's go, then. I used to live here when I was a nipper. My old man worked on the land – it's a bit flat but it's nice.'

Shortly, we arrived at a nondescript junction with a Ramblers sign on to the grass verge. The area was deserted, without a human being or car in sight. We got out to start our walk. Andy assured me that the route wouldn't be muddy (I was wearing domestic shoes) and as usual he was wrong. It had rained recently and parts of the paths were pure mud, but I waded through it without audible complaint. When we reached a wood, the quality of the path improved. After five minutes, it led into an old forest of beeches and oaks. The upper branches had formed a roof which stopped the sunlight.

'Hear that?' Andy said, raising his head. 'A woodpecker.'

At this point I was leading the way, with big Andy behind, bumbling away about a triviality in the past. I was enjoying the walk; perhaps the oxygen from the trees was invigorating me. There was a spring in my step and I found myself happier than I'd been for a long time. Only twenty four hours ago I'd been in Parliament looking at Harry Hetland. This was a big improvement: breathing fresh air and appreciating things that my father and grandfather had known before me.

And yes, a woodpecker was thrumming away, a sound I've always liked. We stopped to look for it. The tree was easy to pick out, but the lack of sunlight meant we couldn't spot the bird, though we moved about a bit in an attempt to see it. Of course woodpeckers are not big and their plumage provides excellent camouflage. We were careful not to get too near. The thrumming usually stops when you're within fifty metres.

'Forget it,' said Andy, ushering me on, 'it doesn't mind being heard, but it doesn't want to be seen. An' it's dead right, too.'

We picked our way over some soggy ground and then I heard another sound.

'Someone's coming up behind us.'

I've been accused of paranoia. I hate being followed, however innocent the follower might be. It's something which goes back to my childhood. My old Aunt Bette tells me I was like that when I was five years old. It's irrational, but I like to see my options. What bothered me now was that ten minutes ago ours had been the sole car at the parking site and now we were being overtaken.

'It's a busy path,' Andy explained. His hands were in his pockets and he was quite relaxed. 'Oh, oh, the pecker's away.'

And so it was. The woodpecker, curiously small for all its volume, was off to new pastures, flying with an undulating motion. It had been further up the tree than we'd thought.

'When I was a boy I climbed these trees. I'll bet my initials are still there.'

'You couldn't write when you were a boy.'

'Still can't.'

That was when things became hazy. I've gone over them a thousand times, but I've never been able to recollect the events with total accuracy. We were on a straight path. It was relatively dark and a fallen tree trunk had blocked our way. These things are ten a penny. I was about to step over it, as thousands of walkers had done, when three things happened almost simultaneously. Behind us a gun fired, there was a thud, and Andy gave a terrible cry fell. I flung myself into the trees as a second shot rang out.

But I didn't fall. I hit a tree offset from the path. I turned to see Andy lying face down on the path as soft shoes ran up to him. My path was blocked by a thick bush growing around the base of the tree.. It would be impossible to get through it without making a lot of noise and the gunman was clearly a competent shot. Already he was beside me, looking down at Andy. He seemed utterly calm about the whole thing and apparently unaware of me, he was six feet tall with a serious gun in his right hand. A bit of bruiser. I noticed his navy suit and red tie and recognised him as one of the two men who'd come into the pub when we were at lunch. I recalled disliking his mask of a face.

All of this had happened in seconds. I was in shadow; he was unaware of me though he must have known I was about. Anyway, I didn't matter. I was unarmed, whereas he had plenty of fire power. A clumsier man was running up behind him.

My position was slightly elevated; the path was low set and the gunman's head was down as he bent to look at Andy. There was no mistaking his satisfaction. In a fraction of a second he'd look up and see me, then he'd kill me. I'd seen this type of idiot before, an outright killer who rejoices in death and will talk of nothing else. The power of life and death was his and he was full of his own importance. Today he intended to talk about two killings.

I was without gun or knife and he was clutching a SIG with which he was obviously expert. It was difficult to believe that he was unaware of me hiding a mere metre to his left, but he was enthralled by the killing. In a moment he'd remember and it would be curtains for me.

Using every ounce of energy, I kicked his head in a foot-jarring motion which almost broke my leg. I have never kicked anyone so hard in my life. My shoes, though domestic, were solidly built. It was a terrible blow. I can feel it yet.

It broke his neck. The rebound flung me back against the tree for a second time, banging my head on its hard surface. My aim had been accurate; the gunman was on the ground, twitching, his head at an odd angle and his mouth open. I had nearly broken my foot. The other man, still out of sight, had stopped running, but then he began again.

At that point, I couldn't tell whether he was running towards me or in the opposite direction and there was no way of knowing if he was armed. The SIG had fallen from the killer's hand and was lying in plain view. If the other man seized it I was dead. I jumped out. My foot gave way underneath me. The muscles had been strained by the kick, and I fell over the path. But my eye never left the gun. I reached for it, grasping it slowly (too fast, and you always drop it) and rolled over to look behind me. A short skinny man was running away. I loosed off a shot that ripped through the twigs and branches.

'Stop!' I bellowed. 'Raise your hands.'

I'd expected him to ignore me but he whirled round, nearly falling, and raised his hands high, looking at me with imploring eyes.

It all happened in just a few seconds, and now the woods were peaceful again. A flock of pigeons which had crashed from the trees were wheeling overhead, though no birds were singing now. Two men were lying dead at my feet and the killer's accomplice was standing with his hands up. The gun was cold in my hand. The trees were spooky and dark. I'd never felt so lonely in my life.

What was I going to do? This might be the pivotal point of my whole life. Should I take Andy's phone and call the cops? That would mean my name and address being logged and that was dicey. It would certainly bring my association with Sir Lance to a complete stop. I'd lose money, but that wasn't remotely important. Cash is useless when you're dead. We're told to be boy scouts and do the right thing, but in this context the only reward was likely to be a bullet from the other side. How many witnesses against Harry Hetland – surely he was behind the shooting – had come to a sticky end? I hadn't the time to evaluate the situation, but this was probably a response from the storage depot. My name and address would put me in a vulnerable position.

I was entirely innocent, but all the evidence said it would be rash to be identified. It looked as though Andy had been killed for taking too much interest in the gold bars. He'd been telling the truth after all. Never a subtle man, he'd probably given himself away several times. The security people must have expected him to come back and had an expensive hit man waiting in the wings. It was all obvious now that he was dead. Unfortunately, I was his associate and that wasn't life-enhancing. I was damned by association and I knew too much.

'Who are you?' I said, hobbling over to the other man.

'I'm just the driver, mister. Don't shoot, please!'

Using one hand only, I searched him and found an ugly knife which I threw away. Then I ordered him to lie flat on the ground. I went back to search the gunman and found a second handgun in a nylon shoulder rig, at his chest, which I removed with some difficulty, I hate dealing with the dead. There were a lot of rounds in his side pocket and a wad of notes, almost a grand, which I stuffed into my jacket. When you're in a tight spot, money is often more helpful than a gun, which was doubtless why he had it in the first place. There was nothing to identify him – a typical hit man. He'd emptied his pockets before going out.

Then I went to poor Andy. There was blood everywhere and I had to take care when I removed his wallet. Unbelievably, it was full of money – fifty pound notes, which I could hand to his sons at his funeral. I left his glasses, his small change and his keys. His phone must have been in the van.

My foot was sore. It seemed I'd sprained something and I was limping as I went back to the driver, who started whimpering in fear.

'Get up,' I said, my voice hard. 'You're gonna take me somewhere.'

He scrambled to his feet.

'Don't shoot me, mister.'

'Now walk to your car. I'm behind you. If you try anything, you're dead.'

At this point I had the SIG in my right hand and the holstered gun in my left which wouldn't look good to any passing walker. I took off my jacket and fitted the holster over my shoulder as I walked, then I held the SIG in my side pocket. It was heavy enough to tear the lining but at least it was out of sight. In front of me, my captive was so terrified that he was stumbling over everything. So was I. The kick had left me lame and perhaps a clever policeman would be able to tell from my footprints that I'd been limping. A bad thing. It would probably take several days to heal and that might draw unwelcome attention to me. Then we were out of the wood and on to the muddy land with a car and Andy's van in sight. Fully two miles of road were visible, with no other traffic in sight. Nor were there any walkers about and that was a bonus. The roof of the pub was just visible in the far distance.

'Is there fuel in your car?'

'Yes, mister. Don't shoot me, mister.'

Five minutes later we reached his car., It was a freshly washed brown Volkswagen Golf, this year's model. and This must have been a professional operation, because the car had been cleaned to remove any traces of its previous use. There might be back-up nearby. I'd have to hurry. With the driver standing with his hands up, I made a point of searching every bit of the car's interior. It was entirely innocent until I opened the boot to find a sniper's rifle with elaborate sights, as well as a carrying case that had been disguised to look like a domestic suitcase. This was definitely a pro job. I lifted them into the rear seat and ordered the driver to get in. I sat diagonally opposite him.

'Drive off,' I said. 'Not fast.'

For a brief moment I surveyed the area. There was no human being in sight, the land was flat, partly waterlogged and the forest seemed a hateful place now that Andy was lying dead on the footpath. I wondered if I'd made the most stupid decision of my life. But it was too late for regrets.

'Go,' I said.

As the car lurched into life I dismantled the rifle and packed it into its case, then I took the second gun and its holster and put them in too, before locking the case. I kept the SIG in my right hand as we drove along the narrow country lane the car bouncing over pot holes and sometimes going on to the verge. The driver was very nervous. We passed only one house and it seemed to be deserted.

'Who are you?' I asked. He was about thirty five, probably Eastern European, with black hair and ears that stuck out at right angles.

'I'm only taxi driver, mister, they call me Jek. I've never done this before.'

A pro answer that enraged me; I almost lashed out at him.

He was dressed to put the mind to rest in a suit with a dull tie, he might have been a social worker or a door-to-door salesman: certainly you wouldn't suspect him of being a hit man's driver. Yes, they'd known what they were doing when they sent this pair on their way.

We came to a road junction where I considered my options. There was no road atlas in the car, so I made the safest choice and took the route for London. We were soon on a busier road with some occasional traffic and there was an improvement in the terrain and cows grazing in the fields. Overlooking the road were prosperous farms and cottages. We were approaching civilisation.

'What was the other man's name?'

'I no' know, mister. They call him Pete.'

'Who is 'they'? Who's paying you?'

'The storage depot, mister. I no' know nothin''

'Who in the storage depot? Who sent you? What's his name?'

'I no' know. He speak to Pete, not me.'

I was ready to sink my fist into his head but there had been enough violence already and it would have been an utterly pointless move. What kind of idiot did he take me for with these soft-soap answers? I recognised subversive training. For the moment he was my prisoner, but he was still working for the other side and there was a risk he'd drive me into a trap.

'What did you say your name was?'

'They call me Jek, mister.'

There was the question of what 'they' had been planning to do with Andy's body. Perhaps that was why the driver had been running behind the hit man. It would have been unwise to leave evidence of their work behind them, so there must have been some kind of plan, but what was it? There was no body bag, nor was there a spade in the car – or perhaps he'd dropped it when I got his master.

'Is this your car?'

'No mister.'

'What were you going to do with the body?'

I should have said bodies, because I was supposed to have been a casualty too, but I couldn't bear to think of that.

'I no' know mister, honest.'

This was difficult to believe, but I let him be. He might well have been mentally deficient. He was certainly acting the part. But he was working for the other side and it would have been insane to remain in his company for a minute too long. Several times I've had to deal with potential killers who say anything to stay alive, but would readily stab my back at the first opportunity. A trained interrogator might uncover the truth, but that was an impossible luxury in the present circumstances.

At any moment the alarm might be raised by a passing walker. It was essential to get off these narrow roads, in case the police sealed them. To be caught hurrying away from a double murder would have been the worst of all options.

And somehow I needed to get home without this idiot seeing where I lived. Soon there would be oodles of detectives working on the case and one wrong move could ruin my life forever. After examining all the evidence, they'd be sure to get this hit man's driver, and judging by his attitude he would squeal like a pig. Ideally, he ought to have been disposed of (and he knew it too) but that would have been one murder too many.

We came to another junction and after ten minutes we joined the A127, a major road that had signs for the motorway.

'Drive sensibly,' I yelled, when he nearly hit a truck whose driver had responded in fury to his swaying on the road. He was so terrified that he had lost his driving skills, or perhaps he had never had any.

Ten minutes later we were on the M25, one of the world's infamous roads, and again I had to yell at him to follow a convoy of trucks, rather than straddle two lanes where he was infuriating other motorists. That kind of driving was guaranteed to get noticed and it was one thing I didn't need. Meanwhile we were rushing towards my home town.

I was in a quandary. If I went to a neighbouring town, I'd have to take transport to get home. A taxi driver would be likely to talk, the railway stations were full of cameras, a bus would have passengers who might recognise me and I would have to carry the case with the guns, because it certainly couldn't be left in the car, or the driver would shoot me when I walked away. So by default, he'd have to take me home. There was nothing else for it.

'Take this slip road, we're leaving the motorway.'

But sanity returned to me after we'd left the M25 and angled on to a minor road. By this time we were three miles from my town. I ordered him to stop in a lay-by where I gave him a note I'd hastily written.

'Can you read that?'

'Yes, mister.'

I spoke very slowly and as menacingly as I could.

'You're going to dial 999 and read it out. Do the 141 thing to hide your identity. After that you may go. You'll read that message and switch the phone off and do nothing else. Do you hear me? If you try anything you're dead. Okay?'

'Yes, mister.'

With trembling fingers he dialled the number and announced

that there were two bodies on a certain footpath. His voice was stuttering so badly that he had to say it twice. Then he switched off the phone.

'Alright. I'm getting out now. Go back the way you came. And never come near me again, do you understand?'

'Yes mister.'

The job done, I got the case out and waited until he'd done a three pointer (he managed to prang the car on a litter bin) and disappeared towards the M25. Then I went to hide the suitcase, limping off with my foot protesting.

11

Aside from a light in the entrance hall, Dalespun Towers was in darkness when I got there at eight in the evening. I wasn't even sure if the great man would be in – he might be dining at the House or with one of his fancy friends – but, it was essential I saw him. He was the only person I could turn to and there was a lot to discuss. At least there were now no servants in the Towers; they were all part-timers. No one could testify that I'd called unannounced. And of course there would be no one to observe the little things that could bring the plotters crashing to earth. Despite his laid back air, Sir Lance had a cunning streak that would surprise a casual observer.

I was in scruffy clothes and my face was stubbly and none too clean. I wore new trainers which were doing little to alleviate the pain of my sore foot. By now, the cops would have prints of my old shoes and fibres from my clothes where I'd slammed into the tree. They would be able to determine my weight and what I'd been wearing. Modern police methods are good, and although I'd left nothing too blatant behind me there were probably twenty minor details that would result a description of me. They might find hairs from my head on the tree. And of course there was always the chance of having been seen by someone who could identify me. Already some cops with hard noses would be making their own deductions from the known facts.

One, Andy had dined at the local pub with an unknown man. Two, the hit man (and yes, they'd know that's what he was) had dined in the same pub and had been with a man who was likely to be his driver. Three, within fifteen minutes, two men were dead. Four, Andy's van was still there but the other car had gone, probably with both survivors inside. No one would want to leave the murder scene on foot in that isolated area. Five, the cops had been tipped off by an anonymous phone call from a point three miles from my flat within fifty minutes of the murder.

There was the question of whether the two unidentified men

had been in cahoots. Always possible, but since the killer had been bumped off by a blow to his head and his gun was missing, it was probable that Andy's companion had seized it and ordered the driver to take him away. They'd find the discarded knife (would my prints be on it?) and they'd note that our footprints back to the car were consistent with a gun-held departure.

Already they'd have the basic picture.

Footsteps sounded in the hall. There was a pause while he checked me and then the door swung open. Sir Lance was wearing a Savile Row suit which had seen better days and an air of weariness which said he could do without any more trouble. Perhaps he'd come straight from the Commons. His face was pinched, though he gave the impression of being glad to see me. But I wasn't fooled. He gave everybody that impression.

'Come in, Mat,' he said, in his posh voice, as though he'd been expecting me. I followed him in. He turned and said with some pride: 'General Douglas is here. He's one of us. You can talk freely.'

But that was bad. All I'd wanted was a heart-to-heart with Sir Lance, and now there was going to be an onlooker – a man I didn't know who might be an inconvenient witness if things went belly-up. By default, the General was likely to take a poor view of my actions. I could see myself getting caught.

'I've had trouble,' I said, standing back.

'Well, we'll talk it over,' Sir Lance said, as though I were complaining about the weather. 'George is a good man.'

'It involves murder.'

He didn't turn a hair. He was an aristocrat, after all.

'This way. We're in the basement tonight,' he said in his plummy voice, leading me into the entrance hall where two suits of armour stood guard as they'd done since I was a boy. For some strange reason the hall had three grandfather clocks, all of them set to slightly different times, which meant a chorus of chimes at every hour. Perhaps Sir Lance felt lonely without that kind of chaos. Ahead of me, he stepped through an insignificant doorway with narrow carpeted steps leading downwards. I felt a surge of irritation and was tempted to walk out. Sir Lance's aristocratic sensibilities were surplus to my requirements. The stiff upper lip act implied my problems were trivial. Why was I risking my future with this effete old man? For all I knew, MI5 had a dossier on him that would spell his doom.

I followed him down the stairs to a surprisingly big room with no windows. It lacked the luxury of the upstairs lounges, though it was twenty times more opulent than my own poor flat. The armchairs looked comfortable, it was brightly lit, and in the corner there were CCTV monitors that showed the approach to the house. So they'd seen me coming.

A man in his sixties rose to greet me. I had a moment of insecurity when I saw his silver hair and bristling moustache. To all appearances, he was a typical General who would stand no nonsense and keep the lesser ranks in their place. Clearly he was no fool, but that was only to be expected. And here I was, dressed like a tramp, guilty of a homicide which might bring his plot crashing to the ground.

'Well, Mat,' he said, in full command of himself, offering his hand. 'I've read your dossier. It's good to meet you.'

I tried to assess the General. He was moderate height, with an intelligent face and a posh voice. He gave the impression that he understood me. It wasn't the first time I'd encountered that manner. At the end of the day, it was all part of a genteel education. There was nothing new about that. Anybody who reaches that rank has to be reasonably smart, but the real question was whether or not I could trust him, but his face didn't give me a clue.

I shook hands, but remained standing when Sir Lance asked me to sit, still attempting to evaluate the General. I'd reached the blindingly obvious conclusion that he wouldn't be easy to push around, but the deciding factor was whether he'd be on my side and there were no clues about that. It was easy for Sir Lance to say that he was 'one of us' but what did that mean? I've never met a General who was not an establishment figure. Such people lack the fire to be good plotters. Most have a natural antipathy for civil killers, and I was one. Also, they have a tremendous amount of power at their disposal. Yet his face was reasonable and his eyes were not unkind, though he didn't look like he'd tolerate any nonsense.

'Mat's had a spot of trouble,' said Sir Lance with great understatement. He offered me a sherry, which I declined. He repeated: 'Take a seat.'

But it was too late to turn back. I told them everything, pacing about and reliving my memories. I omitted nothing. I've seen a lot of things in my time, but it was unpleasant to go into the details again, though I didn't hesitate to give them the unvarnished truth. On the few occasions when I glanced at them, they were staring at me with shock on their faces. Typical desk men. They just wanted to avoid the violence, and hoped the unpleasantness would stay outside their little world. Or perhaps they were just wondering if they'd been rumbled.

When I'd finished, the General asked some questions in a calm voice. He seemed none too ruffled and not antagonistic to me. He was utterly reasonable and I found myself responding to him.

'Why did they shoot him?' said Sir Lance to the General. He was much more shocked. There was serious concern on his face.

'It was the gold bars, surely,' I said automatically, before I realised that his question referred to something a lot bigger. There were a myriad of things in the background and the situation was not what I'd perceived it to be. I didn't have the full facts, or anything approaching the full facts. Certainly the men beside me seemed to know a lot more than I did and might have the answer.

'Yes, that's what it must have been,' said the General in an unconvincing tone, and suddenly my world changed as things began to fall into place. So far I hadn't thought it through.

Why would Hetland shoot a bungler like Andy, who was no threat to him or his organisation? There was no logic to it, and he was a supremely logical man. Now there would be a murder enquiry with scores of cops to contend with; scores of problems he didn't have before. And he was trying to be respectable too.

I turned to the General and said angrily:

'What's at the back of all this? What's it all about?'

His blinked at me in surprise, before becoming a commanding officer again.

'God knows,' he said in an even tone. 'It's Hetland we're dealing with and he's a law unto himself. First, we have to look after you. We don't want trouble.'

'No, we don't.'

The General pursed his lips together and stared at me with narrowed eyes. I could see that he'd had some experience of handling emergencies.

'The big question is, were you followed?'

'Oh no, I kept a watch.'

'Are you sure about that?'

I stood back, shaking my head, aware that he was calling my expertise into question. Fair enough, that was his job and it might bring some light to the proceedings.

'Yes, I'm sure. It was deserted country, there were no followers.'

But he was unconvinced. His calm eyes blinked at me.

'Did any cars go past you? Any at all?'

'Nothing went past on the minor road, nothing.'

'What about the women that went into the pub? Did they have a car.'

They'd had a nice clean Toyota four by four.

'Nothing followed me. I checked.'

'You were lucky. The Golf would have had a tracker on it, no question. Harry doesn't send killers out without back-up. The women were the burial detail.'

He'd solved the mystery and I looked at him with new respect.

'But you did well,' he said. 'Killing a goon with one kick.'

'It was either him or me,' I said, irritated that he had completely missed the point. I might spend the rest of my life inside and he seemed to think that I'd won a coconut. But that was Generals all over. They see things from a different perspective and are singularly unconcerned with the little man's survival.

'Self defence,' said Sir Lance. But then he asked, with a hint of anxiety: 'Which charity shop did you buy your clothes in?'

I'd taken the bus to the next town and changed clothes and shoes in a public toilet before returning in another bus. The service in the shop had been lackadaisical and the old woman at the till had scarcely looked up from her Jackie Collins paperback.

During the entire outing I'd seen no one I recognised and on both bus trips I'd been one of only five passengers.

'What did you do with the old stuff?'

'It went straight into a bin bag and I dumped it at the refuse tip. Nobody saw me. That bit went okay. I went straight home and had a bath before coming here.'

There was a silence. Both men studied the floor, frowning.

'You've done well, Mat,' said the General. 'The thing is to lie low and avoid attention from either Harry or the police. We have to assume that they're in cahoots and will share information. Don't overreact, whatever you do. The situation's under control.'

'Yes, under control,' parroted Sir Lance. 'You've done well.'

I closed my eyes impatiently. I've been involved in more killings than Sir Lance and every one has been a potential disaster. And Harry was easily the most formidable man I'd ever met.

'The murder,' I said, 'couldn't have taken place without identification. We were outside the depot. Andy's face must have been compared with an existing image. They must have photographed us in the van. That means they've got my picture too. They'll show that to Harry. I met him only yesterday under the name of Browne. I can be identified.'

'Mat, you're right to be concerned,' said the General, before Lance could respond., He was still speaking very calmly. 'We'll assume that Harry can identify your face. It never does to underestimate your enemy. But he doesn't know who you are and Lance won't tell him. You are just another face and he's got a million enemies already. Why should he kill you? He certainly won't want another murder on his hands and the oaf you killed means nothing to him. I'd say that as long as you keep away from the depot you're safe. Now let's look at the other side. The cops' point of view. What are the weak points in your armour?'

'Shoe prints. They'll get my weight, though I'm on a crash diet now –'

'Steady on, you can't lose weight that quickly.'

'It'll take several days before they work it out. By then I'll be lighter and leaner.'

'That's possible.'

'– the old clothes and shoes are dumped, they're not an issue. But they'll discover that Andy phoned me in the morning. Maybe no one saw me getting into his van, but a man answering my description lunched with him in the pub before the shooting. On a murder enquiry those points will be investigated. If they give me a grilling they'll work it out for themselves, no matter what I say. Modern profiling is good.'

'Best avoid the grilling, then. Choke them off with an easy answer. Set their minds to rest. You have to stop 'them digging deeper.'

'Yes, but how?' I said.

'Were you seen by any independent witnesses?'

'I don't know. It was broad daylight. He phoned from across the road. They can trace a caller's position to an accuracy of a metre. That means we probably met.'

'Did you take your phone with you?'

'No, I left it at home. And I didn't bring it here, either.'

'Good man. Then you've got to be open about it. He came to see you this morning. There was a short exchange and you refused to go with him. End of story.'

'What if somebody saw me getting into his van?'

The General shook his head.

'They'd need to have door-to-door enquiries to find that person. They won't do that for a minor witness.'

'We hope. They'll ask what I did after that. Telling them I stayed at home all morning is the worst thing you can say to a tec.'

'You're wrong there,' said Sir Lance. 'You went to the shops. My housekeeper got some things this morning. You were in the superstore at lunchtime. I've got a receipt.'

I looked at him. Could things really be that easy?

'That'll fob them off for a day. I dined in the pub with Andy just before he was shot. We were the only ones there – at first anyway.'

But Sir Lance was shaking his old head.

'Mat, identification isn't that easy. Unless you did something to get noticed, the landlord won't remember whether you were sixteen or sixty. You're trained to notice things, but he isn't. If there's an identification parade, you're already in different clothes.'

'My footsteps are at the murder scene. It was muddy.'

'There are three million men of your size – incidentally, watch that sprained foot. If you need to see a quack let us know. Don't go to your own doctor and don't walk with a limp. That's the kind of thing which gives you away. We have our own clinic.'

'A week and it'll be okay. I don't need a doc. So everything's fine then?'

'Of course it is,' said the General. 'Nothing to worry about.'

'You're an honourable man,' said Sir Lance, 'with a blameless record. If you had a string of convictions it might be another matter.'

'So you go to the police, Mat,' said the General, 'as soon as Andy's name is confirmed. You're a bit upset, not weepy, and you'll tell them you refused an offer of work that very morning. Keep it matter of fact, an honest citizen doing his bit.'

I nodded without enthusiasm.

'Now here's an important point. Start the interview by asking what happened to your pal. Think laterally. You have an innocent conscience, you're about to tell them everything you know, but you're all agog with curiosity. You just heard his name on the box and you want to know the real story. They'll smell a rat if you don't. If you've no curiosity about the deaths, that means you know more than they do.'

'A good point,' said Sir Lance. 'This is not an interrogation. You are volunteering evidence, so they've got to be polite to you. Ask them questions. Show an interest. I always say a well-asked question can change a whole interview.'

On the coffee table sat a book about Tax Laws which must have had more than a thousand pages. I wondered how a man as rich as Sir Lance could be bothered with such drivel. I disliked this room, with its low ceilings, dark beams and ancient air. It made me feel claustrophobic. And there was only one way out.

'Andy claimed to have been inside the depot,' I said.

I told them how he'd posed as an insurance inspector and photographed the gold bars, or at any rate, their packaging. I told them that he had always been a chancer and that the goons had probably sussed him out. How, I didn't know. No cameras had been visible from the road, though there were plenty in the backyard. We'd parked near a lot of other cars and drawn no attention to ourselves. They must have seen me too.

There was a pause when I'd finished, then the General began to speak. He spoke clearly but not loudly and I suspected he had good judgement – though whether his ultimate aim was his cause or mine was another matter.

'You've been scanned in the car – no two ways about it. We've had intelligence that he's bought sophisticated cameras. But you're no threat to Harry, as such. It's the Hets, his bodyguards. You need to watch them, and the police.'

'I know.'

'They might well have your photo, but they don't know who you are. Keep your head down and you're safe. The Hets are the kind of low life who avenge a killing. They might shoot you on sight. Keep away from them and you're okay.'

Some of this made sense. The rest was baloney. Of course I recognised the way his mind was working. After a serious alarm it's necessary to calm the troops with some bland assurances. But he looked worried.

'That's great,' I said acidly. 'What about the cops? Will they ignore me too? I could spend the rest of my life inside.'

'Oh, you're probably alright,' said Sir Lance, hurriedly. 'I'm sure there's no evidence against you. We'll go into that in a minute. We want to get the backdrop first.'

'It was a pro killing,' I said. 'We didn't even know we were followed.'

'He's got plenty of experts on call,' said the General. 'There's a lot at stake.'

'Why the hell is Harry stealing gold bars,' I said, 'when he's going respectable? That could stop him quicker than anything.'

'He needs the cash,' said the General, so knowingly that I knew he had to be right. 'There are a lot of things which can't go through a bank. He won't pay the assassin with a cheque, will he? He's got to have cash. And that's what the gold is.'

'Mind you,' said Sir Lance. 'He's still got to turn it into currency.'

'Steady on, Lance. Plenty of small banks will do that for a few percent.'

'Gold's heavy. He'll need a security van and a team of guards.'

'He's got that already.'

I shook my head at this irrelevance. By this time I'd worked out that the General was the boss and Sir Lance was merely his spokesperson. Although I was not entirely reassured, I was beginning to feel better.

'What did you do with the guns?' asked the General, turning business-like.

I told him how I'd packed everything into the case and hidden it.

'Where?'

'In a hedgerow three miles away.'

'Better retrieve them, quick' said the General. 'We can't leave them lying around. Your prints will be on them too.'

I would have been grateful for his concern, but the inflection in his voice told me that it wasn't me but the guns that interested him – his tone had changed at the mention of them. Generals love weaponry and they can never have too much.

'I'll find that receipt for you,' said Sir Lance. 'That will clinch it.'

I was effectively dismissed. The old buffers wanted their confab, but first that meant getting rid of me and that couldn't be done until the weapons had been collected. We all went upstairs. The General put on an overcoat and gloves while Sir Lance got me a receipt for a tube of toothpaste which I folded into my pocket. It was time-dated at 12.02.

'Let me know how things go later in the week,' he said, in his best bedside manner. 'I'm in every night. But keep watch. They might follow you.'

'They just might.'

'Come on,' said the General. 'We need those guns.'

He turned and walked towards the rear of the house, revealing a familiarity with Dalespun Towers which suggested he was no stranger to the place. Outside the back door sat an old saloon car that looked as though it belonged to the village headmaster, the sort of car nobody would look at it twice. Soon we were cruising down the avenue.

'Mat, don't lose your cool. It's a bit of an upset but you can weather it.'

'General –'

'Call me George, this isn't the army.'

'– this is an emergency. They've got enough evidence to get me already.'

'Yes, but they won't, dear boy. By this time Harry will have been in touch with the friendly inspector. He certainly won't want you brought into the thing. And I don't mean that he knows who you are, but he won't want to stir the hornet's nest. That'd be a disaster, with a lot of questions about his involvement. He knows when to lie low. We've seen it before. Be sensible and you're safe. We'll stand by you. We need you.'

'They'll know about me as soon as they see my dossier.'

'The army will never show them that.'

'Oh, they won't?'

'The army will give you a clean bill of health and it won't reveal your history. You're safe. Special Forces won't be mentioned. That stuff's under lock and key.'

'But I'm still in a sticky position.'

'To an extent. I'd say you were in the clear.'

'Does this mean a stoppage?' I asked. 'The other thing's finished?'

'Good heavens, no. We've got important work to do. We need that report. Granted, there's a delay because of this thing, but we have to go ahead.'

'It sounds pretty dangerous to me.'

'Everything's under control. Your report's an option only, a contingency. But we must have it.'

'Yes, but all roads lead to Mecca. No matter what Harry does, he escapes censure. Therefore the last resort becomes more likely by the day. I've seen this before. And it could mean a life sentence for me.'

'The report will not be enacted, but we must have it. I believe Harry can be stopped using non-violent methods. And I think we're going to do it.'

By this time we'd reached the end of the avenue and the Doberman was barking like mad when we passed the lodge. In the middle distance, the lights of the town were spread out and I saw the shape of a London-bound train leaving the station. There were several cars and cyclists on the road. I gave George directions and we moved off.

'So you think you can stop Harry?'

'I'm sure we can.'

'And if you can't we go ahead?'

'Well, that's an option. It may be dangerous, but that won't stop us.'

'The chances are abysmal. It won't work. Turn left here.'

We hit the country road and the General put up the headlights. The town was fading into the background and there were no cars on the road.

'Don't you believe it. These things happen all the time. It's only when you hit presidents and premiers that the odds change. Then you're attacking the establishment and the whole apparatus of the state is against you. The plotter has got to get his guy before he reaches the top. Not after he's arrived.'

'You think so?'

'The evidence is all there, I hope you're still with us?'

'In theory. But we need a plan.'

'Of course we do. That's why we need your report. You know what we need – a list of venues. I grant you it won't be easy.'

'I've already done some swotting. He's elusive So far, his only predictable destination is Parliament and he never goes straight there. He knows there's a risk of getting hit.'

'He's perpetually alert. Keep trying, Mat, you can do it.'

'George, it's better to demonise him in the press. Once the truth is known he's finished. We're both soldiers, we know action can go either way.'

'Oh, I agree. Action's always a last resort. We're working on other things too. Incidentally, this shooting could be his Waterloo. His men have been on high alert all day. Now, what happens here? Is this the lay-by?'

'Yes, but you're driving past it.'

'Just looking, my boy. They may know you got out here. See anything?'

Yes, the old sat nav would pinpoint it in a flash.

'So what?' I said, perhaps I was winding him up. 'You've been telling me all night that Harry isn't interested in me.'

'Yes, but what about the Hets? You killed one of them today and they'll be thirsty for blood. They don't know what you did with the case, of course. Maybe you phoned for a car, or maybe you hid it somewhere nearby. They might arrange a little welcome for you when you collect it. That's the way these fellows think.'

The General started to whistle as he studied the dark hedges and trees. I looked at the area and cursed myself for mentioning the guns. Without a doubt they would have identified the lay-by and could be waiting. On our right there were open fields and I swung my head to the left to see that the footpath was deserted. But I knew in my heart they wouldn't be waiting. At the very least they'd have a parked car nearby; killers are fussy about the getaway. They don't care to walk home.

'It looks alright.'

'Fine then.'

The General did a three pointer and pulled into the lay-by.

I said: 'I did the old army trick; the case is under twigs at the back of a hedge on that footpath, ten minutes away. It's heavy. Better not to wait in the lay-by, you might get noticed. It'll take me a good twenty minutes.'

'Alright, I'll drive about.'

'Do that, and we'll put it in the boot.'

I got out and went to the footpath to find it very ugly in the dark. My clothes kept getting torn on the brambles and wild roses. And my sprained foot began to annoy me. I'd counted my steps on the way back, but that had been in daylight. Now my strides were shorter and I didn't have a torch. The case wasn't where I remembered, or I couldn't find it. For a furious moment it looked as though I'd lost it, until I discovered it twenty steps beyond my position. It took some time to uncover it.

Eventually I got back, limping, just as the General pulled up. I waited until a car had passed and then we lifted it into the boot.

George was amazed at my strength, or so he said, but that was his way of apologising for making me do all the work. I was fatigued and out of breath. The case was heavy and I resolved to carry no weights for the rest of my life.

'Let's see inside,' he said, unlocking the clasps with some expertise.

The boot had no light, but he produced a torch and gave a delighted cry when he saw the contents. The sniper's rifle was a beauty and it was in pristine condition. There were night sights and other accoutrements and he liked the hand guns too.

'Quite a haul. You're not claiming ownership?'

'Of course not.'

In the distance we heard the sound of a car approaching, its lights illuminating the trees at the corner. The General became all business again.

'In you go. I'll get you home,' he said, closing the boot.

'No, I'll walk home from here.'

'Eh? Is that wise? Second walk on the same road? And you've a bad foot.'

'I'll use the footpath. Go home by another route. It'll muddy the boots and tear my clothes, and it's only a couple of extra miles.'

He looked round at the dark night, and then said:

'Well you know the area; best of luck. And thanks for these pea shooters.'

'I didn't want the rozzers finding them.'

He gave a chuckle.

'Listen, don't overdo the slimming. Weaken yourself too much and you'll come a cropper. What have you eaten today?'

'I've had lunch and three cups of tea since.'

He shook his head.

'That can make you look feverish. Knacker of the Yard might notice.'

After a moment he sped off, happy with the armaments in his boot. I wondered what would happen if the cops found them in his car. Would they arrest a General, or would it be nodded through? Rather him than me. An owl hooted nearby and I felt lonely. I had a lot of miles to cover before I got home, but somehow it wasn't too bad. A man had tried to shoot me in the back and I was still alive. I couldn't complain.

12

It took two hours to get back. The footpath deteriorated as it went on and finally I had to go into the fields to complete that stage of my journey. My foot got worse and I found myself cursing at every step. At last I reached a public road, a minor route which fed a village and which was surprisingly busy for that time of night. I hate car headlamps in my face, so tended to stop until they'd passed. Eventually, back at the flat, I fell into a chair and switched on the box to watch the late news.

The bodies of two men had been found in the early afternoon after a tip off. It was given a slot on the national news and was the main feature of the local news. The murders had taken place in possibly the only deserted area near London. The camera panned in to reveal the narrow road Andy and I had travelled, focussing on the pub we'd dined at, and then it swung to the tree lined path to reveal a policeman standing guard at the denser section of the wood.

'The police have not revealed any details of the murders or how the victims were killed,' said the commentator. 'But it is understood that more than seventy officers have been drafted in. This is an unusual case. Neither party had been identified at nine o'clock tonight though it is understood that formal identification of one man is likely to be made soon. The police have appealed for witnesses. They believe that there were four men involved. The murder weapon has not been found.'

During this, a helicopter panned in on the wood but the heavy trees obscured all the details, although some people in silver suits could be glimpsed through the branches. I switched the set off, depressed by the whole business, and went to bed.

13

I was hungry when I woke at six. My diet had scarcely started, but my gut was sore and I was unhappy about my prospects. On the positive side, my foot was a lot better and I was no longer lame. Whatever my other weaknesses, I have a healthy disposition. But that was where it could all go wrong. A half-intelligent questioner could find a dozen holes in my story. I'd have to hope that they'd pay no great attention to a minor witness like me, but with more than seventy detectives on the case it left me in an exposed position. There was a temptation to do nothing, but that would have been a mistake. Sooner or later they'd come for me and that would make it worse

Once up, I switched on the kettle and dressed, then I brought the TV to life. The news came on as I was pouring my tea. One of the bodies had been identified as Andy's. There was an appeal for witnesses. Light-headed, I thought about it.

Then I phoned the cops and spoke to a Constable Smith who was a most considerate listener. I told him that Andy had called on me yesterday and though I knew nothing about the shooting, he was an old colleague who didn't deserve to be murdered and I wished it to be noted that he'd been in touch.

'This will be passed on right away, sir. Would you mind remaining at your phone for the next hour? One of our detectives will call you.'

An hour passed and it wasn't the phone that went but the door bell. Two men had come to see me. The taller of the two was the boss, a Chief-Inspector no less, and he was charm itself, at first, anyway. He shook my hand, thanking me for my prompt call. It looked like being a difficult case and he was grateful to me.

'I'm Herb,' he said, adopting a matey tone, 'and this is Jim.'

Jim raised his head and nodded. It was his only acknowledgement. His boss would do the talking and he would do the menials. I'd have to watch Herb. He looked a shrewd cookie. His eyes flicked over my room and I could tell he was not impressed. Without a doubt he lived in the style of an MP and had some distaste for the utility of my world. At the same time he would have noted that it was relatively sensible. The police don't trust oddballs. Their files are full of eccentric persons whose hands are stained with blood and he could see I didn't belong to that group. I had the kettle on, poured them a cup of tea and offered them a biscuit, though I didn't take one myself.

'Have you been up all night?' I said.

'Well, I'm finishing a shift,' said Herb (so, presumably, had Jim but he didn't count). 'I've gotta work fast at the beginning in case something gets past me.'

'It's a terrible business,' I said. 'What happened?'

'Well we're not too sure ourselves –'

'I got an awful shock when I heard his name on the box.'

'I'll bet you did, sir.'

'I mean, this isn't Andy. He could be a rough diamond but he wasn't into heavy stuff. It sounds downright brutal. How did he die?'

'To be honest, we don't know yet. We've had no word from the post mortem.'

This whopper was told with a straight face, as though he were genuinely mystified. I couldn't see a single reason for it. Why tell me a lie? he was so convincing that I almost believed him myself. He knew that Andy had a bullet in his head, yet he was dispensing bullshit like a politician caught red handed. I would have to be wary of this man. He wasn't as nice as he looked.

'Who was the other bloke?'

Herb raised his hand to stop me, and I knew it was going to go by the book. All of Sir Lance's instructions could be disregarded. No details were going to be disclosed. He would ask the questions and answer none. This was an official visit, and though I had volunteered information and supplied the tea, no quarter would be given. Meanwhile, Jim was holding a portable recorder, a cunning move which gave them a second chance to listen to any hesitations in my voice.

'A total mystery. We haven't the faintest idea. He hasn't been reported missing. Mind you, neither was your friend.'

'Well, he lived on his own. As far as I know, anyway.'

'I see, sir. And you knew the victim well?'

Herb was about forty five and his head was going white with a bald patch in the middle. His hands looked capable and I suspected that he had an incisive mind that would chisel away at a problem until he'd solved it. He was certainly aware of his own importance and it looked as though he enjoyed ordering people about. Despite apparently having been up all night, his shoes were well polished and there was a perfect crease in his trousers.

'I've known him for twenty years,' I said. 'Whether I knew him well is another matter. We were in the same unit in the army – old colleagues. We weren't exactly best mates. To tell you the truth he was a bit of a chancer, and a tight wad too. Everybody who dealt with him had trouble on that score, even his wife and sons. None of them were speaking. Quite sad, really.'

'What was your job in the army?'

Yes, he was astute, a born policeman who didn't miss a trick. Old soldiers are trained in killing. He'd seen it all before and nothing would get past him.

'Mostly clerical work, I'm afraid – not very exciting,'

I could imagine the General's head nodding. Keep it boring, don't get them interested, and above all don't mention Special Operations. Never let them even wonder if you were capable of doing in a gunman.

'What's the story about yesterday morning's call?'

'Oh, that was a wild goose chase. He wanted me to join him in a search for some gold bars that had been stolen. He claimed they were in a depot in Romford. He would pay me a thousand pounds out of his bonus.'

'And you went there?'

'I did not. He never paid me for my last work, not even my expenses. That's Andy all over. If the thieves had stolen the gold they must have been very careless to let him know where they'd put it. And you can't check up on a security depot anyway. I mean, none of us would get through the door and I certainly wouldn't get paid. It was a lost cause.'

'Who was he working for?'

'An insurance company, or so he said.'

'You didn't believe that?'

'Well, I had my doubts.'

'Did you argue?'

'Not really. I'm not that kind of bloke. It was a short call, but I wasn't rude. I listened and said no. Then he was in a hurry to get away.'

'Did you jar him about the money he owed you?'

This had nothing to do with his enquiry, and was probably being asked for voice-check purposes. It would give them a hint of whether I was telling the truth on other questions.

'It was certainly mentioned.'

'Tell me about the previous work you did..'

Again, this had nothing to do with his enquiries, but no stone was going to be left unturned when Herb was asking the questions.

'Well, it's supposed to be confidential, but you're police and it's a murder enquiry. It was a builder's yard in North London. They'd gone bust and the builder had moved half a million pounds of stock into another yard which Andy thought he'd identified. I can give you names and dates later.'

'So he was wrong?'

'Oh, I don't know if he was wrong. He was unable to prove it. So there was no money for us. Or for me, anyway. I think he got his expenses. That was a year ago.'

'I see.'

'If I were you I'd look at that depot – the gold bars.'

'Do you know the name of the firm?'

'No, he didn't give me that, but I would have thought that it was a narrow field.'

'Did he work with crooks?'

'Not that I know of, but I wouldn't have put it past him.'

'He must have. That would explain the gold bars.'

'So you've heard about them before?'

'There have been rumours in the underworld. But we need more than rumours before we can act.'

'You should check that depot. It smells a bit to me.'

He laughed. Big policemen don't take instructions from people like me.

'What depot?' he was half-mocking me. 'You said he was

going to Romford. But did he? We've no way of knowing. He could have gone in the opposite direction.'

'He wasn't that far away when you found him.'

'Well, that's true. Did he have a girlfriend?'

'I've no idea. We only talked for a few minutes.'

'Which pub did he drink in?'

'I don't know.'

'What did you do yesterday, after he left?'

I stared at him for a moment with my mouth open in honest surprise.

'Can't remember, I just sat about the house, I think.'

'All day? Surely you did something?'

'Oh, I remember now – I went to the supermarket. Then I went for a walk.'

'Got a receipt?'

'I usually throw them out,' I said, going through to the kitchen and rummaging in the bin. 'No, I don't have it, sorry. Sometimes I leave them in the supermarket.'

I went back and sat down.

'What time would that be?'

'Lunch time, I think – oh wait.'

I went back and rummaged about in a drawer: 'Ha! Here's the receipt,' I said coming through in triumph and handing it over. Herb stared at it for a moment and then said to Jim: 'Timed at 12.02.'

'I'd forgotten all about that,' I said. 'But I don't see why you need it.'

'Well, it lets us know exactly where you were at a certain time.'

Herb looked around the room in case he'd missed a smoking gun.

'You've been very helpful.'

'Well, he didn't deserve this.'

'Do you know anyone who might have it in for him?'

'Not as such, but he often antagonised people. Come to think of it, that may be why he approached me. Nobody else would want to deal with him.'

'Can you suggest any lines of enquiry?'

'Well, I'd have a look at that depot. I'm sure he was killed because of it. Nothing else is big enough.'

He looked at me and nodded.

'Mr Hill, this conversation is private. You don't tell the press, do you understand?'

'They'll hear nothing from me.'

'Best not to tell anyone. We want wraps on this for the moment. There's one thing, though. Do you mind if I pass your number on to his sons, as a humanitarian gesture? They may want to talk to you.'

'Oh, I'll talk to them, alright.'

'Good man. There's my card. If anything happens, phone me.'

We shook hands and they were gone.

14

From my window, I watched them go to their car. I wondered if Herb would turn to Jim to voice suspicions about me. But that didn't going to happen. They were Senior and Junior and there was no rapport between them. Herb took the passenger seat and Jim did the driving. After they'd sped round the corner, I sat down and reviewed the interview. On balance, it had gone alright. They'd accepted my replies and I hadn't hesitated on any of the points. Nor had Herb asked anything that would incriminate me. Of course this was just the first hurdle and they might be back to clarify some of the detail. That was when inconsistencies would become obvious, though the greater the time lapse the better it would be for me.

Then the phone rang.

'Mr Hill?' said a big voice that was reminiscent of Andy's, though there was a youthful element to it.

'That's me.'

'We haven't met. My name is Carl.'

Herb must have phoned him as soon as he'd left my flat.

'I know who you are, Carl. You're Andy's son,' I said, before expressing my commiserations.

'Thanks. Could we see you? My brother's with me.'

'Of course you can. I'll do anything I can to help,' I said, passing on my address.

'We're in the car. We'll be there in a few minutes.'

It would have been nice to enjoy thirty minutes of peace, but within five they were in my flat. Both boys were nearly as tall as Andy had been and they seemed reasonable blokes. I gave them a cup of tea and they helped themselves to biscuits.

'There are a lot of things we don't understand,' said Carl. 'To put it bluntly, what was my father up to?'

I said I'd seen Andy only once in the last year and asked what he meant.

'Well, there's the money and the safe.'

He was a big lad, perhaps a rugby player and more intelligent than his father. He was certainly fitter and had the gruff manner of a big man. Perhaps the diet was affecting me, but the mention of money and safes made me feel dizzy. If there's one thing Andy hadn't needed, it was a safe, although come to think of it, he'd had a grand in his pocket when he was shot.

'Carl, you'll need to explain that, please.'

'The cops gave us his keys. We went to his flat this morning and found the money, but there was no key for the safe.'

'Do you know anything about this?' said the younger one, Gerry, as though I had organised the whole thing. Of course the boy was big and possibly sounded a lot more aggressive than he really was.

'Where was this money – under the floorboards?'

'Sitting on top of the safe.'

But that was farcical. The idea of Andy leaving wads of money on open display while he was out of the flat was unthinkable. I asked them where the flat was – and was astonished to learn it was in the next town.

'This money,' I said. 'Do you have it with you?'

Gerry reached into his inside pocket and produced a neat bundle of fifties, wrapped with a paper band bearing a bank's stamp. After a moment, Carl produced a similarly marked wad. Both had been stamped by the same London bank. I couldn't believe it, I'd never seen so many fifties before – and of course big Andy had been carrying fifties too.

'Do the cops know about this?' I said.

'No. They gave us the address and the keys. We'd never been there before.

'This is news to me,' I said. 'I didn't know he had a safe; wouldn't have even believed it. Whatever you do, don't tell the rozzers about that money. It's difficult to know for sure, but it's probably gang money of some kind, though I haven't the slightest idea what's going on.'

'And that's what's in the safe?'

'I don't know.'

They looked at me and wondered if I was an old chancer.

Carl said: 'But does that mean he was a gangster?'

'He wasn't,' I said quite truthfully. What gangster would want Andy? 'I'm sure your father was never in a gang. It's probably a payment.'

'Why would anyone pay him that much?'

'For services rendered, whatever they were.'

'We've searched the flat and we can't find the key.'

'I'm not surprised. I don't think it's your father's safe.'

They looked at me.

'Then whose is it?'

'It's probably a stolen safe. Obviously the money's a payment for something, possibly for minding the safe.'

They looked at me again.

'Come on,' said Carl, 'two grand for minding a safe? Gangsters don't part with money that easily.'

'Oh, but they do. Depends what's in it.'

'So it's big, then.'

'It must be. Those big policemen would be very interested.'

They looked at me for a long minute with uneasiness on their faces.

'Mr Hill,' said Gerry. 'Would you like to come over to the flat and see it?'

I nodded, though I'd no great wish to do it. Andy must have been mixing with some colourful people and I'd rather keep out their way. But I was in Good Samaritan mode and could hardly refuse.

We went out to the car, which I was surprised to discover was an expensive saloon with a lovely leather interior. 'It's mum's,' they said, and I made a mental note that the lady was doing well. I took the rear seat while the boys sat in the front.

'We've never really known our father,' said Gerry, leaning over. 'He was a bit of a cuss to our mother. We kept away.'

'I know what he was like.'

'It's a pity, really, but he kind of resented us. An unpleasant situation, but it was never our fault. Now this has happened and we can't make it up. I'm sure he didn't deserve this.'

'He certainly didn't.'

'Mum got a shock when the cops called her. She sent us to identify him. She's very squeamish, you know. But the thing is, we didn't even know him.'

'That can't have been pleasant. How did he die?'

'Shot – they only let us see part of his face.'

'Any idea why he was in the wood?' said the other brother. 'What's going on? There was another man shot too.'

No, he wasn't shot, but I wasn't going to comment on that little trap of Herb's.

'Probably having a walk. He used to live there.'

'Oh, he did? When was that?'

'When he was a kid, I think. His father worked on the land.'

'Oh. What about the other men? The cops reckon there were two other guys.'

'There's been something going on, but I don't know what.'

'I'll bet this has something to do with the safe and that money.'

'If they're going to shoot you,' I said, 'they seldom give you money. I dunno, but it sounds like there are two lots of gangsters here.'

Andy had the bottom flat in a tower block which looked the worse for wear. A lot of windows were boarded up. There was soot around one which suggested that there had been a serious fire. How he'd managed to get the ground floor flat was a mystery. He'd been an able-bodied man who could climb stairs without difficulty. Usually the ground floor is reserved for the disabled. Before we had even stepped inside, I noticed that the flat was crudely furnished, with no curtains on the windows and a naked light bulb hanging from the ceiling. Andy would have it no other way. He didn't go in for domestic niceties. Three concrete steps led to the front door. It would have been easy to reverse a van and offload a safe straight into the entrance.

Carl produced the keys, opened the door and stopped.

'The safe's gone!' he said.

'It was there an hour ago.'

Andy hadn't bothered with a hall carpet and I could see the tracks of the dolly on which the safe must have rested. There were two sets, one going in, the other out.

'Who would steal the safe?'

'If you ask me,' I said, 'the mobster heard the news and

collected it.'

'There was a van in the car park with three men in it when we left.'

That made sense.

'Boys, listen, let's search this place and get out. We might have visitors.'

'We've already searched it, there's nothing else.'

'You checked the floorboards?'

'No.'

'He must have had personal papers and at least one bank book. You've gotta get that, then we can go. Come on.'

The main room wasn't promising, so I went to the bedroom. It was tremendously untidy and had naked floorboards. The only piece of furniture besides the bed was a cheap bookcase containing two books. I recognised that as a false lead. Andy didn't read. With the boys watching, I moved the case. The floorboards seemed solid until I stood on one and heard it squeak. It took a moment to find that it could be prised out from the middle, revealing a dark space underneath. I got out my pocket torch and saw nothing. But the board had often been removed, so there must be something under the floor. I reached under a beam to find, eventually, a cardboard box which I handed over.

'That's his papers,' said Carl. 'And his bank book. But there's no money.'

I made no comment about the money I'd removed from Andy's body. To do so would reveal that I was deeper in the mire than I should be.

'Let's go,' I said, my good deed done. 'This place gives me the creeps.'

As Carl was locking the door, an old lady came out of the neighbouring flat.

'Are you Andy's relatives?'

'Yes, these are his boys,' I said.

'Oh, I can see the family resemblance. I'd like to say how sorry I am. Andy was such a gentleman. He helped me often and nothing was too much trouble. He put my bins out every week. He was so good. I want to go the funeral. When is it?'

But there was no easy answer to that. The boys were polite

and shook her hand, saying that there'd be an announcement in the papers once the police enquiries were finished, but they didn't know when that would be. Then we went to the car.

'I want breakfast,' declared Carl as the car revved up, so shortly afterwards we found ourselves in a coffee shop. I opted for tea and nothing else.

'Did dad have a bad life?' Carl asked me. It was a half-humorous question, which implied an answer in the affirmative.

I stifled my irritation. If Andy was a failure then so was I. You can't pigeon-hole a man's life. Recently a billionaire had remarked that his great-grand children would know next to nothing about him. Perhaps he was a failure too. There are a lot of us about.

'Well, he could be a bit of a cuss, we all can. There was an awkward streak to him, but he wasn't all bad. Some might say he'd had a sad time and that he'd got nowhere. All in all, I'd say he had a reasonably happy life. He was always good company.'

They seemed quite glad that I'd said it.

As I spoke, I wondered at the things that had happened to Andy within twenty four hours of his death. Here was a penniless man with a bundle of fifties in his pocket and another two grand waiting on top of a safe in his flat. And why the safe? Clearly it wasn't his. He must have given his keys to someone who had a lot of clout. Had they sent him out to look for the gold bars while they were moving it in? But why hide the safe in a domestic property where the neighbours would be dangerous witnesses? And what was inside it? The most obvious explanation (and it was probably the wrong one) was that he'd had a hand in its theft and was waiting for an expert to open it. That, of course, didn't explain the wads of money, so it was unlikely to be true.

15

Thirty minutes later, they drove me home and I sank into a chair with my head in a whirl. It was not yet ten in the morning and already too many things had happened. The interview with Herb was most worrying. It was difficult to know whether I'd made the right impression, and I'd had a sense of things happening in the background. In addition, there was the possibility that he'd find out about the safe (the cops are good at that kind of thing) and start looking at me from a different angle. Then there was Operation Garden and that was one thing I didn't need. By this time I had an aversion to the whole thing. Hetland was a smart operator with a brilliant organisation behind him, whereas I'd no great confidence in either Sir Lance or the General. The thought had crossed my mind that they had other things going on, but what was new?

Then there was my diet. Although this was not an ideal time to stop eating, the loss of a few pounds might be enough to swing things in my favour. In the meantime it would have to continue. Starvation would make me less recognisable by altering my face (witnesses might have seen me out with Andy) and I'd always found myself able to think more clearly when I was hungry. Perhaps I was overdoing it, but there was a murder case in the background and that was enough to swing my judgement. So far I'd had three cups of tea that morning and no food since yesterday's lunch.

I needed time to think, but that wasn't going to happen.

The doorbell rang.

I opened up to find a hard-faced blonde woman looking up at me. She was about fifty-five and dressed in black leather..

'So you're in at last.'

'Jane,' I said. 'Come in.'

But this was something I didn't need. Jane was from my old unit. We were of similar ages and had served the same number of years, during which she'd established a reputation as a troublemaker.

'What brings you here?'

She came in and watched as I closed the door. Jane had a penchant for taking things to extremes, though she was actually nothing like as crass as she first appeared. In fact, she could sometimes be inspired. She was not an ideal companion if you wanted to relax.

'Where have you been?' she asked. There was irritation in her voice as she followed me into the flat.

'You know Andy's dead?'

'Yes, I know.'

'I'm just back from seeing his sons.'

'Those big guys in the car?'

So she'd been watching. I hadn't seen her and I usually notice these things. Perhaps I was getting rusty. A little out of touch, or maybe I was just getting old.

'Tea?' I asked, sensing that the immediate future was going to be difficult and that some light refreshment might alleviate some of the prospects. Any more visitors and the biscuits would have to be replenished.

'You really keep a horrible flat,' she said, looking around, speaking in a tone that would have been almost humorous if it hadn't been so deadpan. 'I've never met anyone who can make things so ugly as you.'

I'd anticipated the criticism. She was, perhaps, mildly discomfited at having arrived without notice and was trying to cover it with some carping comment to redress the imbalance. That said, her judgement was probably correct.

'Is your own any better?' I said. 'You should see Andy's.'

'It's worse than this?'

'It is. I had the cop boss here this morning and he never complained.'

'Where's your woman?'

'Oh, she moved out with a young chap.'

'When?'

'Two days ago.'

'Okay, I'll reduce my criticisms by fifty per cent. What did the cop want?'

'A statement. I'm the last known person to speak to Andy.'

'How are the enquiries going?'

'Dunno. He was tight lipped about that. Here.'

She looked at the cup I'd just handed to her.

'Is that meant to be clean?'

'No. Take it or leave it.'

She took it and the remaining biscuit and looked at me with her pale eyes.

'We need to have a talk, you and me,' she said, her tone indicating that this was the real reason for her visit. 'A serious one.'

A talk? That's usually something you get from your woman when she's decided to leave, although I hadn't had one from Adele, not that I was complaining. Anyway, Jane was not my woman, nor had she ever been. Senior officers were also very good at dispensing talks and there you had no alternative but to salute and say *yessir*. However, Jane didn't fall into that category either, which might just give me an excuse to avoid a finger wag. I was under no compunction to tell nanny what I'd been doing or why I'd done it.

'Everybody wants to talk to me. I'm fed up with it. What about?'

'You know what.'

Jane was shorter than average, with a thin figure and a slightly hooked nose which might have been attractive when she was twenty, but now rendered her something less than a beauty. I'd never seen the point of dyed hair when a woman gets on the wrong side of fifty, but I'm no expert. She'd made a career from her sassy comments. Or perhaps she hadn't, and that was why she'd got no further than me.

'Andy?'

'No. Well, yes, Andy, too. Were you at his flat just now?'

'I certainly was.'

'Well, come on, tell me.'

She was in no position to order me about, but there was no point in stalling. Sooner or later the facts would have to be disclosed and I began to talk. She listened attentively when I told her about the gold bars, the money and the safe.

'It must have been gangsters who handled it,' I said, 'and I'm sure they weren't Hetland's. He'd never hide a safe in Andy's flat. He wouldn't trust him an inch, and he's got plenty of facilities of his own. This has gotta be another lot. Small-timers, perhaps, a local outfit. He's been mixing with some rough elements. I don't know what's going on.'

'What size of safe?'

'I never saw it. Not too big, if three men could move it.'

'I'd like to know what was in it. That could be the reason he was shot.'

'You think so?' I asked, surprised. 'If you ask me, it was the gold bars. Can't see how the safe comes into it.'

'Well, I think it's important. Do the cops know about it?'

'The safe? No, not as far as I know.'

'Yes, but will these boys tell them?'

'Oh, I don't think so. They were clutching the money like they'd won the lottery, I warned them to keep mum about it.'

She breathed a sigh of relief and I wondered why.

'That's alright, then,' she said. 'We'll go into that later. I need to know about your recent activities.'

This was said as deadpan as though I'd been caught with my fingers in the till.

I turned to pour myself a cup of tea, resolved to tell her nothing that I'd hidden from the cops. Years had passed since we'd last met and for all I knew she was working for the Yard. Old loyalties might not exist and clearly she was here on some kind of official business. I suspected that she wasn't bothered about Andy, but how could she know about anything else? Fear swelled in my gut. Perhaps she wasn't with the Yard at all. What about MI5? She'd be an ideal candidate.

'Give it a rest,' I said, sitting down. 'Two interviews are enough for one day. I don't need more searching questions. What are you working at?'

She wasn't working, or so she said. Jobs were hard to come by and she knew I wouldn't be interested in the tittle-tattle of her life.

'What about you? You aren't working either. But you've got a report to write.'

'Write?' I said, almost spilling my tea. 'What are you talking about?'

But I'd spoken only to get my breath back. Was I trapped by Sir Lance in a plot so cack-handed that everyone knew about it?

'You can be very untidy, you know. I mean look at that blind, it's not even straight. You've never got anything right, there's always a rough edge –'

'Oh, come on.'

'Somebody came to me last night with a suitcase. It had been badly packed. The contents were in the wrong places. I said two words. Mat Hill. Only he does it that way.'

'I don't know what–?'

'Oh, but you do. It was a sniper's rifle, a beauty, and it had been badly dismantled. You've got to be careful. The thread on those things can damage so easily.'

This was an upheaval. That 'somebody' could only be General George Douglas. It must have been pretty late at night by the time he'd got hold of Jane. Incidentally, she knows a bit about sniping. She's not a bad shot, which might be why George had approached her.

'But I haven't seen one since I left the army,' I said to jar her.

'Oh, really? We're all in this together. Sorting Harry Hetland, or Operation Garden if you prefer. Don't look at me like that. I'm totally alright.'

'Did George mention my name?'

'Of course he didn't. He thinks he's running a tight cell and he never mentions third parties.'

I looked at Jane in her leather suit, holding her cup at an unusual angle because she thought it wasn't clean. It was unsettling, the way she fired remarks at me as though I was working for the other side. And there was no certainty that she wasn't with MI5. That's one thing she'd never admit to.

'And is it safe, this cell?'

'Why wouldn't it be?'

'There are a lot of reasons.'

The face of Mrs Birhandi appeared at the window opposite. She did something to the sink and then stared across at Jane's yellow hair with her mouth open. A moment later she'd called her husband over and both of them laughed, perhaps at my skill in getting myself a blonde companion so soon after Adele had exited my life. I was seated in the shadow so they couldn't see me. Jane had her back to them. Neither of them had cared for Adele. She was Police and hadn't made the effort to be friendly.

'I'm fairly sure it hasn't been penetrated.'

'It wouldn't need to be.'

'No, it wouldn't. First I need to know how you got that rifle.'

'I think it's Harry Hetland's.'

'That's not a surprise. More details, please.'

'Why would you want that?'

'For heaven's sake, you've been in Special Forces. If the gun's got a bad history it can't be used.'

'I'm not sure it should be used.'

'That's not for you to decide. Where did you get it?'

I sat back in the chair and looked at her. She looked like an angry head mistress who had caught me stealing biscuits. I could see that she wasn't going to back down until she'd uncovered every last detail. I hate this kind of thing. She could be wired for sound and any listener would know my involvement, I could be damned already.

'Name someone else in the cell,' I said.

'I'm not supposed to, but we're *ex officio* so I'll do it. Sir Lance.'

'Name another.'

'I don't know any others.'

Neither did I, and she wouldn't tell me if she could name fifty. She probably knew that the old man had recruited me.

'Well, come on. Start talking.'

'Shouldn't you ask George? I think he knows.'

'Mat, just tell me.'

The General knew the full facts. I'd recited them in Sir Lance's basement with no salient point omitted and he was the kind of man who paid attention to detail. Immediately after leaving me, he'd chosen to take it to Jane and had opted to tell her nothing. Perhaps he had been in a hurry, or perhaps Jane didn't question senior officers in the same way as she did me. Apparently no details had been disclosed. Yet she must be alright if the General had gone to her. I decided to come clean.

'It belonged to Andy's killer. I took it out of his car.'

'Where's the killer now?'

'On a slab. I killed him.'

'Good for you,' she said, with a new note of respect. Just like the General, she was impressed by death.

'Is that all he gave you?' I asked.

'What else is there?'

'Two hand guns, a SIG and, I think, an H&K.'

'I never saw them.'

'Where is the sniper rifle now?'

'George took it away. Obviously I couldn't keep it in my flat. It looked brand new, no signs of wear, but I want its history. It might have been involved in a killing.'

'It just might.'

'The serial number's recent. If it's been used at all, it would have been overseas, probably on the continent. There's no record of any sniper hits in the UK. How is your report coming on?'

The report wasn't coming on. And it was none of her business. Sir Lance had commissioned it, paid me, and he was entitled to the results when they were available.

Mrs Birhandi's son, a boy of about twenty, had now appeared at the window and was watching Jane with interest. They must have thought she was a beauty. It was only when you saw her face that you realised she was thirty years older than she'd seemed. Possibly that's why she was so angry.

'Not well, and this Andy thing isn't helping. I can't begin to formulate it. Hetland lives in his own world.'

'He knows there's going to be an attempt.'

'Well, he's on perpetual alert,' I said. 'And he's got serious enemies.'

Jane was nodding. For once we were in complete agreement.

'We're not the only ones after his head,' she confided. 'Harry's never been slow to make an enemy. He's got a double layer of protection around him and it's been organised by an American, a one-time presidential security chief. He reckons Harry's biggest danger is his own guards. So they're being rotated and there's a system for keeping them in check. It sounds like sheer fiction, but it looks like Harry has about a hundred protection officers. They're mostly male and many of them come from Eastern Europe. Nearly all of them, despite the regulations, bear arms. There's a batch of big bruisers who all claim to be killers. Of course they're not employed solely on Harry's behalf. There are two different companies who hire them out to celebrities and such and Harry's name doesn't appear on the stationery. Officially he hires them when required.'

'How do you know that?'

'From the Royal Protection squad. In case you're wondering, I asked no questions and showed no curiosity when I heard it.'

I could believe that bit. She could be impertinent and even rude, but she could also be discreet.

'What were you doing with them?'

'Earning a crust. I sometimes get the odd day's work. About this rifle – where did you actually get it?'

'The killer's car. I doubt if it has a history. Harry probably imported it. He wouldn't want anything incriminating.'

'Yes, but I wouldn't mind having it checked. I might need to use it.'

'You're not going to hit Hetland with that?'

'I won't rule it out.'

'That's insane! You'll never see the light of day again. If you live.'

'Hetland's got to be stopped.'

'Yes, but not by assassination.'

'That's a last resort. There are other measures in the pipeline.'

'Such as?'

'I can't say.'

'So you want me to tell you everything, but you won't reciprocate?'

'Do you think they'll tell me the other measures?'

'Then how do you know they exist?'

'I've heard rumours from senior sources, including the Royal Protection wallahs. There are credible plots to hit Hetland, some of them involving serious figures.'

I looked at her.

'What does that mean? There are others are after him too? You've mentioned it to George?'

'I did. And I think he knew about them.'

'So he's involved?'

'Only in Operation Garden. But there's probably an understanding somewhere.'

Yes, that sounded likely. There would be a lot of winks and nods in the background. Both sides of the Establishment would see eye to eye on that one.

'Would you shoot Hetland with that rifle?'

'I've had to do that kind of thing before.'

'You'd risk your entire future on a near-suicidal scheme?'

'What's new? And who said it's near-suicidal?' But here her voice dropped a tone. 'Let's get down to business. I need some help. I think I've been followed several times. Don't look at me like that, nobody tailed me here. This is in London.'

So that explained why she'd been hiding earlier.

'Several times?'

'Four that I know of, and it's always been a different person. They were trainees. I lost them easily enough. Usually within five minutes.'

Here we go, I thought to myself, sunk before the boat's even launched. Andy was dead and Jane was being followed.

'You've been spying on Harry?'

'Yes, and it wasn't easy. In fact I never once saw him, even when I watched at Parliament. Maybe I've upset the wasp's nest. The ones following me were almost certainly Harry's people. This isn't necessarily an emergency.'

'Why did they follow you?'

'Oh, they follow lots of people, MPs, civil servants and some passers-by. It's part of their training.'

It's an old trick for recognising regular visitors. Many a clumsy tail has got to know the regulars and uncovered a can of worms.

'Did they follow you home?'

That's another problem with yellow hair, they can see you from a distance. An easy target. The trainees would have a field day. She should never have been allowed to do this.

'No, I'm in a tower block. It wouldn't be easy.'

I looked to see if she was serious.

'You were followed four times? That means they were taking a serious interest in you. How do you know they didn't follow you home?'

'I didn't go home.'

'You must have gone home.'

'Well, late in the evening.'

'Then they know your address. There's no other reasonable conclusion. They followed you wherever you went.'

'They didn't. I lost them every time. Amateurs learning the trade. I mean, I'm not entirely daft, I've had years of experience.'

Well, that was true. She had a good knowledge of that kind of thing and it was reasonable to assume she'd see most amateurs off, but this was Harry Hetland we were dealing with and now Jane would be on his files. And there might have been a few absolute experts watching from the sidelines. That's an old trick, fooling your subject with a clumsy tail while you watch from a distance. They'd probably take a few quiet photos and compare them later.

'What exactly happened?'

'Oh, they just followed me from the venue, a Press Conference at Westminster. I wasn't the only person waiting and I'm sure other people were followed too. I wouldn't read too much into it. Just because I was trying to get a glimpse of Harry doesn't mean I'm their enemy. They've no way of knowing I'm in Operation Garden.'

'I'd like to think they don't know about Operation Garden.'

'Of course they don't.'

At this point I recalled Harry coming to our table on my visit to Parliament. From what I could see, Sir Lance and I were one half of Operation Garden and our enemy seemed to have sensed something. I suspected he knew all about the plotters.

'Have you mentioned this to the bosses?'

'Unnecessary.'

'You're dead wrong there. You know the identities and addresses of the main players. If Harry works that out it could affect our life insurance. They must be told.'

123

'I'm not sure.'

'Four times, at least. Four times, you've been followed. It must be done.'

Anybody who had been followed was at risk of being rumbled and while the enemy's interest was probably low key, it was for the bosses to decide if it were harmless or not. Certainly they should be given the pertinent facts.

'They follow every second person who waits to see him. Even if they followed me for the entire day they wouldn't have seen one thing to alarm them.'

'You know the rules.'

Of course she knew them as well as I did. The game might be over. In theory Harry could pick us off at his leisure, a pathetic band which couldn't even be discreet. That said, in the real world of espionage, most of the players know their opposite numbers, or think they do, and somehow it doesn't affect their work. Or perhaps it does. Nearly everything connected with espionage ends in failure. But that's by the way. This would have to be reported to the bosses.

'They might close it down,' she said, 'and I need the money.'

'It's gotta be done. And I need the money too.'

'It's only trainees. A lot of people watch Harry. Reporters, autograph hunters, passers by. There's nothing to link me with Operation Garden.'

'They could've seen the General last night.'

'You're being wild. They aren't staking my flat. I've got eyes.'

'We're against a sophisticated enemy.'

'Well maybe, but –'

'I'm going to go by the rules and report this.'

A look of exasperation, and then resignation, crossed her face:

'Well, if it must be done.'

'There are other things too,' I said. 'What about Big Andy? It's almost certain that the depot's got my picture. Harry's seen me in the company of Sir Lance. They can zero in on all of us. We're all at risk.'

'Oh, we're not exactly rumbled.'

'We wouldn't need to be, but they know something about all of us.'

There was a silence. From her attitude I wondered if this was the real reason for her visit, and the gun was no more than a prop. I got up and looked out of the window, to find myself face to face with Mrs Birhandi. She was washing her dishes and gave me a big smile when I nodded. As casually as possible, I looked at the space between our flats. I could see no shadowy figures lurking in the doorways. What would pro watchers do? They had a lot of options.

'How did you come?'

'By train, and I didn't pre book it. Nobody followed me.'

'You hope,' I said, adding, 'wait there.'

I went out to the landing to find there was no one about. Downstairs, the ground floor was deserted and so was the forecourt. The car park didn't contain any watchers or indeed anybody. I hesitated to look out to the street from the front door. That would let the tail know that he'd been lumbered, at which he would go to plan B and that would not be a good thing. Instead, I went up the stairs to the sixth floor, passing no one on the way, where I studied the surrounding area without seeing one suspect person. So far as I could see, there was no one on the street at all and that was good. If they'd followed Jane on the train, they'd have to keep within visual distance since there would be no local back-up and they wouldn't want to lose her. Perhaps I was over-reacting. Jane was an experienced officer and when she was on the alert she would be difficult to monitor. Their absence suggested they were not on her tail. I went back to my flat and closed the door.

'Anything?'

'Not that I saw.'

'Well, if you're going to report it, you'd better get on with it.'

By this time I was quietly hoping we could forget about it and my heart sank at the fuss that would shortly be unleashed. Nevertheless, I'd started the ball rolling and it would have to be done. I phoned Sir Lance to say I could do with some work in the garden. Thirty minutes later George called me from a mobile with lots of traffic in the background. After listening to a very discreet summary of Jane's problem, he said he'd call at my flat in the early evening.

That meant I was stuck with Jane for hours.

We went out for a light lunch – I restricted myself to one coffee and toast – and was rebuked for my pointless diet. She'd never been on a diet in her life, but lots of her friends had and it never did any good, she said. In fact, they often finished heavier than when they'd started and in my case the loss of a few pounds would fool no one.

'How does Hetland collect information?' I said. 'Can't see him taking calls from informants.'

'You don't know? He's good at that.'

'Yes, but how?'

She gave a superior smirk.

'Oh, he's got a press agency. It does some genuine work too. Of course he owns newspapers. If he thinks you've got something interesting, a reporter will phone and he, or sometimes she, can be quite pushy. They always send money – not a lot, just enough to whet the appetite and they're good at keeping in touch for more info. They've got it down to a fine art.'

'He's some man.'

'Isn't he just. Tell me about Andy again.'

She made me recite the events surrounding his death twice, shaking her head at the whole thing.

'That's nonsense,' she said, 'those gold bars. Hetland would never have them on display.'

'I'm only telling you what Andy said.'

'Andy could be an idiot at times.'

'Yes, but he did have the photographs. I've seen them.'

'Hardly a proof. You can fake anything with a computer.'

'Andy couldn't. But the bars, whether real or not, had a purpose. They got him out of the house when the safe was being delivered. He was being manipulated.'

At this point I became aware that somewhere along the line there was a joined-up agenda. The gold bars and the safe were probably linked, although I couldn't begin to guess what that connection was.

'It could be a coincidence. It's a mistake to see plots in

126

everything.'

'Maybe.'

'But the safe,' she said. 'That's a different matter. It could be the key to a lot of things. Any idea where they'd take it?'

I looked at her in exasperation.

'How could I know that? I never even saw it.'

'I'd like to get my hands on it.'

I found myself wondering what had happened to Andy's photographs, then I remembered that they were in his van and that Herb must have had them in his possession when had he mocked me about investigating the gold bars.

By the time we'd finished lunch, Jane had consumed a salad, two cream cakes and several coffees, while I'd contented myself with one mug of tea. Naturally, I had to pay for the lot.

16

My flat might just have been an ordinary apartment but I liked its unassuming style. There's something about it that relaxes the mind, and the front window gives an excellent panorama of the whole town that many would envy. Even the new blind had been mounted correctly, despite recent criticism, although it was hanging at a slight angle that could be corrected in a moment. Yes, I liked my flat and after the tensions of the morning I would have liked a short rest, but that was not to be.

'Seriously, why would they hide a safe in Andy's flat?' Jane said, as soon as we'd got inside the door.

'I dunno,' I said, fed up with her fixation. 'Who knows what's going on? It's stupid enough to be off the scale. I'm sure he didn't know it was coming, or he'd have been waiting for the money with itchy palms. If you ask me, that was plan B. Then he was shot and they took it away again.'

Of course just because it was off the scale didn't mean they wouldn't do it. History is full of the monumental stupidities that make life so interesting. If everybody was sane and sensible we'd be bored out of our minds. Anyway, it might not be stupidity: possibly there had been nowhere to stow the safe without the risk of a police raid, and Andy's flat was a good short-term refuge, so long as no one talked.

'I see what you mean,' she said, in a more conciliatory tone. Some of her questions had seemed like a deliberate attempt to wind me up, but that's Jane all over.

'It wasn't there long. They moved it within hours.'

'A murder,' she said, 'makes everybody nervous. We've seen that too often. Let me use your computer. I'll look it up on the web and see if anyone is looking for a safe, I've a feeling it's important.'

I powered up the computer with the happy assumption that it would keep her quiet for some time, but that was not to be. In less than five minutes she had located a detail in a press report.

'Here's something. A safe *was* stolen from a warehouse in London. No indication of its contents, but it was definitely nicked. The safe was sent by a Swiss bank and it was addressed to Croften Communications in Romford. It could be the answer to a lot of things.'

She was staring at the screen as though her life depended on it, speaking with such intensity that I looked up in surprise. Perhaps I was getting out of touch, but it was difficult to see how it could be the answer to any of our immediate problems.

'Not much we can do about it.'

'Who knows? But that was Andy's motivation. The gold bars were a side issue. Even he must have known that there was nothing he could do about a security depot. There are two sets of gangsters here. Harry Hetland and some blundering locals.'

She might well have been right, though I had the damnedest feeling that there really were gold bars in the depot. I recalled Andy's visit of the previous day and his photographs. But that raised a lot of new questions,

'Who was he working for?' I said.

'What d'you mean?' she asked looking down, her tone changing.

'Andy's always been the go-between, a fixer. Somebody wanted a safe stolen and didn't know any gangsters, so they got him to liaise with the crooks. He wouldn't have been involved in the robbery, they'd never let him in on the act, but he'd know who to contact. That could be why he was shot. Was he ever associated with Operation Garden?'

'Oh, I don't know anything about that.'

But her voice had dropped an octave and she was on the defensive. The previous night I'd had the impression that both our bosses knew something about Andy, they'd failed to ask questions about him. I couldn't see Sir Lance or George approaching gangsters. They don't speak the same language and neither party would trust the other, so there was a neat little role for Andy. Jane would get him; she'd once worked beside him. And the plotters paid their bills in fifties.

'There's something valuable in that safe,' she said, changing the subject.

'Well, they'd hardly steal a worthless one.'

'Listen, let's do something. Take me to Andy's flat. It's only a few miles.'

So she knew where he lived, and I'd only found out that morning, which might imply there were things going on behind my back. I was less than happy to get involved. A few hours ago, I'd been interviewed by a senior policeman about a double killing and I'd no wish to draw attention to myself by going to the victim's flat for the second time in a day. Anyway, it's stupid to interfere in other people's business, particularly when the link was so tenuous.

'It's locked,' I said. 'I don't have keys and there's nothing to see.'

'Oh, I want to talk to his neighbour, that old woman. Come on.'

I looked at her in consternation.

'What about, oh, the three men? I don't know if she saw them.'

'You don't know much about old women. She's got nothing else to do but look out of the window. She saw you, so the betting is she saw them too. Come on.'

There was no point in arguing. I went out to the car with bad grace. Twenty minutes later we reached Andy's flat for the second time that day. During the whole journey we didn't speak a word. I hate being bossed and she was enjoying my discomfort. There's something of the weakling about me. Most men would have refused outright, but that's not in my nature. I certainly shouldn't have gone; there were many things that could have gone wrong and I didn't fancy explaining my actions to Herb.

'Yes, you're right,' she said, looking at Andy's flat. 'It looks a dump.'

The old woman was quite pleased to see me. I introduced Jane, who went out of her way to be respectful, as an insurance agent who wanted to trace the safe. The old woman said she had seen three men in a grey van, but that was all she knew. At that, a burly man of about forty appeared from the front room to say that he didn't want his mother troubled about these things. There were enough difficulties in life without these questions and the three men weren't nice blokes.

'I understand,' said Jane. 'Did you recognise the van by any chance?'

'Try Furbishers, an' don't quote me.'

With that he closed the door, none too gently.

Back in the car, Jane turned to me: 'Who are Furbishers?'

'A hire company in the old town,' I said, with reluctance. I had no wish to go deeper into the mire, but I was well aware that Furbishers were going to be next on the agenda. Every second person in the old town knew me and it would be insane to draw more attention to myself. 'And I don't want to be involved.'

'Oh, I'll do the talking,' she said, as though that overcame the difficulties. In fact it would be difficult to stop her talking and it was quite possible that the men in blue would be coming behind us asking the same questions. Ours was an unofficial enquiry that could well be seen as muddying the waters.

'Oh, no you won't. They know me at Furbishers. Anyway, they won't open their books without official documentation. I'm having nothing more to do with this.'

'Okay,' she said, surprising me by accepting it. 'I can see that. But let's just drive to their place and have a look.'

This was typical of Jane. No doubt she'd change her stance and start grilling someone when we got there. She had a rare capacity for annoying people.

'No way, I'm not going near their place. And that bloke didn't say it was Furbishers' van. He said try them.'

She turned all sweet.

'We should still have a look. I'm only going through the motions. They probably dumped the safe and ran. I just want to look.'

'Look for it! Where would we look?'

'They'd have to move fast, so it probably went somewhere obvious.'

Here a definition of obvious would have been helpful, there being so many things that could be deemed obvious and so many things that could not. She'd been building up to this. Already there had been twenty references to the safe.

She said: 'After the shooting, they'd want rid of it. It would be too hot to handle. They wouldn't go to another flat – too risky – so they'd head for the Industrial Estate. It had small workshops nobody would look at twice. If it's not local we'll never find it. Try it anyway. I won't go near the hire company.'

I considered an outright refusal, but that would mean being stuck in the flat with an angry woman until George arrived. So I caved in again.

'Okay, but I hate this.'

First I made her cover her yellow hair with a dark scarf, explaining that it was essential to keep a low profile. That made her so mad she stopped speaking to me, which was a welcome bonus. Ideally, we shouldn't have been out at all. If Jane really was being followed we ought to have remained indoors until an executive decision had been made. I reversed the car and a quarter of an hour later we pulled into the industrial estate, where I drove straight to a workshop in the far corner.

'I know this bloke,' I said, while Jane stared straight ahead, studiously ignoring me. 'He knows everything that's going on. Stay in the car. I'll find out if he's seen anything.'

Alex had been in my class at school. He was a middle-aged hippy who pottered about with motor bikes and seemed to lose money at everything he did, while somehow managing to stay in business as The Bikers Bazaar, a would-be workshop which was nothing more than a store for barely functional second hand bike parts. He was a lean fellow with long straggly hair and a bald patch on his crown. I found him at work on an old bike which was emitting smoke like a Victorian chimney. I had to wait until he'd finished revving it.

'They said she was finished,' he said, nodding at the bike. 'A good service and she'll be going like a bird.'

'You certainly know your stuff, Alex.' At that moment the engine stuttered into silence. After two tries it roared into life again. Then he turned it off.

'What are you after?'

'Something daft. Three men in a van with a tail lift. Seen anything this morning?'

His eyes narrowed and he looked at me with interest.

'What's this about?'

'My client's had a theft.'

'Well, there are plenty of grey vans. But I saw one around nine behind that shed there.'

He pointed through a dusty window from which the shed could be seen, an abandoned building with long grass around its walls.

'What was happening?'

'Couldn't see. They were there for two minutes.'

'Thanks. I'll check it out.'

'How come you're interested?'

'It's part of my job.'

'If there's a reward, you could slip me a grand or two.'

'Not on your life. You'd only spend it on motor bikes.'

'What else is there? They're my best friends.'

After a few further remarks I returned to the car to find Jane waiting anxiously. She really was interested in the safe.

'You won't believe it,' I said, getting into the car. 'There was a van over there this morning. I'm wondering if they dumped it.'

'I knew it,' she said, brightening. 'They thought it was too hot.'

The shed was an abandoned factory building which had been closed for years. Its back yard was strewn with rubbish. We got out of the car and picked our way over the debris. The tracks of the van were fresh and we followed them to a section littered with old cardboard cartons. I kicked them away and saw the gleam of metal.

There we found the safe lying on its back. It was pristine, its shiny unblemished surface a sharp contrast to the desolation around us. Clearly we were looking at an expensive article with a sophisticated locking system. It was easy to see why the robbers had stolen it, though I suspected it would be very difficult to open without a key.

'What's in it?' I wondered. 'Do you think it's full of money?'

The safe was space age technology, the smartest one I'd seen for ages.

'Give me a hand,' I said. 'Tip it on its side. See if anything rattles.'

We got our hands under it with some difficulty and despite its weight we were able to tip it to a steep angle.

'No, nothing,' Jane said, as we let it down again. 'It's gotta be paper.'

'That's my bet.'

It was beginning to get dark so she sparked her lighter to check its surface. There was a hand-written number above the maker's name, which was probably the vault number from the bank.

'They've changed the banking code in Switzerland. Items in vaults must be declared if there's an enquiry. Doesn't mean they'll open it, but if there's a lot at stake, the cops can ask the court to have it done. I'll bet the owner didn't want it listed.'

'That's almost certainly why it's been flown here.'

'I'll bet there are megabucks in there.'

'Well, I didn't think it was the golf club accounts. Oh, look at this!'

She was pointing to the underside, where a small tab proclaimed the legend *Hetland Enterprises*.

A blast of icy air seemed to strike me. I was becoming accustomed to the endemic influence of Harry, but even so it was a shock to see his name again. Up until that point, the prospect of the safe belonging to Hetland had been nothing more than a hazy theory, but here was confirmation that overrode everything. I recalled Andy's shooting and was suddenly nervous for my own future.

'This changes everything.'

There was garbage all around us and the lights of the Industrial Estate in the background. Cars and vans were moving about as though it were an ordinary day, but it wasn't quite that.

A theory was developing in my mind. Why would the Hets shoot Andy because he was taking an interest in their depot? What if it was all about this very safe? Presumably a local gang had stolen it from under Harry's nose, somewhere in the chaos Andy had been liaising with them, and they'd shot him in an act of vengeance., Then the thieves had dumped the safe and fled. A safe owned by the biggest hood in the country was lying at our feet.

But had they merely dumped it, or had they telephoned the

Hetland organisation to tell them what they'd done? One anonymous phone call would do the trick, then Harry would be able to collect his safe and normality would return. He might even let them live.

We looked up to see a car driving towards us. Just when it seemed to be on our patch it swung to the right. For a moment I thought that they'd come to collect their safe.

'Let's get out of here,' I said to Jane. 'I don't like this.'

'Cover it again.'

It was the work of a few moments to kick the cartons back into place and then we went back to the car.

'Everything falls into place,' I said, as we pulled away. 'Andy was associated with a gang of idiots who stole Hetland's safe. You don't do that kind of thing. That's why he was shot.'

I drove to The Bikers Bazaar and stopped the car.

'I'd better have another word with Alex.'

Inside The Bikers Bazaar Alex was bent over the bike, though I'd no doubt that he'd watched us from his window. The bike's engine had only started up when I'd parked at his door.

'Did you recognise any of the men in the van, Alex?'

'Never seen them in my life. Did you get what you were looking for?'

'Maybe. If you ask me, it belongs to some dangerous men. I wouldn't touch it if I were you.'

Alex said, 'Oh,' and continued working. I noted a cunning tone in his voice.

'For your own safety, you should forget it's there.'

'Well, my memory's not what it was.'

I went back to the car and drove away. Jane was in a subdued mood.

'We're on to something,' I said, speaking more to myself than Jane. 'I don't know what. But there's a lot at stake.'

I pulled out on to the main road and headed for the flat. We didn't do a lot of talking as we drove back.

17

It was early evening. The street lights were on and there was a chill in the air which heralded rain. I was in a pensive mood. Things were not what they'd seemed to be. The discovery of the safe made a big difference and I had no great faith in the plotters' ability to handle it. Besides, it brought me too close to the action. Granted, I'd undertaken to write a report, but that was the extent of my involvement. I had no wish to be included in the action. Already Andy had been shot and there was sure to be further fireworks shortly. Clearly things were both murkier and more dangerous than they'd seemed and I found myself wondering what would happen next. Certainly Harry was a dangerous man to cross, and all the evidence suggested that he'd want his safe back. So far, the scenario had been vague, but now there was serious evidence and it jarred with me. During the short car journey, I'd watched my mirror for signs of pursuit and seen nothing. Not that I'd expected a tail, but it was reassuring to find there was none. At the flat I unlocked the door to let Jane in and was about to enter myself when a man went in ahead of me.

'George!' said Jane, whirling round in surprise and seeming delighted.

He was almost unrecognisable in a workman's cap and green anorak, though to my eyes the bristling moustache gave him away immediately. His approach had been so discreet that he must have had security training.

'Close that door,' he said, in his commanding voice. 'We'll have a talk.'

'Have you been waiting long?' asked Jane, all concerned.

But the General wasn't the kind of man to utter complaints about trivialities.

'A minute or two. Nothing to speak of. Now, what's the problem?'

'Mat, give us a minute, will you?' said Jane waving me away as she turned to George, putting a hand on his arm as though he were a long lost relative. They began to talk in low voices, like old friends, as I made my way to the front of the flat, rather relieved that I was not involved in their discussions. Throughout my life, I had made it a habit to keep as far as possible from the bosses and that policy had always served me well. Nothing good ever came from being too closely involved. If something went wrong, the lowest ranker was guaranteed to get the blame. I didn't know what Jane was thinking, but she'd have done better to keep her distance, particularly when she'd been careless enough to get followed. I gave them a quick glance. But all was well. They were at the back of the room, engrossed in their conversation, the General frowning at the floor as he listened to Jane. They would be invisible to Mrs Birhandi.

My hands in my pockets, I surveyed the world from my front window, noticing a train pulling into the station. There was nobody within sight of the flat. Then I remembered that this was my home and technically I was their host. Sir Lance had always offered me a sherry on my visits and that was the least I could do for George, the highest ranking figure ever likely to enter the building. My old father always sends me a bottle of Crofts for my birthday. It wasn't my favourite tipple, but it soon got depleted. When I opened the cabinet door, I was surprised at how tidy it was. There was no sherry, nor was there any sign of a bottle of malt I'd bought recently. And not even one glass remained of a set my grandad had given me on my twenty-first. Adele had taken the lot. She didn't even like sherry. I almost let out a cry of frustration. Of course that would have been an irrelevance that George would dismiss, while being annoyed at not getting his sherry. Military discipline had taught me that it was best not to draw attention to yourself. I closed the door and stood up.

'Alright, we'll move you to a safe house,' the General was saying, *sotto voce*.

I turned to the window, studiously avoiding their conversation, but the conversation would not avoid me.

'Mat, would you come over here?' said the General in a voice that was quiet but cutting.

I turned and went to them.

'That safe's got to be collected,' he said, making it clear that I was to do it.

This was a confirmation of my worst fears and I stared at him in consternation. Since I was the only workhorse in the room, the difficulty would have to fall on my shoulders. Certainly neither Jane nor George would be breaking into a sweat to hump that heavy safe to a new venue. It would have to be poor old Muggins. Of course it was an old army trick for the Commanding Officer to issue a blank order and sit back while his sergeants and lieutenants got the job done. But this was not the army.

'George,' I said, sounding all reasonable. 'It took three men with a tail-lift truck to get it there. We don't have those resources.'

'I know it's not easy,' he said, doing his best to sound reasonable. 'But it'll have to be done. And done now.'

Involuntarily, I stood back and looked at the floor. If there's one thing I hated it was someone issuing orders that were impossible.

'Yes, but how will we move it?'

'Think of something, Mat.'

'Come on, you can do it,' said Jane to me in a sweet voice. I'd noticed that she became the little lady when George was about. So far she had not made one impertinent remark.

'You'll need to fetch a carrier from town,' I said, passing the buck.

'Haven't time for that. Got to get it done now.'

'It *is* heavy,' said Jane to George.

We stood in silence for half a minute.

'What if the Hets arrive at the same time? That could be why Andy was shot.'

But I'd said the wrong thing. That wasn't an argument I could put to a General. Infantry losses were acceptable. The safe was more important than me.

'It must be done, and done quickly. Where can we hire a tail-lift truck?'

'There's a garage five minutes away,' I said, carefully omitting Furbishers name. 'But it'll be closed. Anyway, a hire needs proof of identity. You've gotta get one with a strong floor, otherwise the safe will fall through it. Must have proper transport.'

'That shouldn't be difficult.'

Clearly the General thought my objections were little man stuff and could be overcome with a little management. He was going to have it, no matter what was said.

'We'll have a look,' he said, turning to the door, 'Let's take my car.'

'George,' I said. 'We're against heavy odds.'

Only a day ago, big Andy had been shot. That made a difference to a man's mentality. I suspected that the General was a desk man without recent experience of action. He didn't realise the risks involved.

'We'll do nothing rash. Come on.'

Jane turned to me with a look of earnest bewilderment. Maybe she wanted to see my reaction, or perhaps she was delighted with George's attitude, which made me look so inconsequential. Clearly, she wanted the safe but wouldn't be getting involved in the hard work. We both followed the General. That was army discipline. Nobody disobeys a senior officer. Today the General was driving a well polished black Citroen saloon which was sitting at the edge of the car park. I took the back seat and Jane sat in the front. By this time it was dark and the area was deserted. In five minutes we drove past Alex's workshop, where he was still working on the faulty engine.

'Park here,' said Jane, outside the derelict shed. Here the car was conspicuous – visible for five hundred metres in both directions, the only vehicle in that section of the estate. George produced his pocket torch and we followed him to the back yard, to begin searching among the debris. In the dark, it took a full minute to find it in the junk lying about, and for a moment I wondered if it had been removed. George bent to examine it while Jane and I watched for approaching lights. There were some, but mercifully they turned off before they reached us.

'Let's go,' said the General. He was aware of our exposure, too.

'What do you think?' said Jane.

'It's important. In fact, it's vital. Maybe the biggest thing in the whole business. We have to have it. Come on. Better not wait here.'

With some relief, we went back to the car and drove off to a small car park in the middle of the estate.

'I want that safe,' said the General, switching off the engine. 'It may contain things that change everything. It's very important. Nobody, least of all Harry Hetland, flies in an expensive safe like that for nothing. We've got to get it.'

'Yes, George, but how?' I said when Jane made no comment.

'There's a man working in that garage next door,' said the General turning to me. 'He's got a breakdown truck. You can load the safe easily enough, the thing tips back. I say we hire it and get the safe. How much would it cost?'

I stared at George for a minute, impressed by his powers of observation, which were a lot better than mine. Only then did I realise that there had been a breakdown truck beside Alex's workshop. Whether it worked was another matter.

'At least two hundred. Depends where it's going. I don't know if it's roadworthy. It might not be in good nick.'

'Could you drive it?'

'Provided it works. Alex is not a great mechanic.'

'It's a professional garage. Of course it'll work.'

This, I felt, was not an accurate description of The Bikers' Bazaar.

'But I'm not insured. Where would you want to go?'

'It had better be Lance's place, the Towers, although I wouldn't want your garage man to know that. Better offer him five hundred.'

'Yes, but –'

'I've got the money. Obviously you know the man. Spin him a tale, anything that suits the bill. It belongs to your client, you've got to take the truck yourself and you'll be back within the hour. Get him to load the safe. It shouldn't take five minutes. He'll be glad for the business. I'll give you seven hundred in case he gets uppity. Is that alright?'

'George, I'm not insured. If the cops stop me –'

'Mat, you'll drive all the better when you're not insured. And there's no chance of the cops stopping you. When did you last see a patrol car?'

Too often, but George had taken a wad of fifties from his wallet and was counting them as he spoke. I was aware that my objections were mere trivialities beside his Grand Design. Nevertheless, this could get me banned from driving if I were caught.

'Be confident. The job's easy. You merely have to hire a truck and move the safe to the Towers. Less than two miles. Easy.'

'Well –'

'It's three minutes walk to the garage. Off you go. I'll wait here and follow you when you drive past. Better not let the garage fellow see us or the car. There's the money. Go.'

So he didn't want to risk his own identity, but mine could be exposed to the four winds. I opened the door and got out. Three minutes later I was in The Biker's Bazaar, wondering what could go wrong next. Alex looked around angrily when I went in and revved his machine even louder for an ear-splitting second until it stalled. How his hearing had survived for so long was a puzzle to me.

'This is desperate,' I said. 'I want to borrow your truck.'

'That's a pity. It's not available.'

He was in a bad mood with the bike. He'd heard a knock on the engine that spelt its doom and he was seriously angry.

'I'll give you five hundred. I need it for an hour.'

'I don't take cheques. I don't believe in them.'

But his tone had lightened.

'What about cash? Do you believe in that?'

He looked up and his attitude changed in a flash.

'It's the only thing I do believe in. You've got it on you?'

Wordlessly I produced the notes.

'I'll have to drive it myself,' I said. 'You can't come. There's funny people taking an interest. Lives are at stake.'

'Wait a minute. I can't let you drive off uninsured.'

'Seven hundred, then. I'm covered third party by my own policy.'

This last point was likely to be inaccurate; my insurance probably only applied to private cars. He looked at the money, looked away, and then reached for it.

'It's a deal,' he said, leaving the bike on its rests. 'Come on, we'll get the old jalopy on the road before anything goes wrong.'

Outside, we climbed into the truck's cab, which smelt of stale air, dampness, and ancient cigarettes. The floor was littered with old newspapers and some empty beer cans. I doubted that anyone had been in it for a month. After a full minute of cranking it burst into life with a lot of black smoke. To my relief, the engine didn't rev too badly and soon settled into a purr. It might just work.

'She's got a lovely engine,' said Alex, falling back on his sales routine.

'I want to collect the safe from the back yard. You'll have to load it,' I said, looking round in desperation at some approaching lights which turned off about two hundred metres away.

At first I thought he was going to refuse but he was merely looking at the gauges on the facia.

'I'll top up the water and the oil,' he said. 'But we'll load the thing first. What's in it, money?'

So he'd been out for a quick shufty. That was only to be expected. No doubt he'd watched Jane and me. Not much gets past Alex.

'I don't know. It's my client's. All I want is the job done.'

The truck jerked forward and nearly stalled. The clutch was in a bad way, but Alex manoeuvred it out of his drive, switched on a strong rear light and reversed into the back yard where I jumped out and kicked the cartons away until the safe was exposed. Soon Alex had the floor tipped up, a canvas strap around the safe and in seconds it was on board the truck. Then he covered it with an ancient travelling rug (he was aware of the sensitivity of the situation) fetched more straps from a container and made it secure while I watched the road for approaching lights.

'What are you watching for? Who's put the fear of death in you?'

'There are some nasty blokes about. Tell them nothing if they ask.'

He nodded impatiently. Now that the seven hundred was in his pocket he'd be discreet.

Car headlights approached, then turned off to the right. It

seemed likely that this was when they'd come. The night was dark and the local workers were hurrying off, taking no interest in us. Later, things would be quieter. Activity would be noticed and there would be night watchmen to consider.

'Is there enough fuel?'

'Couple of gallons. Depends where you're going.'

'That'll do.'

'Don't go fast, now. Brakes need adjusting.'

With the safe secured, Alex climbed into the cabin and drove back to his garage where he topped up the oil. I could see that he was nervous about whether it would start again, but the engine burst into life at the first turn. Then he waved me on my way. I revved up and jerked forward in first gear, changed into second and nearly stalled, but I've driven some rubbish vehicles in my time and soon got into its rhythm. It was a clumsy old truck, and I wondered when it had last been serviced. Its steering was heavy and the cabin gave the impression of being as big as a house. But I was an old pro. Hadn't the General said that the job was easy?

Past the car park I saw the Citroen pull out behind me. I reached the public road at five miles an hour and pulled out, tremendously glad to be away from the industrial estate. The road was quiet. Soon I was doing a comfortable thirty when a patrol car passed me in the opposite direction. I was surprised to see that it was driven by Adele. Fortunately, she didn't give me a second glance. The truck's steering shuddered like a living thing, the engine was roaring and the screen was dirty.

A minute later I applied the brakes at a red traffic light. At least, I tried to. But there were none. Alex must have been tinkering with them, because the whole system had been disconnected. With a terrible crunch, I slammed into a lower gear and sounded the horn, which made a noise like a transatlantic liner. A car emerged from the right to turn in front of me, then the driver saw me looming towards him and flung his car out of my path, missing me by inches. There was some furious horn sounding from another car on the left that had been about to pull out. By that time I had managed to get the hazard lights on and was through the lights with no damage done. Several pedestrians were looking at me with their mouths open.

Behind me the Citroen was waiting at the red light, all respectable, and after that brief moment of mayhem everything returned to normality, though the second car overtook me, blowing its horn, while the driver shook his fist in tribute to my bad driving. I shared his sentiments entirely.

There was nothing to be gained by stopping. The entrance to Dalespun Towers was less than three hundred metres away and it would take me off the public road into a different environment. I continued at ten mph and turned past the Lodge and its angry Doberman to drive up to the Towers, getting slower and slower until at last I stalled it at the back of the buildings. I staggered out, drenched in sweat.

The General parked behind me and got out of his car, looking pleased with himself.

'Good man. You've done well –'

'It's got no brakes!'

'Who needs them? You did well. Most impressive.'

'I could have killed people back there.'

But the General wasn't troubled by such trivialities. As far as he was concerned, the operation had been a complete success, apart from some minor squeaks from the infantry. Against all the odds, a heavy safe had been seized and delivered into friendly hands. George belonged to a world where everything was ordered and in control. His silver hair and eyebrows showed a serenity which did him proud. He was not bothered by my anger. If I'd killed someone at the lights, my life would have been ruined. I'd have gone to jail and I doubted if I'd have received any sympathy from my bosses. But that's the way of the world. I'd seen it all before.

By this time a bemused Sir Lance had joined us. He was the only titled person present and the least impressive in appearance. I suspected that George had phoned him in advance. The battered truck was a strange contrast to the splendour of Dalespun Towers. After some words with the General Sir Lance said:

'Mat, we've got a fork lift here. I'll show you where it is.'

'Will it take the weight?'

'It's heavy duty, I believe.'

It was ancient, but in good condition. Nearly all fork lifts are battery operated and won't function unless they've been charged, but by a stroke of good luck this one had a petrol engine and it started at the second try. I've used fork lifts in the past, and after loosening the straps on the safe, I got it into a storeroom. I moved fast, all too aware of the possibilities of car lights coming up the drive, either belonging to the cops or someone else. If it was Adele, I'd be down for every charge in the book

'Well, Mat, I have to congratulate you,' said George, almost smiling as Sir Lance locked the storeroom door and I made my way back to the truck.

'I'll have to take this back. It can't be left here. What should I do at the lights?'

'Does the handbrake work?'

'Not enough to make a difference.'

'Well, just take it slow.'

'Its number might have been reported to the cops – those irate motorists.'

'No, nothing's been reported,' he said, still in good spirits.

'How do you know that?'

'It's got no registration plates.'

The General thought this was most amusing. I looked and saw that he was right. It explained Alex's initial reluctance to do business. With a bit of luck, the local band of gypsies would get the blame for the whole thing. Shaking my head, I climbed into the cabin, started the engine and looked out of the open door at the General.

'I won't follow you,' he said. No, Generals didn't do escort duty. Obviously, Jane wouldn't be coming either, but that could be regarded as a bonus. 'You'll need to walk back to your flat. On your way, my man. Best to get back while all's well.'

This was a dubious; all might not be well, but I got into the cabin and drove off, going all the way around the Towers and out by the Lodge at five miles an hour. By some miracle, there was no traffic on the road and the lights were green. Shortly I turned into the Industrial Estate, watching to see if there were any lights outside Alex's garage. I stalled the truck on his forecourt rather than risking knocking his building down.

'You weren't long,' he said, looking at me anxiously. Yes, he had known about the brakes. 'Everything alright?'

'The brakes are bad,' I grunted, determined to make no further comment. It would be best if Alex didn't know about Dalespun Towers.

'I was thinking about that. I'll have to get them fixed.'

18

The following day, I reviewed everything from the peace of my flat. At long last, I was alone and glad to be. The chaos of the past days seemed to belong to another world, though I was still not at ease. Perhaps my diet was too severe. Perhaps it was unnecessary and unlikely to fool Herb for more than a minute. However, its rigour would make me more alert and that was a different thing altogether. It was best never to over-eat or over-drink when people were looking for you. When you start to feel good, you get arrested. Prison is full of idiots who let their guard down in the pub. Nevertheless, I was ill-tempered and finding it difficult to concentrate on my work.

There had been no questions about Andy's van from Herb. No doubt it had been moved to a laboratory and was undergoing tests. They'd find traces of my clothes on the passenger seat, but those had been destroyed and there would be nothing to link them with me. They that say murderers are odd people. Often that's true of their victims, too and it was certainly true of Andy. Only he would have been stupid enough to impersonate a loss-adjuster while driving an old battered van. Most people would have hired a shiny new model. Andy's old banger would have raised the suspicions of any security guard in the world.

Then there was the question of how they'd identified him on his second visit to the depot. The General had said something about Harry Hetland being into sophisticated cameras, but I'd seen none and I was sensitive about these things. No one had walked past our parked van. The number plate had not been visible from the big building and there'd been no sign of watchers. I didn't like that. A killer and driver had been summoned at short notice and that would only have happened if Andy had been positively identified. How had they done it?

It was a quarter to eight and outside the roads were at a standstill.

There were things in the background that didn't make any

kind of sense. I went for a walk to run over the whole scenario in my head, crossing the road to reach our public park. It was looking well. There were a lot of birds singing and nobody about. Was it feasible that a security depot would have a hit man and driver on hand on the off-chance that Andy would reappear? Did they reserve a room for them and provide coffee and buns with the proviso that they must be ready to scramble at a minute's notice?

No, to both.

For a start, there would be too many witnesses, and that was intolerable. It would have been impossible to hide two men in that restricted environment; soon everybody would know and all it would take was one blabbermouth. Perhaps the killer had just happened to be in the area at the time. These things do happen, but would a hard-nosed boss tolerate the chance of him being absent when he was needed? No, that wasn't on either. So the killer must have been summoned at short notice, and since he was heavily armed it was a fair bet that he hadn't come far. Road trips would be kept to a minimum. The last thing Harry Hetland would want was an employee to be caught with guns in his car.

Therefore it followed that the killer was stationed nearby. That made good sense for Harry. There was a depot to be protected, to say nothing of a hundred other treasures, which might even include gold bars. Every empire had its enemies and some form of security, and Harry had more enemies than most, of whom the police were the tamest. His biggest threat probably came from the murky world of gangsters, and since they'd be armed, his security would be armed too.

So somewhere near the depot there must be a house, workshop or office that could house a whole security team. An army of one has its limitations. There would likely be an arsenal of weapons and a pool of cars and drivers. Jek might have been a fool, but he'd been trained. He had known how to deflect questions and he'd been skilful in shadowing us; Andy had never dreamed he'd a tail.

I'd covered a half mile along the park's periphery path and there was still no one about. The path angled towards the car park where my car was waiting in its space, ready to go. It had crossed my mind that Adele might have removed it with her duplicate key. But all was well. I'd intended to drive off but I hesitated when I saw the snarl-up on the main road. Both lanes were still blocked and the prospect of a road trip in the late stages of the rush hour was unappetising.

Back at the flat, I changed into a crumpled suit, shirt and tie. Then I put on a pair of blank glasses that made me look like a myopic librarian and got out my old black brief case.

I was about to go back to the car when I found myself hesitating. Andy had been killed when they had identified his car. Why should I take the risk? My bicycle was a better bet. Cycling was now very cool and it often gave the option of overtaking stationary traffic. Yes, I'd go by bike. The exercise would do me good and it was less than ten miles. I got my bike out, checked the tyres, and started pedalling. A round trip of twenty miles would be a doddle. The traffic was lighter now, though there were two halts for road works. I hit the industrial estate in just over an hour. I followed another cyclist past the depot with my eyes fixed straight ahead, apparently taking no interest in the big building. As on my previous visit, there were cars parked on both sides of the road. It was strangely moving to remember that this had been Andy's last journey. Beyond the security fence was a second, smaller building which I hadn't noticed before, a small narrow structure with three floors. There was little more than one room on each – a peasant skyscraper. It was called Croften Communications. Croften Communications! The safe had been consigned to that very company. On the top floor there was a glint of glass behind glass.

A hundred metres on, the cyclist turned right and I found a place to padlock my bike. Then I took my case and walked back to Croften, looking at the cars on both sides of the road to see if the killer's car was there. It wasn't.

Harry had been cunning when he had set up Croften Communications. The entrance was untidy, there was grass between the slabs and the front door hadn't been painted. Against the far wall, an old banger of a car sat on a jack with a front wheel missing. It looked as though it had been there for a long time. But there was a hint of money, too. The door locks were bank quality and the lintels were reinforced with metal.

I rang the bell and the door was opened almost immediately by an athletic man of about thirty who was wearing shaded spectacles. There was a closed door behind him and I could hear a radio playing a pop programme.

'Morning, sir,' I said, reaching into my case and producing a small poster. 'I'm from the Council. We're looking into problems of harassment in the work place. Would you mind displaying this in your staffroom?'

He looked at it.

'Okay.'

'It's harassment we're concerned about. Do you have a problem with that?'

'No.'

'Well if you do, our help line's at the bottom.'

'Okay.'

'Make sure it's displayed, please.'

'Okay.'

He was dressed in dark trousers and a top that looked too tight to hide a weapon, but he was a heavy alright, possibly with an Eastern European background. He closed the door with a firmness that meant he would say nothing further. I turned and went to the depot, where I repeated the procedure with the guard at the barrier. He, too, said okay and put it beneath his copy of the *Mirror*.

Then I went to the bottom of the street, turned right, and then right again. The industrial estate was built as a series of rectangles, with the depot and its huge building occupying the bottom section. I walked on with my head down, taking no apparent interest. So the killer had probably come from Croften. It seemed as though it was the base for Harry's security section, and they might have surveillance equipment on the top floor that had been able to register Andy's car. There was something missing, however. Transport. They certainly didn't park on the street, so there had to be a handy fleet of cars somewhere. Past the depot, I found the answer. A narrow strip connected Croften's back door to the street. It was two cars wide and there were six cars facing out on its top side. None of them were the killer's vehicle.

So now I knew.

By this time I was in full view of the top floor. From the corner of my eye, I saw movement as someone turned to look at me, but it didn't matter. I continued unhurriedly, taking the next street on the right, which was out of their range and within sight of my bicycle. A thought came to me. Herb has dismissed the gold bars as irrelevant, though he'd plainly heard of them. Surely the cops knew about Croften Communications, and also that the unidentified gunman was one of their employees? To an extent, the CID enquiries were little more than window dressing. The killer wasn't authorised but he was tolerated. I, meanwhile, had killed the killer and that was a different matter.

It was quite likely that Croften would want to bump me off too. I hadn't exactly been asking questions or making a nuisance of myself, but I'd been sitting in Andy's car yesterday and I'd killed their man. Jek would have given them all the details. Perhaps they'd stored my image when they'd seen me walking up the street a few minutes ago. My spectacles and tie might fool them, but maybe they'd see through my disguise. Now I'd been at both their doors.

I got home by lunchtime, after taking a circuitous route to ensure I wasn't followed. Then I switched on the computer to continue my research on Harry Hetland.

19

The previous morning Harry had addressed a bankers' breakfast that was widely covered by TV. His speech had been cautious and understated. There were no attacks on the Government. It was well delivered; his voice training had turned him into a good communicator and he'd made no extravagant comments or gestures. All the news programmes showed excerpts, usually as the third item on their bulletin. Since the first item was an African coup, the second a bungled heist in which four would-be robbers had been arrested, that made Harry's speech the first item of interest to most UK viewers. Good PR. A specialist news channel showed his arrival in a family saloon, alone with a chauffeur on a busy street where several security guards were to be seen, two of whom were undoubtedly plain clothes cops. His car door had been opened by his personal secretary, who was carrying a brief case which probably contained the speech. Two uniformed police waited in the background where a few celebrity-hunters had gathered. Harry was known to have left the building at nine, but there were no details of his exit or of his other morning activities. He had next been seen arriving at the House of Commons at one thirty. There wasn't a clue about where he'd been in the interval.

I had a bad afternoon studying the internet. My stomach was rumbling, making it difficult to concentrate on the screen. I'd eaten almost nothing since my lunch with Andy, and I wasn't too happy about it, though it was encouraging to see I'd lost a little weight. Obviously I ought to take something more substantial than tea, but that might kill my resolve. When I could take no more I went for another stroll in the park. This time there were several people about, including three dog walkers. I walked around it twice, reversing my direction the second time to make sure I wasn't followed.

At seven o'clock, unable to relax or concentrate, I went for a longer walk around the periphery of the town, which must have taken about an hour. I wasn't followed, and, thus encouraged, I went to the river footpath and made my way towards Dalespun Towers. It was a moonless night and while walking on the riverbank, I tripped over a root and banged my knee. It was irritating rather than painful, and probably a result of my crash diet. My reflexes were dulled and I hadn't reacted quickly enough to the obstacle. Cursing silently, I sat down to rub my knee, and saw a big man go past me, walking stealthily and looking ahead with an anxious air. He seemed entirely unaware that I was sitting at his feet. Had he been following me?

I counted to ten and hobbled back. He hadn't been carrying any fishing gear and hadn't moved like a walker. He'd had a sturdy build. On the plus side, he hadn't been holding a gun. A hundred metres from the town, I climbed the embankment and leaned against a tree for twenty minutes before he came back. He was looking around, but he was entirely unaware of me. After fifty metres, he left the path and went down to the river where he was out of sight and where, presumably, he'd been when I first passed. Perhaps he was an innocent fisherman, but perhaps he was something else. Most fishermen watch their rods and not the passers-by.

After twenty more minutes, I rose and continued up the embankment until I reached an overgrown path I'd known as a boy. In those days a score of us had played around the river, but now the young spent their time on the internet and the path hadn't been used for ages. I moved slowly for home, glancing behind me occasionally and seeing no one. Half way there, I stopped at a corner shop to buy a bar of chocolate. I was tempted to buy two and save the second for tomorrow, but that was best avoided. As I stepped back into the street, my luck turned bad. I bumped into Hazel.

'Mat! What are you doing here?' she exclaimed in delight, as though she were greeting a lost relative.

She was dressed in an outfit that resembled the colours of our local bus company, a choice which made an unhappy comparison between her shape and one of their double-deckers. She was casting predatory eyes on me.

'Just having a walk,' I bleated weakly. 'Getting some fresh air.'

'Has Adele been in touch?'

'Adele? No.'

'She's having terrible trouble with Bob. His wife had a row with her and scratched her face.'

'I'm sorry to hear that –'

'But they're still together.'

'Oh, well, as long as they're happy –'

'That's one thing that –'

She was speaking at her usual volume but I was no longer listening. A man was signing to me from across the road, in economical gestures that I had scarcely noticed at first. Something about his frame seemed familiar but it was only at my third glance that I recognised General George Douglas, complete with cloth cap and false beard. Of course now that Jane was installed in a safe house, he was having to do the donkey work himself. He was pointing to a car fifty metres away, a red Fiat. Plainly he'd been driving around the town to locate me, which probably meant that something had gone wrong again. I remembered my visit to Croften Communications and the man at the river.

Muttering an excuse to Hazel, I hurried to the car, aware of her eyes boring into my neck. I'd been weakened by hunger and now I'd erred by drawing her attention to the Fiat She might mention it to Adele and that was one thing I didn't need. The CID had probably been in touch with the local station to check up on me and it was best to avoid any more interest in my affairs. Maybe I ought to give up my stupid diet.

20

'They're on to you,' the General said in acid tones as I clambered into the car. 'You were seen at Romford this morning.' He didn't sound pleased.

'How do you know?'

'Their emails.'

'You monitor them?'

'Sometimes. You were seen in disguise at a communication place.'

'Croften Communications. The safe was addressed to them.'

'Absolutely idiotic! What were you thinking?'

'I needed to know.'

'Not exactly subtle, was it? I told you to keep away from Romford. There's a car with two men outside your flat. You're going to a safe house.'

This was an uppercut which would change my lifestyle in one unwelcome swoop. The pressure was building and the prospect of a safe house should have been welcome. But it offered no comfort at all. I'd seen too many of them and every one was a dead loss. Their very name was a misnomer. Few were actually safe, and they always had some kind of limitation. It was all daunting, particularly when Harry was the smartest opponent I'd ever seen. Already his men were at my door, and had it not been for my walk by the river they'd have had me. How had he traced me? How could he have been so efficient? Surely this was spelt Waterloo for Operation Garden? The plotters had been rumbled. It was time to wave the white flag. Unfortunately, there was no likelihood of Harry respecting it.

The Fiat burst into life and I looked around to see the bright figure of Hazel watching me with her mouth in an 'O' shape. She was certain tell Adele, and that wasn't good either. I gave her a wave and looked ahead to see that George was taking the road to London. A moment of panic swept over me. The metropolis holds no attraction for me, and being there would put me deeper into the heart of their plot, while leaving a lot of dangerous data in my wake.

'No, not yet!' I protested. 'Give me half an hour.'

The car slowed.

'Why?'

In fact there were a myriad of reasons, none of which I was going to share with him. Once inside my flat (and they'd get in within minutes) they'd have my cards and my papers. That would give them enough details about my life to launch as assault that wouldn't miss. I know how these things work and Harry was sure to be better at it than most.

'I've got a computer full of Harry Hetland, That's a death warrant.'

He looked in his mirror, pulled up, and said icily:

'Did you hear me? There are two bruisers outside your flat!'

'They're the least of it! Do a U-turn. I need to go back.'

But he didn't move.

'What are you going to do?' he said.

'I'll have to get the laptop out.'

'You can't. They're at your door.'

'There's another way in. I've got an escape route. Gotta have one. I've been in too many scrapes. I gotta get that computer.'

'Surely you're using security software?'

'Won't stop them for ten minutes. There's too much on it.'

'And you can get in without alerting the Hets?'

In fact, my alternative entrance was the front window and I'd used it only once before when I'd locked myself out. The idea of a second entrance was largely nominal, but I wasn't going to tell him that.

'I think so.'

'Very well, then.'

The General seemed like a quiet man who avoided extremes, although he was involved in an extremist plot. His reactions were ordered and controlled. He looked in his mirror and waited until the road was clear before turning back into the town at a sedate speed. I had difficulty recognising him in his cloth cap and false beard. He looked like an artist on his way to paint a landscape.

'I can do it in five minutes,' I said.

'Bully for you. What do I do?'

'Just wait for me.'

'I'm not prepared to drive past them again.'

'You won't need to. Take the second right.'

'This is safe?'

I grunted in assent, remembering that like all modern Generals he was a desk man. Had I asked that question, he'd have rebuked me for losing my nerve.

He indicated and I said:

'I'll grab my things. Can't risk leaving incriminating evidence. There's usually a parking place in this street – there's one.'

The car came to a sedate stop. This was a minor street with no pedestrians and poor lighting. Some of the houses in it were three hundred years old, and had housed farm workers. They were not attractive buildings. Once they'd all been owned by Dalespun Estate.

'I don't like this,' said George, looking round, no longer angry. 'These are heavy odds.'

'You're right there.'

'If I have to move, stay in this street. I'll drive back.'

'Will do.'

I got out of the car, put my hands in my pockets and strolled back for fifty metres before turning to the right on to an ancient lane barely wide enough for a car, which rose at a gentle angle towards the flats. There were houses on both sides with TVs flickering in every window. The lane got steeper as I reached a point about fifty feet from its junction with the main road, where I knew the Hets were waiting. There seemed to be nobody about, but it would have been unwise to assume that they didn't know about the lane. I stood for a moment to make certain that I was alone, then I put my foot on Mr Grimshaw's wooden fence and climbed on to his garage roof. The garage was a flimsy building which didn't look as though it could take my weight. I knew it was essential to keep to the edge until I reached the far corner, where I was able to move on to the roof of the Smith's lounge. Their TV was loud but that only meant their roof was thin. Then I approached the far corner which abutted my flat.

The panorama of the town was all around me, a prosperous market town with loads of lights. A man standing on somebody else's roof could have been spotted in a flash by somebody with night sights, but I was out of sight of the nearby lane and that was all that mattered.

Three feet up, a fair-sized pipe jutted out of the wall and I had to get on to it without making a sound. It was an inconvenient leap and if I didn't make it, there would be an audible creak in the room below when I stepped back. The trick was to approach it boldly and let the momentum force you against the wall just long enough to grab the window sill above it. Despite feeling a bit feeble, I managed it at the first try. I got my right foot on to the flat's overflow pipe and clambered on to the sill itself. The left upper window's catch was always off. If I opened it, I could reach down to unfasten the main window. It was easy, and it went like clockwork. I was inside without a single hesitation. It did help that there was someone waiting outside to shoot me or more likely to kidnap me. The shooting would come later.

I got into the darkened flat, disconnected my laptop, folded it down, and then went to my bedroom to pack a suitcase that could hold the laptop, some clothes, my papers, and the money I'd taken from the bodies. Money was very important. I needed it to survive, and would be able to accomplish very little without it. It was also something that officers 'forgot' to give their troops. Shortage of money kept us dependant on the chain of command. But I wanted some independence. My life might depend on it.

The landing outside fed two other flats. It had been abused by countless tradesmen who were forever lifting its boards to adjust the electricity, the gas, and the cable TV. As a result, the floorboards were ill-fitting and noisy, their tongue-and-groove detail long destroyed. I'd just reached my bedroom (the room was still in darkness) when they creaked so loudly that I thought someone was standing beside me. There was a heavy person outside my door.

What pathetic luck!

I stood back as someone attempted to turn a key in the door, but it didn't open. There was a big sigh as it was withdrawn. Another was inserted and, after much turning, withdrawn. More creaks, some snorts, and now something new was happening: a lot of scraping, a pause, and then more scraping. The lock was being picked, presumably by an expert. I'd never been able to pick a lock. Shortly he (I guessed that it was a heavy man from the weight of his footsteps) was going to be inside the flat and I was unarmed.

There was a small alcove to the left of the door, a supposed cloak room. I could hide there, but it was essential to have a weapon. I remembered an axe handle in the cupboard of the next room and I grabbed it in seconds, taking care to avoid the creaking floor boards. Returning to the alcove, I could hear the sounds at the lock continuing, accompanied by creaks and barely audible mutterings. Perhaps he wasn't an expert after all.

Then the lock turned.

The door opened two inches.

There was a pause. The visitor, in no great hurry, was getting out his gun and possibly a torch. The door swung open, obscuring my view. When it closed I saw the outline of a big bruiser looking into my room with his torch aimed at the floor. He glanced in my direction, but saw nothing because I was at the back of the alcove. Had he flashed his torch at me, I'd have been dead. He was undoubtedly a pro and very cautious. It would have been crazy to make a move while he was listening. But he wouldn't wait forever; eventually he'd have to move.

When he took a step forward I took one too and walloped him on the back of the head with the axe handle. The thump was loud. He let out a grunt and began to fall. I dropped the handle and grabbed him as best I could to prevent him hitting the floor at full volume. There were neighbours to consider and it would be a mistake to alarm them. His jacket tore but I'd slowed his descent. There was a thump, of course, but it could have been a lot worse.

He was face down on the floor. His gun – another SIG, this time with a silencer – was lying on the carpet and I grabbed it. Then I turned him over to see that he was about thirty, breathing heavily and almost snoring. His mouth was open and his eyes were flickering. That wasn't a good sign. I searched him., He had a second gun holstered around his chest like Andy's killer, a knife in his belt, and a wad of notes in his inside pocket. I took them all, and a container of ammo. He began to mutter words in a foreign language, as though he'd been having a long conversation with me. His eyes were still flickering which might indicate brain damage, or that he was coming round. I wasn't medically trained. in I pulled him into the middle of the floor, opened the door and dragged him out. He was very heavy. Following first-aid procedure, I left him lying on his side.

Once the door was closed I moved fast, terrified that someone would come down the stairs and start screaming when they saw him. Then I'd be trapped by a hundred police. Adele would be able to describe the bruiser's assailant with no difficulty.

Grabbing the suitcase, I tossed in the money as well as the weapons I'd seized. Finally I put my laptop on the top and locked it. Time was rushing past. The idiot outside was muttering loudly, either dying or waking, and the General would be getting impatient. Then I became aware of another problem. I couldn't get the case out of the flat. Plainly it couldn't be carried when I climbed out, and it couldn't be dropped on to the lounge's roof without breaking the laptop and causing the Smiths to raise the alarm. It took another minute to find a rope, which I tied around the handle. As I was doing this I heard a loud moan from outside the door. My assailant seemed to be complaining of a sore head. Surely soon one of the neighbours would come out to investigate. Back at the window, I made a discovery. A bullet had struck the wall and flattened out. He must have fired when I hit him, and now there was a lovely display of lead on the wall. It had been a soft-nosed bullet, designed to cause the maximum physical damage.

I opened the window and lowered the case on to the flat roof. Then I climbed out myself and closed the window. I was in such a hurry that I almost fell at one point. I grabbed the sill and dangled by my fingers until my feet found support. Twenty seconds later I was walking slowly with the case in my left hand. Near the bottom of the lane a small gang of yobs were standing, smoking fancy cigarettes. We nodded to each other as I passed. I doubted if they'd remember me. Then I turned into the main street. George saw me coming and had the boot open by the time I arrived at the car. Shortly we drove off.

21

'I've got another two guns for you,' I said as the General pulled away.

'Eh? You don't keep guns in your flat, do you, for God's sake?'

'No, I had a visitor while I was there.'

'I wondered.'

'He broke in. I'd to wallop him on the head. He didn't look good. His eyes were wild and he was muttering to himself. I dragged him on to the landing and left him.'

'This is getting too violent.'

'If he's a goner I'll be in big trouble –'

He looked at me.

'Then you'd better call an ambulance.'

'That'll bring the cops –'

'If he dies, it'll certainly bring them.'

'My instinct would be to do nothing.'

The General dropped down a gear and accelerated up a gradient, being careful to keep within the speed limit. Then he nodded.

'Well you're an experienced man...'

We were silent as the car paused at a roundabout, then I dropped my bombshell:

'There's a bigger problem. How did that heavy know where I lived?'

'Hetland has the police in his pocket. They'd get you address from your car number.'

I shook my head at his smug answer.

'How would they know that? I didn't go to Romford in my car, I went by bike.'

He swung round to look at me in surprise.

'You didn't? Now that's a rum one.'

'A very rum one. It implies your security's been breached.'

I looked at him from the corner of my eye but he was staring at the road again.

'Any chance he was a run-of-the-mill burglar?'

'With two hand guns and a knife?' I didn't mention the money. 'Not very likely.'

'No, I suppose not. What was his object, do you think?'

'I'm in line to be kidnapped. It's the safe, of course. They must be desperate.'

'Yes,' he said, glad to get on to his favorite subject. 'So you should keep your head down and get on with the report.'

'My dearest wish.'

We joined the main road and accelerated towards London.

'How are things going?' I asked. 'Garden things?'

The General didn't look as if he would respond, but then he said:

'Harry's beginning to lose his cool – I think we're making progress.'

'What about the safe? What have you done with it?'

'Forget it, Mat. It'll take time.'

'Yes, but you're not going to leave it at Dalespun, I hope?'

'Oh, it's been moved.'

So they were organized after all. It would have taken a bit of maneuvering and some good transport, but at least the job was done. We drove in silence for five minutes and then the General laughed.

'I've solved your problem. They must have had a report from Herb. They know you were the last to see Andy before he was shot. He gave them your name and address.'

'I hadn't thought of that.'

'That's the trouble with the cops. You don't know where it goes.'

No, you certainly don't. I remembered that Herb had been reluctant to explore the gold bars angle. In fact, he'd been complacent about everything. Given that he must have known all about Croften Communications, the whole thing had been a farce.

'I'd be willing to bet that Herb will be back at your flat with more questions.'

'You think he's outright working for them?'

'Well, I wouldn't say that, but we can assume he's in their

pay. You're at the heart of the action. They'll send him round as soon as the dust's settled. He knows you killed the Het but he can't prove it and I don't think he'll try. Instead, he'll let them deal with you and you may never be seen again. We have to choke him off. We don't want him at your flat door before ten tomorrow morning –'

'To find I've bolted.'

'Exactly. That wouldn't be good. He could post you as a missing person and have all the cops looking for you. Best avoided. As I said, better choke him off.'

'How do I do that?'

'There's a service station coming up. We'll go in for a coffee, and you can phone from there. Better tell a neighbour you're off for a fortnight. Anyone you can call?'

'Yes, Mrs Birhandi.'

She'd believe me too, after seeing me with Jane.

'After that you'll phone Herb. Hmm, better think of something to say.'

The service station had been mobbed by a bus party and what looked like a rugby team and we got the only spare table. I had some tea while the General frowned into his coffee and asked me questions about the Herb interview. I could see that it wasn't going to be easy. A phone call about nothing would only make him suspicious. Eventually George came up with a plan.

First I phoned Mrs Birhandi and told her that I was going off for a fortnight to sunny Spain. She giggled and told me that I was a fast worker.

Then I phoned Herb.

A woman with a deep voice who said her name was Tanya asked how she could help. Judging by the noise in the background, phones were ringing and a lot of talking, it seemed as though I was through to the incident room itself. I was dismayed by the volume of human activity. It was difficult to see why the case hadn't been solved in the first hour. It must all be a façade. Every one of those seventy officers must know about Croften, to say nothing of the Harry Hetland connection. I asked for Herb and after some questioning, was put through.

'Well, Mat, how's it going?' he said, all affable.

'That depot,' I said. 'I've remembered its name –'

'Depot? What depot?' he was genuinely puzzled, or seemed to be.

'The one Andy was going to visit, about the gold bars –'

'Oh, I remember now.'

'– It's Northern & District.'

'Northern & District? I'll just write that down,' he said. It didn't sound as though he would.

'You asked me to phone if I remembered. I'd investigate it if I was you.'

'Well, we'll see.'

No, he wasn't going to bother.

'Incidentally, I'm off to Spain for a fortnight.'

'Eh? While we're tramping about in the rain, some people have all the luck. Keep away from the Senoritas now.'

And then the call was over.

'Sounded fine,' said the General, who had been leaning over to hear. 'At the very least, he isn't interested in you.'

But I wasn't too sure about that.

22

The safe house was an apartment near central London which must have cost a fortune. George took me up in the lift to the fourth floor where I found myself in triple glazed luxury, looking down at a busy London street. It had a fully equipped kitchen, a bedroom and a lounge with a big TV on the wall. I'd never seen this quality of safe house before.

'How long will I be here?'

'Till the job's done.

'How long is that likely to be?'

'Sooner than you might expect. Days, possibly.'

'Days?' I asked, wondering if I could have the report ready in that time.

'Yes, a few days. Get on with that report. It's urgent. We may need an emergency option. Look at that first. He's in serious trouble. We can't let him get away at this late stage.'

I glanced at the General, wondering how he could believe Harry was in trouble, after reading the man's history. Hetland had come out of jail for manslaughter and was now a major player in the nation's affairs. According to my notes, he'd been questioned seventeen times about major crimes, including killings, and had survived every one with impunity. That was a decade ago, of course, but no doubt even the most persistent of cops would take that into account before closing in with a case that might rebound on them. That's if the cops weren't in Harry's pay in the first place, and I suspected that all the top ones were. Several times in the last few years, he'd had close calls which he'd handled with aplomb. Not one had reached the public's notice.

And his men were camped at my door.

'Well, I'll certainly look at that. On the face of it, any option I can moot would mean the operative being captured.'

'List it anyway. We've got a lot of facilities. Poison gas, grenades and sniper rifles – all of them foreign and with no apparent connection to us.'

'Yes, I noticed that,' I said, with a sinking feeling, all too aware that Jane or myself were pencilled in for the hit. That would have to be avoided. He certainly wouldn't be doing the field work himself.

I decided on a ploy.

'But George, that kind of thing depends on the agent. I need details about them first. I'm not prepared to be the assassin myself, and I doubt if Jane will be either. We're both past our best. We've been pensioned off.'

George nodded, but I might as well have kept silent. Minor squeaks from the infantry wouldn't influence his plans for a second and there was a lot at stake. This was like Alex's breakdown truck all over again. Although I'd refused to drive it, when push came to shove, I'd got into the cabin at the first command.

'Write your report, man, and we'll worry about that later. I want that report immediately. I've got one of my own of course, but I'd like to see what you can come up with. Perhaps we don't need it, but we must have it. We have to be ready for anything. Keep your head down and for God's sake don't let them catch sight of you again.'

'I'll get on with it right away.'

'Good man.'

'Who knows I'm here?'

'I do. No one else.'

'How can I contact you?'

He pointed to a group of small cartons in a corner of the lounge.

'Pay as you go phones. There's a re-order number on each box. Prefix it with '07' and that's my number – just activate the thing and dial. I don't want to be bothered with trivialities. If I don't answer, you'll wait until I phone back. Then you'll destroy the phone. Don't use one twice. Take the battery out and throw it in the bin in the basement. Don't leave it in here for five minutes.'

'Okay. So I just get on with the report?'

'That's it. You're completely safe here, and isolated from all distractions. Oh, I'd better give you some cash for food. How about fifty? You're hardly going to need to eat a lot on a diet.'

I waited until he'd gone, then I searched the flat to discover it had been expertly cleaned. There were no papers in the bin and no food in the fridge or any sign that there ever had been. In fact there was no indication that anyone had ever lived there. The doors had no scuff marks, nor was there wear on the handles or any erosion on the light switches. In the kitchen there were tea bags, coffee and muesli in unopened packs. I went to the bedroom and put my face into the bed linen to discover it was new. In the bathroom there was wrapped soap in the trays and the towels and the toilet seat were new. The whole flat had been recently painted and it was free of electronic bugs. I stood back and thought about it. Without a doubt it must belong to the Home Office. It was unlikely that a small group of men, however rich, would have so many facilities, George was using a perk of his rank.

I made tea and ate the chocolate bar I'd bought on my way back from the river. My body heat had melted it in my jacket, but it tasted fine.

Then I unpacked my case, plugged in the computer and got on with my research. I started with Croften Communications and discovered that, like many things associated with Harry, they were bigger than they'd first appeared, turning over millions every year. They had branches in seven countries, including China, and they specialised in the transfer of data and 'other security interests'. There was no mention of Harry Hetland in the list of major shareholders (their base was in New York) and they seemed to be trading nicely. The firm was not strong in the UK and they seemed to be looking to expand their influence. At the first glance, it seemed very respectable, but everything associated with Harry Hetland did until you started digging.

23

The buzzer went at nine o'clock on the following morning.

'It's Jane. Let me in,' I heard when I lifted the intercom. Her voice was almost drowned by the traffic which was curiously inaudible behind my triple glazing. This was an interruption I didn't need. How had she known where to find me when George had said that only he knew about the safe house? More to the point, what had I done to deserve Jane? I pressed the entry button, then shut the laptop. I opened the door in time to see her step out of the lift, looking as fierce as ever.

'How did you know –?' I began, but she pushed her way inside.

'Forget that. I've got to get something out of my flat. You'll need to help.'

'I thought they were watching it,' I said, suddenly angry. 'I thought that's what the fuss was about.'

'I've left something behind. I have to get it.'

We all make mistakes, but to have left something of value behind spoke of sheer incompetence. I'd had enough. Somewhere at the back of my mind I knew that I was costing the plotters a fortune. The report was still not ready or even properly begun. This was going to interrupt it again.

'Then contact George.'

'I can't. This is desperate!'

I hesitated. We were both agents, pledged to assist each other and all emergencies that had to be resolved. To send her away might bring the whole edifice tumbling about our ears and that had to be avoided at all costs.

'Tell me more,' I said, albeit with bad grace.

'I've got to get a file out – it's sensitive.'

There was something different about her, and I realised what it was. She had dyed her hair startlingly black. The yellow tint had gone, no doubt in response to the current situation. It seemed that Jane was incapable of adopting an neutral colour, but had to fly between extremes. She'd gone from bright blonde to jet black.

'They will have got into your flat already.'

'Believe me, they haven't.'

I looked at her and wondered if I was going off my head. The notion that an organised gang would keep a watch on her without breaking into her flat was ludicrous. They were the most expert hoods in the land. They were certain to have ransacked Jane's home for clues. If they'd spotted something of value, they would keep watch in case she tried to retrieve it.

'Forget it. We can't take on the Hets.'

'I've got to get it out of the flat. This is an emergency.'

'What's in it?'

'Can't say, but it's vital. We can't let *them* get it.'

'Jane, if the Hets so much as see me, my feet won't touch the ground.'

'We can do it. There's a taxi waiting.'

She'd declared an emergency and driven through the rush hour to get here. I had to react to that. A crisis couldn't be scrutinised in its early stages. I'd have to do it.

'Alright,' I said, weak-willed fool that I was. 'I'll do it.'

'Come on, then!'

'I'll get my shoes on.'

In the bedroom I put on the shoulder rig with the H&K under my jacket, grabbed a wad of notes and slipped my shoes on. When I emerged Jane was standing with the outer door open, ready to run.

'Use the stairs, they're quicker.'

Whatever our faults might have been, we were both fit. An elderly couple waiting for the lift on the floor below looked at us in amazement as we galloped past. My leg seemed to have recovered, although there was still an occasional twinge. Outside, a taxi, was waiting on the pavement with its hazard lights on as the rush hour traffic filtered past. The driver, a middle-aged chap who seemed reasonably smart, saw us coming. He threw the door open and began to merge with the traffic as only a taxi can do. Despite Jane's change of hair colour she was still easily recognisable. So was I. Harry's gang were proven killers and they were waiting.

Not being one of Jane's inner circle, I'd never been to her flat, or even seen it. I was in no position to discuss tactics. However, she was a pro and her judgement would have to be relied on. In theory it would be possible for me to walk away if I didn't like the look of things but it seldom works that way. She was sitting beside me, getting angry at the stationary traffic.

'Does this involve Operation Garden?'

Her face froze and she looked away.

'That's privileged information.'

'Is it hidden?'

'Yes, it's well hidden.'

I sat back in the seat as the taxi crawled another twenty metres. It would have to be very well hidden to escape the kind of people who were waiting for us. Perhaps there'd be a limit to the number of personnel, but I expected at least one watcher. He or she would probably be one of the foreign killers and they were dangerous. Despite myself, I'd been impressed by the discipline shown by the intruder in my flat.

'Listen,' she said. 'We're headed for a charity shop. I'll get out and get something to disguise us. Stay in the taxi. They'll remember two of us –'

'Okay. An overcoat for me. I want to keep this jacket on,' I said, all too aware of the H&K under my arm. 'You've got money?'

'Yes.'

We turned into a side street and pulled on to the kerb beside a charity shop that was just being opened by a thin woman in black. Jane was out in a second and disappeared into the shop.

'Women!' said driver turning to me. I suspected he was one of George's tame assistants. What other driver would wait in the rush hour while she fetched me?

'Can't keep 'em out of a clothes shop,' I said.

'My missus has so many I can hardly get in the room.'

'I know the feeling.'

The meter ticked away and it was ten minutes before Jane emerged with a bundle of clothes which she could barely carry. I got out and lent a hand. The purchases were placed on the back seat, the door closed, and we moved off after she'd given new directions. Jane produced something from the bundle which looked like an eastern sari, and started to wrap it around herself. She ordered me into an overcoat sitting on top of the bundle. It was not a British-style overcoat. I didn't know where the thing had come from and it was difficult to get into. Clearly it had been made for a very tall man and would trail on the ground when I got out, but I saw no point in arguing, particularly when the driver was paying more attention to us than the traffic.

'Get your hat on,' she said.

By this time she was almost unrecognisable, in the sari and a bright red hat. It was difficult to know whether she was supposed to be an Indian or a drama student, though it would fool all but the most serious of onlookers. We might have a chance after all. My hat was too big, but I folded the inner band to make it stable on my head, though it would certainly blow off in a breeze.

'Is this the place, missus?'

I looked up to find we were in a crowded car park with a substantial tower block at the far end, marked Nelson Tower. There wasn't a vacant space in sight but at least there seemed to be nobody hanging around. Of course, there wouldn't be. They'd be in a car watching people going in and out, or perhaps they were already inside her flat. Either way, they'd have a phone pre-dialled to their HQ.

'Yes, wait here for us –'

'You pay me first, pet. I've done a lot of waiting.'

There was a delay while she paid him. It was a lot, and he agreed to wait for ten minutes. The meter was still ticking. I don't know where she had got the money. We got out.

'Walk slow,' she said.

No danger of my doing otherwise. I was walking unsteadily on my tiptoes to keep the hem of the coat off the ground. My calves were already sore. Jane took my arm as I made painful progress towards the tower block, aware of the driver's eyes on the back of my neck. He suspected that we were up to something, and he was dead right, but nobody else gave us a second glance. There were many oddly dressed people in London. In fact I saw two couples who made us look almost staid.

'Do you see anybody?'

'I wouldn't expect to. Not here.'

There were all kinds of cars parked around us, including some vans and at least two vehicles with no wheels resting on bricks. Nearly all were unoccupied, though I saw solitary occupants in two of them.

'Which floor are you on?'

'Sixth. We'll use the stairs.'

'No, we won't, not dressed like this. Take the lift to the eighth.'

'Approach from above?'

'Yes, slowly. You've got your key?'

'In my hand.'

On the forecourt a post van and two cars were parked illegally. They were all vacant. I bent towards Jane and I allowed my eyes to flick over the nearest cars in the park. I saw several occupants, none of whom seemed to be looking at us, though that went for nothing. I looked for a solitary bruiser, a Het, and saw nothing alarming. We were just another dizzy couple, and I was walking unsteadily, offering no challenge to man or beast. However, a professional might take a keener interest. It might have been a little late for revellers to be returning from a party.

At the door, we stopped to let a Chinese couple through, before we reached the lifts where several people were standing.

'Damn,' I said softly. The central lift was out of order and it was stuck on the sixth floor. Jane saw it too and she squeezed my arm. This was too much of a coincidence. If they had jammed the lift on the sixth floor, they would certainly have ransacked her flat. That meant they were probably still there, otherwise the lift wouldn't have been parked on that floor.

'Abort?' I said in an undertone, hoping she would see sanity.

'No!' She spoke so fiercely that an old man looked round at us.

There were several people in the foyer, including a black couple waiting for the lift and a group of Indian women with several children who were arguing with each other. There was no sign of the Hets, but there wouldn't be.

'We're not backing out now!'

But this was bad. It would be insane to arrive while they were searching the place. Did she actually want a showdown? I wondered what was in the file to cause such desperation.

'Then I want out.'

She swayed uncertainly, incongruous in her sari.

'Stay there. I'll go up and see.'

But that would be the height of folly. Any watcher in the car park might have paid no great attention to the fool in the long coat or his sari-clad companion, but if she went up in the lift while he remained in the hall, that would be a cause for curiosity. Something slightly odd was going on and although it wouldn't be deemed an emergency, there might be a call to the sixth floor.

Then the lift doors crashed open. Six people came out and I pressed in behind her. She looked at me in surprise but there were people about and she said nothing. Eventually the lift stopped at the eighth floor and we both got out.

'What are you doing now?' she demanded.

'Do you want me shot, standing down there like a wally?'

She looked at me and was silent. I could see the file meant a lot to her.

'What are *you* going to do?' I said.

'I'll walk past. I just want to see.'

So she didn't have a plan after all. Two floors down a team of Hets were probably searching her flat. They would certainly find her file. This was a classic no-win situation and we were at risk of being trapped.

'Would they recognise me in this?' she asked.

'I wouldn't risk it.'

We were speaking very quietly; the sixth floor was a mere thirty steps away.

'We'll both walk past them,' I decided. 'Have you got a gun?'

She had. I got the H&K out and held it in my right pocket with my finger on the trigger. We didn't want a shooting match either. There could be no winners in that scenario.

'Nobody's using the stairs,' I said, speaking even more quietly, remembering that sound bounces off concrete walls and carries for a surprising distance. The Hets might have heard us already. 'We'll be a sore thumb.'

At that moment there were sounds from below. A door opened, a man said something, a woman said cheerio and footsteps sounded on a lower floor. By the pace of his footsteps, the man was going to use the stairs.

'Come on,' said Jane, half running down the stairs ahead of me, her shoes making clacking noises on the concrete.

By this time the man was on his way down to the sixth floor and we paused to listen to a short conversation. A man with a foreign accent was saying something about the lift being out of action all day. He sounded like a big bruiser. The walker made a comment and went on down the stairs. I looked at Jane. Despite the odds to the contrary, it sounded like the lift had only one man on board. Presumably he was pretending to work while watching Jane's flat. But was he the look-out while the rest of his team worked in the flat?

Before I could do anything, Jane dashed on ahead, her gun in her right hand. She was desperate. On the sixth floor, the central lift door was jammed open. Jane practically jumped in front of it, gun raised, looking very odd in her sari. Then I was beside her and a bruiser was standing with his arms raised and a stricken expression on his face.

I said: 'I'll take over. Get your door open.'

I glanced at her door, noting its reinforced design and that it was hung on a metal frame with a high quality lock. It seemed intact and undamaged. How she'd managed to get such a fitting in a Council Tower was beyond me.

I turned back to the bruiser. He looked like a heavy weight boxer, and thick too. He had a broken nose that gave his face a puffy look and his shoulders were so broad that his overalls didn't quite meet at the top. There were several empty cans and a *Daily Mirror* at his feet. Some of the electronics had been detached from the lift to give the impression of work in progress. His gaze was alternating between Jane and me and he seemed contemptuous of us both. He could probably have killed us with one blow, and it seemed as though he was looking forward to doing so.

'You,' I said, keeping my voice down, aware of how sound could carry in a tower. 'Get out of there and lean on that wall with both hands against it.'

At first I thought that he'd refuse but a spasm of fear crossed his face when he looked at my gun. He lumbered out and put his hands on the wall. His big body blocked the walkway. If anybody should come we'd be in trouble. Without a doubt there were weapons on him. A phone began to buzz in the lift. I ignored it. There was no way I could have answered it, though it had chosen a suspicious moment to ring.

'Are you alone?' I asked, forcing the gun against him.

'Yus.' It was a kind of grunt; he was not, apparently, an English speaker. I didn't believe him for a moment. I looked at the junk in the lift. There had to be at least two of them. Perhaps the other guy had gone to fetch something.

'What's keeping you?' I called to Jane with some impatience.

'They've gummed up the lock!' She sounded demented.

'Heat the key with your lighter. Sometimes that works.'

And sometimes it doesn't, I said to myself, giving the bruiser another fierce prod with the gun while I reached into his side pocket. He turned out to have an SIG in there, which I put it in my coat pocket. I found a knife in a scabbard on his belt. If his equipment was consistent with that of his fellows, there would still be a holstered gun under his jacket, but it would be difficult to remove it without giving him a chance to get me. I kept him standing against the wall.

Then something wonderful happened, the first piece of luck on the outing. Jane's door clicked open. The big bruiser looked up and flexed his muscles but I prodded him with the gun before he could move. He'd waited until we were both distracted by the open door and now he'd lost the opportunity.

Speaking quietly I said: 'One false move and I'll have to send a wreath.'

He was still leaning against the wall, but now his head had drooped in an attitude of failure. That was no reason to relax. Boxers have a way of hitting you on the nose when you think they're down. Sometimes, he glanced my way before looking away quickly. I was careful to keep outside his range, well aware that he could kill with one blow.

Then Jane was at my elbow, a look of triumph on her face

and her sari in disarray. She was carrying a silver file case. It was a high security file. I'd seen several in my time, though I'd never had one in my own possession. Obviously Jane was higher in the echelons than I was. She had several plastic ties in her other hand.

'Get down on the floor,' I said to our captive, giving him a prod with the gun.

With a sigh of resignation, he lay down while Jane expertly tied his feet and wrists. I stood back with the gun aimed at his head. His eyes kept returning to me. In the background, I could hear the sounds of people moving about on the stairs below. Sometimes a lift door would slam and sometimes people spoke to each other and laughed on other floors. Sounds carry in a tower block but none of them were close to us.

'There's a gun under his shoulder. Get it.'

Quick as a flash, Jane's hands searched for the weapon, found it, and handed it to me, there being nowhere to hide it in her sari. When I put it in my coat pocket, the lining began to tear under the weight of both guns. She pulled a wad of notes from his inner pocket

'Wait,' she said, going back to her flat and returning with a shopping bag into which she placed the file and the weapons, though I kept my H&K.

I said: 'Lock your door and go.'

She closed the door and the lock clicked. Somehow we'd been successful. All we had to do was get back to the taxi and celebrate. We looked at the fallen bruiser for half a second.

'Listen, pal,' I said as Jane hurried down the stairs. 'I haven't gagged you because you might choke to death. You're not going to make a sound for the next ten minutes or I'll come back and shoot you. I've killed more people than you have. I'm good at it. I'm an expert. Do you understand?'

He nodded, but I didn't trust him for a minute. It was essential to hurry. I went down the stairs, holding my coat up in case I tripped. This was the difficult bit. It was one thing to be coming home in fancy gear after a late party, but any watcher would wonder why we were leaving in the same garb after a mere ten minutes. That was enough to give us away. Jane was waiting for me at the fifth floor, righting her sari and doing something to her hair. The shopping bag full of guns was at her feet. We continued down at a sedate pace.

When we reached the second floor, we looked through a window which overlooked the car park.

'The taxi,' Jane said. 'It's gone!'

I peered out. It wasn't where we'd left it, but perhaps the driver had found a parking place. There were a number of similar vehicles around. I was scanning the area to see if it was elsewhere, when she half screamed: 'Oh!'

Five big men in dark suits were walking towards the tower block, the one at the back carrying a shopping bag. There was another bruiser at the entrance to the car park, and a people carrier was looking for a parking space. The five were trying not to look too conspicuous, walking in single file. Their leader gave an old lady a greasy smile while the man behind him tried to summon a grin.

24

The alarm must have gone off when we left the taxi. Perhaps it had been the unanswered phone in the lift. Even so, they'd been quick.

We hadn't been all that clever. Surprise anyone with a gun and they're likely to cooperate, big bruisers included. But now the situation had changed and we'd lost the advantage of surprise.

This was Jane's home ground. I hoped that she was familiar with the tower block and knew all the exits. No doubt she had a contingency plan, perhaps even an emergency route in mind, though the gang of five would be at the entrance before we'd be out of the tower. We couldn't let them see us. But her face was stricken. It looked as though she had no idea what to do. We'd lost the initiative and all we could do was surrender or die. The latter being the end result of either option.

'Move!'

It was too late to run. Then the unbelievable began to happen. Jane threw the window open and let out a piercing scream which must have been audible a mile away. I felt like joining in. Then she pulled a gun from her bag and fired three shots into the air. From the distance I heard more screams.

Fair enough; we had been advised to create a diversion when in a tight spot. I'd done it myself and survived. But firing shots into a London car park isn't the best of ideas unless you can get out in seconds, and that was one thing we couldn't do. One problem with a diversion is that it can rebound on you

I'll say one thing. Whatever the limits of their intelligence, the gang of five were quick on the hoof. This was sheer ballet. One moment they had been doing a sedate three miles an hour, the next they were all gone except the leader who had spread himself on the ground, having no handy hiding place. He was looking up with an anxious expression. The others were hiding behind cars with a grace which would have inspired a modest acknowledgement at Covent Garden. They had their guns out and an old woman was screaming.

A bullet hit our window. It was a good shot, bearing in mind that it had come from a hand gun which had just been seized from a holster. Time to go. We ran for the stairs as another two bullets shattered the glass. I had an afterimage of the leader rolling to the side and yelling for a cease fire. This wasn't the Ukraine. You didn't fire guns in a London car park, unless you were Jane. It was frowned on and you could get years in chokey for your pains. Soon there would be a hundred police asking questions with the dreaded Armed Response Unit in attendance. That meant that the entire area would be sealed off for hours. The net had tightened.

We stopped on the first floor.

'Get these stupid clothes off,' I said, getting rid of the coat and hat. But was it that easy? Dare we leave them behind? One drop of sweat could identity us for ever. I picked up the coat, wrapped it around the other things and pushed it into her shopping bag. Outside, the car park had become deathly calm and the five men were in urgent conference, keeping their heads well down.

'Walk slowly,' she said. 'Six feet behind me.'

I hadn't intended to draw attention to myself. We made it to the entrance hall, where a number of people were watching the gang of five and paying no attention to us. The gang's leader was holding a mobile phone to his ear and seemed to have turned to stone. The others were behind a car watching the windows above us. They didn't look too happy.

Remaining causal, Jane turned right into a service corridor, a dull, smelly place covered in dust. Then we were suddenly coming out of the back door into the refuse section. It was a depressing area which demonstrated the worst of modern times.

In a shooting incident, the first thing the cops would do was isolate the locality. All roads would be closed and no people or vehicles would be allowed in or out of the area. Passing trains would be diverted. Even airliners on their way to Heathrow would have their flight path altered. The cops love this kind of thing. An Inspector might even get a TV slot to calm the public's fears. Then there would be a long delay while the Armed Response Unit got their boots laced. Next the head honchos would have a conference, a plan would be agreed and they'd zero in on the seat of the disturbance. Except that quite possibly they wouldn't. Perhaps no cop would raise his head within shooting distance for hours, because no operatives could be placed in a risky position. Committees have agreed on this and the rules are set in stone. Thus the entire compliment of perhaps a hundred men and women would remain out of sight until the situation could be deemed safe for them to make an appearance. During this time, the net would be tightened, people on the periphery would be ordered out of their homes and moved to community halls with armies of social workers adding to the confusion. There have been cases where nurses and first aid people have been allowed access to the crime scene while the police were afraid to show their faces. Such is our modern world. In some ways, it's an extension of the old police policy of waiting until the fight's over before arresting the winners.

'We'll go to the canal,' Jane said.

But that was bad. Canals go in straight paths, they are flat, and you can be seen for miles. For a start, everybody on this side of Nelson Tower would see us.

'No, it'll be sealed.'

'There's a way under it – into the next estate.'

She was walking faster now. Behind us there were a number of doors into the base of the building, probably leading to storerooms. This area was set below the level of the surrounding lawn. We passed a number of wheelie bins with a lot of litter and graffiti before climbing the embankment, where we stopped to look at a section of lawn with some kiddies' swings and entertainments. A path led towards the canal, the banks of which adjoined the area. Freedom was about two hundred metres away.

But we remained where we were.

A Het in a dark suit and baseball cap was standing in the middle of the lawn with a frown on his face as he looked into the sky. He hadn't seen us.

'Back,' said Jane, and I didn't need to be told twice. We were in full view of the tower, but that was the least of it. The Het had been looking at an approaching helicopter. No doubt it had already been aloft and had been directed to the emergency. It wouldn't come within shooting distance, but that was immaterial; it would be loaded with high quality cameras, and it would record every detail in glorious colour. Whether he knew it or not, the heavy on the lawn had now had his portrait taken and was on police files. Had we'd gone on to the lawn we'd have had a starring role beside him.

Back at the building, we tried all the doors, but they were locked.

'What the hell are we going to do?'

'We'll have to lie low.'

This was a terrible prospect. We'd have to hide for hours and there was a big risk of capture. And where could we hide? I looked at the wheelie bins, but surely they'd be searched.

'There's got to be somewhere we can hide.'

By this time we were back in the service corridor. It was still deserted. In view of the emergency, it would probably be checked shortly. The cops would phone and order all service doors to be locked.

'Where can we go?' she sounded despairing.

There were two doors off the corridor which led to storage units which were little more than big cupboards.

'The outbuildings are our only hope,' I said. 'Where are the keys?'

'In the Caretaker's office, the other side of the hall.'

'No good.' That would mean being seen.

I opened the back door and heard the copter again. It would probably be there for hours

She said: 'What are we going to do?'

'Run for it. Put these coats over our heads. Get under the canal –'

'Too late.'

The door opened and the Caretaker came in. He was a bloke of about forty, dressed in a boiler suit. He stopped when he saw us.

'Fred, it's just me.'

'What are you doing here, Jane? Or shouldn't I ask?'

The caretaker was a medium sized man with an easy-going face. He had a sloping chin, he was going bald and there was a hangdog expression about him. He seemed well disposed to Jane.

'What's going on out there?'

'There's been a shooting. Some big men are running around.'

'They're still here?'

'They're away now, most of them. They got into a car and drove off. Mr Todd on ten says he saw them stopped by the cops. They had guns; more cops came –'

'So they aren't all away?'

'I don't know,' said the caretaker. He didn't seem too bothered. 'We got one trussed up outside your door-'

'Fred, you've got to help me. Will you lock me and this man in one of these outside rooms till it's over? Tell no one.'

He stood back.

'Well now, Jane, I didn't know you were that fond of men.'

'Oh, come on, Fred.'

'I can't do that.'

It was just our luck to get a man who didn't do deals.

'Fred,' I said. 'Jane is an undercover policewoman. She's involved in government business and this is important. These men tried to kill us. You'll have to hide us until the emergency's over. I'll give you a hundred pounds. I've got it here. I'll give you another hundred when you let us out again.'

'That's a lot of money, but –'

'Fred you'll have to do it,' said Jane. 'And you mustn't tell anyone.'

'Oh I don't talk, Jane. You wouldn't believe what goes on –'

'Give us a room we can hide in, perhaps a storeroom with a lot of stock. We're professionals. We know how to hide. We won't let you down.'

'You're hiding from the police too?'

She adopted a sweet tone.

'For the moment, yes. But we're really on the same side.'

'Well, you can't ask me to do that, Jane. I don't hide things from the police. That could get me sacked and I'd never get another job.'

'If we're caught,' said Jane, 'I'll say nothing about you, I promise. We'll say we had a duplicate key.'

'That'll hardly do.'

'Yes, it will and we're not going to get caught anyway.'

During this exchange I'd reached into my jacket and taken five twenties out of my pocket. His eyes kept returning to them. We all need money.

'Here's your cash,' I said. 'We'll cause you no trouble.' He reached out and took it with some enthusiasm. 'Have the police phoned you yet?'

'The police? No.'

'They will soon. Say nothing about Jane or me. You've never seen us, right?'

Now he was nodding, seemingly anxious to please, but he didn't seem to trust us one bit and I didn't trust him either. We were entirely at his mercy.

'Hang on, I'll get the keys,' he said, hurrying off. The door swung shut and we were alone again.

'Is he alright?' I said to Jane.

He might be reporting us at that very moment.

'I don't think he'll shop us.'

'He wouldn't need to.'

She said: 'The cops are going to watch this place when it's over.'

'So will the Hets. That idiot was watching the canal.'

'You heard Fred. The cops stopped their car.'

'Means nothing,' I said. 'I'll bet they'll be free by tomorrow.'

'Thanks for coming up with that money. I'll pay it back.'

To our relief, Fred came back, walking past us to the door, which he opened and looked out. It seemed that he was the kind of plodder who erred on the side of caution and hadn't reported us. Having taken our money, he'd tolerate us in a half-hearted way.

He said: 'Come on, it's clear.'

I could still hear the sound of the copter, and there was nobody else about. Jane was holding her shopping bag tightly so that Fred wouldn't see the guns inside. Everything was happening too slowly. Soon the place would be swarming with police. Fred opened a door that had a high security self-locking system. He switched on a light to reveal a fair-sized room with a low ceiling, which contained office desks, filing cabinets and chairs which had obviously been stored for years. Everything was covered in dust and there was an ancient boiler in the corner which probably acted as a spare. I didn't fancy it much, but it was a refuge.

'Will this do you?' he asked, as though we were in a position to argue.

'It'll do fine.'

'I'll have to leave you here for ages. I'll come back when it's all clear. Is that okay?'

'If we go,' I said, 'we'll leave your money on that boiler. Is there a floor brush? I don't want them to see our prints in that dust.'

'There's one over there. I've got to go. Things are happening.'

He stepped out and closed the door and that was the last we saw of him.

'Well, this is a pretty mess,' said Jane.. 'Stuck in here.'

'I said this would happen, if you remember.'

'Don't rub it in.'

I realised that she must have thought that my supposed talents would be enough to make it work. Why did everyone depend on me? Jane put the shopping bag on a desk and we both looked at the room. There was a solitary light in the middle of the ceiling, casting dark shadows. The room was bigger than it had seemed at first. There was a lot of furniture stored along its length. Not a good thing. It was the kind of place that the police would either ignore or search thoroughly. There would be no half measures. Some potential hiding places presented themselves, but none were good and any half competent cop would have us in seconds. Unless we could find a natural hiding place it would be near impossible to dodge them. There was years of dust under foot and our prints were easy to see. I picked up the brush and began to sweep the floor while Jane explored the room. It would have to be swept twice.

'Were the Hets after your file?' I asked.

'No, they don't even know about it.'

'So the entire operation was to catch you, not the file? Why are you so valuable? What gives?'

'I don't know. I never dreamed that they'd have an interest in me.'

'What's the file about?'

'It's classified. I can't say.'

I went on sweeping the floor and thought, feeling like a blind man beside an ocean being told there was no water nearby. The idea that so many Hets would be employed to pursue a minor witness was risible.

'Then there's something else. You've been involved in a previous plot.'

'Absolutely not. I've never even heard of a previous plot.'

'Well, can you explain their interest?'

'I can't. Maybe they'd have the same interest in you if you'd stayed home.'

Like me, Jane has had some training in interrogation. I was aware of telltale signs which hinted at evasion, but nothing of outright fiction. She was giving the impression of being mystified by it all. I noticed that she'd abandoned her proclivity to overstate her opinions, which hinted at a major shift in her attitudes.

'Well, what about this morning, then? Did they tail you?'

'You mean when I came for you? No.'

'Was the taxi driver okay?'

'He must've been. I thumbed him down in central London. I know he ran off, but that was nothing to do with the Hets.'

But that was a lot to believe. No casual driver would have remained outside my flat door while she fetched me. Despite her comments, the driver had been a pro and he'd been shrewd enough to get away before the trouble started. I wondered what was in the file and decided it was best if I didn't know.

'I don't understand this.'

'Neither do I. What happens now? Will the cops do the Armed Response thing and isolate this place for hours? We could be stuck here for a day.'

'They've got a carload of Hets. They might move in right away.'

'Right, better hurry. That floor will have to be swept again. I'll do it.'

25

In fact, I discovered that the room had several possible hiding places. The most promising was two ventilation channels (it had apparently once been a boiler room), under the ceiling which went back for some distance. On the debit side, they were little more than a foot high, but we could tolerate that. Helpfully, they'd been fitted with grilles which were lying on the openings. Someone had knocked them flat, possibly because the room had become too smoky. Once in the recess with the grille up, we would be well hidden. The cops would have to force them before they discovered us. Of course there were minor difficulties. The recesses were both at ceiling level and there were no step ladders, but I could lift Jane up to the left one and then climb into mine via the adjacent wall on the other side of the room. I'd have to switch the light off before I went to my own place and that would involve some difficulty, though Jane's lighter would provide enough light to get me into my hiding place. We had brushed the floor twice and our prints were no longer visible. However, the very fact that the floor had been swept might be deemed suspicious. We'd have to hope they wouldn't look too carefully.

For a long hour we stayed near the door and heard nothing. Searches usually came at the tail-end of an incident and were often conducted by a specialist team who hadn't been involved in the earlier stages. So we delayed going to ground, as it would be an endurance test to be confined in so small a space.

'This thing escalated,' I said, 'when you moved to a safe house. Up until then they were only mildly interested in you. The safe house let them know you're valuable.'

'And how would they know about the safe house?'

'Because you disappeared. It was a major change to your lifestyle, something that was guaranteed to interest them. They were watching you all along.'

'You could be right.'

'That means they probably saw George arrive with the gun,

too. The plotters have been rumbled.'

She made no reply.

Time passed slowly, and although there was utter silence outside, it seemed best to go to ground. So far as we knew, no further shots had been fired, no copter had landed and there had been no police sirens or shouted commands. It might almost have been an ordinary Sunday morning. Yet there were probably a hundred police in hand. The car park would be full of their vehicles. I imagined that several personnel carriers, each containing at least twenty cops would be waiting in the background while a quick assessment was made of the situation. Almost certainly a specialist team was checking the Towers and getting a lot of hassle from its residents. No doubt they'd be examining the bullet holes in the first floor windows and taking statements. The emergency would be difficult to understand. Gunfire from the Tower and gunfire from the car park, but what was it all about? The whole thing had fizzled into nothing and nobody had been hurt, so it didn't look like gang warfare. According to the caretaker, a carload of Hets had been captured, but they were unlikely to be helpful. Of course they'd be in possession of unlicensed guns, which was guaranteed to get the low ranking cops excited. What their bosses would make of it was another matter. Eventually, someone would crack and they'd know the truth. Ultimately their enquiries would focus on Jane. The sabotaged lift would be notice, as would Jane's reinforced door and the fact that she'd been missing for a day. All that meant it would be a long time before they got down to searching the outbuildings. That was a bad thing. The greater the delay the more restless we would become, and the more easily we could be captured.

I got Jane and the shopping bag into her recess and then switched off the light. It would have been nice to break the bulb so that the searchers would have to rely on their torches but I had no step ladder to reach it. Anyway, that might be counterproductive. If they fetched a step ladder to replace the bulb, they might use it to check the ventilation ducts too, and that would be the end of it all. It took me three tries before I got in and only after I'd scratched my shin on the rough edges.

'You alright?' asked Jane.

'Yes. Put up your grille and we'll stay here forever.'

'Okay – maintain silence from now.'

I was not claustrophobic, but I hated a restricted space with no rear exit. Perhaps I was paranoid, but I felt it was nice to have a handy escape route, and now there was none. The vent was dusty, though I was lying on the long coat, which I had taken from the shopping bag, and had some protection from the cold concrete. I lay face down, finding it difficult to move my shoulders. It was easy to bang my head on the ceiling and my feet were uncomfortable. It was like lying in the barrel of a cannon. Yet it had to be endured, and these complaints were mere trivialities. The real fun would start if Harry got his hands on us.

I must have fallen asleep out of sheer boredom when I heard voices outside. A group of people were talking. They didn't sound very interested in each other or anything else either. I shook myself awake. I had pins and needles in both arms and my feet were stiff.

'Watch!' said Jane warningly. Perhaps I'd been snoring.

A key turned in the lock and the door opened to reveal three men and two women in police uniforms. After the darkness, the daylight was bright and I had to close my eyes for a bit. The light went on, then they came in and closed the door with a bang.

'More junk,' said one of the men in a disgusted voice. All five of them gathered round the office tables. The smaller woman sat on a chair, but seeing the dust everywhere she stood up and began to shake the marks from her uniform.

'That chair's five hundred quid,' said the biggest man, grudgingly.

'Everywhere you go it's money. And it's never used, either.'

'Offer the Caretaker a tenner to put it in your car,' said one of the men.

'No, he's straight,' said the first speaker. He'd seen a lot. 'That kind of guy could report you.'

The chair was a swivel one. Someone swung it round and let it spin.

'That's not five hundred,' said the girl who'd sat on it. 'That's designer stuff, best leather. It would probably be lovely if you got the dust off it. It'd be a thousand, maybe more.'

'Well we're not here for the furniture,' said the other woman. I thought that she was the sergeant. 'Everything okay?'

They looked round the room in silence.

'The only thing's these vents,' said the smaller man.

I held my breath as all five looked at me.

'And how did they get into them?' the sergeant said, bored and disinterested.

The man walked up, saw my foothold in the wall and appeared in front of me, striking the vent with his fist before falling back to the floor with a yelp.

'Are you alright?' asked the sergeant, without sympathy.

'It's my knee –'

'Well, you should know better by this time. Come on, before you break your bloody neck.'

One of them opened the filing cabinet and shook her head while someone else looked in the desk.

'Nothing.'

'No surprise there,' said the sergeant. 'Well, we'd better get back to the boss. I hate these bloody hoods.'

Hoods, did she say hoods? Were the Hets running the show? Surely the cops weren't openly consorting with hoods? Or perhaps Harry's head of security had thoughtfully sent someone round to advise. That meant we would still be in danger, even after the last cop had gone home. The Hets had watched Jane's flat when she'd gone to a safe house. After the recent shenanigans they'd certainly watch Nelson Towers. Had we endured this long wait only to find ourselves back at square one?

The police left the room in single file. The younger woman looked round at the leather chair before the door closed with a bang.

There was a sound from Jane's grille.

'Stay,' I said.

That was how you got caught, leaving your refuge too soon. They could be back for a lot of reasons. The statistical chances of catching someone on a surprise return were high, and apparently there were hoods about who might want to confirm their findings. And the girl had liked the chair. Yes, we had a lot to lose if we relaxed our guard.

26

An hour must have passed before we spoke and when we did it was in whispers. By now it had to be dark outside. Most of the cops would probably have gone, though the Hets would no doubt be lurking nearby. But the caretaker hadn't come with the all clear and that was worrying.

But it was time to go. I was feeling feeble, weakened by my diet. Neither Jane or I had benefited from our incarceration. Our limbs were sore and if we waited too long we'd only get weaker.

My grille wouldn't open. The idiot policeman had jammed it into the duct and I couldn't pull it in. That left me with no alternative but to force it outward, risking it falling on to the concrete floor. The thing had jammed so tightly that I had to use a lot of force. I banged my fist against it until there was movement. Then it jammed again. More punches, but it still refused to budge. Eventually I hit it hard and it fell out. My arms were constricted by the width of the vent and I couldn't catch it in time. It fell on to the floor with a crash that seemed deafening.

'Don't move,' I said.

We waited for at least fifteen minutes. The room was in total darkness. Then I began to wriggle out. When my head and shoulders were free, I turned upwards, facing the ceiling, and somehow got my feet out without falling. Then I dropped on to the floor, so stiff that I nearly injured myself.

'Are you alright?' asked Jane, worried at the sound of activity.

'Give me a light.'

After a few seconds the lighter shed some welcome illumination on the room. I switched on the light, took a non-swivelling chair and stood on it while I got Jane extricated. No easy matter, but at least the grille didn't fall. Then we got out the shopping bag with its rattling guns.

'What are we going to do now?'

'Run for it. Better watch ourselves, though. There could be

more Hets about than ever.'

'Perhaps that's why Fred's stayed away.'

'I'll leave his hundred on that stove.'

It was essential to keep to out part of the deal. It would stop the other fellow squealing.

Was there a heavy waiting outside? That's what made the Hets so difficult to deal with. It was possible to predict the cops with some accuracy, but the enemy thought laterally and had taken me by surprise too often. It would be stupid to walk into the arms of the Hets. I feared that they'd have the whole place ring fenced by now.

'The door doesn't squeak. I'll open it.'

There was artificial light seeping under the door, indicating that the big world was still out there. I opened it by an inch. Cars were hooting, people were talking and planes were flying.

Jane said: 'On you go.'

I opened the door a few inches. Outside, it was dark, though lights were shining on the precinct which seemed deserted. There had been some rain. Our field of view was limited and the shadows might conceal an observer.

'Wider.'

With the door wide open, I risked putting my head out, hoping there wasn't a Het watching from the far side. But everything seemed calm, with no one in sight. Jane joined me and we peered into the shadows for one long minute. At this late stage, a mistake would be fatal.

'Grab your things and go.'

Jane went out with her shopping bag, staying close to the wall while I closed the door. Our bridges were burned. We couldn't return without the caretaker's key and it would have been insane to leave the door open. The precinct was illuminated by a series of big lights which lit the entire area as if it were day. Any observer would be able to spot us from a long distance. We adopted a regulation pace, moving purposely, but not fast, and trying to appear as calm as possible. Somewhere in the background, kids were playing football, but that didn't mean that things had definitely returned to normal. We walked against the side of the building, where we'd be unseen from the tower block and shortly we were masked by an army of wheelie bins to the north side where the footpath extended towards the canal.

The precinct was low-set and it was impossible to see beyond the immediate area. Ahead of us the path rose up the embankment into the open. This was the bad bit, where we'd be exposed to the world. Not speaking, we walked on, gradually emerging, to see a big heavy man with a baseball cap about a hundred metres away, barely visible in the darkness. His clothes were soaked, he face was glum and he was bored out of his mind – fortuitously, or he might have noticed us as we shrank into the background. This was the idiot who'd been staring at the copter early in the day. In near despair, we retreated to the wheelie bins.

'What do we do?' Jane said.

But there was hope. I'm an old hand and lighting's one thing I know about.

'Ten minutes. I'll fuse the lights.'

There are several ways to do it and I know them all. They'd be on a ring circuit and it would be easy to blow the entire array. My Swiss army knife was not ideal, but it was a good one and it would do the job.

'I'll scout around,' she said.

I nodded. Better to have Jane on the prowl, than leaning over my shoulder finding fault with my work. Scouting was her strong point. She'd move quietly, she was dressed in black and she'd merge with the background. Also, she might be able to see what the Hets were up to.

I found a big light surrounded by wheelie bins which would shelter me from prying eyes and I worked on it. Within ten seconds I had the metal cover open, placing it gently on the surface as I bent to study the interior wiring. An inner plate with five cross-head screws had to be removed to reveal the actual wiring. I encountered my first problem. It was in shadow and the colour coding was difficult to see. The whole thing would have been simple enough if only the colours had been more decisive. Eventually I worked it out and wrapped my handkerchief around the knife (which would now be live) to disconnect the power. It had been crimped on to a connector and there was a high voltage present. The light above me went out, though the rest were unaffected. Then a voice said:

'What you doin', mister?'

'You again?' I said without turning, recognising the voice. 'Shouldn't you be in your taxi, Jek?'

'I more than a taxi driver, mister. Turn round.'

It was the little man who'd driven Andy's killer, crouching among the wheelie bins. He was dressed in dark tight-fitting clothes and aiming a gun at me. There was a look of terrible triumph on his face.

I said: 'It's nice to see old friends again.'

'I not your friend, mister. I'm your enemy.'

'Where did you come from?' I said. 'I didn't hear you coming.'

'I was scouting about, mister.'

I said: 'Put that gun away.'

'No, mister, I won't, mister. You gave me worst day in my life. I thought I was dead. Now it's your turn.' He'd started speaking quietly but his voice was becoming louder. Anybody in the precinct would hear him. Soon the big heavy on the lawn would come to investigate.

'Oh, come on, I let you go.'

'You think I'm a nobody, a fool. I hate you.'

A bad situation was getting worse.

'I can give you money,' I said. 'We can do a deal –'

'I don't do deals with scum, mister!'

And he lashed at me with the gun, hitting my face with a blow that knocked my head back and dazed me for a moment. Various things seemed to be happening. He was leaning forward to see what damage he'd done to me and I glimpsed Jane behind him swinging a heavy object. There was a thump and he fell to the ground. Quick as a flash, Jane reached down and got the gun.

'Thanks – search him.'

I tried to move and half fell. It was becoming obvious that diets and violence don't mix. My face was wet, there was a fair amount of blood and my nerves were tense.

'Are you alright?'

Jane began to search Jek. I put my handkerchief to my face and watched Jane find an H&K in his holster and a knife in his belt. Then she took a wad of notes from his inside pocket. All of these were flung into the shopping bag.

'What happens now?' she said. 'Can you go? Are you alright?'

Of course I was alright. I was an old soldier. I took the pen from my pocket and looked for the live wire again. Using the pen's plastic body, I pushed the wire across until it touched the negative. There was a bang, the half-melted pen flew out of my hand and all the lights went out. The darkness was lovely.

'Come on.'

I got to my feet, holding the handkerchief against my face and we began to jog. In the dark it was impossible to see where the heavy was. I let Jane lead. Her eyes were better than mine and she didn't have a wound on her face. I was stumbling and she knew the area best. We ran across grass, keeping clear of the footpath where the heavy was most likely to be. At one point we passed a man coming in the opposite direction but he ignored us. Then we were under a bridge – the canal? Shortly we were in a new locality, with street lights and honest people about. Out of breath, we slowed to a walk and turned a corner to see a bus about to leave. Jane ran ahead and we got on board. The driver gave me a dirty look, no doubt thinking I was a drunk. The back seat was empty. Jane looked at my wound and said something about getting it attended to. I kept the handkerchief to my face and tried to look bored.

'Is it sore?'

People always asked that question. But I couldn't say whether it was sore or not. How do you quantify pain? Certainly I was uncommonly glad to be free of our recent problems. My heart sang to be away from the Hets.

In due course, we reached a high street and disembarked. Jane got a taxi to take us to a clinic, an expensive place often used by the Department, where they make a show of taking your name and address and medical history. The doctor seemed very competent. She put seven stitches into my face and though that was less pleasant I wasn't inclined to complain. Jane paid in cash, got another taxi and had me delivered to my safe house. Fortunately, we'd remembered to remove my shoulder holster with its H&K before going into the clinic. It was quite a thought that Jane had sat in the waiting room with enough guns in her bag to start a war. When we arrived at the flat, she was all set for coming up with me but I refused. Worse things had happened to me. A good night's sleep was all I needed. And I didn't want Jane around in case something else went wrong.

27

Five minutes after being deposited at the flat, I got into bed. It was a comfortable one and was most inviting. I couldn't believe how much I needed a long rest. The activities of the day had been dreadful. It was difficult to believe I'd survived, and now all I wanted to do was rest. In the back of my mind, I was mulling over the prospect of leaving the plotters forever and retiring to a peaceful shore on the other side of the planet. Mat Hill was getting too old for the fray.

Then the doorbell went.

I stared at the intercom in fury. Had Jane had come back, walking into my life as though she owned me, forcing me yet again into another crazy situation that would do no good? I did the sensible thing and ignored it.

Then it went again and this time it was continuous.

'Hello,' I said, reaching for the intercom.

'Let me in,' came the sharp voice of General Douglas and he sounded as if he were disgusted with me. Plainly my problems for the day were far from over.

Wearily, I touched the button, put on a house coat that had been in the wardrobe and opened the door in time to see the General step out the lift, immaculate in a light overcoat and soft hat with an Eton tie just visible. But there was a frown on his face and his silver moustache was bristling with anger. He marched into the flat without acknowledging me.

'Where were you today?' he said, swinging round as soon as the door was closed. Throughout my life I had dealt with angry officers and they had never bothered me. All I needed do was say as little as possible and stick to the rules.

'On an assignment.'

'Your orders are to write a report.'

'I have a duty to brother officers in an emergency.'

He looked at me with narrowed eyes, frowned, then took a seat. I remained standing. He must have seen the bandage on my face, he couldn't miss it, but we lived in a man's world where such trivialities are ignored.

'Tell me.'

I was weary and couldn't bear to relive the day's disasters, but the General had to be obeyed. I recited a summary of events, omitting nothing about the Hets, during which he gradually relaxed. He was even nodding by the time I'd finished.

'So it was you at Nelson Towers. I might have known. Is your face bad?'

'A few stitches. I've seen worse.'

'You're walking wounded until that heals. It'll a bit obvious among the unwashed.'

'Nothing I could do about it.'

'You'll have to see a quack again, that's obvious. We'll provide one. Whatever you do, don't go back to that clinic. Did they take your details?'

'Jane gave false ones. They weren't bothered. She paid cash.'

'Did she, by Jove? Someone will be round to ask questions. It's too well known. And that was a big thing. Sit down man, relax. I won't keep you.'

With some reluctance, I took a chair and was surprised at how uptight I was. My muscles were so tense that it was difficult to move. I also had a sense of nausea, perhaps because of the diet or because of the sheer strain of surviving.

'Why did you go to Nelson Towers?'

'You'll have to ask Jane. She declared the emergency.'

'Are you still on that stupid diet?'

'Technically no. Today's starvation was enforced.'

He touched his nose, frowned at the floor and then chuckled.

'This Nelson Towers thing's been big. Another nail in Harry's coffin. Seven of his men have been caught with guns –'

'But they aren't his men.'

'Well, not officially, but the connection is known. He was directing them. They've even recorded a phone call from him. He's in trouble.'

'He'll get out of it.'

'We'll see.'

George might have been a smart man, but I couldn't

understand his tendency to think that Harry was finished or even in trouble. The facts spoke for themselves. Harry Hetland had been in difficulties on countless occasions and had never once looked back. In reality, twenty years had passed since he'd been convicted of a crime. Now his influence had grown and he'd be a match for any prosecutor in town. Also, he'd become a very wealthy man who could bribe his way out of anything. To my mind, Nelson Towers was a minor problem. Harry was a proven survivor.

George sat back and began to talk. Usually he wouldn't discuss Operation Garden, but for a change he was downright garrulous. Of course, it had to be on a night I wanted to relax.

'This business has been all over the news. It happened at the wrong time and must have put him in a spot of difficulty. We know he's tried to pressurise the police, and it hasn't worked. He's not directly involved, of course, but any in-depth look will expose him to the four winds. It could stop him running for the top. If he can't keep it bottled then he could even land in jail, which would suit us just fine and dandy. But the top cops are in his grasp, so maybe he can swing it. Mind you, they loathe him too, we've always known that. It's touch and go. This is the kind of thing that could do him down –'

'They'll get a bullet if they waver.'

'To an extent. But down the ranks there are plenty of officers who hate his guts. Shooting their boss might be a bad career move for Harry. The lesser ranks have got scores to settle. Some of them would do anything to bring him down. He's in trouble. That car load of bodyguards were armed, and they're all in custody. Even worse for Harry, two of them are helping the police about another murder.'

I nodded, not surprised. The Hets had shown no subtlety. They'd acted like a secondary police presence. And the remarks made by the female sergeant, which I'd overheard, implied that the cops at Nelson Towers had been cooperating with them. But Harry's head was far too cool to panic over a triviality like Nelson Towers.

'I'll bet none are charged.'

'Well, as I understand it, their guns have been confiscated.

Their existence can't be denied, so they might *have* to be charged. The trouble is that they don't have you lot, though they can work out your identity for themselves. Jane's flat is a giveaway. They'll know who she is and they'll get your description too. Incidentally, Herb's been very quiet at the old town. Nothing much happening or going to happen. Just what we expected; shortly it'll be run down –'

'And poor old Andy's death will be forgotten.'

'Exactly – just another casualty who didn't need to be shot. That's what started it all. They erred. The *threat* of the bullet was all that was needed. It was about that safe, of course. The damn thing was that they could have captured him and got the safe without any bother. Now it's all gone wrong, and they don't have the safe either.'

'Have you got it open yet?'

'We're working on that,' said George, clamming up. Plainly he didn't want to discuss it. 'Now, you've got to keep your head down. You've stirred up the hornet's nest. Both Harry and the cops are on your trail. Better not to leave the house.'

'What if Jane arrives with more trouble?'

'I'll look into that. We'll do your shopping for you. Make a list of everything you'll need. A Mr Cordiner, not one of us, will call on you tomorrow at ten. You'll give him the list and it'll be delivered before noon. Don't let him in here. Keep him at the door and don't say one unnecessary word. Take the stuff, say thanks, nothing more. Understand?'

'Okay.'

'Tomorrow you're going to work on your report. You've had several close calls. By now, you must know more about Harry than anyone alive. Make a note of everything, including the trivia. It's amazing what you can learn from it. Things are urgent and we can't let him get away this time. You've got to work. Are you up to it alright?'

'A good night's rest and I'll be fine.'

28

It was nine in the morning. A week had passed and I'd almost completed a report that might just please the plotters, though it underscored the difficulties in the best military jargon. George had sent a doctor to treat my wounds and shortly afterwards I'd been supplied with a false beard to hide the damage. I could go out without drawing attention to myself.

When the doorbell went I couldn't believe it. Jane was in my flat with yet another emergency.

'Get your things,' she said when I'd closed the door. 'They've got George.'

She was dressed in a black trouser suit and her hair was actually a neutral shade for once. There was a whiff of panic in the air.

That was what I couldn't stand about Operation Garden. Neither Sir Lance or George seemed to bother about security, and it was a dead certainty that Harry knew all about them. Underneath their fancy talk was laxness, a total lack of discipline that made a mockery of their aims. There had been no briefings for this kind of thing, or any other emergency for that matter, and now it seemed that we were leaderless.

'How do you know?' I asked, not moving, irritated that she was ordering me about again.

'Sir Lance. They grabbed him this morning at seven. Come on!'

This was all the proof I needed that, despite her insistence to the contrary, Jane was more deeply involved in the plot than I was.

'How did *he* know?'

'One of his servants phoned. Come on, we can't spend all day talking! We'll go to George's right away. I've got a taxi waiting at the door. Better take a weapon.'

Yes, that seemed like a necessity. Despite my reluctance, an emergency was an emergency and I'd have to respond to it, a minute later we were hurtling down the stairs and out to the taxi which drove off immediately.

General George Douglas owned a house with three floors in central London. It was a terraced building on a narrow street of houses. It was an olde worlde area, and it wasn't possible to park in the street, though I noticed that George had underground parking. The building itself seemed utterly calm. There wasn't the slightest sign of an emergency. As the taxi drew to a stop I looked around, but saw no obvious watchers or anyone resembling a Het. At the opposite end of the street, another taxi was disgorging a group of girls who looked as though they'd been out dancing all night. It was typical of Jane, who'd claimed to know no more than me, that she knew George's address and was able to direct our driver to the exact house.

I waited until she'd paid the fare before getting out, having no intention of making a target of myself. Just about anybody in the street could photograph us, and although I was wearing my false beard, I didn't fancy being on anyone else's data bank. Harry would certainly have been able to predict our arrival, and it was all too likely that he would have an observer on hand. In fact it would have been careless of him to do otherwise. He would be able to get a good view of the team and see what a sorry lot we were.

We shouldn't have been visiting his house at all. Sir Lance should have come to mine or Jane's safe house for a conference, but naturally the great plotter hadn't thought of it.

Presumably the alarm had been raised by George's servants and it seemed best to keep out of their way. If things went wrong, and that was all-too likely, they could be dangerous witnesses and the time had come for a little damage-limitation, though perhaps it was too late for that. Since the servants had approached Sir Lance rather than the cops, they must have been aware that something was going on. Theoretically they were on our side, but that was no reason why they should be placed in a position to identify us.

As it happened, the door was opened by Sir Lance himself, who seemed his usual calm self. We went into a brown varnished hallway. There was no one else in sight.

'This way,' he said, indicating a doorway. I stood back to let Jane lead the way into a big front room. It was cold and looked as though it hadn't been changed since the Victorian times. There was a lot of bric-a-brac which confirmed that George was a rich man. Sir Lance was dressed in a pin-striped suit which must have been twenty years old, and seemed totally unbothered by the events. He was brushing some cigar ash from his lapel when he closed the door.

Jane said: 'What happened, Sir Lance?' I noticed that she addressed him in the obsequious tones she used for George.

We were standing in the middle of the room. There was an unlit chandelier above our heads. The curtains at the front window were open to the street and anyone could have seen us.

'Shouldn't we close the curtains?' I asked. 'Or use another room?'

'Oh,' said Sir Lance, who hates cloak and dagger stuff, 'petty precautions. I can't be bothered with that kind of thing. Take a seat. No one can see in.'

Like two erring pupils visiting the headmaster, Jane and I sat down on a cold sofa while Sir Lance took a seat opposite us.

'The doorbell went at five to seven this morning. George's man answered and four big men pushed their way in. They went straight to the breakfast room and ordered him to come with them. He wasn't allowed to take his coat or hat. They had two taxis at the door with their engines running and he hasn't been seen since.'

So they'd been well briefed. They knew where the breakfast room was; they'd seized their man and departed. Hetland's organisation was superior to the plotters alright.

'What did they say?' I said. 'Did George know them?'

'As far as I know, nothing was said. I don't know if he knew them.'

'Have you got the police?'

Sir Lance shifted and looked past me.

'George wouldn't want that. There's not a lot they can do. And we wouldn't want them looking too closely at things in his background, would we?'

'For heaven's sake, his life's at risk,' I exploded. 'You've got to get them.'

But Sir Lance was unflappable.

'A high level decision's been taken. That's the way George wants it. He gave me explicit instructions.'

This kind of thinking wasn't uncommon in kidnaps and it was almost always wrong. By the time the enemy had captured the leading player, the game had ground to a halt even if the other players weren't yet aware of it. But I was the lowest rank present. What could I do?

'Where were you?' I said.

'The Towers. I've only just arrived.'

So he must have phoned Jane before he left. I hoped he hadn't used an open line. If Harry knew enough to kidnap our leading player, it was a fair bet that he had someone listening to the phones. That meant they would probably be able to find Jane's safe house.

'Anything odd in the last few days? Funny phone calls?'

Sir Lance raised his hand to stop me.

'Leave that, Mat. I haven't done any questioning yet. Best if the servants don't see either of you. I'd like to keep you both out of this.'

It was a bit late for that. Obviously Harry knew everything about our pitiful little group and I didn't doubt that he had all the plotter's secrets at his fingertips.

'What do you want us to do?' asked Jane, giving me an angry glance then smiling sweetly at the great man.

Sir Lance reached over and removed a pocket-sized device from the table which looked like an electronic compass.

'George was aware that he might be kidnapped. He's got a ring which transmits his location. That's the Finder. See if you can get him.'

'That's got to go to the police,' I growled. 'The two of us are no match for the Hets. George's life is on the line.'

'Now steady on, Mat,' Sir Lance said, taking out his snuff box. 'We've got to be careful with the police. Some of them are in Harry's pay. And they'll wonder why George should have a thing like that. It looks like he expected to be kidnapped. We don't want any awkward questions. Anyway, Harry would know about it in ten minutes. They might cut George's finger off and we'd be back to where we started. '

This might have made sense to Sir Lance, sitting in a comfortable drawing room, but I knew what it was like to be kidnapped. His attitude was nothing less than a gift to the kidnappers. To put the General's survival in our hands was ridiculous. If the cops were all that untrustworthy (and surely they weren't all that bad) it could be given to the army. George was a General, after all and they were entirely independent.

'It isn't reading anything,' said Jane.

'Oh, perhaps he's out of range. Anywhere within a kilometre and you'll get a signal.'

Arithmetic had never been my strong point, but in a city the size of London (and there was no certainty George was even in London) that made the odds about one hundred to one. Not very good. Ideally, the device should be taken up in a copter until a hot signal registered.

I said something about this, but naturally it was dismissed.

'We could try some of the Hets' strongholds,' said Jane, ignoring the fact that we didn't know where any of them were.

'Yes. Well, I'll leave that up to you. With your experience, you have an advantage over me. I'll back you to the hilt. Use your ingenuity and you won't go wrong. Don't take risks. It's best not to phone me. Here's some money. I'll have to go. Do your best, will you?' he said, handing what looked like a grand to Jane.

A minute later we were out in the street and the big door closed behind us.

'You're getting old and grumpy,' she said, turning to me 'That was embarrassing. He's an old man and you were quite rude to him. Oh, there's a taxi.'

So George's life was at stake, but it was my manners that were at fault.

'Leave it! An empty taxi outside George's house? Have you lost your marbles?'

She saw my point immediately, though she wasn't pleased. She walked to the end of the street in a huff, with me following in her wake. There were several people about, though none who looked like observers. Perhaps the Hets weren't taking us too seriously. They were on a winning streak, after all. The taxi drove past, its driver ignoring us.

'Where are we going?' Jane asked, turning to me as though I had a plan. What a question! It was clearly impossible for two people to search a city the size of London and there was no certainty that George was even there. Nor had I any faith in the Finder. There would probably be no signal if the hostage was in a basement, which seemed likely. Harry Hetland was not accident prone. He limited his risks. George had thought that he was desperate, but I wasn't so sure about that. Big Andy had probably been shot as a warning to the gang who held the safe. And now they'd kidnapped George, who had it in his possession. This was a serious situation.

'Somewhere near Nelson Towers,' I muttered.

This was a gut reaction, because Nelson Towers was a place we knew the Hets had been recently. They'd summoned quick reinforcements, which might mean they had a presence nearby.

'We could take the tube –'

'Not on your life! A taxi, but not that one. You might get a reading.'

She nodded, displeased again. Ten minutes later, we found a taxi being driven by a Jamaican girl, and were on our way. Because of the Hets' presence, neither of us had any wish to approach Nelson Towers, yet here we were, driving into the area looking for one of their field offices. What we were going to do if we got a positive signal was another thing altogether. No doubt Sir Lance would leave that up to us.

'This is ridiculous,' I said. 'Don't you get it? They'll torture George until he tells them where the safe is. There's nothing we can do about it. They'll be on full alert. And how can we fight them? They're winning hands down. They've got complete knowledge of the group, they're heavily armed and they've just kidnapped the boss. They've known about him all along. What else do they know –?'

'Leave that, we've got a job to do,' said Jane, waving her hand to dismiss my point. As always, the only item on her agenda was the current job. Nothing else mattered. She'd no wish to hear my views. As far as she was concerned, all we had to do was find the General. Simple.

'Kidnapping the General!' I said. 'The whole thing's been reduced to a farce.'

'George and Lance are old men with no experience of this. They've been brought up to believe that their servants will give them all the protection they need.'

'Sir Lance doesn't even have any servants, well full-time ones.'

'Maybe not, but even you wouldn't expect a security guard at his door.'

No, but I'd expect him to show a little more sense.

The taxi lurched to the right and soon we were within sight of Nelson Towers.

'We're blown,' I said, speaking calmly in the hope that she would listen. 'The plotters have been infiltrated. By rights, Hetland shouldn't know who George is. When Sir Lance took me to the Commons, Harry Hetland himself came up to speak to me, Harry Hetland. He might have even wondered if I was the hit man. I reckon we should resign.'

She shrugged in contempt.

'After we find George.'

'Yes, after we locate George. If we locate George. If he's still alive when we locate him. That's provided we're alive too. Look at the influence Sir Lance has. He could go to the Home Office or the Army and get something done about it, but no, he's put it on our lap.'

'You're not running this. You don't know the facts.'

'No, and the ones I do know are frightful –'

'Is this where you want?' asked the driver, looking round. We'd been speaking quietly to prevent being overheard and hadn't been watching our progress. Already we were in the car park of Nelson Tower. A place with unhappy memories.

Jane looked around in some surprise and shrank into the seat. Clearly the device was reading nothing.

'No, sorry, take us to –'

She looked at me, unable to remember any other venue. Neither could I, but then Jane said something about another tower about a mile away. The taxi drove through the car park and sped off. It had been more than a week since the fiasco but they might still be watching and we might well have passed an observer, though I had seen no one. But of course, I'd seen none on our previous visit either.

'Any readings on that thing?'

'No, nothing.'

'The driver's going to think it's odd, driving in and out of tower blocks. We'd better give her an explanation of some kind.'

'Yes, I'll say something,' she said, leaning over to say that we were Social Workers searching for a missing patient.

Of course there was no reading when we reached the next venue. We began a long circuitous tour that took us through housing centres, industrial estates and office blocks as well as a score of odd places, including the docks. In fact, most of the time we were stopped by traffic lights and snarl-ups. This was a tour of the rough areas and some of them were like third world sites.

'We don't even know if that thing's working,' I complained. 'Who set it up? Has it been tested?'

'We've got to keep trying. It wouldn't be fair to walk out on George.'

Slowly, the taxi turned into an area of warehouses that I'd never known existed. Some of them were derelict and some were used for storage with trucks being unloaded by fork lifts. The street was a long one, deserted in places. Finally we ended in a traffic jam, where a group of workmen were digging up the road.

'Why are we here?' I said. 'There's nothing to stop them taking him to a fancy hotel. Maybe Harry's got a house in Mayfair.'

'We'll just have to keep trying.'

'They could have had him on a plane by eight. Harry's got an airline.'

'I know.'

After two hours, our driver objected and we found ourselves on the pavement in a godforsaken part of the city, after Jane had handed over a fortune in notes.

'What do we do now?' she asked. 'Go back to Sir Lance?'

'We might as well finish this section first.'

Then we were in another taxi, continuing the endless search. This time we drove with the window open, in case the metal body of the taxi was masking the signal. We were losing track and twice duplicated areas we'd been in before.

'This is pointless,' I said. 'We can't outguess Harry Hetland without more details. And we won't get those. I say we go back to Sir Lance.'

'I think so too.'

The taxi turned into a new locality and we leaned forward to look at yet another anonymous tower block, when Jane said:

'I've got a reading.'

29

On the Finder's screen, an arrow indicated a sharp right turn while the text at the top flashed 'out of range'. I looked in the direction of the arrow and tried to remember what lay there. But that was too simplistic. The range of the device was supposedly one kilometre, but that didn't mean that George was a kilometre away. He could be nearby in a basement or any one of a dozen warehouses. It might be a mistake to drive half a mile to the right.

'Should we stop the taxi and get out?' asked Jane, all agitated.

We looked at each other. Plainly we were entering enemy territory of one kind or another, with a probable Het presence. Standing on the pavement looking at the Finder didn't sound like a healthy prospect.

'Take the right. Then we get out.'

Jane leaned forward to give the instructions and the taxi did a right turn on to a deserted street crammed with parked cars. We got out and jogged in the required direction. It was a rundown area and not ideal. We risked being noticed long before we got to where the arrow was pointing. I also recalled that George had thought that the Hets might shoot me on sight.

'Are we still out of range?'

'No change,' she said, looking at the Finder in agitation. 'It's still flashing.' By this time we'd covered a fair distance. I shook my head in frustration. I had a deep distrust of those sort of things. We could be reading someone's burglar alarm, or the instrument could be malfunctioning.

'Not too fast,' said Jane. Perhaps we had been overdoing it. We were getting some curious looks from passers-by. We crossed a road and continued into a street with some shops and garages. Since it was fully a kilometre long, our quarry should have been within view, yet the screen still declared him out of range. A fair distance away, there was a junction with a busy road where the traffic was stopped in a typical London snarl-up. We were halfway there, when Jane looked at the Finder and said:

'It's moved.'

According to the display we were a lot closer to our target. The out of range text had gone but the arrow had turned almost ninety degrees.

'He must be in a car on that road,' Jane said. 'What are we going to do?'

So far as I could see, the only option was to let him go. Two pairs of feet are less than adequate when it came to catching up with a car. It was maddening to have achieved the near-impossible and now we were going to lose him again.

'A taxi?'

Perhaps we'd been too quick to leave our taxi, but it was too late to do anything about that. Besides, how would we get a taxi to follow a car? That sort of thing only happened in films, and we were dealing with the Hets. Taxi drivers are notorious for talking, too, and if anything went wrong that was one risk too far. I looked to the left. We were standing beside a garage which sold second hand cars. Jane turned too.

'We haven't got that kind of money.'

'They sell bikes too,' I said. 'Give me your grand. Walk to the end of the street. I'll join you.'

Without a word she handed me the bundle and walked off. Of course it was no longer a grand. A substantial sum had been paid for the taxis.

In the garage's forecourt there were several reasonably priced bikes, though they were of the boy racer variety and that wasn't what I wanted. My eye alighted on a conservative model which looked as though it had hardly exceeded sixty in its life, with a silent exhaust and comfortable-looking seats. It was cheap, too; the boy racers wouldn't be seen dead beside it. There were no pushy salesmen about so I walked into the garage to find a man glaring at me from under a car.

'I'll buy that bike if it works,' I said, pointing.

He put a spanner down and crawled out with bad grace . Perhaps he was fed up with tyre kickers, or just he was having a bad day. I suspected that the bike had been on sale for a long time and that there was a long list of non-buyers. He went into his office and returned with a key, which he inserted into the ignition. It started at the first turn and didn't make a lot of noise when I revved it. That suited me to the core. It would have been impossible to be discreet with a bike which made more noise than a volcano.

'Eight hundred,' I said. 'Write me a receipt, and I want two helmets.'

But nothing is ever easy. He held some of my notes to the light to see their watermark, and then he took his time to find the bike's log. I don't recall him uttering one word. A long time passed before I revved into the street to find Jane waiting impatiently beside the main road, which was jammed solid with short-tempered drivers.

'You took your time. He's almost out of range.'

But she put her helmet on and flung a leg over the machine without hesitation. We crossed the road at the first opportunity and began a gentle overtake of the stationary traffic, which extended into the far distance.

'It's getting stronger,' she said, and I hesitated, having no wish to be up against their rear bumper. Possibly they'd seen pictures of us. It was essential to be discreet, even while we were on a motor bike and wearing bike helmets.

Further ahead, we discovered that the traffic jam had been created by road works, and that the temporary lights had failed. There was some angry hooting. I looked along the line of vehicles to see two black people carriers, each containing several people, about three hundred metres ahead.

'That's them,' I said. 'The black cars—'

'Don't go nearer,' Jane shouted. 'They'll be watching.'

They certainly would.

With a bit of luck they wouldn't spot us at this distance, though they'd certainly be alert to a tail. Fortunately, there was a big truck partly obscuring us and a couple more bikes in the queue which would help confuse the issue.

Jane said: 'What do we do when they get there?'

There was no answer to that. Obviously they were moving George to a new address. As long as we could find it we would be in a strong position. Perhaps we could give the address to Sir

Lance, or possibly we could invent an emergency and have the police raid it. But the Hets didn't take chances. George was being escorted by at least one other car and there might be other security details nearby. It would be best to approach with an open mind and select the best option when the facts were known.

A patrol car arrived, approaching on the wrong side of the road. A constable got out and began to direct the traffic. That meant that this must have been deemed a serious situation. It was very seldom that the cops got out of their comfortable cars. Our lane started to move and I saw both black cars drive off. Then we were stopped to let the oncoming traffic through. I advanced to the front as Jane complained about losing the signal. Of course the road ahead would be clear. Once past the road works there would be little traffic to hold us back.

After an age, the cop waved us on and I purred along the road, careful not to go too fast. We had no insurance and it was essential to avoid the Hets' attention, but I didn't want to lose them either. We were on a main road which led through some prosperous areas. There were BMWs and Bentleys at the road side and some expensive shops to excite the interest of the passers -by.

'I've got a signal again. Keep going.'

We weren't in biker's clothing, but that wasn't an issue on this particular model, though it was something which might cause the Hets to look at us twice. I drove near the side of the road and a few cars flew by.

'Faster! Oh, it's going to the right,' exclaimed Jane.

But that wasn't good. It meant that George was being taken out of London. Once they were clear of the town, they could select a minor road and that would make it difficult, perhaps impossible, for us to follow them, an old trick. And there was the question of how many Het cars there were. We knew about the two people carriers, but there might be additional vehicles. Harry wouldn't want anything to go wrong at this stage and he'd good cause to be nervous.

We were approaching a major road junction where there was a queue of traffic, including buses, trucks and scores of private cars. The road to the right was one I knew well. It led to my home town. I edged towards the front.

'To the right here,' said Jane. 'Oh, they're out of range again. I've lost them.'

The lights turned green, the traffic moved and I swung on to the dual carriageway, which was busy. The traffic was slow and there was no sign of the black cars. I gave the bike a burst of power to find that it accelerated like an overladen bus.

'Anything?'

'No. Keep going.'

But the road was too busy. There must have been a hold up further into town, as both lanes were crowded with slow vehicles. As far as I could see, the two black cars were well on their way. I remembered about something that recent events had driven from my mind – fuel. It brings out the stingy side in a dealer. My apprehension was correct. The gauge was at zero.

'We're almost out of fuel,' I yelled.

'Shit.'

Of course I didn't know the vagaries of the gauge. There might be enough for sixty miles, or it might sputter to a stop in a minute. There was no point in stopping now. I recalled that there was a service station two miles ahead where George and I had had tea on our way to the safe house. I continued along the carriageway.

'Reading anything?'

'No, lost them.'

Two trucks were blocking us and we had to move at their speed until the way was clear again. When we reached the service station I swung in, filled the tank and paid the bill in cash, which lost us another three minutes. Then we were off again, but there was little hope of catching the people carriers. They would be miles ahead of us. I opened the bike to seventy but shortly had to reduce my speed to the pace of the rest of the traffic.

'You know where they're going, don't you?' Jane shouted above the noise and the wind blast.

'I think so.'

'The safe must still be there.'

'George said it had been moved.'

'Yes, but has it?'

I wasn't exactly happy with this turn of events. At home they'd been looking for me. It was probably just as dangerous as Nelson Towers, though perhaps my absence of more than a week had dulled it down a bit. Of course it gave me one advantage. I knew Dalespun Towers fairly well. I also knew where I'd put the safe. The Hets would need something more robust than people carriers to take it away. Heavy transport would be required, although Harry could probably arrange that with one phone call.

Near the town, we took a slip road from the dual carriageway on to the old road where we passed a roundabout. Quarter of a mile ahead I saw the walls and front lodge of Dalespun Towers, looking rather dull. I was moving at a more thoughtful speed.

'I've got a signal.'

Just then a passenger bus, bound for London, emerged on to our road and I reduced speed. I was in a biker's helmet, but somebody might recognise me and it would be a mistake to be seen near Dalespun Towers.

'Go in?' I said, and when she didn't answer I drove past the lodge at thirty mph with the Doberman barking at us. His master, old Walter, the sole remaining gardener, would be at home for lunch. I reduced the revs and drove up the tree-lined drive.

'They're here,' Jane said. 'I've got a strong reading. You can see their tracks.'

I'd seen them too and I wasn't entirely pleased with this turn of events. At the very least, there would be several armed Hets in the vicinity, and they wanted me dead. I had no intention of committing suicide. At the second last bend before the Towers, we saw the cars through the trees. There were two of them parked by the roadside. I switched off the bike, letting it coast on to the verge where I held it until Jane got off. I left it on its rests and took my helmet off – it might protect my head but it stifled your hearing, and that wouldn't be helpful. We were just out of sight of the cars, though they might have caught a glimpse of us. I got my gun out and we began to approach from the trees. Then we paused.

'See any of them?' I said in a whisper.

Jane had better eyesight than I had. She peered for some time.

'No. They must have taken him to the Towers.'

It looked as though they had approached on foot. The cars would have been too obvious. They'd probably found the safe already.

'Right, come on.'

But she hesitated: 'What are we going to do?'

'I don't know. Have a look.'

Then she put her hand on my arm as a warning.

'There's someone in the front car.'

In the rear window there was a shape which could have been a person. But after watching for a minute we saw no movement. It certainly didn't look like one of the Hets.

'It's alright, I think,' Jane said.

'Okay, let's go.'

There were trees on both sides of the road and we slipped across to the other side to make cautious progress under their shelter. The advantage of that was that we were in shadow and it wouldn't be easy for our quarry to see us. But there are pitfalls in every step. It was easy to stand on twigs, which made a lot of noise and were difficult to avoid.

We reached one of the cars and found it deserted. The engine was hot and there were several cans of coke on the back seat. We kept our heads well down and watched on all sides for movement. Birds were singing in the trees, making a lot of noise. Everything was deceptively calm.

'See anything?' Jane whispered.

'No. They'll be at the Towers now. Come on.'

We went to the leading car.

'It's George!' said Jane, after looking in the back window. And so it was. At first I thought he was dead, but he was just staring forwards without seeing us. His hands were tied. Jane tried to open the door and found it locked, as were all the doors. She rapped the window but the General just stared ahead.

'Drugged,' I said.

'We've got to get him out.'

We both turned to look in the direction of the Towers and saw no signs of activity.

'Okay,' I said. 'Got to smash a window. Anything else takes too long.'

'But the noise!'

'Nothing we can do about it. I'll get a boulder.'

It took a matter of moments to find a big stone. In the past, I've found there's no point in trying to do it quietly and anyway two or three quiet blows might attract more attention than a solid one. I stood back and smashed the rock through the driver's window at the first attempt. All the birds stopped singing and a flock of pigeons flew off. With the front door open I unlocked both back doors. There was a mobile phone on the dashboard, which I put it in my pocket. Jane was standing outside with her eyes trained on the road.

'Are you alright, George?' I spoke as though to a child. 'Out you come.'

But he looked at us without understanding. I remembered that his hands were tied and I cut the plastic strips which bound them. He had perfectly manicured fingers. He looked at me with no intelligence in his eyes, as though he were watching an incomprehensible play.

'Manhandle him out,' I said, angry at this new problem. 'Give me a hand.'

We turned him sideways and got his feet in the right direction, then I got behind and pushed until he was almost out. Next I went round and we got hold of his arms and forced him to his feet. He half fainted when we tried to make him stand. That would have been a disaster, as we might not have been able to get him upright again. With his arms around our necks we half-walked him to the bike, leaving the car doors open and looking back every two steps to see if the Hets were coming.

It took an age to reach the bike.

'Get him on it, don't let him fall,' she said. By this time George seemed to be coming round and was almost standing of his own volition. We got one leg over the bike and then he was seated. I got on board and we began an agonisingly slow journey George the front lodge, pushing the bike, Jane supporting him all the way. As soon as we starting moving, he'd fallen unconscious again, his head lying to the side.

Being unfamiliar with drugged Generals on motorbikes, the Doberman went into a frenzy as we approached. I rapped on old

Walter's window until he came to the door to look at us with expressionless eyes. He's a very calm old man, and because of my beard, he had to look twice before he recognised me.

'This is Sir Lance's best friend,' I said. 'We've got to help him.'

'Happen you want the quack?' Walter comes from the West Country and is difficult to follow. He might have said 'Do you want Doctor Dark?' There's a Doctor Dark in town.

'Just get him inside.'

With some difficulty, the three of us got him off the bike and made our way into the lodge, a sorry place with small rooms. I pushed the table back and we laid George on the floor, where Jane stuffed a jacket under his head. He'd seemed to be on the point of waking when we lifted him but now he'd returned to unconsciousness.

'Hide the bike,' she said, and I went out and moved it to the back of the lodge.

Inside, I found old Walter rubbing his hands anxiously and keeping as far away from Jane as possible. His house was a terrible mess. There were bottles all over the place and some dinner plates which looked as though they'd been lying on the floor for weeks. Presumably he thought she would object to his untidiness, but Jane was peculiarly tolerant of chaos. It was half civilised places like mine that she objected to.

'Phone the cops,' I said. 'It's got to be you, Jane. If they work out it's me or Walter they'll come in here. Dial 999, say you're the secretary of Dalespun Towers and that there are men ransacking the outbuildings. Put on a posh voice.'

'I'm no good at that.'

'Do it! Whatever you do, don't mention guns.'

'Okay.'

She reached for old Walter's phone, and though she wasn't a great actress she made a convincing enough job of it, saying that Dalespun Towers was being raided by robbers.

Shortly afterwards, two patrol cars with their sirens wailing drove past us. It looked like Adele was driving the second one. The General was snoring at our feet.

'Make some tea,' I said to Jane. She switched on the kettle

and started washing some cups. I looked down at the General and wondered if he was dying. The tea had been intended to revive him but it looked like he was in need of more serious attention. Old Walter was still rubbing his hands and watching us.

Then another patrol car with three cops on board went howling up the drive.

'George doesn't look good,' said Jane, looking at the patient.

'Is he bad? I said in an undertone. You weren't supposed to discuss a patient's welfare within their hearing, even if they were unconscious. Bad news from an incautious observer might cause a relapse.

'I'm no doctor. Better get him to the clinic.'

'He should be coming round by now.'

'They've overdosed him. He'll be out for a while. I hope he's alright. We need a car, or a van. Can you steal one of their people carriers?'

Old Walter looked up in surprise at the proposed theft. But he'd never talk. He has what are known as 'learning difficulties' and wouldn't be deemed a reliable witness.

'Not with the cops milling around, we can't. There's going to be trouble soon. They'll see that broken window, and the back door's wide open. They'll almost certainly call here when they come down the drive. We have to get out before that.'

'How?'

There were four of us in the room, but that didn't stop me from feeling lonely. Everything we'd done so far could be undone with the arrival of the police. Knowing the cops, they'd enjoy their visit to Dalespun. It would make a big change from the druggies in the council estates and there would be many interesting things to see. At the present moment, the leader of the Hets would be arguing his case but there was a limit to how long that would take or how successful it would be. Then they'd go to the people carriers and start noticing things.

At that moment a phone rang in my pocket 'I stole it from the car,' I said, taking it out. It was an expensive model and it took me a few seconds to find the right button.

'How's it going?' asked a very calm voice.

'Not too bad, thank you. Everything's under control.'

'Have you been successful?'

'There's been a little difficulty—'

'Ah now, I believe we're speaking at cross purposes. Or perhaps you are being evasive. What is your name?'

'Browne, with an e, Bob Browne.'

'Browne... Browne? Ah yes, Mr Browne. I thought we would speak again. Did you enjoy your visit to the Commons?'

'I did, and it was nice to meet you.'

'How gratifying. Could you elucidate as to why you are using this phone?'

'That's a long story, Mr Hetland. I can tell you that there are a lot of cops here, but I'm sure you wouldn't be interested in all those details.'

He gave a sigh.

'Oh, but I am, Mr Browne. But we'll have to leave that till later. May I suggest you keep the phone? An opportunity may arise to communicate on a future occasion.' It went dead.

I switched it off, suddenly drained of energy. Too many things were happening and it was difficult to keep track of them. Meanwhile, the General was lying on the floor, looking like death itself, and there was the question of what the police would do next. Any moment now a patrol car would pull up at the lodge.

'That was the devil himself,' I said by way of explanation.

Jane said: 'We have to get a van, quick!'

'I've got a —'

At that moment I heard the sound of a heavier vehicle. A big police van drove past the lodge with its blue light flashing.

'Did you see that?' said Jane in delight. 'That's the meat wagon. The Hets are heading for the slammer. The cops have got them. They're under arrest.'

But this was something we didn't need. I'd only intended to scare the hoods. Now that the cops were involved it would mean detailed enquiries which might embarrass every one of us. For a start, they'd see the safe. And Jane and I were in the loop too.

'We have to move,' I said. 'I've got a car in the car park.'

'What about the key?'

I produced it from my pocket.

'Walter,' I said. 'Look after George for us. Jane and I will be back in five minutes. Don't let anyone in and don't leave the house, okay?'

He nodded and looked at the General, none too happy. Whatever his talents he was not an ideal medical orderly.

Jane started the bike and I got on the back. She was decidedly unsteady and I was relieved when we finally revved into the car park, which was barely a mile away, and found the old banger in its familiar place. It started at first try and I drove towards the lodge with Jane behind me. She put the bike round the back and I parked the car at the front, there being nowhere else to go. I hoped to that hell the cops wouldn't come for the next three minutes. Then we hurried in.

Old Walter hadn't moved and looked up in relief.

''E's still sleepin'.'

George didn't look good. His face was drained of colour and his breathing sounded funny. I wondered if he'd deteriorated a little. In a moment of inspiration, Jane loosened his collar, but it didn't make a difference.

'Get him moved before anything else goes wrong,' she said, *sotto voce*.

I went out and got the passenger seat adjusted so that it went straight back into a crude camp bed. Then all three of us carried the General out and got him strapped in. He seemed to wake up for a moment, then he fell asleep again. Jane put something under his head for a pillow. They'd certainly given him a heavy dose. At one point I thought that a car was coming up the drive, but it was just a faulty exhaust on the main road.

'Walter, you'd better lock the house and go back to your work,' I said.

'Oi'll do that.'

'Don't go near the Towers. There are cops everywhere.'

He nodded. Walter wasn't daft, he'd thought of that too.

'Oi'll go to the veggie garden.'

'Do that, Walter. Bye.'

A thought struck me and I went behind the lodge, pushed the bike into Walter's garden shed. I locked the door. It would have been a big mistake to let the cops find it. I shoved the key through the letterbox and got into the car.

Jane sat behind me as we moved out to the public road. So many things could have gone wrong, but we were still alive and heading back to London.

30

The General was snoring and showing no sign of coming round when we got to the clinic. Jane went in to summon help while I backed the car into a bay at the back in an effort to create as little fuss as possible among the people in the waiting room. George didn't look good and I was concerned that he'd deteriorated during the journey. I didn't know how Jane negotiated his entry since she'd no money, but almost immediately two orderlies arrived with a stretcher and removed the patient. They were very discreet and were clearly experienced at extracting drugged patients from cars.

'Is he safe here?' I muttered, when Jane returned.

'It's the best we can do.'

'He didn't think this place was secure.'

'I know that.'

'You'd better contact Sir Lance.'

'A bit difficult, he'll be in Parliament. We're the people on the ground. We make the decisions.'

Jane wanted to stick to the rules, but this was a situation which demanded some thought. If Harry Hetland knew about the clinic (and almost certainly he did) he could remove George with ease. At the very least, Sir Lance should be informed. The plotters had their own medical facilities and George could be whisked off to somewhere safer. Of course Sir Lance didn't want phone calls, but with the future of the operation in the balance that would have to be ignored. We were George's only protection and we were tired after a nerve-wracking day.

'What happens now?' I asked. 'Do we stand guard?'

'Looks like it. Better go to the waiting room.'

I hated waiting rooms. The idea of wasting time reading ancient magazines was insufferable, but I was a professional, or at least supposed to be. Jane and I sat apart so we could watch both sides. There was an old man waiting in the far corner who kept letting out great sighs as he read his copy of *The Times*.

Behind me, the receptionist worked at her books. I watched the car park through the glass doors. After about thirty minutes, the doctor who had treated me called us through. I saw her look at me, but my false beard confused her. She seemed to have recognised Jane alright.

'He's comfortable,' she said. 'But we'll have to keep him in overnight. 'We don't know what the substance was and he's had a heavy dose. All being well, I can release him tomorrow morning. Not before.'

That meant he was at risk for the entire night. I'd hoped against hope that they'd have an antidote, but nothing was ever that easy.

'Is he going to be alright?' asked Jane.

'Yes, I think so. He has a healthy frame. We'll just have to wait and see.'

The doctor went away and we returned to the waiting room. After a couple of minutes Jane signed to me to go out and we began to talk.

'I'd better stay here all night,' she said. 'I'll do guard duty, it's the least I can do. It'll look odd if we both wait. I've told them he's a relative. I need to go home to sort some things. Will you wait for an hour till I come back? You can go home after that.'

'Of course, take my car. But home? Are you going to Nelson Towers?'

'Oh, no, to the safe house.'

'Fine. Here's the car key.'

'Thanks. I'll be back shortly.'

I returned to the waiting room where I found a *Daily Mail* and passed the time doing the five-star Sudoku. I felt a bit of a heel, leaving Jane on duty through the night, but she'd volunteered and I was drained. It occurred to me that she and George might once have been lovers, or perhaps she'd been his bit on the side. They addressed each other with some familiarity and I'd noticed that she was almost always pre-informed of our instructions. She'd negotiated his entry into the clinic, which implied a familiarity with both the patient and his money. Certainly she must have known something of his financial affairs to get him into a bed. A private clinic wouldn't be easily fooled when it came to money.

As it happened, more than two hours passed before she returned, handing over the key and saying:

'Any news?'

'No, nothing,. Do you want me to watch while you get some dinner?'

'Dinner? Oh no, it's okay. I'll wait in his room, they'll serve it there.'

'It's going to be a long wait.'

'Oh, I can cope. It'll be no worse than the telly.'

'Well, that's true. I'm off, then.'

'Yes, you've done well.'

A rare compliment.

I went back to the car and drove off. My safe house had no parking facilities, so I had to leave the old banger in an expensive car park. I went into the flat and had a long bath while I thought things over. Tomorrow, I knew, there would have to be some changes.

31

On the following day, I walked to the General's house at twelve noon, a quiet time for the elite residents of the street. There were no cars about and I was the sole pedestrian as I made my way to his door and rang the bell for a brief, almost apologetic, half second. He opened the door personally and gave the impression of being glad to see me.

'Come in, Mat. I was just thinking about you.'

'How are you, General?'

'Oh, fit. They released me at seven this morning. I've got to thank you. Jane says you were a great help.'

'It was the least I could do.'

He took me to a room at the back of the house with a warm fire and several armchairs. There was a vase of flowers on a plinth, which indicated that there were servants about, though there was no sign of anybody and he'd answered the door personally. Perhaps his servants were all part timers who did a couple of hours in the mornings. Copies of the morning's newspapers were sitting on a coffee table, a bottle of malt whisky sat beside a tumbler and it seemed that everything in George's world had returned to normal.

'Was it bad for you, George? Were they violent?'

But you didn't ask a General that kind of question. The stiff upper lip had never been more obvious.

'Well, it wasn't a good situation, but I survived. Mustn't complain. It could have been a lot worse.'

'Have you got a headache after that drug?'

'Earlier on, but I'm alright now.'

'What about Jane. Has she gone home?'

'Jane? Oh, she's about somewhere.'

His tone had changed and I got a sense of defensiveness. So perhaps they really had once been lovers. It would explain how she'd known about my safe house, and so many other things. As always, I'd been the only person who hadn't know what was going on.

I hesitated for a moment. It seemed only right to tell him about the phone call from Harry Hetland, but suddenly I found myself reluctant to broach the subject. Possibly it was irrelevant. I liked the idea of having my enemy's phone as a souvenir, and almost certainly the General would order me to hand it over. Possibly Harry and I would never speak again but sometimes it was helpful to have a line to your opponent.

'Does this little incident change anything?' I said.

'Eh? Why should it change anything, Mat, my boy?'

'Because Harry Hetland knows more about the group than I do.'

His expression changed immediately. I was expressing sentiments which bordered on the disloyal, and he didn't like that kind of thing. A steely note crept into his voice.

'What makes you say that?'

'Come on, George, we've got to be frank with each other. His men have raided all our houses. They were even at Dalespun yesterday. It's time to call a halt.'

The General blinked at me as though I'd gone off my head.

'Not on your life, man. He's the biggest threat to peace in the Western world. The job's not done. And it'll have to be done.'

'Tell me about the safe.'

An expression of outrage crossed George's face, as though I'd asked to see his bank statement.

'I can't tell you anything about that,' he snapped.

'Why wasn't it moved from Dalespun?'

The General looked at me and chuckled.

'Oh, but it was.'

Slightly shaken, I said:

'So yesterday was all about nothing?'

'I don't know what you mean by nothing, but the safe was certainly moved within hours of you getting it there. Under duress I misadvised Harry's men. I'm glad you got me away before they discovered that.'

'I see. So they were searching for it when the cops came.'

'Exactly, and it wasn't there.'

There was a silence while we looked at each other. I had

unsettled him. He was no longer sitting back in his chair and he'd lost his sunny disposition.

'I know what's in it,' I said.

'Oh, might I ask what?'

'Incriminating files from his early years. Publish them and he's finished.'

The General gave a humourless chuckle and looked at me with shrewd eyes. I'd never been able to impress a Commanding Officer.

'I suspected it from the beginning,' I said. 'Harry's organisation's getting too big. His management techniques aren't up to it. That safe could blow him out the water, yet he had it sent by ordinary freight when it should've come by special courier, a disaster that's going to ruin him. You've been reading his emails, you found out about it. Andy was brought in to liaise with a team of robbers to have it stolen. The robbers were out of their depth too. No doubt Andy forgot to tell them about Hetland and they got a fright when they found out. Harry was blazing mad and Andy got shot. And now you've got the safe, the worst possible scenario for him.'

'Forget it,' said George, unimpressed. 'I can't possibly comment.'

For a moment there was silence. I reflected that the room was a drab place which offered no more contentment than my own poor home. On the wall behind George's head there was a painting which must have been two hundred years old. It was of a gloomy old man, no doubt one of his forebears. He didn't look intelligent, but no doubt he had been rich. What was the point of living in the past?

'I want out, George. I can't take any more.'

This had an electric effect on him. He sat forward, frowning.

'Eh? Out of the Operation? Not on your life. I won't hear of it. You've done well. You can't quit on the field.'

'I'm not on the field.'

I almost said that I didn't trust him any more. Andy's death had upset the apple cart. It could have been so different. Now I knew that it was the plotters who'd had it stolen. There was something mind boggling about the gang putting a stolen safe in

Andy's flat with two grand sitting on top. In fact they must have been refunding their fee for an item which was too hot to handle. As soon as they'd heard that Andy had been shot they must have got it out and dumped it before the cops (or the Hets) arrived. I could hardly blame them. Then Jane came to send me to the Industrial Estate where we had just happened to find it. They hadn't frank with me in case I blamed them for Andy's death. I couldn't decide whether the gold bars were real or virtual, but they'd played a part in events too.

'Think it over, man. It's important work.'

'There's an understanding between you and Harry Hetland.'

'That's preposterous!'

'Yesterday they kidnapped you. Subsequently they lost several men to the cops and failed to get the safe and yet here you are, sitting in the same house with no security and nothing to stop them coming back. A truce has been declared. You're off the danger list.'

'There are things you don't know.'

'Now there I agree with you. Anyway, George, it's been an exciting time and by some miracle we've all survived. In two hours, I've got a doctor coming to take my stitches out. After that I'll move out of the safe house. I'll post the key to you.'

There was a silence. I'd said my bit and the General wasn't going to comment. He wasn't pleased, but he didn't want to fall out with me either. There was a chance he'd need me again so he'd keep his options open. I'd been in these situations before. Military commanders can be very shrewd at times.

'You can't go back to your home town, you know. They're looking for you.'

'Oh, I know that. And I also know they aren't looking for you, but good on you. In the meantime, I'll go elsewhere.'

The General nodded and stood up. He was going to put his best face on it, a nice polite parting to keep the options open.

'Well, I've got to thank you, Mat. You've been a tower of strength. Maybe we'll meet sometime. I hope so.' The good PR was coming to the fore.

'Thanks, George, and I wish you all the best, too.'

At this point I felt he should have offered me some money.

I'd been working very hard and endured a lot of unpleasantness, but he showed no inclination to do it and I didn't bring the subject up. He took me to the door, remarking that the weather was looking a lot better and that I should take the opportunity to get out of town. I agreed, we shook hands, and I turned into the street which was as quiet as ever.

It took less than an hour to walk back. I went with my head down, none too pleased to be isolated from the group I'd made a conscious decision to quit. I was sure my judgement had been correct, but now I didn't have their protection and that made me vulnerable.

I let myself into the safe house and started tidying the place in the best regulation manner, wiping my prints from the door handles and putting all the rubbish into a black plastic bag. There was a lot of money in my case, some of which I'd removed from the Hets, some from Sir Lance and some from Andy. It would give me some freedom, though I wouldn't spend it lavishly. It would have to last for a long time.

The doctor and his assistant arrived on time, removed the stitches from my face and declared themselves reasonably pleased with their work. I'd have a scar, but it wouldn't be obvious. With time it might disappear; my false beard, which I'd glued on as soon as they had finished, was perfectly acceptable. They didn't know what to make of me. I was an ordinary man in an expensive flat which wasn't mine but they asked no questions. They'd seen a lot. I signed their papers and they were gone.

I went over the whole flat again, making a final check. Then I left, taking my case and leaving the plastic bag with the rubbish in the basement. I went out to the busy street and posted the key to George. After that, I got into the car and drove out of London.

32

I went to Portsmouth on the A3, twice going off the road to walk in anonymous towns and twice driving along country roads to make certain I wasn't followed. At Portsmouth, I took the ferry to the Isle of Wight and booked into a quiet hotel on a cliff top in Shanklin. It was heavenly. Almost every day, sometimes before breakfast, I'd walk to the neighbouring town of Sandown, a round trip of about ninety minutes, during which I'd meet all kinds of walkers, nearly all of whom would nod to me. It was a splendid lifestyle. The Isle of Wight had always been a civilised place and I'd never found it more congenial.

A week passed, and I was walking along the shore road, having taken a sandwich and tea in one of the eateries, when a group of people came out of a hotel. There were three blokes and five girls, heading for the beach and making a lot of noise. One of them was fat and wearing a bright yellow top over red stretch trousers which were fully challenged by the size of her bum. I wondered if there could be two Hazels in the world. But I knew that there was only one, and that the real world had intruded into my life again. I was about to dive into an amusement arcade, but she saw me.

'Mat, what are you doing here?'

'Oh, Hazel, how are you?'

'Mat, everybody's looking for you at home.'

'Eh? I've been away on business, Hazel, what –'

'We thought something had happened to you. The police have been at your door. Adele was quite worried.'

'The police? What were they looking for?'

'I don't know, Adele didn't say. You should have told us you were going.'

'I haven't been away all that long.'

'I hardly recognised you with that beard. Is that a scar on your cheek?'

'Just a scratch.'

'Have you been here all the time?'

'Oh, no. Just for the day, delivering stuff to a hotel. How long are you here?'

'Till tomorrow. It's a pity you're going, you could have joined us.'

'A pity.'

'Adele has fallen out with Bob and he's gone back to his wife. She couldn't get into your flat. So she's had to stay with me. She can be very difficult, you know.'

'Yes.'

'When are you coming back?'

'Shortly, but I might have to move. It's the work. I'll need to run, Hazel. I'm with a bloke in a van and he's waiting for me. We're due on the ferry in a couple of hours.'

I hurried off, turning to wave as I went round the corner. This was a disaster. Adele would know as soon as Hazel got back. If they wanted, they could trace me easily enough. My car number at the ferry would give them all the information they needed. But were they sufficiently interested? Perhaps it was only Adele who was taking an interest. My worry was that Herb had come back with more questions. That would be more serious.

My first inclination was to get off the island immediately, but that might be interpreted as running away and might give them the excuse to put me on the missing persons list. Hazel was going back and the coast would be clear again. I'd stay for the meantime.

33

The following morning I awoke too early. Outside dawn was breaking and there was a blissful silence from the kitchens which suggested that the morning staff hadn't arrived to start their work. The silence made the hotel seem like a morgue. It was always comforting to hear the sounds of breakfast mingling with the cheery talk of the staff. But I couldn't complain; I'd slept relatively well, though now I was wide awake with no prospect of getting back to sleep. There was nothing else for it but to get up. I decided to take my walk to Sandown an hour earlier than usual, intending to take the cliff path on the way out and return by the coastal route.

The morning was cool and the night air hadn't yet lifted, but those things didn't disturb me when I was walking. I liked the cliff top. It was one of my favourites, with its sweeping panorama of the sea, which today was electric blue. A big ferry was making its way to an unknown destination, accompanied by a host of seagulls. Even at that time in the morning there were a number of dog walkers about and we gave each other courteous nods.

Thirty minutes into the walk, my phone rang.

But it wasn't my phone; it was the one I'd taken from the Hets. Perhaps I should have discarded it, but it was a trophy of war and I'd been reluctant to part with it. Only now did I realise that Harry would know I'd resigned from the operation. Its tones brought me out in a sweat, a reminder of the violent world I was trying to forget. In a moment of panic, I considered throwing it away, but that would only raise the eyebrows of the various dog walkers, so after a moment's pause, I answered it.

'What are you doing, Mat?' asked a familiar voice. It was the first time he'd used my real name. I didn't know how he'd got it, but I wasn't surprised.

'Oh, I'm having a walk, Harry.' I tried to sound as natural as possible. 'I'm at the seaside.'

'Good for you. There is wisdom at the seaside. It is the giver of life. Our forebears emerged from it and it has soothed the nerves of many a troubled soul. I can hear the seagulls. Are you happy?'

Hetland's voice was unusually calm. He seemed to be speaking from a sound-proofed room which revealed nothing of his whereabouts. He gave no hint of the cunning I'd heard on previous occasions. Nevertheless, I looked in all directions to see if the Hets were creeping up on me while the boss distracted their victim.

'Yes, I'd say so.'

'I envy you. It must be nice to walk by the seaside.'

'What's stopping you? You could buy a fine house on the coast.'

Perhaps I was being a little cheeky. My father always said that you should reply to people with the same courtesy as they'd shown to you. Harry was a celebrity. The least I could do was be polite. The voice on the phone sighed as though I had a simple mind and couldn't understand the pressures at the top.

'Oh, I've a house beside a river. I'll go there soon. Pressures of business and politics are driving me out of my mind.'

'A lot of people wish they had your problems.'

'Well, that may be true, but my world, I fear, is crumbling. Major flaws have been found in my motivation. My career has been planned badly and I no longer have a clear objective. I shall have to rethink my goals.'

Why was Harry telling me this at six thirty in the morning? He was a problem I didn't need.

Someone approached from behind, but it was only an old man with two German Shepherds, who gave me a friendly nod.

'Flaws...rethink,' I repeated, trying to catch up. 'Who found the flaws?'

'Oh, I did, they were self evident. I'll have to retire from politics. What do you say to that?'

At the side of the path there was a bench provided in memory of some old codger, which gave an excellent view of the sea. I looked around and sat down, then realised I was being stared at as I turned to see a black backed gull watching me from a pole.

'Well, it'll take the heat off you,' I said, seeing an end to my troubles. At the very least, it would render further action unnecessary. Sir Lance and George would congratulate themselves, call a halt to their plot and I'd be free again.

But why was he telling me this?

'That is doubtful. I suspect I'll be very vulnerable without my political cloak. As long as I was a competent politician I had a certain control of events. The powers that be couldn't foreclose on me without interfering in high politics. Had I been of lowly status it would have been different. Soon I'll be yet another businessman. My affairs will be subject to scrutiny and I may not survive. They can go a long way back with their enquiries. I've been able to stem them in the past, but their files are never destroyed. Sooner or later a bright cop will make a name for himself by looking under the carpet.'

'Does the safe have anything to do with this?'

'Ah, the safe. I don't know what's happened there. Every day I dread a bombshell, but it never comes.'

'Perhaps George messed up.'

'Well, that's a distinct possibility. It wouldn't be the first time, either. I don't know what's going on. It's a worry. Maybe they can't get it open. Do you know?'

'I don't. They never tell me anything.'

'No, they wouldn't. I fear the cops will come soon.'

'So what, Harry? You've led them a dance since you were twenty.'

'You're overstating. There were been times when they almost had me.'

He sounded seriously depressed. There were distinct pauses between his comments and his voice was totally lifeless. Even a series of acting lessons couldn't achieve this level of doom. He'd make Hamlet seem quite cheerful.

'It doesn't look that way to me.'

'I get a kick out of some things, but I'm still a failure.'

'You're no failure. You're a celebrity, a multimillionaire. But you've got to tell me, what are the major flaws?'

'You wouldn't understand. My driving force has always been to reach the top. Sir Lance and the General were terrified of me getting there. Their fears were exaggerated, but that wouldn't stop me. What has stopped me is an inescapable truth, I don't have the aptitude for it. I couldn't cope. I'd have a nervous breakdown.'

'No, you wouldn't. There's no such thing now.'

'Well, acute depression, then. The same thing with a different name.'

'And you're a depressive?'

'I fear so. My mental profile is not all it might be. Do you sometimes feel your sanity under threat?'

'All the time, but what's sanity? You should see a good doctor.'

Now that I came to think of it, Harry was a classic example of a manic depressive. He was highly competent and far-sighted, but prone to moments of extreme self doubt. Of course, he had no home life and no friends. Presumably once he had attained a certain degree of wealth, his psyche had begun to wonder about his motives.

'Is there such a thing? You are speaking to someone with a lot to lose. If my head gives me uncertain signals, I cannot direct my affairs. My enemies could take me to pieces. My past would be exposed in an unfavourable light. I'd die in jail.'

'Harry, surely you must have expected that. You can't fool all the people all the time. There have been too many victims, too many killings –'

'Killings?' said Harry, sounding angry. 'Name one so-called victim who didn't deserve to die. I've killed no bright sparks or contributors to the better life. There is far too much sentimentality associated with the dead. We all have to die. If I have removed some dull people from this fine land then I have done it a service. I honour the great and the good. The unworthy get their comeuppance. The Shakespeares and the Milton would be safe under me.'

'But –'

'I do not fear to kill. It is my abiding strength. It's only the mediocre who condemn me, largely because they are aware of their own banality. So wrong. Can you name any great man who doesn't have blood, as they'd put it, on his hands? Julius Caesar, Napoleon, even our own Churchill. I make no apology for my executive decisions. I don't fear death and I don't fear to kill.'

'Oh.'

'And what about my business empire? I am the greatest tycoon in the UK and I've built it from nothing. I didn't come from a privileged background. I came from zero. Do you know that PhD students have written papers about my expertise? I am deemed to be genuinely creative. My management techniques are original. They're the best in the country, perhaps the world. In politics, I could probably have improved the Civil Service had I reached the top, though there I speak with some caution.'

'Oh, you've done well,' I said, stifling an urge to remind him that he was in the unique position of having a private army to ensure his customers paid on time. After his outburst there was a short silence.

'And yet you are not feeling well?' I prompted.

'That is so. I don't apologise for the past. The future worries me.'

'And you don't have a side kick to take over.'

'Exactly. I'm unwinding things. I don't know what to do next. I've sent my bodyguards away. They weren't pleased. I had to give them cash settlements. They had to go. They were far too costly and far too violent. There would have been a scandal. That business at Nelson Towers was the last straw. And they knew too much.'

'I can see that. What about your American advisor?'

There was another pause of several seconds.

'You're well informed. I didn't know that he was common knowledge. Gone too, I'm afraid. He despaired of me.'

'Harry, I'm a layman. I know nothing, but I'll stick my neck out and tell you to get medical advice. You need a competent doctor. There are experts who can help.'

'And who will arrange this for me?'

'I don't know. You'd have to do that yourself.'

'I can't do that. Would you do it?'

A flock of oystercatchers flew overhead, uttering their peculiar call. I stared out to the sea in consternation.

'Not me, Harry. We're on opposite sides.' I knew that as soon as he was 'cured' he'd deal with me. No, sir. I'd walked out on

George. There was no way I'd trust Harry's tender care.

'Irrelevant. That'll be over by the end of the week. And you have left the plotters. I'd pay you well.'

'I know nothing about medical things.'

'All the better. Swot it up in a day. There are agencies which provide facilities. I'd pay good money. You'd have to make certain stipulations. I'd want to be treated under another name, and the doctor would have to be good. I'd want one security guard present at all times. You'd be my choice. There would have to be a letter of confidentiality from the doctor and absolutely no records could be kept.'

'Harry, I can't do that. I'm an ex-soldier, not a secretary. Get your own people to do it. What about the tall man, the baldy bloke?'

Harry snorted in irritation.

'That's one thing I can't do. History is full of leaders who have erred by trusting their aides. I won't make that mistake. You won't appropriate my assets, you know your place and you can get out of a hole when you need to, whereas letting my managers know I was going off my head would be downright suicidal.'

My eyes swept over the sea to the big ferry. I shook my head in frustration. There was something hypnotic in his voice which almost convinced me, but in a lifetime of bad decisions, agreeing to this would be my Waterloo.

'No can do, Harry. Sorry.'

There was a long silence. I said: 'hello?'

'Alright, I accept your decision. Continue with your walk.'

'Continue? How do you know –?'

'You're seated somewhere, probably on a bench. The background sounds are static. Get on with your walk. We remain enemies.'

34

Two days passed. The skies were dull and the rain was bouncing off the hotel roof with some force. I sat in my hotel room, reading a paperback, with a cup of tea in my hand. I had no problem with the weather. In the afternoon it would be dry, and I was planning to go to the Luccombe coastal path and walk for a couple of hours, listening to the jays calling to each other.

Then a sharp insistent rap said someone was knocking on my door

It was Jane.

'So here you are,' she said, without any sense of being glad to see me. She came in and looked around. The hotel was not expensive, but it was competent and my room reflected that. Every morning a team of smart women gave it the treatment.

'Not bad,' she said, then spoilt it by saying, 'George is looking for you.'

'What does he want?'

'It's all over. Harry's caved in, or at least he's disappeared. There's a small detail to be completed. Just a little safeguard to make sure he doesn't come back.'

'One small detail?'

'You'll need to come back. Some things need tidying.'

'I'm not a tidy person..'

'You're safe with us. We'll look after you.'

It appeared that they'd been having a talk about me, and one, or perhaps both, her bosses had zeroed in on my insecurities. A nice touch, that. *We'll look after you.* Meaning, of course, that they could get no one else to do whatever it was. Even Harry himself had suggested that I had the ability to get out holes, though surely I was a mere amateur compared to him. The damnedest thing was that I didn't rate myself at all. I'd never once shown a trace of original talent in my life. I didn't know why I was still alive.

'This was supposed to be over by now.'

'Don't rub it in. You and I have something to do first.'

'How did you know I was here?'

'Oh, we've always known you were on Wight. George knew the day you went over. Finding the hotel was another matter. But here I am.'

Undoubtedly she'd driven around the car parks until she'd spotted my car. That's the thing about life. The past always catches up with you.

'You've found me, so I'll come. But there should be enough details in that safe to blow Harry out of the water. I want out of it as soon as possible.'

Jane was shaking her head.

'It's not that easy,' she said, doing her best to look wise, her old stance as the female warrior forgotten. 'They're all in code and difficult to collate. Harry's good at that kind of thing. They're hardly a publishing sensation in their present form.'

'But you've still got them? They haven't been handed back to Hetland?'

'Of course we've still got them. Pack your case. We need to be back by five.'

I didn't move. I'd noticed an urgency about her, and I don't like getting told what to do,

'What kind of deal has George done with Hetland?'

'I don't know if it's a deal. Certain threats were issued.'

'Are you going to hit him?'

'No, that's not on the cards.'

'Okay, I'll come.'

35

Back in London, the safe house was unchanged. Two interior doors were still in the positions I'd left them, there was a fine layer of dust over the kitchen sink and outside the traffic was thundering past in triple-glazed silence. It was four thirty in the afternoon when I dumped my case on the bed. After that I went straight to the General's, resigned for anything and not too happy about it. This wasn't a fashionable hour and the select street was devoid of all activity. In fact, I was the sole walker. There were no bicycles or cars and nobody was working in their garden. That might just mean nobody was watching, but I wasn't too sure about that. When I rang the bell, the General himself opened the door and showed me through to the back room, where Sir Lance was sitting in an armchair. He looked up at me with an anxious glance.

'Have a nice break?'

'Yes, you could call it that.'

'I've always liked the Isle Of Wight.'

'One of my favourites.'

The General glanced at me and then looked at the fire. He was looking better. His pallor had returned to a healthier colour, though he seemed a little pinched and worried. I was aware that something unpalatable was going to be placed at my door. I cursed myself for getting back into their clutches.

'Mat, we've got one thing waiting for you,' he said, getting business-like. 'It sounds more difficult than it is. You'll have to get something out of Hetland's flat. He's away at the moment, a speaking engagement in Birmingham. Jane will go with you.'

'What is it?'

The General looked at me to see how I was taking it.

'A metal file. It's rather desperate, actually.'

'You're sure it's there, and recoverable?'

'Yes, to both.'

'If it's important, it'll be in a safe.'

'That's exactly where it is. We've got the combination number.'

My head jerked back in astonishment.

'How did you get that?'

'No details, Mat. But our electronic people are the best. This is pukka.'

'Good. Numbers can be changed of course.'

'We know what we're doing. He's in big trouble. Some of the Hets have been flown home and he's missed a week in Parliament – never happened before. His things are being run down as though he's finished. And he may be, though it's too early to crow about that. We've got enough incriminating data to kill his political hopes. But he's had low spots before and survived. This is the *coup de grace*.'

This was said deadpan and I'd no doubt he believed every word of it, but I wondered why Harry, of all people, would have a file in his possession that could destroy him. If he was running things down, surely it would be hidden in the vault of an obscure bank. And how did George know it was inside his safe?

'How the heck can we get into this place?'

'Oh, there's a way in. At least, there is now. An exit is also an entrance. In some respects Harry's not unlike you. He likes to have more than one way out. And he's got it. Have a look.'

He handed me two photos. One was a wide-angle shot of the back wall of a building, an unremarkable place with no windows in view. The second was identical, except it showed ladder built into the right side of the wall, which stretched to the heights without safety rails or embellishments. The building was several storeys tall. I looked at the first photograph and saw that the ladder was covered so effectively that no one would guess it was there. The cover was probably spring loaded. It was in its open position in the second photo. Yes, it looked like a handy escape route.

'That's his back door. His emergency exit,' George said, and being a General he had to digress. 'No planning permission for that, eh? Health & Safety would have something to say –'

'Sheer paranoia,' muttered Sir Lance. 'There must be umpteen better ways out. Very unsubtle.'

I wasn't sure I'd apply that description to Harry.

George was chuckling: 'Our psychologist reckons that his head's deteriorating. That ladder was installed only last month. It's a dangerous escape route. His mental health isn't good.'

The plotters were surprisingly accurate. How they'd discovered the ladder was a mystery, but they'd done it and of course there really was a question about Harry's sanity. At this point, I probably should have mentioned his phone call, but that would mean admitting I had his phone. It seemed best to say nothing. The plotters were staring at the two photos and I was getting an ugly feeling about my own immediate future.

'He can't cope,' said Sir Lance. 'He's on the retreat.'

'Exactly,' said George. 'This is when we've got to hit him. We want you and Jane up that ladder to get the thing. We know how to get in. You're trained, you can do it. We know how to spring that ladder open. I've had a team do it every day in the last week without a single problem. It's a doddle.'

Typical General. Doddle or not, he wouldn't be climbing it himself. But there were far bigger problems.

'You're sure?' I said. 'There's the minor difficulty of getting into his flat once you've reached the heights. You've got the know-how?'

They both nodded with something approaching glee.

'It's been tested,' said George.

'And someone actually got in?'

'They got it open, Mat. I didn't want them to go in. That's for you and Jane, you're the experts. I could hardly ask techs to open his safe.'

I looked at the two old men sitting in front of the fire. Apart from the newspaper, there was nothing in the place that wasn't at least fifty years old, myself included. Was this how the real world worked? Were these old buffers more tech-aware than Harry Hetland?

'I see.'

I couldn't be bothered to ask more questions that would only attract trite replies. I'd have to go. It had already been decided, and Jane was involved, though she was not discerning when dealing with the bosses.

'The flat'll be empty?'

'Correct. He has no partners. Like many a cold-blooded dictator before him, he prefers his own company. And that's his undoing. He knows that there are a lot of people out to get him – gangsters, politicians and of course us. He's constantly distracted and he can't concentrate on any of them. Ironically, he thinks we're the weakest of his foes. He's going to get a surprise soon.'

'We hope,' I said, then realising that was cheeky, I added, 'Of course he will.'

'Jane knows what to look for. She'll take care of things once you get in.'

At that moment Jane came in, without knocking. I think she'd been listening behind the door.

'I've got clothes and shoes for you,' she said to me. 'Better get into them and we'll go.'

'Go? Now?'

'Yes,' said the General. 'No time like the present. We know he's in Birmingham tonight. He's due to give his talk in thirty minutes and even he can't be in two places at once. We'll never get another chance like this.'

36

The evening was dull with a hint of rain. We took a taxi to a nearby street and walked slowly to the lion's den. Harry's penthouse was in a short cul-de-sac, a crafty move that eliminated all passing traffic and reduced passers-by to the barest minimum. No mean building, it occupied the full length of the street. There was a Revenue & Customs office on the opposite side, making his apartment the only domestic dwelling in the area. Before leaving, George had shown me more photographs of the building and the apartment's plan. It covered the fourth floor.

'This file,' I said to Jane, 'it's the code to the safe, right?'

'I assume so, and don't start.'

'How do they know it's in the safe?'

She gave an angry snort and began to walk faster. Of course I shouldn't have asked that question at the beginning of the outing, but my doubts were serious. Despite a few dicey moments, the plotters hadn't done too badly, but this smelt of desperation. In all likelihood the safe and its contents were useless without the code and that was why they'd brought me back. The likely basis for our raid could be nothing more than Harry's emails, and that was enough to make anyone nervous, particularly since he probably knew they were being monitored.

We were wearing black tight-fitting clothes that were supposedly knife proof, though there was no record of Harry's victims ever having been knifed. On top, we had light raincoats and I carried an attaché case. Ostensibly we were two office workers on our way to an appointment. We walked apart as though we were less than friends.

'Well, it's all clear,' Jane said, with a hint of tension when we reached the mouth of the street. I didn't know what she meant. There was nothing clear or unclear about it. Perhaps she was merely trying to be positive.

But I was surprised by the character of the building, with its generous windows and impressive frontage. The three lower floors were offices, some of which were still lit. Two women were studying a paper on the second floor, a group were bent over their screens on the third and there was a taxi leaving the front door. These offices were not necessarily related to Harry's enterprises, but were merely paying a high rent to enjoy his facilities. The upper floor seemed to be in darkness.

'Not bad,' I said in grudging tones, noticing that there were two entrances, one with a big frontage and two sliding doors and another on the far right was insignificant-looking and could easily have been mistaken for a caretaker's door. We knew, however, that it was the route to the lion's den itself. To its left, a slip road descended to an underground car park, firmly sealed with a steel shutter.

I let Jane lead. Harry might be in Birmingham ready to deliver a speech but it was unnerving to be stealing up to his home. It was only our military training which kept us going. From day one we'd been taught to obey orders. That was fine when we were eighteen, but doubts grow as the years pass. How many squads of soldiers had been despatched to certain death in the face of an enemy advance? It had to done. To save his army, the Commander had to check the enemy and ultimately his judgement was correct. But it was still a shame for the squad.

'So it's go then?' Jane said.

We approached the big door casually. By this time, the taxi had gone and the vestibule, all smart and business-like, was visible behind the glass. The lights were shining, but no one was about. The doors sighed open when Jane put a card to the slot and we walked in as though we went there every day in the week. So George's electronics actually worked. I couldn't help feeling that it would have been nice if they'd failed, killing our mission on the spot. Overhead, a discreet camera surveyed us. To our right lay the doors to several offices, twin elevators, and a carpeted stairway which soared upwards, exactly as expected. Without a pause, we went through a service door to the back.

'Alright?' Jane mouthed as the door closed behind us. I gave no indication of having heard her. It didn't matter, but there was a small camera against the ceiling that she'd forgotten. I lifted her up and she attached an electronic device to the cable which would render all the cameras unstable for the next twenty four hours. We swung to the right into the toilets, which were camera free. We stuffed our coats into the case and hid it in a storage cupboard. Now we were dressed in figure-hugging black suits and looking like cat burglars.

We went straight out to the back of the building, closing the door behind us.

'Alright so far?'

'I think so.'

The back street was long and narrow and bereft of almost any object. It was also completely unlit and looked as though it hadn't been used since the builders went away, though there was a heap of cigarette stubs at my feet. First we went to the right hand corner, where Jane worked at the cover for a few seconds before jumping back when the cover flew open, revealing the ladder.

'Well, that went alright,' she muttered.

Straight as a ruler, the ladder soared up to the heights. The rungs were rock solid and didn't budge when we pulled at them. Judging by the scuff marks, it seemed they'd been used several times. I shone the torch at my feet to see if anyone had fallen off.

'What do you think?'

'Looks okay,' I said regretfully, giving a heartfelt sigh.

We stepped back to the far wall and looked for the top floor but it was out of sight. One of the peculiarities of the building was that there were no rear windows other than those in Harry's suite, which meant we wouldn't be seen by the office workers, though there was always the risk a smoker might come out for a puff.

'Alright?'

'Looks like it.'

'Go for it.'

Technically Jane was the boss, so I went forward to the ladder. It was exactly vertical, with each rung a full handbreadth from the masonry. Harry must have had a good head for heights, but of course emergency exits aren't designed for immediate comfort. An exit is also an entrance, and I had a funny feeling that Harry knew that better than the plotters. Putting on my gloves, I wondered how safe it really was.

'Here goes.'

I began to climb. My shoes had non-slip soles, my gloves an excellent grip and even the figure-hugging suit was reassuring. Certainly I was well kitted for a good ascent, but I'm not a good climber. Uncertainty made me grasp each rung too tightly while reaching for the next. The first ten were easy, but I found myself clinging a little too tightly when it came to the next ten. It was best not to look down, but just kid myself that I was only a few steps up. I was obsessed with the certainty of death if my hands (or feet) should slip. After thirty rungs, the drop seemed to be dragging at me. By this time I was moving slower, looking at each rung before I reached for it. If Harry had a booby trap, it would be up here. It was in his nature to have a surprise for the intruder, but perhaps he wouldn't risk it. The surprise might kill him in an emergency and he didn't take personal risks. I was out of breath when I reached the safety rails. The final steps were at an inclined angle which led to a flat landing. I sat down and looked back and was astonished at the height. Jane was out of sight on the street.

Turning, I looked in at the glass door behind me, to see an elegant room, big enough for fifty people. A bit extravagant, given that Harry didn't entertain and had never been known to have had a party. It was unlit, but I could see oil paintings on the walls, including a weird abstract, landscapes, and a modern drawing of a lion. Not surprisingly, there were none of humans. Obviously Harry didn't admire that species. A computer with a wide screen sat on a fancy desk. . Several armchairs and couches were aimed at a large, wall-mounted TV. I could just see that the end wall was covered with books. I tried to remember the plans for the apartment, but the details were lost to me.

I turned as a panting Jane appeared, gripping the safety rails, her cheeks red with effort. She hurried away from the drop with unsteady steps.

'That was awful.'

'It was.'

'It'll be worse going down.'

Perhaps it would be, but we had a lot of things to do before we faced that ordeal. In reality, the exit might be more of a pleasure. She sat down to rest, then turned to look into the flat.

'That's some room.' But she was only speaking for comfort. She'd looked to see if we were alone. Nothing else mattered.

'And it's free of Harry,' I said.

'We hope. Do we start now?'

We both hesitated. The room seemed to be innocuous, but it was best to be cautious. Nothing should be taken at face value.

'Better have a gander first,' I muttered, reluctant to go in.

The entire apartment was inset within the building's frame, with a path around its border to facilitate window cleaning and other utilities. We walked to the far end, covering a fair distance, looking in the windows without seeing anything of a discouraging nature.

'The Bank of England's easier,' Jane complained.

Back at the sliding doors, we looked in for a long time. The apartment's splendour made Harry seem superhuman. No cushion was rumpled and no chair had been sat on. We tried in vain to get an insight into his security. It seemed unlikely there'd be none, but where was it and what was it? Jane had a gizmo that came up with zero at every test, but could we rely on it? It had been specially designed and was supposedly capable of detecting the slightest emission. But Harry might be ahead of the plotters. That was enough to make anyone nervous.

'Go on,' Jane said.

I got the tools and began to work. There was a palm-sized remote in my hand of polished alloy, with several buttons and a numerical display. This, too, was handmade, probably in the same lab as Jane's device. It was capable, in theory, of tapping into a digital interface. Apparently it had been tested on this very set-up. I don't know how. It seemed unlikely that they'd clambered up the ladder. Of course, in this age of wi-fi it was possible to read a lot from a safe distance. Perhaps details of his system had been logged.

'Doesn't seem to be alarmed,' I said, not believing it.

'It might not be,' she said, more by way of comfort than anything else. 'It's an emergency exit.'

I was sure that Harry wouldn't want alarms howling when he made his dangerous descent. Intruders could drop things, or shoot him while he was on the ladder. Much better to make a silent retreat which would let him negotiate those dangerous rungs without distraction. But that didn't make sense either. The ladder went to a sealed back yard. He'd have to run through the building before he reached the outside world. Not exactly a smooth exit, and distinctly dangerous if he was under pressure. Usually Harry was a lot more efficient than that. Perhaps he had another trick that had so far eluded our bosses.

My gadget's purpose was to instruct the digital master to unlock the door. Lights had been flashing on its screen for some time, and it seemed that it wasn't happy about things but suddenly the screen went green.

'It's ready?' Jane said.

'Looks like it. Open?'

'Yes, yes, go on.'

I pressed Enter.

There was a click and the doors slid open, causing the curtains to flutter like living things. The room, full of mystery, was waiting for us. No alarms were blaring.

'I'll lead,' said Jane, but she hesitated for a moment before stepping forward, walking slowly and watching her reader. She was well inside before she said:

'It's okay.'

With some reluctance, I went in.

'I'll get the door.'

She reached behind the curtain, and pressed a switch. The doors closed.

The safety rails were sited in such a way that they were out of sight. It wasn't a bad exit. Harry could be on the ground before his attackers knew what was happening.

'Are we alone?' Jane mouthed, going to a door which opened to reveal pristine toilets. If we'd triggered a silent alarm, a gunman could have been hiding there to surprise us. There were no other hiding places, though we had a cautious glance behind the couches. Then we went to the main door.

At this point, Jane produced a camera which was suspended from her wrist. She photographed the room.

'Right, come on,' she said, opening the door to reveal a wide unlit with a white carpet. Almost involuntarily, we stepped back to rub our shoes on the sitting room's floor. It was best not to leave tracks. By this time we had pocket torches in our hands. Jane took another photo. To my mind this was a piece of nonsense. George wanted shots of the whole apartment; typical military meddling that I'd have ignored in a flash. We should have been in and out as quickly as possible with no distractions tolerated.

We began to check the rooms to find them as impersonal as furniture showrooms. Shortly we were in Harry's office, where we saw the safe which was the object of our raid, but we continued on our way, to photograph the remaining rooms.

Harry's bedroom boasted a modern bed with a tasteful duvet, all neat and tidy with a full length mirror beside the walk-in wardrobe. The walls were wood panelled and they were immaculate. Sir Lance and George had both said that Harry had no personal servants, but it seemed unlikely that he made his own bed. Perhaps a team came in for an hour every morning, but how would that fit in with his busy life? Did they have their own keys? Would Harry give anyone a spare key? The whole thing was a mystery.

For a moment, Jane lay face down on the duvet before rising, shaking her head.

'No one's slept in that,' she said,.

Nothing about Harry surprised me. Maybe he didn't sleep.

'Clothes,' she said, spotting the omission and opening a walk-in wardrobe. There were surprisingly few outfits. The en suite toilet was empty too.

There was a fancy bathroom with a lot of colourful towels and a kitchen with facilities I couldn't imagine Harry ever using. Finally, we came to the biggest room of all. It had a dance floor and what looked like a fully stocked bar. By this time I'd lost count of it all, but I'd noticed that there was only one bedroom. Nobody but Harry was intended to sleep in the flat. And since he didn't use the bed there was the question of where he slept. None of this was reassuring.

We reached the end of the corridor, where a glass door revealed an outer hallway with an ultra-modern lift and stairway.

A plinth with flowers sat in a corner and to the left a door led to the outside path for window cleaners and maintenance. Jane aimed the camera and took a final shot.

I was about to turn away when something came to me.

'The lift,' I said, gesturing. 'It's up.'

'I know,' she said, her voice hard. 'Ignore it. Let's get the job done.'

We went back to Harry's office, where the safe was mounted on a plinth. Elsewhere in the room there was a desk which looked as though it had never been used. No papers lay on its surface, though there was a telephone on the right hand side and a computer on a desk beside it. Two abstract paintings hung on the wall. I looked in the bin and saw nothing. The shredder was empty too. Everything was too tidy.

Jane had the security code on the back of her hand. She punched in the numbers as I stood in silence, listening to every click and looking forward to a hasty exit.

'It's blank!' she exclaimed. 'It won't open.'

'Try again, slowly. You're nervous.'

The procedure was repeated.

'It's no good. I'll check the numbers –'

'Don't bother,' said a calm voice. 'I've changed them.'

Harry Hetland was in the corner with a gun in his hand. He had been sitting behind a screen. He wore his customary dark two piece suit with neatly pressed trousers. No doubt a jacket was necessary to hide a gun holster. I recalled that he'd said we were still enemies.

'Against that wall, please. Hands on your heads.'

We did as instructed and looked at our captor with a tremendous respect. He was completely relaxed. The gun was steady in his hands and his eyes were flickering over us with nothing more than a casual interest. He was certainly in control of the situation and there was no sign of the mental problems he'd complained of.

'Mat, very slowly, and do nothing stupid, take your gun out by the handle and slide it over the floor to me, one hand only.'

Keeping my left hand on my head, I unzipped my top, lifted my H&K out of its holder and slid it over the floor where it stopped three feet from his black shoes.

'Now, you'll do the same, Jane. I can see the outline in your jacket. Do it very slowly. Try nothing. I won't hesitate to kill you.'

She compressed her lips, lowered her head and slid her gun beside mine.

'Now, pull chairs over and sit against the wall where I can see you.'

In one quick movement he bent down and seized our guns and put them on the desk. Yes, he was in total command of himself.

'Where are Sir Lance and George tonight?'

When neither of us answered he aimed his gun at me.

'I don't know,' I blurted. 'At home, probably.'

'Mat, Mat,' he said with infinite sadness. 'A lifetime in the military and you still don't know your bosses. Never get into a state where you don't notice things; it's fatal. I don't know where they are, but I'm certain they're not at home. Perhaps they're having dinner with the Archbishop of Canterbury – or, no, they're not that high up, more likely they're having tea with an accommodating vicar. When Knacker of the Yard eventually gets round to asking a few questions, I'm sure they'll have a good alibi. After a little head scratching, they'll even admit to knowing you. Sir Lance will recall that your father worked at Dalespun and that you weren't a bad chap, though you lacked ambition and were a bit dull. Being a dull fellow himself, he's sure to have noticed that.'

He pointed his gun at Jane

'I don't know about you, Jane, my dear. I've a feeling that they won't admit to knowing you. George will be quick to point out that more than thirty thousand personnel have served under his command and it's difficult to remember every one of them. When shown your photo, he'll stare at it for some time and admit with an air of puzzlement that he's seen you before but the where and the when escape him. And of course he's got the excuse that you've changed your hair colour.'

I still had a knife in my belt, but it would have been folly to go for it. Harry hadn't tied us down. He was keeping his distance, but I doubted if I'd gain much from this omission. He was wary of us. He was elated at our capture, but he knew that we were dangerous and there were two of us to his one.

He turned to me, all business-like.

'Mat, when I met you in Parliament, I had the feeling we'd met before. I still have that impression. Your voice is familiar. Would you elucidate?'

I lowered my head. The past never went away.

'A long time ago, in your printing company. I was the Microsoft man.'

Harry, a man who was rumoured never to display emotion, threw back his head and laughed.

'Of course you were! I've puzzled over that for years. You made a great impression on me. What was going on?'

I stared at him, reluctant to recount an event in my life that still rankled, but I couldn't defy the man with a gun.

'A robbery that went wrong. I had to rescue an old mate who got stuck. He got away and I had to bluff my way out.'

Harry shook his great head and I saw the vestige of a smile.

'So it was all a bluff?'

I gave a sad nod.

'Who was your friend?'

'Big Andy. He was accident prone. Your man shot him at Romford.'

Harry gave another laugh. He knew all about it: 'Yes, a big chancer.'

'He didn't deserve to die,' I said, but the complaint was lost on him.

'I'll hand it to you, Mat. I nearly closed the operation down. An MP pirating *Windows* would have been a bit over the top. I'd made millions out of it, too. I almost had a heart attack when you said you wanted to inspect the plant.'

'It's best forgotten.'

'You're right there. And of course you made no money out of it.'

'That's correct.'

'You are a fool, Mat. You rescued a friend and didn't get a penny. I'll bet the plotters have forgotten to pay you too.'

'It doesn't matter.'

'No, it doesn't, does it? Well, this little conference is finished. Incidentally why did you come tonight?'

'You were due in Birmingham.'

'Ah, I'm almost sorry for you, depending on the plotters. That was last night. There was nothing booked for tonight. That was a journalist's error. You'd think even Sir Lance would check that.'

He raised the gun, aimed it at my chest and pressed the trigger.

37

Everything came to a standstill. Harry had fired at my chest. I awaited the searing pain that is said to precede oblivion. But the trigger made an uncertain sound. Perhaps it had jammed or the magazine had been maladjusted. Maybe it was just a bad round, but the results were the same and I was still breathing. Immediately, his eyes lost their look of concentration. He dropped his gun to the carpet and looked at the desk where our two guns had been placed. His body swerved towards the desk, as his eyes, wider now, with the beginnings of real alarm, returned to me in the desperate hope that I was paralysed with fear. But I was and I wasn't. I'd tensed myself for death, but now fate had offered me another chance. My feet were under the chair against the wall and I launched myself with the single-mindedness of a missile, well aware that Harry mustn't be allowed to seize another gun. Indecision crossed his face. He was closer to me than the desk and he could see that he wasn't going to make it, so he turned to repel me, but I was going too fast. I collided with his chest and he fell backwards over a chair and thumped heavily on to the carpet. Harry was a fit man and younger than me. I couldn't allow him to make a recovery. I smashed my fist into his face with a weak blow that did no good. Then I grabbed his head and thumped it against the floor in a series of blows which must have been audible throughout the building.

'It's alright, I've got him,' said Jane, and I turned to see her tying his ankles with a plastic tie.

Harry seemed to be unconscious. His mouth was open, there was some blood on his face and he looked seriously ugly.

'Turn him on his side, or he'll choke,' she said. In fact this sounded like a good thing, and I've a tendency to obey orders, so I hefted him on to his left side without a second prompting. Then I began to search him while Jane tied his hands behind his back. I removed a notebook and his wallet, seeing that it was well filled with cash. Then I got his phone and wrist watch, as well as the inevitable shoulder holster and its H&K. There was a knife attached to his belt and a lot of keys in his trouser pockets.

'Are you alright?' said Jane to me.

'A bit shattered.'

'Sit down for a minute. You've done well.' A unique comment from Jane.

'Search him again. He's worth the watching.'

I sat down and watched the room swirl around me for a minute as I got used to the idea of being alive. It was ironic that a month ago I'd felt life was becoming a bore. Nothing was ever right.

Jane came over with a miniature gun.

'Look what I got from him.'

It was a plastic weapon in dull colours which fired .22 bullets. It was easily hidden and capable of delivering death to the unwary, the kind of thing that scanners might not register, though they'd read the bullets. She put it in her pocket and turned to look at our captive, who seemed to be semi-conscious.

'Do you want brandy?' she said, turning to me.

'When I get home.'

She nodded and frowned at Harry.

'What the hell do we do *now*?'

Having captured the enemy, we'd exceeded our instructions by a mile. Clearly we couldn't leave him trussed like a chicken. To release him would be a bad career move. The matter would have to be referred to our bosses and I'd a funny feeling they'd be as perplexed as we were.

Jane reached for the desk phone and then looked at me.

'Better not. They can trace it.'

This was a momentous situation. Someday there might be a court of enquiry and to have phoned either Sir Lance or George would establish our identity. At the very least, Jane and I were housebreakers, but we were anonymous ones and it was essential to keep it that way. If Harry should die, there'd be a lot of questions to answer. So far as the law was concerned, he was an innocent man as well as an eminent one. The whole purpose of our raid had been to get something from the safe and there we had failed, though we'd captured the monster himself.

'In that case,' Jane said, after a long pause. 'It'll have to be verbal.'

But that meant going back to the bosses for a decision. One of us would have to guard Harry. It would have to be me. After a pause I said:

'Nothing else for it. Take his wallet. And his keys.'

She hesitated.

'I could use *his* mobile and destroy it after.'

'Not on your life. It's probably monitored.'

'Okay.' She looked at me. 'Will you be alright?'

'No reason why I shouldn't be.'

'Well, give me half an hour.' She looked at her clothes. 'What about this cat suit? A bit obvious.'

Her original coat was in the attaché case on the ground floor and in the present situation it would have been unwise to be seen there.

'Get a raincoat out of his wardrobe. Throw it over your shoulders.'

She nodded and returned in a minute with one of Harry's coats. It was far too wide, but she found a way of pulling it in and it wasn't too bad.

'I'm going,' she said, tightening the belt. 'I'll lock the door behind me.'

'Take the stairs.'

She nodded. Lifts are best avoided in dicey situations. Then she was gone.

I wanted to go too, but that wasn't an option and I braced myself for a lonely wait. By this time, my captive was half awake, glancing at me quickly before his eyes glazed over. He might have been semi-conscious or fully alert. Certainly there was danger in the air. I was a troubling presence to a man who'd pulled a trigger to kill me. He could hardly beg for mercy from me. But what were his intentions? Why shoot me in his own apartment? Even if it were to be redecorated he couldn't hide the traces of murder. Being an expert in death, he knew that better than anybody. The most likely explanation was that he was leaving forever and didn't care about leaving disorder in his wake. His face gave me a pang of fear whenever I looked at him.

Like everything else in the apartment, the office was a showroom. It had never once been used. There were no papers in the filing cabinet with packing material still on some of the chairs and when I powered up the computer it showed no sign of use. So the whole place was a fake. Any half intelligent officer should have known that from the start. We'd risked our lives on a false errand that had almost killed me. In reality, George had no way of knowing what the safe contained. He'd been sold a lame dog. No doubt Harry had planted enough false clues to lead him astray and but for his jammed gun Jane and I would be dead. Again I checked the captive and stood facing him as I wondered what to do next.

'Stay very still, mister,' said a familiar voice from behind me.
'So it's you, Jek?'
I couldn't believe it. Where had this creep come from? Only seconds ago, there had been no one in, or near, the doorway.
'Drop your gun, mister.'
I let it fall about three feet in front of me, seeing that Harry had suddenly become very alert and was looking behind me with interest.
Slowly, Jek emerged, keeping well to the right. He was aiming a gun at my head and looking at my gun on the floor. Jek was a peculiar person to be associated with Harry. He had seemed capable of doing undemanding jobs, and thus by virtue of his limitations was a safe assistant who'd never usurp his master. At this point he was indecisive, well aware that we'd beaten him at Nelson Towers, and also that I'd killed a previous gunman with a kick.
'Stand back, mister.'
I stepped back.
'Further.'
'Get on with it, you idiot,' spat Harry in icy anger, irritated at the pace of things. 'They'll be here in seconds. Move!'
Jek's hand darted for the gun, but his eyes were on me and he missed it. Then he made a second attempt, his own gun pointing all over the place as he grabbed it. He was just out of range, and my shoes were soft.

'Loosen me, you dolt, or they'll have us!'

Slowly Jek put both guns on the desk and started going through his pockets for a knife as though there were no hurry. Harry's face grew red with exasperation. Jek couldn't respond to the situation. He seemed physically incapable of doing things fast. He was apparently terrified of me and kept watching me with wary eyes.

'Get on with it!'

I'd lost and it was my own fault. The whole apartment should have been searched as soon as we'd tied Harry down. We'd never addressed the question of where he'd come from and the obvious dangers it posed. The shock of events had driven standard disciplines out of our heads and now I was paying the price

There was another blaze of anger from the captive, before Jek produced a pocket knife and cut the plastic ties, moving the knife slowly in case he cut his master, while keeping his eyes fixed on me. Then he stood back as Harry tried to struggle to his feet, his face a mask of pain and rage.

'Help me up, you idiot!'

So he was injured, or at least unwell. I'd pummelled his head and caused him to lose consciousness. Wordlessly, Jek extended his hand and helped him rise, which Harry did with some difficulty, rubbing his back, his face seething with anger. By this time I'd slowly retreated to the back of the room.

'Come on!' he shouted at his lackadaisical assistant as he hobbled towards the door. 'The brown Golf. Go!'

As Harry limped past me, he swung a blow at my face, but it barely connected. For the second time in an hour, I'd thought I was dead. He could have grabbed one of the guns from the desk and shot me, but I think he was too shrewd to leave a body in his wake if Jane was coming with reinforcements. Warily, I watched him limp into the corridor followed by his rescuer, his icy voice issuing instructions:

'Get that power off, all locks on. We're going.'

For once, he'd lost his cool. After being captured, he was free again and was so preoccupied that he'd forgotten the guns on the desk. A big chance for me. I could have rushed out and stopped him, but I didn't feel like it. My nerve had failed too. Twice I'd danced with death and I didn't fancy trying my luck for the third time.

When they were gone I sat unmoving on the chair for a full five minutes, trying to come to terms with it all. Then I went over and looked at the guns. Harry's was useless, so I put it in a drawer and took the H&K in my sweaty grasp, taking the magazine out and checking that it was operational. But I could do nothing more. For another five minutes I returned to the chair, during which there was silence from the corridor. For some reason I had no great curiosity about where they'd gone It was sufficient to know that I was alone. Even so, I had heard no sound from the front door.

But they didn't advise you to hang around after serious conflict. In fact, they were quite definite about it. Get away while you're still alive. I got to my feet and went into the corridor to find it dark and deserted. First, I leaned against the doorway and listened as intently as I'd ever done in my life. There were many distant noises: car horns, a police siren and a truck revving, but they were all outside the building. The apartment was utterly silent. Then I went to the front door to find it was still locked. No problem – Jane had the key and she'd be back soon. I turned to go back, then stopped and whirled round.

The lift was still in place. The escapees hadn't used it! In an emergency, with the risk of the cops, or at least Jane, arriving, they'd used the stairs. But they couldn't have done. Harry had been limping and four flights of stairs would be a problem even if he weren't in a hurry. Were they still in the place after all? Clutching the gun, I ran to the first room to find it serenely calm, with a view of London's lights through the sliding door. Had they passed through it on their way to the emergency exit? Was Harry fit enough to descend four storeys on an open ladder? But it refused to open when I pressed the switch. I applied my remote to the electronics and read zero voltage. It was as dead as a fossil. Nor was there any give when I put my shoulder to the glass. Some doors had an emergency facility which overrode the bolts – in fact, the fire authorities insist on it – but Harry never bothered with rules, and it wasn't pretending to be an emergency exit.

So the power was indeed off and the locks were on.

And that meant that Jane would be unable to open the front door.

Of course, sounds didn't carry well in a carpeted environment. I hadn't been all that attentive but their voices had disappeared within a few seconds. Back at the office, I looked along the corridor with an ugly idea forming in the back of my mind. Was there a secret section? There must be. Where else would he sleep? Somewhere nearby, there were facilities to switch the locks and turn the power off. Jek must have come from there, as had his master a few minutes earlier. Jane and I had looked in every room and seen no one. Our inspection had been quick but it was unlikely that we would have overlooked two men lurking in the shadows. That explained Harry's fury. Jek had been the back-up, the plan B. He'd been so ineffectual that it had almost failed. That was the trouble with dopey assistants.

My head was buzzing. The place was in darkness, but to save my life I'd have to make a methodical search of the whole apartment. Obviously it would be best to start in Harry's supposed bedroom. It was promising. When I shone the torch on the floor it was possible to see some mild depressions near the right wall that might have been footprints. Lying down with my eyes a few inches above the carpet, I saw undulations that went towards the blank wall.

It was just about impossible to hide a secret door in a modern house. The wall had to be designed to hide spaces for hinges, with gaps on all sides to prevent jamming. That was true of this singularity. The walls were wood panelled to hide the shape of the door. It was six feet from his bed, handy for a quick exit if he did ever choose to sleep in it. It was against the exterior wall where it wouldn't intrude too sharply into the next room's space.

This might be the secret section, but where was the trigger to throw it open? There was a mock fire place with a mantelpiece adjacent to the supposed door. I put my gun down, and pushed on it. Nothing happened. There was an edge underneath which gave a good grip but it didn't move when I tugged. So there must be a safety switch. I spent three minutes looking for it. Eventually I found an interruption to the skirting board which showed mild signs of wear. I pressed it with my foot while pulling the mantelpiece.

Bingo!

There was a click and a door swung open to reveal a dark passageway which stretched ahead for some distance. There were no signs or sounds of the escapees, but there was a man smell which suggested someone had been there for some time. This must be his real lair. At long last, I'd made a discovery.

But it would be stupid to go in. I had lived too long to take that kind of risk. Let the enemy move first. Harry was injured and might be licking his wounds. He wasn't in a condition to face the external ladder and hadn't used the lift. The reference to the Golf could have been a false clue that I'd swallowed to my peril.

I went back into the white-carpeted corridor and checked the front door to find the lift was still in place. Did that mean he was waiting for me? Was it likely that he'd remain in the building while he knew Jane had gone for reinforcements? I was holding the gun tightly, utterly vexed by the problem.

Back in Harry's bedroom, I hid behind the bed, gun at the ready, for all of ten minutes without hearing one sound. Then I crawled over the bed, confirming Jane's statement that no one had ever slept in it, but what did that matter? The secret section was the vital thing and despite my earlier resolve, I'd have to go in.

Silently, I approached, keeping as close to the wall as possible.

Cables dangled from the ceiling. It had been roughly constructed with untrimmed wood holding the structure in place. Only to be expected. You can't hire competent craftsmen without becoming the talk of the town. Instead Harry would have had to use his own unskilled labour force. The Hets came to mind. At least he could have been sure of their discretion. They'd laid a strip of thick carpet along the centre of the passage to reduce the sound of footsteps.

Six paces in, I found a control board which probably governed the security, a steel box with several switches that were operated by a key of some kind. There were a number of legends around the keyhole, but there was no sign of the key. No doubt he'd grabbed it when he had passed. Given time, I could probably have taken the thing apart and got the power on, but aside from my Swiss army knife I had no tools.

Ten paces on the passage widened into a room, where an untidy bed lay against the far wall. There were several phones on a table and a group of CCTV monitors. The pillows on the bed were filthy and the sheets looked as though they hadn't been washed in a year. Jek's bedroom, I said to myself, but I was wrong. It was Harry's. His suits hung on a rail with a selection of shirts. On the wall there was a full length mirror with a number of lights around it. Above the table there was a set of switches, a bedside light and a computer manual. Harry always seemed so clean. But this was his secret. The fancy bed was a showpiece which had never been used and the whole apartment was a sham to hide his secret.

Here was a man who aspired to be Prime Minister. He had spent millions on his way up, but he slept in circumstances which most people wouldn't tolerate. It was clear evidence of his psychological flaw and would be mocked the world over. This didn't look like Ten Downing Street. His comments on the phone had been true. He had probably spoken from this very room. Of course he wasn't unique. Any psychologist would say that there were many examples of this kind of behaviour. It was a well documented syndrome. A descent into what the patient sees as their gut reality, a place where there's no luxury to confuse the mind. Hetland viewed the world from a base position.

Next door there was a toilet and bathroom, both filthy, and next again, an untidy office with sheaves of papers. Then another untidy room, possibly a lounge, with a TV, two half-eaten sandwiches, and several foil containers which looked like carry-outs.

I went out of the section and walked back to the front door where the lift was still in place. There was no sign of Jane. What was keeping her? Harry's snide remarks about our bosses dining with a vicar could probably be overlooked. They were most likely in George's house. Surely they wouldn't abandon me, unless Harry instigated a little pre-arranged counter attack of his own? He was certainly capable of it. His stratagem in the apartment suggested that he had contingency plans for everything except jammed guns. This was a dangerous place and sooner or later something would happen. I'd need to act soon.

Back in the secret section, I walked into the final room, which had a portable bed, a TV and a couple of magazines about cars. A jacket in the far corner looked like Jek's. This room seemed to have been used sparingly and the pillows were almost clean.

At the end of the passageway I found a silver pole stretching down from the ceiling. A fair amount of flooring was cut away around it and there no safety rails. It went all the way down to the floor below where a second pole made a similar descent. So this was his getaway – a set of fireman's poles which doubtless went to the garage in the basement. Against the wall there was a ladder beside each pole, a two-way system which allowed access to the flat without the use of the lift. Beside me, a ladder rose to a loft above.

After a moment's pause, I slid down the levels.. The poles seemed secure, though one had a bit of play. It was an effective mode of travel.

In the garage there were four or five cars, none of them flashy. There was no brown Golf, though there was a black people carrier, but that was of little interest to me. I went to the exit to find it sealed like a bank vault. A curtain of metal shielded me from the world and there was no way it would open. My torch located several switches but they were all inactive and my remote found no electronic activity. Clearly I was locked in.

Back to the ladders. I climbed to the fourth floor and went to the front door again to find it still depressingly deserted.

Where was Jane? Surely something had gone wrong. By my reckoning it had easily been ninety minutes since she'd left. Even if the bosses had decided to abandon me, which I doubted, she'd have returned. But the front door revealed nothing.

Of course she'd know immediately that something was wrong and the apartment was a dangerous place to enter. But what would she do next? Difficult to be sure. She might report back to the bosses, or she might climb the exterior ladder to the first room to find that the door was also sealed. I went there and saw nothing.

I wondered if I was panicking. It could take many forms, and I'd had a stressful day. Certainly I was not thinking straight.

Another thought struck me. If Harry had switched off the power from the secret section, how had he opened the garage door? There must be either an auxiliary power supply, or he was still in the building. I went along the corridor and opened all the doors so that I'd have a chance of hearing any movement. Then I asked myself what the chances were of a second secret section? Unlikely. The known section seemed to account for all the free space.

But what was I going to do? Every avenue had been a dead end. It was beginning to look like there'd be no rescue from outside, until I remembered there was still one thing to be explored.

Returning to the section, I went to the fireman's pole where the solitary ladder rose upward. This could be nothing other than an escape route, a secondary exit which avoided the main apartment. I clambered up to find myself in a cramped room which smelt of sawdust, with walls of ill-fitting hardboard. The room contained only one thing – a step ladder to a skylight window. My hands shook with relief when I saw it. All of Harry's security was based on the principle of keeping people out. Granted, this had trapped me in the building but that was a side issue. The skylight had to be an exit that led to the external ladder. It was Harry's escape route, and it would release me into the real world again.

I turned the lever, and the skylight opened with a burst of fresh air to reveal the lights of London. At long last I was within an ace of freedom.

A group of people dressed in black with the look of junior army officers, were coming towards me. They had seen me open the window.

'Is that you, Mat?' said Jane.

38

At long last, I was back in my own flat and it was just as I'd left it on the night the Het had broken in. Throughout my career I had spent most of my life away from home, but it was always pleasant to return to a familiar environment, even though it was mediocre and covered in a fine layer of dust. I removed traces of the Het bullet from the wall, washed some dishes that had been lying in the sink for the duration and gave Mrs Birhandi a cheery wave when she appeared briefly at her window. Then I sat down to read the paper, where a small article on page five was headed *Harry Hetland Missing.* – It was not a sensational piece; written in conservative language, it referred to 'worry' among his aides about his absence without going into details. Nevertheless, it hinted at exposures to come.

But I wasn't going to get a chance to relax. The real world always intruded.

The phone rang and it was one man I didn't want to hear from.

'Hello Mat. Herb here. How are you? There's a couple of things I need closure on. May I come over for a couple of minutes?'

With some relief, I noticed the absence of a threat in his voice. I said to come over right away. Now that Hetland was missing, Herb could hardly be working for the devil, which that meant the second interview would be a lot less onerous. At the best of times, disguising the truth from a cop was a difficult business. It was reassuring that there were no complaints in his tone. I'd always regarded him as a Het sympathiser, which was possibly a little unkind. At the end of the day, he was a cop with a difficult job, though I'd no doubt he'd taken the odd bung from Harry.

The doorbell went an hour later, and I found myself facing Herb with two cops standing behind him. He was frowning at me and didn't respond to my cheery greeting.

'Come in,' I said, but already I could tell that it was not a friendly visit after all. There was going to be trouble.

They didn't move.

'You're coming down to the station.'

'Might I ask why?'

For a moment there was no response. A man of Herb's importance perhaps found it irksome to answer questions from minor members of the public.

'To assist us with our enquiries. Come on.'

'Am I under arrest?'

'You will be soon if you don't move.'

'And I thought this was a free country, too.'

Soon after I was in a patrol car which took me to a big station in London. There was a cop beside me, a cop driving, and Herb ensconced in the front passenger seat, a glum overbearing presence who seemed to inhibit his men. Plainly he was enjoying their discomfort, and never once spoke. In fact, no one spoke for the entire journey, though the police radio was on, revealing a host of cock-ups which made me shake my head.

At the station I was taken to something they called a 'waiting room' and locked in for about two hours, which seemed like an age. No doubt this was part of the softening process, designed to upset the victim. It gave me a chance to get my head in order. Even so, I was getting ready to blow my top when, eventually, two young policemen took me to a room on the third floor. Herb and two men in uniforms were sitting at a desk facing an empty chair. I sat in the chair and by this time I was seriously angry.

'I'll make no comment,' I announced, 'until my lawyer gets here.'

Nine out of ten prisoners probably say the same thing and no doubt Herb had his own way of dealing with it. He didn't move a muscle when I spoke.

'We'll have to place you under arrest, then,' said Herb, unbothered.

I said nothing.

'Did you hear me? I'll have to place you under arrest.'

'I heard you.'

There was a silence and then one of the men said: 'Mr Hill,

we don't believe you've been entirely straightforward about the double murders. We just want you to answer some questions.'

'Then get me a lawyer first.'

'We want to keep it as simple as possible –'

Plainly Herb was the boss and the two men were specialists brought in for the occasion. Judging by his bulging case, the one speaking was a legal advisor and the other, who had no paperwork, might be one of his lieutenants. Both were overweight with double chins and neither of them looked too bright.

'You grab me and lock me up for two hours. That's supposed to be simple?'

'We're entitled to do that.'

'And I'm entitled to a lawyer.'

'Have you any idea how much trouble you're in?' said Herb, taking over again and leaving us all in no doubt about his seniority. It occurred to me that I might be framed for the whole thing. After all, I'd terminated the goon with a kick to the head. There might be sufficient forensic detail to charge me with that.

'That's why I need a lawyer.'

He rocked back on his chair for a moment, mad at my attitude.

'Listen to me carefully,' he said, and now he was trying a new tack, his voice oozing with false sympathy. 'There has been a double murder. There are heavy odds at stake. Some of your previous testimony is at variance with the known facts and under these circumstances we're empowered by the law to look into these things.'

'Yes, and that's why I need a lawyer.'

Herb glanced at his black notebook and looked up. Apart from the pad and pencil, there were other things on his desk including what looked like an A4 photo.

'You complained of being locked up for two hours. Getting a lawyer will add another two hours.'

'So what? The day's ruined anyway.'

'You're being impertinent.'

I said nothing.

'You'll *have* to answer the questions.' He was almost

pleading. 'I'm sorry to have kept you so long, but my colleagues were late.'

I was silent. By this time they should have launched their attack and he hadn't flung one question. Standard procedure would be to shock me and then break my resistance with a barrage of incriminating facts. But they were holding back. That had to mean their case was dodgy. This was a delicate situation in which their weakness had to be protected. So far I hadn't budged. Of course, I'd had some training in interrogation. Not very much. I'm no good. But they were even worse.

'You have to co-operate. We know a lot about you.'

Yes, that was an old one, ideal for a kid burglar. But I had been around a while.

'I demand a lawyer.'

Without a doubt, the photo on his desk was crucial to their agenda. Perhaps it was the shock tactic they'd intended to throw in my face. Never mind that there might be traces of me in Andy's van and possible prints on the driver's knife, they had neither my samples nor my prints. But the photo was another thing altogether, potentially explosive. It was intended to rock me on my heels. Unfortunately it was concealed under the black notebook, though Herb gave it some rueful glances. It was likely to be shot of me sitting in Andy's van outside the depot, which they'd say proved I'd lied in my previous statement and that I'd been present at the murder. Perhaps they'd scanned us from Croften Communications, where someone had ordered us to be shot. It would be doubly damning for Herb, as it revealed his association with the killers. Granted, the cops accepted video evidence from all available sources, but a photo like that would raise a lot of questions about Croften. An HD shot of the victim and his companion? Why had the camera zeroed in on the murder victim in the last seventy minutes of his life? Police enquiries should have focussed on Croften immediately. But no doubt they hadn't been questioned, and there wouldn't be a word about them in the black notebooks. Herb must have known that they'd sent the killer and he must have known, too, the place was full of guns and heavies. If that line of enquiry was logged Croften would be done for and so would Herb. That was why I was facing three men; three witnesses who would say I'd never been shown a photo. It was there to shock me. A little garnishing to make me talk. It would no doubt be shredded and all references to it omitted from their notes. They certainly wouldn't want a defence lawyer there who could confirm its existence and upset the apple cart.

'Alright,' said Herb, standing up and looking angry. 'You're going back to the waiting room while we fetch one.'

'I'll choose my lawyer from the list,' I said.

But the man with the bulging brief case had to have his say: 'Mr Hill, this is an informal meeting. You are not charged with anything. You came here voluntarily' Did I? 'And you are not under any threat. All we want are a few simple answers.'

This was the one to watch, the wheedler who said there would be no charges. He wasn't the boss, he spoke without authority and his assurances were meaningless.

'I've been snatched and threatened with a charge. That says it all.'

'Mr Hill, we're trying to solve a very distressing case.'

There was a silence and then Herb said: 'Take him away.'

But hadn't George said to choke them off at the first opportunity? Once the defence lawyer arrived, I risked going deeper into the mire. In a double murder that was no place to be. It was time for me to fire my own broadside.

'Did you investigate the security depot?'

Herb had been rising but he sat back again. The suspect was beginning to talk, which was exactly what he wanted.

'This is a double murder,' he said, reaching new heights of smugness. 'I leave corporate matters to the accountants.'

'I'll tell you who owns it. And I don't care if there's a Bishop on the Board. It's Harry Hetland. Je owns Croften next door too.'

'Really?' He lowered his gaze to the black notebook and the photo. The suspect was singing at last, proving his judgement had been correct all along.

'And the unidentified body is one of Harry's killers. But I'm sure you know that already.'

Herb moved the black notebook and seemed about to lift the photo, but something changed his mind. He looked up:

'You seem very well informed.'

'Don't tell me you didn't know that.'

But a big man like that seldom misses a chance to talk you down.

'I'm not going to tell you what I do and don't know. I want to get to the bottom of this violence.'

His eye returned to the photograph, but he hesitated. Beside him, the two men were looking at the table and avoiding my gaze. They'd become aware that my attitude was wrong, that I wasn't quite the victim they'd thought I was.

'Why not blame it on Harry Hetland, then? He's disappeared.'

'It's you we're interested in.'

'Did you know there's been a team investigating Hetland and his associates?'

Herb gave me a stern frown.

'Mr Hill, we'll ask the questions –'

'If you look carefully, you'll find out a lot of things about them. I was a member of the team. I've been in his secret section. I've seen them take his black notebook and his phones. My bosses even have his safe. They know all about the depot and Croften Communications. It's a can of worms. Apparently he's been bribing some of the top cops, too. You wouldn't believe it. At this very moment it's being collated by a team of lawyers.'

Herb's face darkened in disbelief and then uncertainty.

'Name one of them.'

'You know I can't. But I'm sure they'll be in touch shortly.'

'So you *were* a Special, then?' he said, sounding defeated. He must have mulled the matter over and concluded I wasn't, and it had been the biggest mistake of his life. The two men beside him looked like they were getting ready to run for the door.

I said nothing.

Herb stood up with a grim look and said: 'Take him down.'

I turned and saw that the two young cops were still standing at the back of the room with their hands behind their backs, trying to ignore their boss's humiliation. They were at my heels when I walked out. In the background, the trio were having an urgent conference while Herb ripped the photo into small pieces. I had a feeling they were no longer thinking about me. In less than ten minutes, a cop arrived and drove me home.

39

The following morning was mild. There were few clouds in the sky and it promised to be a fine day. I ate a leisurely breakfast, read the paper which said a top cop had been suspended and smiled at Mrs Birhandi. Then I opted for a walk; a real one, not the short jaunts I'd been reduced to in recent times. I thought I could go to Dalespun and walk around the entire estate. As a younger man, I'd often done it in three hours, but today there was no hurry and I could have a modest picnic beside the river. The prospect was so appealing that I threw the newspaper aside and got out into the big world. First, I bought a couple of sandwiches and a fruit drink from the corner shop and stuffed them into my pocket. Perfectly happy, I sauntered off. What more could anyone want in life?

'Mat.'

I turned to see Hazel running after me. I'd erred in walking past her shop. Today she was clad in a mauve outfit. The trousers were nearly bursting, revealing thighs like oak trunks. 'Have you heard from Adele?'

'Adele? No, I've just got back. I doubt if she'll trouble me again.'

'That's just where you're wrong, Mat. I've had to put her out of my flat. She's nothing but one long moan. She's trying to get back with you, and she doesn't even like you, she told me herself.'

I laughed.

'That's not on. I like the single life.'

Hazel opened her mouth to tell me that the single life wasn't all it was cracked up to be, but, realising she'd said it all before, she closed it again.

'Well, Mat I wanted to warn you. She isn't a good companion. You're far too nice to be with her.'

Her voice was getting louder. Several women with shopping baskets were hanging around.

'Oh, I don't know. Did you get back from the Isle of Wight alright?'

'Yes, it was great. Where are you going?'

'Off for a walk in the sun.'

'Oh, I wish I was going with you.'

Eventually I got away from her. I followed the route I'd taken on the abortive motor bike ride almost a year ago. First I went past the lodge, where old Walter was weeding a flower bed and I stopped to thank him for his help with George.

'That boik's still round back,' he said, in an accusing tone.

I'd forgotten all about it and made a mental note to consult Sir Lance when the opportunity arose. Then I walked past the Towers which seemed utterly deserted. When I was at school there would probably have been ten people working inside it. Now old Walter was the only full time employee. My route took me through the trees. I had to take care to avoid the potholes which were now in such a poor state that some residents in the Estate made a detour of five miles to avoid them. No doubt that suited Sir Lance, who valued his privacy.

Near one of the road junctions I stopped to listen to a woodpecker, and spotted it high in a tree. The memory of Andy's death was so strong that I almost looked over my shoulder to see if a Het was creeping up on me. After a minute, the pecker fell silent and I walked on.

Forty minutes later I reached Riverburn Cottage, the house I'd broken into in error. It had seen better times, but was no doubt a comfortable home to its tenants. The door had been repaired and was in good order, though of course it was only the lock that I'd damaged. As it happened, there was a woman in the garden. I didn't remember if she was the one I'd alarmed on my raid, but she gave me a pleasant nod. I reached the public road and walked along it for two miles until I reached the Estate's north road. There was a disappointing river there, a tributary which joined the large river just short of the Towers. It ran beside the road, lacked the volume of the big river, and was seldom visited by even the most fanatical of fishermen. After about a mile, I sat down on a hillock beside a pool to eat my sandwiches. I shook some crumbs on the grass and watched the finches darting in to seize them. Then my eye caught sight of Riverbar Cottage, where I'd smashed the window. It wasn't all that far away, since the road followed the river's meandering path and bent back to a position that was little more than half a mile distant. Sir Lance had sold it to a Mr Goodal, possibly to raise money for his plot. The new owner was in residence, too; I saw his car beside the porch. And then I was struck by a thunderbolt.

It looked like a brown Golf.

So far as I knew, brown was not a standard colour for that model of car. For a long time, I mulled over the tremendous coincidence in front of me. Perhaps that shade was available on the continent and a foreign family had rented the cottage for a break, or it was a trick of the light that had rendered a false shade of brown After five minutes of watching I couldn't make up my mind. Surely to high heaven it wasn't Harry Hetland? Certainly he had the panache to hide on his enemy's estate where only the most obdurate of policemen would look, and Riverbar Cottage was so wonderfully hidden. Only oddballs like me would have a picnic in such an obscure place. But did that mean it really was Harry? Very unlikely. Even he wouldn't take that risk.

By this time, I'd slid down the embankment to avoid being spotted. You didn't take chances when you might be dealing with Mr Hetland, though I doubted if he'd be looking out of the window with a sniper's rifle. I'd finished my sandwiches and two carrion crows had arrived and were fighting over the crusts. On the other side of the river a stoat was foraging on the meadow, its black tipped tail clearly visible as it searched for its dinner among the grass. It was the first one I'd seen in twenty years.

Then I stood and laughed at myself. The sun was glinting on the car's paintwork and I saw that it wasn't really brown after all. Harry had certainly flitted to a far off country, where he'd soon be planning an audacious heist, or perhaps not, as he had sufficient money to keep him in luxury for a lifetime. However, he'd shown little penchant for luxury in his secret section.

I walked back to the road and hesitated. In two miles I would have completed my circuit and reached Dalespun Towers. But that meant being isolated for ten minutes on a road which was exposed to Riverbar Cottage, and I just didn't fancy the idea. It was unlikely there was anything unfriendly about its occupants, but I felt uneasy, so I turned and went back the way I'd come. On a lovely day like this, a few extra miles were nothing. It was the nicer route anyway, and I was enjoying the walk.

Who could say what Harry was doing now? He had his own airline, which no doubt gave him a lot of perks with airports. It was likely that he'd planned a number of emergency boltholes. The last thing he'd do would be to remain in the UK with the highest number of CCTV cameras in the world. Everyone knew his face. But the man had a nose for the unexpected. Only he could move about London with near anonymity. His own staff had seldom known his arrival times, he had been driven in smallish cars which never attracted a second glance and even his arrival at Parliament had been uncertain. I tried to remember his words to Jek as they had been leaving the flat. Was it the black or the brown car? On the Wight phone call he'd said that he had a house by a river, but what did that mean? Half a million cottages fitted that description and he owned a lot of property.

The phone was ringing when I got back home. It was Jane. For once in her life she sounded friendly.

'Mat, what did you do with that motor bike you bought?'

'Nothing. It's still at the Lodge. Old Walter jarred me about it this morning.'

'Okay, I'm just doing the books. I'll say it's in stock.'

'The books? You should know better. This isn't the Civil Service. I'd sign for the lot and keep the change.'

'If there's any change to keep. You're not entirely daft. Where were you? I've been phoning for hours.'

'Walking the Dalespun Estate.'

'Well, that's better than doing the books. Did you see Sir Lance?'

'Aside from Walter I saw no one.'

'Listen, I still owe you for that two hundred you gave the caretaker. I'm going past in the early evening. I'll call.'

'I'll be in.'

Actually, the two hundred had been removed from one of the Hets. It seemed a bit unkind to take it from Jane. In fact, I'd forgotten all about it. I'd probably take half, but it would be a mistake to refuse it altogether. That would establish that I was flush with money and you didn't tell that to the people who do the books.

I made some toast and tea and then spent seventy minutes trying to do a crossword which refused to accept my answers. Perhaps the walk had tired me, or maybe the build-up from the recent shenanigans had affected me, but I settled back on the couch and slept.

40

The bell went and I found Jane at the door, dressed sensibly for once in an almost-demure two piece suit with a red silk scarf which didn't exactly lighten the frown on her face. This time she uttered no complaints about me or my flat, though she made no attempt to reply to my greeting as she led the way in. She was carrying a black attaché case. As luck would have it, Mrs Birhandi was working at her sink and her head went up in interest. Now that Jane had dyed her hair she would be deemed to be yet another girlfriend, but that was a mere triviality. What was causing so such tension in the air? Jane was walking too fast, unbothered by the untidiness of my room. Had the cops sprung back with a raft of charges against us?

'Have you been in touch with George or Sir Lance?'

I looked up in surprise.

'No. I've no reason to do that.'

'They're not answering their phones.'

So she had their numbers. That hadn't been offered to me, though I did have two of Sir Lance's. Of course that explained why she was 'going past' my house in the early evening in a smart suit. She must be bound for Dalespun, whether for a celebration beano or not, I couldn't tell. Certainly I hadn't been invited. But I know my place and I don't complain.

'Won't Sir Lance be at the House?'

'He's at home today. George is with him. We're finalising the books.'

So that's what was in the case.

'Old men. they'll have left their mobiles behind.'

'Well, not George'

No, not George. He'd have the phone in his pocket and he'd know how to use it. But Sir Lance was another matter; his would be languishing in his office in Parliament. A man who doesn't like fuss or the modern world wouldn't welcome its intrusions. And he wouldn't know which buttons to press.

'Try the land line. The transmitter could be down. It wouldn't be the first time.

Without a word, she lifted my phone and dialled a number from memory. Clearly she was disturbed and I was beginning to feel uneasy. Her hair had been cut by a stylist, who'd managed to persuade her away from the mad army look, and apart from the frown she was looking well. The phone rang and rang.

'No good,' she said, putting it down. 'I've tried it twice already. He always answers. Why are you looking at me like that?'

Ugly thoughts were returning in a rush. Maybe I'd been wrong and the brown Golf couldn't be dismissed so easily. I remembered that one of my old Commanding Officers hadn't believed in coincidences. And when it came down to it, neither did I, not with our enemy on the loose.

'I may have seen Harry Hetland's car,' I said, feeling a fool for not doing something about it. 'I'm not sure.'

'Where?'

'One of the Estate cottages, but Harry would never come here –'

'Wouldn't he? When was this?'

'Lunch time. But Sir Lance would never sell a cottage to Hetland.'

She looked at me and her face hardened still further; she already knew that this was trouble.

'The sales are handled by an agency. Hetland could have bought it under another name.'

'But the cops are looking for him,' I protested.

We stared at each other for a long minute.

'Have you got a gun?'

'No. Have you?'

She shook her head. 'What do we do?'

What indeed? If it really was Harry's car then it was probably too late to do anything. Even so, it was unlikely he'd be so crass as to come to Dalespun when half the world was looking for him. And all for the dubious pleasure of settling old scores? Of course, gangsters take a different view on that subject. There was something seriously wrong, or at least potentially wrong, when the commanders weren't answering their phones.

'Head for Dalespun. Not by car, the river path.'

'There's probably a simple explanation,' she said, not moving.

'It's a nice day. They could be having a walk.'

A shake of the head.

'It would have to be a long one.'

'Well, it might be. Better check it out. It'll be a laugh if we're wrong.'

But Jane wasn't for laughing: 'Alright, come on. What are you doing?'

'Getting some plastic ties,' I said, stuffing them into my pocket. 'If you can't shoot your enemy, you can tie him up.'

'You could be right,' she said, and we went for the stairs without further comment.

As we were leaving the building, I looked out of the glass door and caught the reflection of Adele approaching from the opposite side, looking ungainly in her police uniform. What a time to arrive! She stopped when she saw me with Jane and I was careful not to turn round. As the door opened, I saw her reflection as she turned away. Jane had saved me.

Then we were in the open air, walking to Dalespun, but not by the quickest route. There was an unspoken agreement between us that a little subtlety was required. She took my arm as we headed for the Public Park which abutted a good footpath beside the river, loved by many of our visitors who like to feed the ducks. Today it was deserted, with nobody about to hinder our progress.

'How can you be sure it was Hetland's car?' she asked, frowning. 'He's got scores of cars and he'd be insane to come here.'

I talked about the brown Golf. We both agreed that it was probably a coincidence. Any car could be re-sprayed, and anyway there could well be hundreds of brown Golfs if you knew where to look. Quite possibly the colour had been nothing more than a trick of the light. Of course it would have been insane for Harry to come here. But was he sane? We recalled the curious secret section and reminded ourselves that he was a gangster, and gangsters do strange things. Sometimes their mindset demands revenge, and that was not sanity. I narrated the phone call on the Isle of Wight.

'Weird, calling you at six. What was he doing the previous night?'

'I never thought of that.'

'Well, I'm no shrink, but I'll bet it was something nasty.'

Yes, that seemed likely.

The main path ceased at the end of the park and we went on to an unmade track which continued beside the river. Technically we were now on private land, but Sir Lance doesn't grudge access to the river, or indeed any part of his vast estate. Jane complained about the mud. She wasn't dressed for this kind of terrain and it was damaging her shoes – of course it was my fault. The whole thing was ridiculous and we were now moving slower.

'This is the best approach.'

'Not today, it isn't. Not with me in my good shoes, dressed like this.'

'I just don't fancy the main drive if Hetland's about.'

She said there was a limit.

'Best to have a silent arrival,' I said, trying to sound wise. 'A quick shufty, without being seen. A car's too obvious and this isn't too bad, really.'

By now we'd reached The Colonel's Pond, where the river forms a great pool on which two elegant swans were watching us. There were trees on both sides, some of them ancient cedars, which rendered it into a picturesque setting that attracted visitors from all over the country.

'If it's Harry's car,' I said. 'And I'm not sure it is, then it'll be driven by Jek, the half -wit who caught me in Harry's flat.'

'I enjoyed bashing him –'

'This way.'

A small path, nothing more than a trail, rose up the embankment. It was a little known route to Dalespun, now rarely used and known only to a few old timers like me. We were both fit and neither of us slowed for the incline. Under the trees, Jane stopped and cleaned her shoes with a tissue while I looked around and saw nothing to be alarmed about. For a few minutes we walked on until the shape of the Towers emerged among the twigs and branches. Seen from this angle, it was a majestic building. We stopped at the edge of the wood, keeping under its shadow.

'See anything?' she asked, suddenly all tense.

But I couldn't. There was nothing remotely alarming about the vista. The big building had been there for more than two centuries and it looked like it would survive for another two. No windows were broken, no doors were open, nor was there any sign of intruders or violence. There was even a light on in the main lounge, though that raised the question of why the phone hadn't been answered.

'Looks okay.'

'Better check the back.'

This was a sensible suggestion and we stepped back into the trees which partly surrounded the house and extended to the back. It wasn't quite the back, in fact, but the west side. It gave us a view of the back and we were there in a minute.

'Would you look at that!' Jane wailed.

41

Jane was in front as we stumbled forward to see a brown Golf, unremarkable and ordinary, parked on the red gravel beside one of the back doors. It was the only car in sight. Around us everything was deceptively normal. Crows were calling, pigeons were cooing and an audacious family of rabbits were feeding on the far lawn. We looked in all directions to see if we were being watched, then we stepped back into the trees.

'It's not a kidnap,' Jane said, her face grim. 'It can only be revenge. We have to save them.'

I had no problem with her observation, though I wondered about the last bit. The phones had been unanswered for too long. But perhaps there was hope, Harry's car was parked quite openly at the door and possibly there was a prosaic reason for his visit.

'Sir Lance objects to petty precautions!' I muttered, remembering his comments when George had been kidnapped.

'Maybe he's changed his mind,' she said. 'We'd better go in.'

But we were unarmed and Harry – if that was who it was – might have plenty of fire power. It was never wise to jump into a bad situation without first collating the facts. And we had none. How could Harry have known that Sir Lance and George would be here at this time? Why was his car still here? Of course, he'd always known things. His tentacles ran deep. The previous secretary had probably supplied information and perhaps the current lady augmented her income by continuing the tradition.

Intuitively, I knew there must have been a lot of planning in the scenario. Obviously he'd bought Riverbar Cottage some time ago, and we'd intruded into a well plotted event that had the smell of a madman's revenge.

'Come on,' Jane said.

At the back door there were windows overlooking the immediate area. Calmly, we walked from the trees, our feet crunching on the red gravel as we passed the Golf. On an impulse, I tried its door to find it unlocked, and gave it a quick search while Jane stood and watched. There was a trove of gadgets inside, but no guns. Perhaps there were some in the boot, but I was reluctant remain in the open for a second too long. Harry might be watching and it was a bad policy to take risks when he was around. I shook my head and we went to the door.

Jane turned the handle and it opened immediately, a certain sign of trouble. All the outer doors at Dalespun are on latch locks and are secured at all times. That rule has been extant since I was a boy. Possibly Harry had left it unlocked for a quick retreat, but who had opened it in the first place? We were in a corridor beside the old kitchen, where the walls were lined in white tiles. The kitchen had once boasted a staff of four, but now it was redundant. The whole aura of the place was deteriorating into heroic failure. To our left, a varnished timber stairway led to the floors in the main tower. Slowly, Jane advanced to the end of the corridor, where she stopped and threw a questioning glance at the open door ahead. Beyond it lay the entrance hall, with its elegant furnishings and fine carpet. In normal circumstances that door would never have been left open.

I signed for her to come back. At long last my mind was beginning to work. Harry was probably aware that Jane was expected and he'd have a little welcome waiting for her. Already he might know she was inside, though he might be unaware that there were two of us. The outer door would have caused a minor shift in the air which would tell an ambusher all he needed to know. Perhaps he hadn't expected an entry from the back, but no doubt he'd be able to encompass that in his plans. Certainly it would be hazardous to step into the entrance hall.

'Hear anything?' It was a very quiet whisper.

A shake of the head.

But that wasn't good either. It was far too quiet. The very silence spoke of treachery. Walking backwards, we retreated into the corridor. At that point I considered using the back stairs to the next floor, so I could come down the main stairway on the other side. But Harry would be difficult to surprise and the stairs would creak.

I saw a shadow on the door at the entrance hall.

'Down,' I gestured, and we made a silent drop.

We were lying on our bellies looking at the open doorway with anxious faces, well aware that we'd been stupid. This was how you got killed. We were unarmed and vulnerable. To my reckoning, there was someone making stealthy movements within two metres of the door's left side. Our position was indefensible. We should never have entered the house. A plan should have been formed before we'd left the trees. Of course, Harry wouldn't know we were unarmed. The very fact that we'd entered showed a boldness which implied some kind of back up. He knew that we were survivors and he might hesitate to challenge us face on, but there was nothing to stop him leaving the house by any one of five back doors and attacking us from the rear. The door behind us was unlocked, and he would easily be able to open it and shoot us with impunity. Almost certainly the shadow belonged to Jek. It was unlikely that his boss would be so clumsy.

'Stay,' I whispered to Jane. Perhaps she couldn't hear me but she knew to maintain her stance. I crawled back to the door and locked it as silently as possible, sealing the catch so that it couldn't be opened, even with a key. Then I went to the stairs, and walking on the extreme left, got to the first floor. I was greeted by an open door leading to a museum piece of a dining room, with eighteenth century furniture and a table spread with ancient crockery. It was a showpiece to delight visitors on Open Day. The far door was also open, possibly to circulate the air.

I cursed myself for the creaks I was making. Except I wasn't making them. The sounds continued when I stood stock still.

Someone was ascending the main stairs from the other side. I got behind the door to watch from the gap at the hinges. The main stairs were wider, with greater strain on their timbers and they presented a challenge that the back stairs hadn't. Very slowly Jek came into view, staring at the floor, placing each foot with great care and wincing when it sounded. He held a gun in his right hand, his lips were compressed in concentration and he had a fanatical look on his face.

I waited until he put his left foot forward before chopping at his right wrist with all my force. He gave a cry as the gun fell to the floor with a crash. I swung at his face but he dodged to save himself, leaping back on to the landing and revealing an unexpected agility. But he couldn't be allowed to get away. Grabbing the gun, I was on to him as he straightened and delivered a wallop that sent him tumbling down the stairs with another yell. He seemed terrified of me. I leapt behind him, intending to stop at the doorway, but my momentum was too great and I found myself in the entrance hall, my finger itching on the trigger. I'd have been dead if Harry had been waiting, but against all the odds, there was no one in sight. It was early evening and the hall was in shadows.

'Get up, you fool,' I shouted, keeping as close to the wall as possible, in the hope that I wouldn't make a target for his master.

'Don't shoot, mister, please!' Jek said with a great wail.

The entrance hall was big. It was comprised of three sections joined into a single unit, lined with a lot of doors, all closed, and it had a fair amount of furniture against its walls. There were two suits of armour and three grandfather clocks. It fed a total of three stairways and three corridors that would offer a lot of cover to a man with a gun. This was a dangerous place to be.

'Where is Harry?'

'I no' know, honest.'

I'd heard that before. Jane came through, moving fast, watching all the angles and seeing nothing. My gun was aimed at Jek, but we couldn't stay here, both in the same region of the house, giving Harry the opportunity to get at us from any angle. By now he'd know exactly what had happened and precisely where we were.

With a quick movement, Jane removed an H&K from Jek's holster and aimed it at the idiot.

I nipped across the floor to look into the lounge. The lights were on, but there was no indication that anyone had been there recently. Everything was orderly, with no sign of violence. Of course the room was big enough for fifty people and there were many hiding places behind the furniture. Harry could be waiting with a gun.

Too risky to stay. I went back and said to Jek,

'Where is he?'

Jek was lying on the carpet, looking at me in terror. His teeth chattering and he was apparently determined to say nothing. Jane had searched him and removed a lot of objects, including a knife and a wad of cash. Then she tied his hands and feet with my plastic ties. His terror reminded me of the event in the woods when he'd been party to a murder. I had a nasty feeling that the same was true again, but where were the bodies? You can usually smell the dead and there was nothing in this part of the house.

Meanwhile Jane was active.

'Right, Mat,' she said, standing up, 'we're going down to the basement. This might not be a pretty sight.'

I didn't move. That was where they'd be and it might well not be pleasant. There was also the possibility that Harry himself would be there and that was a good reason for holding back. All my instincts were against it, not least because the basement had only one exit and that wasn't enough for me. The phones had been unanswered since Jane had left London more than an hour ago, during which time Harry could well have made a little surprise for us. And he wanted us dead.

'Better get Harry first,' I said, in a weak plea. 'We could be trapped.'

But she was shaking her head at me.

'We've got guns. We'll go now.'

There was no arguing with her. I nodded reluctantly and followed her with my finger on the trigger, watching for any suspicious movements. When we were in the vestibule we found the basement door open. The stairway was lit and now I felt the smell of death. Jane was going slower now, hesitating for a moment at the doorway, while I looked behind to see only the figure of Jek watching us from the floor.

'Come on,' Jane said, as she descended the stairs. I followed. The basement was fully lit and I stepped behind her to see the display of death.

George and Sir Lance were both seated in arm chairs facing us. Their hands were on their laps and their heads were propped by cushions into an upright position. Their faces were chalk white and their jaws were hanging lifeless. It was a sick display and must have required assistance from Jek.

Suddenly, Jane turned and brushed past me, running up the stairs in a fury. I followed, relieved to get away from the disaster around me. In the entrance hall, Jane ran at Jek, who had been sitting up, perhaps trying to get away. She struck him with a terrible slap which knocked him down and made him scream.

'Murderer!' she bellowed. 'You murderer!'

A new drama began to unfold, with Jane banging Jek's head on the floor while he squealed like a pig. There was no point in urging caution. She was too far gone to listen and I was not prepared to intervene. Sir Lance and George were dead and if we weren't careful we'd be next. The rumpus on the floor was giving Harry all the cover he needed. It played into his hands and he thrived on chaos. I'd suspected that Jane had once been George's lover. Perhaps her feelings still ran deep, though the best of us could be driven batty by a senseless killing.

But I wanted to survive.

I'd almost forgotten my own situation. It was too easy to let detail swamp my consciousness and that could be fatal. I went to the far wall with its expensive wallpaper, selecting a spot with some furniture behind me. I was beside a magnificent arch that led to the ballroom, big enough to take a bus. It was decorated with wooden carvings which must have taken a lot of skill. In my father's time there had been balls with a hundred guests and a small orchestra.

Something minor happened, a change in air pressure which indicated the opening of a distant door. It had to be Harry. He must have gone out to surprise us from the rear, and having found the door locked he was now returning. I crouched against the wall, making myself as small as possible in that darkening hall, aware of death approaching in stealthy footsteps.

Hetland would know we were in the west side of the hall and would assume we were armed. He'd know that we had seen the bodies and that would give him some strange pleasure. Now it was our turn. The drama on the floor would provide him with sufficient distraction to creep up on us. Outside, the sun was setting and there were shadows all around. Night was falling and it was becoming darker by the second.

Jane was still banging Jek's head on the floor.

Then I saw that Harry beside me, motionless and utterly calm. He was waiting in the shelter of the archway, where he'd made sure he was a limited target. There was a gun in his hand and his head was up. He was obviously fascinated by the disturbance and there was pleasure on his face as he watched. For a few moments his eyes flitted to the lounge and over the Hall as he looked for me, but I was still crouching in the shadows, all but invisible. He was unconcerned by my absence.

By this time Jek seemed to be unconscious but Jane was still belabouring him. Her back was to me and she was shouting so loudly that I couldn't warn her. Anyway, it was too late for that. There was no gun in her hand. Possibly she'd dropped it. It was never good to be defenceless in front of Harry. Certainly she was in a bad position. The slightest sound from me would only draw fire from the monster.

Then Harry did a surprising thing.

He moved the gun to his left hand and lifted a vase from an adjacent table, which he on threw in one careful movement towards Jane's head. A direct hit. The vase was fragile and it burst into a hundred pieces as Jane fell to the floor. His aim had been perfect. Fortunate, too, that he'd struck her with the vase, otherwise he'd have fired with fatal results. Everything became silent. Harry's sleeve swished as he transferred the gun back to his right hand, looking pleased with himself. His head was high, his hands were steady, and he feared no foe. Then his head swivelled around the entrance hall, eyes narrow, as he wondered where I was. He must have known I was in the building and he must have known I was familiar with the place. He'd heard us speaking and he'd reckon that I'd got Jek in the first place. But where was I?

Then he found out.

I fired, aiming at the white of his hand, which was a clear target in the darkening hall. It wasn't a good shot. I missed, but in an amazing fluke of luck, the bullet caught the barrel of his gun, making it fly out of his hand and tumble to the floor.

A rare moment: I'd taken him by surprise.

Harry wasn't so good with the unexpected. There was a fatal hesitation, then he reached into his jacket for the ubiquitous spare, but I was on him before he could grasp it, hitting him with such force that he was flung against the opposite wall. He turned to strike me but I banged my gun against his forehead and his head rebounded against the wall. His eyes danced in alarm and for the briefest moment there was panic in his eyes. He tried to kick me and missed.

'You contemptible fool!' I spat, hitting him on the side of his face, well aware that there would be other weapons on his person. 'Get your hands on your head. Make one move and I'll kill you.'

I was trembling with anger.

'Immaterial,' came his utterly calm voice. 'I am finished, anyway.'

In the background, Jane sat up and put her hand on her head. Then she turned to look at us.

'Why all this? Why kill Sir Lance and the General?' I exploded, angry at the disaster all around me. Sir Lance and the General were dead in the basement and nothing would ever be the same again. Despite that, the monster was standing in front of me, completely unbothered. Perhaps he was even proud of his actions. His face was relaxed and his eyes were shrewd

'Oh, they were due it. And so are you.'

His eyes had a cold insolence about them which defied me. I was tempted to strike him. I knew people who'd have done just that, but he was fitter than me with an expertise in killing that was unequalled in my experience. And of course that was what he wanted. He was trying to goad me into action. I would be unlikely to survive the encounter. But I was keeping well back and I kept the gun trained on him.

'You're a fool,' I said. 'You could have got away.'

'There was unfinished business. I had to deal with you first.'

'Contemptible!' I repeated.

But he rather welcomed my contempt. I recalled that he'd scorned a polite compliment in the Commons. This was a man with a serious disdain for me and possibly the entire human race.

Jane had been sitting up in the middle of the floor watching us. She looked dazed and kept touching her head. Her gun was lying on the floor beside her, but she seemed to have forgotten about it. Harry, on the other hand, kept glancing at it. Jek seemed to be unconscious, and now Jane was looking at his master, who was a different kind of entity. She had a strange respect for rank,

Harry was the king of all gangsters and she had nothing to contribute to the dialogue.

'What do you intend to do now?' he said to me, raising his head with a smirk. His hands were still on his head and despite his comment about being finished there was no defeat in his eyes.

It was a valid question. My head was numb and I didn't know what to do. The whole thing was a repeat of the calamity at his flat and this time we couldn't summon help from George. Harry watched my eyes go to the phone, an ancient model which sat on a black varnished table three paces away.

'If I were you, I wouldn't,' he said, with a knowing look. 'Knacker can be very clumsy at times. We might, God forbid, finish up in the same cell.'

He'd been here before, with nothing to save him but his wits, and he'd gone on to become a rich man and a celebrity. Without question he was already mulling over a number of possibilities, feasting on my weakness and getting ready to launch an offensive. His eyes flicked to the floor beside us and then back to me. Perhaps he hoped for a diversion, but Jek was flat on his back.

Perspiration gathered on my forehead. Something would have to be done. The military answer would have been to shoot him and go. A little bit of tidying and the cops might never know we'd been there, though that was a big risk in this high-tech age. Jane and I had passed nobody on our way, and at the very least I could depend on her discretion. The corpses would be discovered by the housekeeper in the morning and, as always, the cops would fill a hundred notebooks without getting all the details. But that was dicey. Sir Lance and George deserved something better.

'You're a loser, Mat, you know that?' Harry said, irritated by my silence. 'All of this hassle, and I'll bet you haven't made a penny.' In fact I'd accumulated quite a few wads, but he'd regard that as petty cash. 'If you're not careful you'll end up in toothless poverty like most soldiers. I could negotiate a windfall with you and we might go our own ways. Not as friends, but as respectful enemies. Later you can talk about how you dealt with life and death at Dalespun.'

'If you're into life as well as death,' I said, my voice bitter.

'Then raise George and Sir Lance and I'll let you go for free.'

Harry gave a mirthless laugh, glad that I was talking. That meant the possibility of a deal.

'I'd only have to shoot them again. I can give you fifty thousand. I have it with me. Put a couple of bullets through the windows and you could say that I escaped after a fight.'

But the way he'd dismissed the deaths was the stuff of insanity. This was a man who had been well on his way to being Prime Minister. Fifty thousand? You didn't say that to a man with a loaded gun. It was inviting him to shoot you and collect the loot.

'Not on your life.'

'You're so stupid,' said Harry sighing in despair of me. 'What are you going to do? We could be here until hell freezes over. It's going to be dark soon. You're a most indecisive person.'

I was aware of that. The shadows had lengthened and I could barely see my captive.

'Jane,' I said. 'Would you switch on the lights?'

For a moment there was silence, then she said: 'Right.'

She rose and tottered across the Hall. There was a quick movement from Harry.

'You've lost again,' he said, swinging a gun at me. A moment ago his hands had been on his head. I'd seen just a flick of motion and now there was a small plastic gun in his hand, of the type that Jane had found in his flat. I didn't know where it had come from. Perhaps it had been hidden in the sleeve of his jacket. It spat fire, but the room was dark and I flung myself to the side and was unhurt. I fired too, but he'd slipped into the doorway and was running fast to the end of the corridor. I could have followed and shot him dead, but there had been too many deaths already. A moment later, a door slammed and Dalespun Towers settled into peace.

Suddenly he was gone and it was a tremendous relief. Had he remained, it would have been necessary to kill him. That, at least, had been avoided.

Light flooded the hall when Jane found the switch, revealing Jek in the middle of the floor. His eyes were blinking.

Jane sank on to a chair, staring ahead with unseeing eyes.

'Are you okay?' I asked, remembering the blow to her head.

'I'll live,' she said. 'What are we going to do?'

I got out my phone, though I was still aiming the gun into the corridor Harry had taken. On an impulse I looked out of the big window on my left, to see the tail end of the Golf disappear into the darkness. It was going none too fast and swerving to avoid the potholes.

I put the gun down and dialled 999. I couldn't help noting, wryly, that after all the fuss, the plotters were dead and we'd failed to take care of Harry. Now the Towers would be full of cops and we'd have a lot of explaining to do. What's new?